immed

FAMILIAR
STRANGERS

By the same author

Fiction
TRUTH LIES SLEEPING
THE DISTANT LAUGHTER
THE SLIPPER AND THE ROSE
INTERNATIONAL VELVET

Autobiography
NOTES FOR A LIFE

Biography
NED'S GIRL (the life of Dame Edith Evans)

Screenplays include:
THE ANGRY SILENCE
THE LEAGUE OF GENTLEMEN
SEANCE ON A WET AFTERNOON
THE L-SHAPED ROOM
THE WHISPERERS
THE RAGING MOON
ONLY TWO CAN PLAY
KING RAT
INTERNATIONAL VELVET

BRYAN FORBES

FAMILIAR STRANGERS

Donated by the author.

HODDER AND STOUGHTON
LONDON SYDNEY AUCKLAND TORONTO

The lines of poetry on page 138 are reprinted from 'The Age of Anxiety' in the *Collected Longer Poems* of W. H. Auden by permission of Faber & Faber Limited and Random House Inc.

British Library Cataloguing in Publication Data

Forbes, Bryan
  Familiar strangers.
  1. Forbes, Bryan
  2. Moving-picture producers and directors –
  Great Britain – Biography
  791.43′092′4   PN1998.A3F55

ISBN 0 340 24360 0

for Bunter, Sheila, Brickman, Eve, Roger and Louisa
— familiar friends in times of need.

"Many a man commits a reprehensible action, who is at bottom an honourable man, because man seldom acts upon natural impulse, but from some secret passion of the moment which lies hidden and concealed within the narrowest folds of his heart."

Napoleon i, *Maxims*

1

IT WOULD HAVE appalled Theo even to have contemplated that his final resting place would be Slough. As a matter of fact it would appal me to die in Slough, since I can think of few English towns that depress me so instantly; Theo's body must have welcomed the consuming flames. Even the name 'Slough' – a constant source of confusion to foreigners – conjures up an Orwellian present. *Sluff* is how most strangers understandably pronounce it, and they get closer to the pictorial truth than the correct *Slau* as in *sow*, which in itself is hardly a celebration of our perverse language.

To be accurate and to calm his ghost, Theo did not die in Slough. He died in a rented bed-sitting room in a Victorian mansion with Gothic pretensions just off the neighbouring Englefield Green, a small and relatively unspoilt hamlet bordering Royal Windsor Great Park. He died alone, and from the coroner's report it is conceivable that his death took place on Christmas Day. The body wasn't found until the New Year. Nowadays, England being morally and financially bankrupt, we treat ourselves to longer and longer national holidays and nobody, not even the proverbial milkman, noticed poor Theo's absence from the festive scene during the six-day hangover that now dignifies the birth of Our Lord. Eventually his landlady stirred herself to enquire when one of Theo's three neutered cats expired on her doorstep. Using a house key she doubtless had no mandate to retain, she entered Theo's section of the building to find him long since dead.

He was lying across his spartan single bed clutching an ancient hot-water bottle to his chest, rather as a victim of religious persecution embraces the true Cross. Rigor mortis had set in, driving his fingers into the perished rubber of the bottle. Rusty water had stained his striped pyjamas, giving her the false impression of a dried chest wound sufficiently

9

realistic at the time of discovery to send her into hysterics. An electric fire was burning at full strength and the atmosphere, I gather, was somewhere between a sauna and a charnel house. In all events, the body had started to decompose and it was with difficulty that the ambulance men prised him from the cheap mattress and took him to the mortuary.

It was hardly a fitting exit for one of England's most distinguished men of letters, somebody widely tipped for an eventual O.M. I don't suppose I would have had any prior notice of the tragedy before the obituaries appeared, for we were not close in the decade preceding his death, but by coincidence, or possibly a premonition, I had sent him a Christmas card that year. The local police found my seasonal greeting by the side of Theo's bed, and since I had appended my address and a vague invitation for a long-overdue reunion in the New Year, it was me they contacted to identify the body. We were related on my father's side of the family.

I drove to the mortuary at a speed that evoked rage and frustration from my fellow road users, but it was not a day to be hurried. When one is past fifty death seems all too close for comfort and the deaths of our contemporaries an almost weekly reminder that we are on the wrong side of the insurance statistics.

Much to my surprise the mortuary proved to be a pleasing example of modern architecture. I think I had been expecting some Burke and Hare establishment reeking of formaldehyde, but the entire building was air-conditioned and the only detectable scent that of freshly-polished floor tiles. There was also a refreshing lack of bureaucratic red tape and indeed, Mr. Pollard, the official who greeted me, behaved with more warmth than your average British hotel keeper.

My first impression was that Theo looked younger than his years, but as Mr. Pollard explained, death, unless it comes violently, often achieves this cosmetic effect. I was reminded of the famous death mask of Napoleon, a leader whom Theo greatly admired, I might add. The skin was truly wax-like, the face babyish, plumped, the lips slightly curled and suggesting a smile, though I noticed that he had lost more hair than me and that what remained looked as though it had been artificially coloured. Theo was a great one for patent medicines, believing anything he read in those health magazines he subscribed to, though I suspect he purchased them for the frolicking and, to my mind, always unattractive nude photographs of middle-class families engaged in improbable games.

"Satisfied, Mr. Stern?"

The tone was that of a tailor soliciting approval for a final fitting, and was hardly the right choice of word in the circumstances. I nodded, since I always believe in humouring minor officials. One can't be too careful as 1984 draws near.

"Perhaps you'd be good enough to say it then, sir."

I stared at him, then back to Theo. I had no idea what was expected of me – was I supposed to produce an instant wake, murmuring some suitable eulogy or prayer?

"We have to observe the statutory requirements required of us," Mr. Pollard continued, in the same faintly condescending voice, revealing in his thin smile a complete set of grotesque false teeth. These, more than the presence of poor Theo between us, gave me a jarring glimpse of life on the other side.

"I'm sorry?"

"We have to formally identify the deceased person, Mr. Stern. The law requires it."

"Ah, yes. Of course. How stupid of me."

"Take your time, sir."

"That is, or rather that was, my relative."

"I'm afraid we have to be more precise than that, sir. We need the full name of the departed. You say to me, 'That is Mr. So and So' – or, at the other extreme, 'That is Miss So and So, or Mrs.,' according to the marital status, adding if you wish, 'to the best of my knowledge and belief'. It saves any possible misunderstanding thereafter."

I repressed a desire to giggle. I felt Theo would have enjoyed this part of the proceedings – my discomfort and Mr. Pollard's delivery – for he had a sardonic sense of humour when it suited him.

"Right," I responded. "Well, we must do it by the book. That is my second cousin, Theo Gittings."

"And . . .?"

"And?"

"Did I detect the merest hesitation, Mr. Stern?"

"No, I don't think so. Did you?"

"Just a whisker, I fancy."

"Well, it wasn't intentional. I mean that *is* Theo."

"Can I suggest that – just to be on the safe side – we add the words 'to the best of our knowledge and belief'."

"Our knowledge? You mean my knowledge, don't you?"

"Yes, you've got me at it now, sir."

"Okay, I'll say the whole thing again, shall I? To the best of our – my – knowledge and belief, that is my late second cousin Theobald Gittings. How's that?"

"Perfect, sir. You said it very nicely."

I felt I had passed the audition and the role was mine.

"Now then, sir, unless you'd like to linger, I think we can tuck Mr. Gettings away."

"Gittings," I murmured.

"Quite so." His manner became brisker all of a sudden, as though he had been caught out in some shameful act.

"What happens now?" I asked. "Is there to be a post-mortem?"

"That is on the cards, I believe. What was his line of business, your cousin?"

"He was a writer," I said. "Quite a famous writer," as the sheet blotted out Theo's face and the drawer slid back into the wall.

"Wrote books, did he, sir?"

"Yes."

"I've always thought it was a nice hobby, writing. 'Course, I could write a few tales myself, if I had the time. You see it all here."

"I'm sure."

"Oh, yes. Death be not proud, what price glory, et cetera."

"Very apt."

Perhaps he detected in my voice that note of coldness professional writers employ when their craft is so lightly regarded. At any given gathering one can always count upon being button-holed by some would-be author and told that,

12

were it not for the pressures of more important business, 'I could write a book.' It sometimes seems there is an Irving Wallace lurking inside half the population.

I signed the necessary papers in triplicate and drove away, thinking of the complexities of other people's lives. What sort of ambition or necessity leads the Mr. Pollards of this world to spend their years filing the dead? It's easy to say, somebody has to do it, but that is never the complete answer. I am aware that there was never any shortage of applicants anxious to break the Pierrepoint family's monopoly for the job of public hangman, and whilst Mr. Pollard was a long way down the line of spectators to human misery, there is no escaping the conclusion that suffering is addictive.

That last glimpse of Theo stayed with me as I drove through Datchet, past Windsor Castle walls, and headed for Runnymeade and the London road, fully intending to return straight home to my chambers in Albany. I live alone, in what used to be called 'style' in less egalitarian times; a fairly routine existence, set in my ways, as the expression goes, since the death of my wife. I answer correspondence in the mornings, venture as far as the Garrick for lunch – the whole day a slow gathering of energies for the nightly stint at my Carlton House desk. I am always fascinated to read about the working habits of fellow writers, envying those who are most creative in the early hours. I find comfort in noting the eccentricities of others – their superstitions soothe me, for I share many of them. We are all programmed, we know what pressure points to touch, working like acupuncturists in reverse, seeking to reproduce the pain of past creative bouts. At various stages in my career I have made determined efforts to break away from my self-imposed drudgery, but like an old-time convict, I have found the ball and chain of routine has proved too strong. Even if I break the links I have no idea where the frontiers of freedom lie. I know my own limitations. I am not content with them, but I am enslaved by them.

Theo was totally different. Secretive by nature, he could seldom be drawn to discuss his own work in progress or his working habits, but over the years I gleaned enough to know that our distant blood relationship pulsed through separate artistic veins. We had both lived through the pen (or in my lazy case, the electric typewriter) and to that extent we were alike, but in thinking of his death I realised we had little else in common. The memory of his calm, dead face troubled me. A vague, nagging doubt, such as parents experience when they drive away for a dinner engagement leaving children alone in the house. I had left something undone and it wasn't until I came to the intersection leading up the hill to Englefield Green that I realised I had one other task to perform.

I had no idea at that point which other members of our far-flung family would eventually appear out of the woodwork (grief and avarice frequently leave the same visiting card), but I was aware that poor Theo still had the power to shock from the grave. I didn't really give a damn about the relatives, for they had never appreciated his true worth, but I did care about his reputation. From time to time he and I had discussed our literary estates, not too seriously, for Theo shied away from illness and could seldom be persuaded to attend a funeral or even a memorial service. We talked about some loose arrangements such as people do when they are in the best of health. I would look after his papers, he would look after mine, whoever went first – that sort of thing. It was never a formal undertaking and in my own case, since I have a horror of files and old letters, I had no real cause for concern. As to the rest, I am indifferent. I never had Theo's mania for the trivia of one's life. I would rather people speculate than be certain.

With Theo it was another story. I remembered something he had once said to me during the war when nobody was spared the inconvenience of sudden death.

"Have you ever given a thought to the skeletons?" he asked.

"Skeletons?"

"Yes. The proverbial kind, that rattle in cupboards."

"No, I can't say I have."

"I think about them all the time."

"Perhaps you've got more than me."

"Perhaps. It isn't the number, it's the quality of them."

"I'm sure yours are superior to mine."

"I doubt that."

It was one of those passing conversations we think little of at the time, but like certain social diseases they lie dormant just below the surface, erupting when we believe we are completely safe.

Although, as I have said, Theo and I had drifted apart in his final years, there had been a time when his friendship meant much to me. Perhaps I was not being totally altruistic, perhaps my predatory writer's instinct shared the honours with my concern – at this remove, and bearing in mind what later came to light, I can't be certain. In any event, I turned the wheel of my Mercedes and headed up the steep hill, changing gear to protect his memory.

2

I PARKED MY CAR on the grass verge outside the house where Theo died. It was set back from the road, the front garden protected by a crumbling brick wall daubed with the inevitable graffiti. Its daily dose of dog pee had caused the words to run, but I could still make out the message – ENOCH RULES OK. The garden itself was over-run and when I entered through the small iron gate I had to duck to avoid the branches of a weeping birch. The house had been converted into two separate dwellings, the original large front entrance split in two, so that now two front doors stood side by side, both glassed and both badly in need of a lick of paint. I hesitated, not knowing which bell to push and eventually pressed both of them. I had never visited Theo there when he was alive.

Why is it that houses where there has been a recent bereavement seem to have an aura surrounding them? Was it just my imagination, or merely the general gloominess of the façade that made me shiver as I stood waiting? Distant shouts reached me from a group of boys kicking a football about on the green. I heard the yap of a small and, even sight unseen, boring lap dog.

A few moments later one of the doors was opened a fraction. The dog pushed its repulsive face through the crack. A rodent-like head with eyes protruding like burnt sultanas, it exuded hatred – yapping and urinating simultaneously as it advanced towards me. I took a step backwards to avoid my trousers being fouled.

The woman in the doorway had certain marked similarities to her repellent pet, in that her head was out of proportion to the rest of her body. The effect was further distorted by a mass of Carmen rollers in her hair, fixed so tightly that they exposed areas of pink and scurfy scalp.

"Yes?"

"You don't know me," I began, speaking louder than normally in order to pitch my voice above the incessant yapping of the dog. "And please forgive me for disturbing you without warning, but I'm a relative of the late Mr. Gittings."

"Yes?"

"As a matter of fact I've just come from identifying his body."

"Oh. Shouldn't have thought that was necessary. I saw to all that."

"Well, the usual red tape, I suppose."

"I found him."

"So I was told. It must have been a great shock."

"New Year's Day."

"Not a very pleasant beginning."

Her dog had a bladder capacity out of all proportion to its size and by now was killing what remained of a cankered privet bush, all the while fixing me with its maniac eyes.

"That's enough, Elsie," the woman said. She slipped the chain from the lock and opened the door. "You've done your business like a good girl, now just be quiet."

The animal was suddenly, blissfully silent, but stood transfixed, one front paw raised as though petrifaction had set in.

"My name is Stern," I said. "I'm sorry, but I don't think we've ever met before."

"Davis. Mrs. Davis."

"Well, obviously, Mrs. Davis, you were very kind to my cousin. And on behalf of the family I'd like to thank you for that."

"I did what I had to do."

"Had he been here long?"

"Seven years."

The conversation was getting nowhere. She was not the kind of woman who volunteers information.

"Has anything been done about his things?"

"I haven't touched anything," she said, immediately on the defensive. "Not a thing. Apart from stripping his bed. I had to do that; it wasn't sanitary."

"I'm sure you did everything properly. But obviously, at

some given time, things will have to be sorted out. Forgive my ignorance, but did Theo . . . did my cousin own his part of the building, or was he renting it?"

"The house is in my name. The late Mr. Davis left me well cared for."

"So, presumably, you'll want to rent it out again as soon as possible?" I had an idea Mrs. Davis could best be approached through the cheque book.

"Well, naturally, although I'm comfortably off, I can't afford to let it stand empty for long."

"No, that's why I thought I ought to call. To try and be of some help."

"Tell me your name again."

"Stern. Anthony Stern. I'm a writer, like my late cousin." I paused. We authors always live in expectation that mention of our names will immediately elicit a smile of delighted recognition. Mrs. Davis was obviously not a patron of contemporary literature. "Not such a distinguished writer as he was," I added.

"Yes. I read a couple of his. He always gave me copies. Deep, I thought. Not exactly my cup of tea. All right for people who like that sort of thing."

"Did he ever mention me to you?"

"He might have, yes. Yes, the name is slightly familiar. Not that he was a great talker, and not that I ever pried. He respected my privacy and me likewise."

"I'm sure he appreciated that. Look, I don't want you to be bothered in any way, but somebody has got to tackle the business of clearing out his personal effects. D'you think I could take a look around? I think I must be his closest surviving relative. His parents died years ago and as you know, he was single."

"Yes, he was a very bachelor sort of man. You want to go inside, do you?"

"If that's possible."

"Into his rooms?"

"Yes."

"They're not very tidy. He was a regular payer, but not a great one for tidiness."

18

"All the more reason," I said, "for getting things sorted out."

She regarded me in silence for a few moments. "I hope I'm doing the right thing."

"Well, naturally, if you want to come with me I've no objections."

"Yes. Yes, all right. Well, I'll get the key. One can't be too careful these days."

"I quite agree."

"Come on in, Elsie. If you'll just wait here." The animal produced one last spatter before following her back into the house.

My first encounter with Mrs. Davis added to my bewilderment concerning Theo's last years. What could have possessed a man of his intelligence and distinction to bury himself in such a backwater with such a crone as his closest neighbour? I had no idea at that point what his financial situation had been. Although his novels never figured in the best seller lists, his sales had been respectable over the past decade, two of the novels being required reading for exams. I had never imagined him to be poor, yet the house seemed to be the last retreat of a man of declining means. The Theo I remembered had liked living well, had driven a hard bargain whenever his services were required for a Hollywood stint and was always a generous host with a nose for the best wines and cuisine. It seemed incomprehensible that he would choose to exist in such mundane surroundings, devoid of any stimulating conversation. Where Mrs. Davis was concerned, the effort of maintaining day-to-day politeness, however minimal, would have been too much for me.

It wasn't that the house was squalid, or that Mrs. Davis was slovenly. The house was merely depressing and his landlady the sort of neighbour I would take a sea trip to avoid. That is what really puzzled me as I waited for her return. I remembered Theo as a witty, gregarious companion, somebody who enjoyed the cut and thrust of debate, a man of pronounced opinions and unafraid, indeed anxious, to air them.

I was still pondering these contradictions when Mrs. Davis reappeared. She opened the adjacent front door and led the way. The conversion had obviously been done on the cheap, for Theo's door gave on to a narrow partitioned hallway, the staircase rising steeply to the upper storey he had occupied. The place smelt damp; I got an immediate impression of neglect, but nothing, not even my own fertile imagination – for which I have often been taken to task by my critics – had prepared me for the revelation of his bedroom, the room in which he had died.

Mrs. Davis stood to one side and made no attempt to cross the threshold.

"As I said, tidy he wasn't."

I shall need all my restraint to describe the state of his bedroom. Perhaps I should start by evoking the memory of Miss Haversham's fabled room in *Great Expectations*, for that was the comparison which leapt into my mind at first glance. The squalor was horrendous. Admittedly, there were no dead rats or decaying wedding cake, but the room – of average size – was crammed from top to bottom. Stacked all around the single iron bedstead were piles, three or four feet high, of old newspapers and magazines, the top layers faded with age. A desk was pushed tight into one corner and alongside this, without an inch to spare, was a cheap wardrobe, itself so full that the door had been forced from one hinge. Both the top of this and the desk were stacked high with an assortment of bric-à-brac: filing boxes, books with their spines broken, jam jars full of pencils and old coins, here a mass of what appeared to be old bus tickets, there a collection of cigarette tins, numerous ashtrays, bottles of patent medicines, batches of manuscript, a large biscuit tin overflowing with rubber bands, one shoe with a tea cup pressed into the heel, the saucer somewhere else serving as a receptacle for cigarette butts that had been smoked down to the filters. There was scarcely any room between the foot of the bed and the chest of drawers facing it. The top of this was also heaped with debris, and behind the bed Theo had massed more old newspapers, lining these up to form a crazy shelf on which he had arranged more books. The whole scene resembled a police photograph of a room that had been deliberately wrecked by intruders, and the curious thing is that I saw it all in black and white, just like such a photograph, all the colour bleached out. To tell the truth there was very little colour in that room, for everything had a dull sheen of dust over it. What clothes I could see were crammed in an open corner cupboard and looked like the garments one sees on second-hand stalls. It was one of the saddest rooms I have ever been in.

"See what I mean?" Mrs. Davis said. "'Course, I was never allowed to clean it up. Hated having anything disturbed."

"Didn't he have any help?"

"They never stayed."

"It's amazing," I said.

"There's two other rooms and the usual."

I followed her through into the tiny kitchen. In stark contrast to the chaos of the bedroom, this was bare except for the essentials, and betrayed the fact that this was where a bachelor had prepared his solitary meals. A few recipes cut from newspapers were pinned over the sink, and I noticed that the only objects that seemed to belong were three cat bowls with the names of their owners inked around the sides: Billy, Fluff and Mr. T. Lying beside one of the bowls was a toy mouse, the tail bitten away.

There was a sitting room adjoining, comfortless and furnished in appalling taste. Over the mantelpiece was a framed photograph of Theo taken during his undergraduate days at Cambridge. As I looked at it, the old expression, The Lost Generation, came to mind.

"Did he leave a Will?" Mrs. Davis asked.

"I don't know. I suppose that's one of the things I shall have to look for."

"He always talked about leaving me his grandfather clock. Not that I'm counting on it, mind, but that's what he used to say."

"Well, I'm sure if that was his wish it'll be honoured."

She brightened at this. "Would you like a cup of tea? I should have asked you before."

"Yes, that would be very welcome."

"I'll make it downstairs in my pot."

As she retreated I heard her call to the dog, "Go back, Elsie precious. You can't climb these stairs with your little legs, and this isn't the place for you."

I went back into the bedroom and eased my way to the desk. I had no idea where to begin, and in any event to examine another person's private papers is always distasteful. I would hate to be a policeman. Few of us make adequate preparations, for the myth of immortality is the hardest to discard. So much of what we leave behind for others to uncover betrays us. Happy the people whose annals are vacant.

I stared down at the cluttered desk. There was an open box of manuscript, the top page scribbled over with Theo's corrections. Work in progress, that would never now be finished. Then I saw a copy of my own last book, a review copy as it happened, presumably sent to Theo by some over-enthusiastic literary editor who thought that the family connection would maybe produce some controversial copy. It had the look of a book that had never been opened.

Not one of the drawers in the desk was locked, and I opened two or three at random and was appalled by the task ahead, for it was obvious at a glance that Theo had no system. I sifted through an assortment of unpaid bills, some months overdue, and my immediate thought was that he had died penniless and felt guilty that I had allowed us to drift apart. A moment later I came across a bundle of uncashed cheques and some quick mental arithmetic dispelled my first fears. Most of them were dividend cheques, and even to my untrained eye I could see that they represented sizeable investments more than sufficient to take care of his creditors. It was the first paradox of his secret life.

I turned my attention to the bedside table. Lying open on it amid a welter of odd scraps of paper was a school exercise book. I saw that the exposed page was dated at the top – December 22 – and I sat on the edge of the bare mattress and began to read the handwritten entry beneath.

10 a.m.   Got up. Felt very slightly sick. Made cup of choco-
           late. Laid and lit fire in lounge.

11.05	Ate porridge before the fire, felt very cold. I have been dreading this day, although I know it must be faced.
11.20	Practised deep breathing until feeling of dizziness wore off. Shaved and dressed.
1.20 p.m.	Caught train to Euston. What compelled me to make the journey? Was it merely the agony of expectation? I should know, but I don't. Didn't notice the train rocking so much as usual. On arrival at Euston I went to the snack bar and bought a cup of tea, cheese and biscuits and two mince pies. I quite enjoyed the rest and the bustle of the station. It's the season, of course. Everybody going home. Home for the holidays. Home.
3.45	Took various bus routes, then the Tube to Swiss Cottage. Was pushed several times. Noticed that most of the staff are black. Train filthy, seats ripped. Felt dizzy again and had my first cigarette of the day. Middle-aged woman shouted at me – I was in a non-smoking carriage. Extinguished cigarette but did not apologise. The episode unnerved me.
4.20	Had difficulty finding A's address. House next door has been pulled down since my last visit and this confused me. He kept me waiting on the doorstep for at least five minutes before answering my ring. Gave me a Dubonnet and said I could not stay. He had another appointment and it was too dangerous. Said the whole thing was impossible and had to end. Made a fool of myself by pleading. All to no avail. I was stupid to go in the first place. He explained he no longer received at home, that it was madness, the place was being watched. This may have been just to scare me, but I am past scaring. Anyway it ended. I left before he did since he refused to be seen with me. Walked part of the way back to the station then felt dizzy again and hailed a taxi.
7.15	Arrived home. Fire out, of course, and too tired to re-light it. Felt terribly lonely. Dog barking incessantly. I've made such a mess of it all, doing all the wrong things for the right reasons, or do I mean the other

way round? Too tired to think it out. To bed with a hot water bottle.

I covered the notebook with some magazines at the sound of Mrs. Davis returning. She brought the tea on a tray, together with a plate of digestive biscuits. I needed the hot comfort the tea provided, for the unheated room had chilled me. I had to concentrate to hear what Mrs. Davis was saying.

"He was a good payer, I couldn't fault him there. And a real gentleman, of course. One of the old sort. I suppose, in a way, it's quite something to have a famous person die in your house. He was famous, wasn't he?"

"Yes. Not famous like a footballer or a pop singer – times have changed – but very distinguished."

"'Course, some people get a morbid pleasure out of that, don't they, like living in a house where there's been a murder. I mean, some people will pay more for that."

"So I've heard."

"Funny, isn't it?"

"People can be very odd," I said.

"I did think of ringing the local paper. I expect they'll want to interview me, seeing as how I was the one who found him."

"D'you think we could put on the fire?" I said. "I find it very cold in here."

She pulled an ancient electric fire into the open space by the door.

"It was on when I found him. Like a furnace in here. Been on for days, you see, and of course the you-know-what – well, to be crude, the smell, you know."

"Very unpleasant."

"Yes. Gave Elsie a nasty turn; she wasn't herself for days. They sense things, don't they, animals? And of course she's highly strung. On account of her breeding. She's pedigree."

"I could see that."

"Yes, lovely little thing. Would you like another cup? Plenty in the pot."

"I can see why he stayed with you all those years," I said. "You obviously spoilt him."

"I did what I could. I did my best."

24

"Was his rent paid up to date? Because, if not, I'd be only too happy to take care of that. Until things are sorted out."

"He owed a month," she said quickly, and I knew I had found the way to her heart.

In the short time I had been left alone in the room I had made certain decisions. I knew I had a task ahead of me. There was the funeral to arrange, of course, but beyond that – beyond the dismal formalities – I had the feeling that my instincts had been sound. It's difficult for me to speculate on my true motives at that moment, for in the rush of the day's events I had experienced a variety of emotions. Perhaps uppermost in my mind were horror and pity, for the state of the room, the way in which Theo had obviously spent his declining years, was something my imagination had not previously embraced. They say that an author's inventions always outstrip reality, but I have found most human acts too dreadfully obscure for us to pronounce judgment with any finality.

Yet there was something else, no more than a vague uneasiness. The last entries in Theo's journal hinted at a muted nightmare. The fact that he had used words like 'dangerous', 'madness'; that he had written 'I am past scaring'. Most journals and diaries are banal, pre-edited versions of our daily lives that we write from habit rather than conviction, but in Theo's case, from the little I had read, there were undertones of quiet horror. The careful tabulating of exact times suggested he had a need to record everything, as though he was aware that time was running out in more ways than one. A writer never knows when the pool of his imagination will allow the submerged evidence to surface. I had come to that house to protect that portion of Theo's memory I knew better than anybody else, but now I needed more time alone to think things through, and the presence of Mrs. Davis was too distracting. I gestured towards the desk.

"Look, there's going to be a post-mortem, but once that's over and the necessary authorities have been granted, I'll sort through this lot. In the meantime, perhaps you'll allow me to pay you two months' rent."

I wrote her out a cheque there and then, and she willingly

agreed to my suggestion that the room be left completely undisturbed. While she removed the tea things I pocketed
Theo's journal, then we locked his portion of the house and
exchanged warm farewells under the weeping birch, the small
dog still performing urinary wonders as I drove away.

Let me quickly deal with the mechanics that set this account
in motion. The post-mortem revealed nothing untoward.
There were the usual signs of deterioration in some of the vital
organs commensurate with his age, but the final verdict was
that all-embracing comfort, 'death by natural causes'.

The funeral was a simple one. I placed In Memoriam
notices in *The Times*, the *Daily Telegraph* and the *New Statesman*,
in addition circulating the Cambridge newspapers since I
thought it possible that some members of his old college
might care to pay their last respects. In the event the
mourners numbered eleven. Apart from Mrs. Davis and
myself, there was a representative from the Arts Council
whom I vaguely knew, but the rest were all strangers, and
although I carefully noted their names when the short
cremation service was concluded, they meant nothing to me.
There was no family and I was therefore spared the embarrassment of even a token wake. The young clergyman who
conducted the service introduced a brief element of farce into
the empty proceedings by referring to Theo as 'our sister who
has just departed' before recovering the thread.

There was talk of a memorial service in the Abbey, but
nothing came of it. Theo's publisher, acting with an enthusiasm seldom visible when Theo was alive, announced that he
was 'privileged' to rush reprints of four of the best-known
novels into the bookshops, but within months I noticed they
had been remaindered on the station bookstalls. I dare say
Theo will have to wait another decade until the next generation evaluates his true worth.

His bank contacted me revealing that he had not only left a
Will but, surprisingly, had named me as his Executor. It was
a simple document. He asked me to make suitable provision
for his three cats, a request I could not honour, for one had

already expired and the other two had vanished, as animals sometimes do when their routine is broken. I went through the motions of placing advertisements in the local news-agent's, but Fluffy and Mr. T failed to reappear. There were a few other minor bequests to charities he had supported and a donation to the Festival of Light (a typical piece of cynicism on Theo's part), and I was instructed to apply the residue of his estate for the preservation of his manuscripts and private papers. In particular, he left detailed procedures for the future handling of his journals, charging me to ensure that they were not to be published for twenty years after his death. I was given full authority to dispose of the remainder of his effects in any manner I thought suitable and to deduct such reasonable expenses for my pains as the situation demanded. He had not made any provision for the anxious Mrs. Davis, a fact I successfully concealed from her, and I used my discretion where the grandfather clock was concerned.

I took the precaution of telephoning her in advance before paying my next visit to the house. She greeted me with some-what flirtatious warmth and a tray of tea already prepared. I had the suspicion that his bedroom had been altered slightly, but the chaos was still such as to defy the perceptions of a Maigret. Having finished her tea and biscuits I managed, by a series of increasingly obvious hints, to penetrate her thick skin and she eventually grasped that I would prefer to work alone and undisturbed.

"You just treat it like your own home," she said, as though Theo's squalor was the natural habitat of writers.

In the interval since my previous visit I had had ample opportunity to consider the scattered evidence in that last volume of Theo's journals. It did not make happy reading. I now knew what I was looking for, but since there was no system to Theo's various collections it seemed a waste of time to impose one of my own, and for the first few hours I delved in haphazard fashion, throwing away whatever was patently of no lasting interest.

I was again dismayed by his dismal wardrobe, for I remembered he had once been what we used to call a 'snappy dresser', immaculate when the occasion demanded. But the clothes I found jumbled together that afternoon revealed no trace of past elegance. One drawer contained a quantity of sports clothes – rugby jerseys, socks and shorts, all soiled. I found this curious because like many of us who toil by the pen he was not one of nature's hearties. Yet another drawer in the same battered chest was crammed with lederhosen, decorated leather and the like, and these seemed to my inexpert eye to be in a variety of sizes.

I have said that I knew what I was looking for. But let me correct that. I *thought* I knew what I was looking for.

I knew only too well that by the time he was in his twenties Theo had settled for being homosexual. The popular description now is 'coming out of the closet', but in the period between the wars nobody 'came out' publicly except debutantes, and for good reason, since queers were still the blackmailer's favourite quarries and I stood sad witness to several of my contemporaries' suicides.

Theo was reasonably discreet, as far as I could tell. On those occasions when we openly discussed the subject he revealed little of his affairs. He would merely say, "I came across a new friend the other day who I think might amuse you," and on two or three occasions he invited me to make a threesome for dinner. I never found his companions even faintly amusing. They all seemed cast from the same mould: rather bovine youths, who drank his wine like draught beer and scarcely uttered, though, presumably in an effort to justify his choice, Theo would laugh immoderately at their unsophisticated jokes, granting them a wit that was scarcely discernible to an outsider. I found such evenings trying. Not that Theo was 'camp' in the theatrical sense, or at least he never parodied his tastes when I was around. He dressed, as I have related, with stylish conservatism, and never gave any clues in his published novels.

So in my preliminary search through the contents of Theo's room I was prepared for revelations of a certain kind, but I confess that I was surprised by what I actually found. There was no clever attempt at concealment – the first box of photographs I came across was stored inside an ancient fibre suitcase, still festooned with old Cunard labels. It wasn't even

28

locked, though the hard-core stuff was under a layer of family snapshots which might have diverted a casual searcher.

I suppose, if I am honest, what surprised me most was not the easy discovery but the nature of the discovery. There was a selection of more or less standard poses showing fellatio and anal penetration between youths dressed partially in scouting uniform, presumably stock items that can be purchased in most dirty bookshops. It wasn't until I came across a batch featuring Theo himself that I was forced to acknowledge that perhaps I had never known him at all. They were amateur efforts, some of them taken in that very bedroom by flashlight that had bounced back from the shiny surfaces of the walls, giving them a milky appearance. In almost every case they showed Theo clad in football gear, complete with studded boots, bent across the laps of various middle-aged men wearing a form of Nazi uniform. They had obviously been taken over a long period, for Theo's appearance was noticeably different in many cases: I noted changes in the colour and style of his hair and the fact that he had acquired a paunch between sessions. Equally, his 'military' companions were seldom duplicated. None of them could be said to be oil paintings; they looked like their real-life wartime counterparts, dreary little men who had had all pleasures blotted from their faces.

Immediately I had brought them to light I felt compelled to check whether Mrs. Davis was anywhere in the vicinity. I went into the kitchen and made myself a cup of black instant coffee from a half-empty jar I found in a cupboard. Looking at the cat bowls, I found myself wondering whether Mr. T and his companions had ever been silent, unimpressed witnesses to the events depicted in the photographs. My novelist's brain began to map out the stage directions that must have accompanied such tableaux. The conjectures proved accurate, since I was later to establish that Theo recruited his contacts by a variety of pen names and box numbers, and it was therefore safe to assume that in the majority of cases his midnight Nazis were total strangers. They must have come to the house and mounted that steep staircase to the upper floor. I imagined Theo offering them a glass of sherry or, more bizarre, a cup of hot chocolate that he seemed to drink in preference to tea or coffee. Then, presumably, they got down to the serious business. Did Theo greet them already wearing his football gear? Did they ever exchange their real names? Was there a scale of charges to be haggled over before trousers were dropped? My imagination was not broad enough to supply all the answers. What I could believe, looking again at the photographs, was the bleakness of it all. I hope I am not being unduly sentimental about this, applying my own conventional standards out of ignorance. I may have got it all wrong. Perhaps it wasn't as joyless as the photographs suggested. Perhaps human loneliness is so complex that the unthinkable can, for a few brief moments, be transformed into an act of compassion.

And Theo? What post coitus emotions did he endure? Did he go straight to his desk, feed a clean sheet of paper into that ancient portable and commence another of his polished, elegant paragraphs – the creative impulse regenerated by sexual fulfilment? I have heard it is quite commonplace with footballers and boxers, and Edmund Kean is reputed to have sampled up to three whores immediately prior to one of his major performances. A highly successful playwright once confided that whenever he fell victim to our recurring complaint, writer's block, he resorted to masturbation. "Nothing like it for clearing the brain. It's the guilt, you see, old man. You feel so bloody guilty afterwards, especially at my age, you have to get back to work. And of course one doesn't have to be polite afterwards. That's what I always hate about conventional sex. To have to waste so much time romancing the creatures. You can say goodbye to yourself so easily."

I don't know how many hours I spent in Theo's room that first day of discovery. I became grimed with newsprint and dust, forgetful of time passing, unaware of hunger, and it wasn't until Mrs. Davis suddenly reappeared, spruced and drenched in a sickening, cheap scent to invite me down for supper that I returned to the world of the living.

I accepted as graciously as I could and endured her small talk over a meal of curry that in itself was justification for the Race Relations Act. Her own brand of loneliness was of the aggressive kind, as though some of Theo's sexuality had seeped downstairs and impregnated the flock wallpaper of her garish apartment. Her conversation, when she was not probing for details of the value of Theo's estate, was saturated with innuendo that I found as bitter as the coffee she served.

As soon as was polite, I excused myself and returned to Theo's room. I packed two suitcases, filling one with the pornography I intended to burn, and the other with selected bundles of letters and documents together with some forty of the identical exercise books he had used for his journals. I had tidied up the worst of the debris and parcelled most of the tattered magazines for eventual collection as salvage. I dare say that would have been the end of it had I not, at the last moment, been drawn to flick through the pages of an old copy of *Country Life*. My initial interest was to compare the price of houses in the Sixties with current values. A photograph fluttered to the floor, falling face downwards. I picked it up and found myself staring at a man who had once featured on the front pages of every Western newspaper. It was the face of a once handsome youth gone to flab; a weak face, the lips moistened in a smile devoid of any warmth. Written across the photograph were the words *To Theo with too much love*. One corner was torn, obliterating most of the signature, but I had no difficulty in identifying the face. It was a photograph of Guy Burgess.

3

THEO REALLY BELONGED to the turn of the century. Connolly once described him (in an otherwise uncomplimentary lead review) as an 'Edwardian monument to the English novel', a remark which prompted a particularly arid correspondence in the *Times Literary Supplement*. He was often spoken of in the same reverent tones as Forster and Beerbohm, though his output was considerably more than their combined efforts and he had no time for either of them. He dismissed Beerbohm as a dilettante and felt it was an outrage that he had been knighted. "He should have had the decency to refuse it," Theo said, "and been satisfied with a widow's pension. That was more his mark." He was no less scathing about Forster, dubbing him a 'back passage to India' and was never so angry as when a critic bracketed him and Forster together.

I can understand how difficult it was for his critics to net him, for it was almost impossible for a complete outsider to get his true personality down on paper. He seldom gave interviews, and although he could have written his own ticket for any of the television talk shows he was seldom seen on the box. Unlike Willie Maugham, Theo never had a constant male companion and thus the gossip columnists were denied the field of innuendo and, in those far-off days before the dawn of the permissive society, were forced to scatter their clues with circumspection. "Hell," he used to remark, "hath no fury like a homosexual critic who senses that his more exalted victims are getting away with it," adding that, "Although it has always been an unwritten law that everybody closes ranks when the yahoos advance on the camp, there is little mercy shown to those within the city walls."

Theo gave no personal clues in his published works. He wrote elegant prose, being closer to Henry James than most of his contemporaries and his narratives centred on a way of life that has long since disappeared. He shared, with Hartley, a belief that the past is a foreign country where people do things differently. He had an affinity with the past, a hankering for time lost, searching back for an age of innocence that probably never existed but which seemed preferable to the world he was compelled to inhabit. The major novels, fourteen in all, were spaced out at regular intervals, and those readers who care about such things will doubtless have noted that the majority of his plots deal with unrequited love. The novels constitute the bulk of his output, but he did publish two collections of essays, both of which were taken apart and degutted by Leavis, thus ensuring that the other critics over-praised them.

Within the family he and I were both regarded as misfits, I perhaps less so than Theo because I was more recognisably successful. My novels, though never accorded the respect that Theo commanded, sold in far greater numbers, especially in paperback editions which many of my relatives favoured since, as one of them put it, 'you don't feel it's such a waste of money'. My mother, who regarded Theo as a second son, remained steadfastly sorrowful about his lifelong bachelor status. "Such a pity," she would say, "Theo never found a nice girl. They were all too flighty for him" – betraying her own sex *en masse*. In her later years she found it convenient to embroider her basic fantasy and spoke knowledgeably of Theo having been jilted. "It broke his heart," she would confide. "That's why he took up writing." Somewhere tucked away in her memory, like the small lawn handkerchief she always kept up her sleeve, was a folded misinterpretation, easy to mock. It satisfied her moral sense of the order of things and I dare say that in her true innocence, typical of her class and generation, her inventions were no more reprehensible than the realities of Theo's secret life. I was sometimes tempted to explode the myth in her presence, but lacked the killer instinct that divides families more easily than the axe. There is always a point when the attitudes of the previous generation make paper Lizzie Bordens of us all.

She was, I am sorry to say, a snob without a glimmer of

justification, for we were not even *nouveau riche*, we were just plodding middle-class ordinary – though, as my mother remarked, bending many a bored ear, she came of 'good stock'. There was always the unspoken implication that she had improved the bloodline without any assistance from my father. Even as a small child I detected the heady aroma of my mother's pretensions, sometimes as strong as the Chanel No. 5 with which she drenched her ample bosom when she and my father had 'an evening out' – a Masonic dinner or one of those annual obligations, so revered in close communities, known as The Mayor's Open Day. We once entertained a canon to tea, and this sent my mother into a frenzy of pre- and post-exaltation.

My father suffered in silence, never challenging, giving no sign that every fresh obsession of my mother's was a criticism of his personality. They were bound together by the conventions of the time, for divorce in our family was akin to leprosy: those who strayed, no matter how distant the relationship, were for ever struck off The Christmas Card List – my mother's equivalent of the Almanach de Gotha.

For reasons that time has partially obscured, I spent most of my school holidays with Theo and his parents in their large house outside Norwich. It was called Westfield, a dark Victorian horror with 'later additions', as the estate agents say. Whatever else may have displeased my mother regarding the character of Harry Gittings, Theo's father, the size of his home and the life style he affected weighed heavily in his favour. By our own standards the Gittings were rich. They took holidays abroad, they kept two horses, had a housekeeper, a maid, and ran a car. Harry Gittings was a senior partner in a long-established firm of country solicitors, a profession where the pickings have always been substantial. Naturally, the fact that he was a member of the legal profession impressed my mother. Out of his hearing and careful of her company she would often inflate his standing, referring to him as 'our barrister relative'. I suspect that Harry Gittings retained scant knowledge of the day-to-day workings of the courts. Early on in his career he had taken stock of his own abilities and concentrated on the intricacies of the laws

pertaining to Death and Estate Duties. He enjoyed a reasonable reputation in his field and was certainly never short of
elderly widows for clients, all of whom had seen their
husbands laid to rest and lived on to enjoy what Harry
salvaged for them. My father, giving one of his rare verdicts,
once pronounced that Harry sailed close to the wind. In my
then innocence I took this to mean he had nautical leanings.
He was a man of many parts, taking a keen interest in the
local community, a church warden who rode with the local
hunt and was on the Board of Governors of the County
Reform School for wayward girls – of which more later.

Theo was an only child, born prematurely by Caesarean
section in France, Harry Gittings having insisted that his wife
accompany him on an exhaustive tour, 'doing' the châteaux
of the Loire. More than anything else, the Gittings' travels set
them apart from my own family, for we seldom ventured
further than Bournemouth and then always putting up in
what the British term 'private' hotels. I cannot recall that
they were ever private or merited being named hotels, but
they came halfway between my mother's pretensions and my
father's income. For many British families most of the year is
a storing of the energy necessary to survive a British holiday.
We journeyed by train, second class, and took a taxi from
Bournemouth station. Every morning, rain or shine, we
would troop down to the beach and hire deck chairs to stake
our claim to a section of the over-crowded sands. My brothers
and I would immediately start to acquire third-degree burns,
assuming the sun shone, or else streaming colds, when the
sun did not shine. Occasionally, accompanied by father, we
would thread our way through the crowds to sample the icy
qualities of that holy stretch of grey matter known as the
English Channel. My mother would sit, protected from the
sun by a large flowered hat, a fugitive from death in Little
Venice. All around people would be struggling to change into
swimming attire, hopping on one foot, swathed in towels,
knickers and trousers entwined around their ankles, bras and
vests quickly crumpled and concealed – a series of prudish
conjuring tricks not yet mastered, so that at times when one
looked up through the heat haze the whole beach seemed to

35

be populated with a tribe of voodoo dancers.

Such were our dismal summer holidays, and it was with mingled fear and relief that I escaped most years to Westfield: fear because of justifiable suspicions of Theo's father, and relief because for a few weeks I could be relieved of my mother's suffocating concern for the proprieties. The moment I arrived at Westfield Theo entered into an unspoken conspiracy, giving me a relationship I never enjoyed with my twin brothers. There was an element of hero worship, of course, and a feeling of superiority since my brothers were never invited. Perhaps I was quieter than they or, improbable though it now seems, perhaps I gave the impression of being better mannered.

Theo was my senior by some three years and yet the age difference was never apparent to me, and I cannot recall that he ever used it to his own advantage, or condescended to me. I suspect that Theo was somewhat undeveloped, for he had been kept apart from children of his own age. He reputedly suffered from chronic ill health as a child, and as a consequence never attended school until he was in his late teens, but instead had a series of tutors, few of whom lasted longer than six months. Illness fascinated me, and I envied Theo what I imagined was a halcyon life free from the drudgery of the classroom. He never seemed particularly sickly during the holidays we spent together, and it wasn't until long after those early years that I pieced together the many clues and came to realise that his reported weaknesses were mostly his mother's inventions – a form of self-protection she had devised to keep him with her.

I don't suppose I am alone in my habit of finding literary comparisons with real life; a chance sentence from a favourite book can transport me back through the years in an instant. I have long cherished what I believe to be one of the finest novels written this century: Ford Madox Ford's *The Good Soldier*, that ironic tale of passion and deceit, so evocative, so erotic that it puts most of today's fiction to shame. It begins with the words 'This is the saddest story . . .' and whenever I re-read it my thoughts surge back to Westfield, and I can see as clearly as I now behold the bowl of freshly-cut roses on my desk the image of Theo's mother, pastel-shaded, her face too heavily powdered, her eyes blurred as though she cried too often, lifting thin hands to her throat in a constant, nervous gesture, and always speaking in a hushed voice. I never saw her laugh when Harry was present, unless it was in anxious response to one of his coarse jokes. At the dining table her eyes never left him: she was like some inexperienced umpire at Wimbledon, terrified of making the wrong call. Away from Harry she would relax and take an interest in our childhood games, but she always seemed to have one ear cocked for his return; the sound of his latch-key in the front door was sufficient to transform her. If this now sounds melodramatic, I cannot help it. She lived in a state of perpetual tension, torn between an unhealthy concern for Theo and terror of her husband. There was an atmosphere of fear about that house, a sense of things happening off-stage, as it were – things which, to a child, remained unexplained but which nevertheless made themselves felt in everyday life.

Looking back, I can fill some of the blank squares in the then unsolved crossword of our immature lives. I remember one occasion when Theo and I had the house to ourselves for a whole afternoon. His parents had both gone to some garden party and the housekeeper had the afternoon off. We were put on our honour – a promise given loosely and immediately disregarded. It was inevitable that with the insatiable curiosity of the young we should jointly settle on the idea of invading the holy of holies: Harry Gittings's study, or 'library' as it was generously termed.

I think I turned the door handle. There was a stillness about the room – forbidding, as though the personality of its regular occupant had permeated the very fabric of the walls. Facing us was a tall, mahogany, glass-fronted bookcase, its shelves housing the standard collection for solicitors, a uniformly bound set of the Law Reports. The partner's desk in the same dark wood stood in front of a leaded bay window, and beside the desk was a brass ashtray with a half-smoked Havana poised on it, the tip black-sodden and flattened. I have always found this a curiously repellent sight.

Committed now to total folly, I advanced into the room

37

and unprompted by Theo performed what to his eyes must have seemed an act of unparalleled heroism. I went and sat in his father's chair behind the desk. The leather seat was dimpled from his weight and emitted a soft fart as it was depressed. This reduced both of us to helpless laughter.

"Don't touch anything," Theo said, when he had recovered. "Don't leave any fingerprints." He was an avid disciple of Sexton Blake.

I took a grubby handkerchief from my pocket in the best traditions of that super sleuth and gently tried the centre drawer of the desk.

"For God's sake!" Theo said. He had not moved further than the doorway.

"They won't be back for ages."

"Well, I'd still better keep look out."

He advanced a few more paces into the room, standing to one side so that he could keep the street under observation.

The centre drawer contained some blotting paper and pens. The heavy scent of stale cigar smoke was making me feel queasy, but Theo's continued timidity spurred me to other acts of bravado. I took a fresh cigar from the drawer and placed it gently between my lips. Theo covered his eyes.

"I'm not at all satisfied with your behaviour," I growled in an unconvincing parody of his father's voice.

"Put it back, put it back," Theo moaned.

I complied because my nausea was stronger than my boastful intentions. I tried another drawer. This was deeper and had dividing sections in it. I saw what I at first thought were some rags in the nearest section. I poked at them.

"What're you doing now?"

"Nothing. Hey, look at these."

"What?"

"Come and look."

Theo edged closer to the desk and peered into the drawer. "What are they?"

"Knickers," I said. "Girl's knickers."

We stared at them.

"They must be your mother's. Why does he keep them in his desk?"

"I don't know," Theo said.

"Let's see what else there is."

I pulled the drawer further open, revealing the back section. This had a lid to it. I lifted this. The first thing we saw was a small, square packet with the emotive word *Durex* printed on a violet background. We were not so innocent that we did not immediately realise the implications of such an astounding discovery. On Saturday mornings when my brothers and I paid our fortnightly visit to the barber shop, we were always drawn to the same word engraved across a small mirror to the rear of the salon. Waiting our turn for the chair, we had observed the furtive transactions whereby the self-same packets changed hands without a word being spoken between barber and customer. Further evidence came our way when we picked up discarded packets on the Common, that sparsely-grassed arena of sexual initiation for many of my contemporaries. Total knowledge had come when a sixth former inflated a sample of the forbidden wares and floated it across the Assembly Hall during morning prayers, a crime of such enormity that he was caned in front of the entire school before being expelled. Although I had never carried out such advanced experiments myself, the grapevine of smut had ensured that I had a rudimentary knowledge of the true function of the damning objects. Even to say 'French letters' aloud was considered daring, suggesting a world of such blazing depravity as to pass all comprehension. To think that such seemingly innocent articles, so close to the Christmas balloons that exploded on the holly tips when batted between us, could hold the key to the ultimate sexual mystery inspired feelings of the keenest intensity. We were triggered into instant tumescence whenever the subject was discussed.

"God!" Theo said.

"Your father," I said. "He uses *them!*"

"God," Theo repeated.

I lifted a corner of the packet with a finger nail, exposing the flaccid white skin of rubber. It was like lifting a heavy stone and finding something loathsome beneath. We both stared at it. I think that, simultaneously, we arrived at the same inescapable conclusion: Theo's father, although patently past his prime by any standards we normally applied, still indulged in the sins of the flesh. And of course the idea was repugnant to us, as well as fascinating – more repugnant to Theo than to me, because it naturally followed that his mother was on the receiving end.

The packet lay on top of a large white envelope. "D'you think there's anything else?" I whispered. It seemed right to whisper in the presence of such mysteries.

"What else could there be?"

I took the question to be rhetorical and, once again using my handkerchief for protection, slid the envelope out of the drawer. Then I lifted the flap with a pencil. Inside were half a dozen postcard-size photographs. Using the pencil as a lever, I pushed the top photograph into view. It depicted what I took to be a French legionnaire sitting on a garden swing, the ropes of which were entwined with flowers. He was wearing a legionnaire's peaked cap and black socks, but apart from these two items he was naked. He was not a particularly healthy-looking specimen and had a reedy body, but he was endowed with a truly enormous penis standing out from his groin at a forty-five degree angle. Kneeling between his legs was a nun. At first I thought she was praying to be spared rape, and then I realised that her mouth was resting on the tip of his penis, the lips parted as though she was poised to take a bite.

We stared at the picture in silence.

Although neither of us were strangers to reproductions of the nude female body and had often discussed the more prominent attributes of the opposite sex, the revelation of such blatant male sexuality – the visual evidence of adult life in the raw, albeit not fully understood (since we were unprepared for and had no comprehension of fellatio) produced in us feelings of excited revulsion. Whereas lust in the abstract, lust directed towards those demure female nudes we searched for so diligently in forbidden magazines, with their sweet pointed breasts and hairless genitals discreetly shadowed, was without conscious depravity, the evidence now before us pointed towards a world of satanic proportions. Had we chanced upon the photographs in some natural setting the immediate effect would have been the same, but we would have been spared the true horror of connecting the sexuality with anybody we knew. But there, in that cold room, Harry's holy of holies, there was no such escape route. The tunnel towards maturity had not yet been dug. The evidence was conclusive. It was Harry's desk; nobody touched it, therefore the photographs could not have been planted.

Fear smothered our further curiosity. We had seen enough. The envelope was hastily replaced, the packet of contraceptives carefully positioned as we had found it, the drawer shut and then wiped of all incriminating evidence by my less than pristine handkerchief. We crept out of the room, went through the house and into the garden. Neither of us could find the right words.

"I think," Theo said finally, "I think he must have bought them in France, don't you?"

"Probably."

"On holiday."

"Yes."

"As souvenirs."

I nodded.

"Without mother knowing."

That thought hadn't occurred to me, but as Theo searched my face for confirmation I hadn't the heart to disagree.

"I'm sure Mother doesn't do that."

"She was a nun," I said, as though that was the perfect explanation.

"A real nun, d'you think?"

"They have temptations, too." For the first time in our relationship his advantage in years was not so apparent.

"Wasn't it extraordinary?"

"Yes."

We walked up and down the garden path.

"What d'you imagine it does to you?"

I couldn't answer that. "Maybe it's only in France," I said, trying to be helpful.

4

I SEE NOW, HAVING read and re-read the journals, that
betrayal was Theo's life's work. In the end I honestly
believe that what killed him was the incurable drug of
deceit itself. Even his published work, the external evidence of
his view of life, so carefully sifted and 'cleared' by his peers,
was an industrious fabrication. He deliberately chose to lead
everybody away from the real trail by concentrating on
themes bleached of all political content. All those books, all
that application over so many years, and not a single clue that
could be isolated and used against him. One has to have a
grudging admiration, and if logic revolts against the evidence,
releasing the inevitable questions as to why he was never
exposed, one has only to turn to the post-mortems held for his
erstwhile companions in arms – Philby, Burgess and Maclean
– to see how openly most of the people who shouldn't be
fooled can be fooled most of the time.

My knowledge of Cambridge in the late Twenties and early
Thirties was acquired second hand. I missed any personal
exposure to the 'loss of innocence' Theo's generation
experienced and which he recounted to me. He was eighteen
when he went up to Trinity in 1929, the very year that Philby
became an undergraduate at the same college. Burgess didn't
arrive until the following year.

I suppose, looking back, I was the most deceived, for in
those formative years I doubt if anybody was closer to Theo:
nobody, to my knowledge, shared his confidence as I did.
Both our families survived the sullen aftermath of the
1914–1918 war. Harry Gittings, having escaped the trenches
with a staff appointment, picked up where he left off – there
was, after all, no shortage of widows to comfort and advise.
His practice flourished as never before. My own father was
not so fortunate. He was gassed, and although he made a

recovery was never the same man again. More by good luck than compassion his old job – that of a quantity surveyor – was kept open for him. He was able to tread water, but that was all. Any plans he might have had for sending me or my brothers to university were never spoken of again. My mother lapsed into another of her periodic declines and their relationship became a bitter truce easily broken. Whenever she saw a crack in my father's thin armour she would lunge to draw blood and somehow she was always at her most dangerous when comparing Theo's advantages in life with my own. Her maternal instincts had always been spread thin; she was never so happy as when she was describing the difficult circumstances of our births. "'Course I never wanted children," she would say. "I wasn't built for them. The doctors said it was a miracle I ever came through" – this with a sidelong glance at father – "not that some people gave any thought to my feelings in the matter. Too intent on their own pleasures."

My brothers found some compensating comfort from the fact that they were twins, being alike in temperament if not in looks. I was never close to either of them, for they lacked any urge to escape from the environment I found so stifling. I thought of Theo as my brother and longed to emulate his attitudes towards life. I gradually came to understand part of my mother's sad snobbery, her sense of outrage that she had missed out on things, and for self-protection I became the Switzerland in the family Europe, surrounded on all sides by hostile forces that I willed myself to ignore.

I began writing at an early age, first as a form of escape, and before the age of seventeen I had completed two turgid and, happily for my future reputation, unpublishable novels. They drew heavily on my limited experience of life, but since I had neither the wit nor the sophistication to be objective, the results were predictably puerile. At the time, I laboured in the belief that I would shortly be challenging Arnold Bennett. Every publisher in London was bombarded with my soiled manuscripts; only one replied with any compassion and a few sparse words of encouragement, and these sustained me for many a fresh attempt. I finally accepted defeat where the novels were concerned and started to write short stories. Here I had a modicum of success and was able to place two of them, since in those halcyon days there was a surfeit of small magazines only too anxious to fill their pages with cheap submissions. I seem to remember I received ten and sixpence for one and a cheque for a guinea for the second, and that the cheque bounced. However, I had proved my point: I was capable of being published. The sight of one's own work actually in print is perhaps the most potent drug for a writer, and my resolve never faltered from that moment. Because of our reduced circumstances I was forced to leave school at sixteen and find a job to help supplement the family income. Armed with my published works I attacked the local newspaper, and must have been sufficiently brash to overcome the editor's reluctance to hire anybody in those depressed times, for I was taken on as a glorified tea-boy. I was deliberately, grotesquely sycophantic to everybody in that grimy establishment, and the ploy paid off, for I was finally allowed to handle those assignments that the rest of our small and jaded staff scorned. I covered weddings, funerals and the local Petty Sessions, turning in copy that was seldom less than purple and was inevitably subbed unmercifully.

It was a boring and in many ways soul-destroying period, but marginally better than the nine to five occupations that my twin brothers willingly embraced. At least I was not chained to the routine of a shop assistant; I had a reasonable amount of freedom and although I loathed journalism at the level I was exposed to it, I was not completely separated from my chosen vocation.

This was the same year Theo went to Trinity. He was the only person who gave me any real encouragement with my writing. Without his understanding I doubt whether I would have stayed the course, since my further short stories slid down the same slope as the novels. Rejection slips corrode ambition after a time. It was Theo who urged me to look outside my own immediate circle.

"The trouble is," he said, "your novels and stories aren't about real people. Or, put it this way, they're not about people anybody wants to read about. Your characters don't have any sexuality. They're neuter." I listened to his criticism with a respect I accorded to nobody else. "What you've got to write about is what's happening up here at Cambridge. Kiss your suburban background goodbye, forget writing abut life in a Bournemouth lodging house and young love triumphant. That's gone, all that's old hat."

"It's all right for you. You're at Cambridge."

"Well, live vicariously through me. I'll give you some copy. The next time we meet I'll give you a plot that'll make your hair stand on end."

"What sort of plot?"

"Life in the raw."

"Meaning sex?"

"Sex comes into it. I mean, sex comes into everything."

"Have you done it yet?"

"It?"

"You know."

"There are some things one doesn't boast about."

"Don't be rotten. We always said we'd tell each other. We had a pact, remember?"

"Well, I will tell you, but I'm in the middle of it. I'll tell you the unhappy ending."

"Why will it be an unhappy ending?"

"Because those are the only affairs worth having."

Ever since our fateful exploration of his father's study, the topic of sex had obsessed us. I had lost my initial advantage where Theo was concerned, partly because of my semi-detached environment and partly because of the age difference between us. I was just turned sixteen when Theo went to Cambridge and there were little or no opportunities for experiment in Little Venice. There were two secretaries at my place of work, but one was married and the other, although only her late twenties, seemed almost as old as my mother. I met girls of my own age, but none of them was emancipated and any fumbling approaches I made from time to time were hastily and conclusively repulsed. I lived in a fever of expectation, starting every fresh assignment for the paper with my imagination recharged, able to convince myself that in the best tradition of a foreign correspondent I

45

would be exposed to voluptuous temptation. The effort of sustaining the image of a foreign correspondent while covering a church jumble sale or a Rotarian lunch daily proved too much and I remained resolutely virginal.

It never occurred to me to envy Theo in the way that my mother sought to envy the Gittings's entire way of life. As the years went by my admiration for Theo became a lifeline. We still spent holidays together and I was no longer tongue-tied at his family meal tables, and could even, on occasion, raise a smile from Harry Gittings with my descriptions of life in London. But I was in no doubt that there was something faintly sinister about him. His speech had a curious delivery, precise, somewhat sibulant and pitched low, maybe a professional affectation he had developed to impress his clients. Having begun by ignoring me completely, I think he grew to tolerate me. I spent Christmas with them the year of Theo's first term at Trinity and was amazed by the amount and variety of food on the festive table. The first time I ever tasted venison, Harry Gittings carved it and after lunch on Christmas Day he offered me a small cigar.

"I don't smoke," I said. It was a white lie because I had several times attempted to puff my way through a Gold Flake stolen from my father.

"No vices, eh?"

He cut the end of his own cigar with a patented penknife which, he demonstrated, could only be opened if held at a certain angle.

"Given to me by a grateful client."

He licked the end of the cigar in a way I found curiously unpleasant. Our conversation took place in his study and it took all my concentration to refrain from staring at his desk; memories of that extraordinary afternoon came crowding back.

"One should always have one vice," he said after the first inhale. "I mean, where would I be if everybody was perfect? Vice of one kind or another paid for your Christmas lunch." He regarded me as somebody in a witness box. "I understand you're not going to university like Theo."

"No, sir."

"Why is that? Don't you want to go?"

"I don't think my parents can afford it."

"No, I don't suppose they can. D'you want a glass of port? You do drink port, I take it?"

"Oh, yes," I said. I didn't, but there was something about his attitude towards me that provoked a spurious courage. He poured two glasses from a decanter and pushed one towards me.

"Put down before you were born."

"Very nice," I said.

"Port is never nice. It's either superb or undrinkable. Remember that. This particular port is superb. Otherwise I wouldn't serve it. Tell me more about yourself."

"I'm a reporter."

"Enjoy that, do you?"

"Well, I don't intend to make it my career."

"What do you intend?"

"I want to be writer. I've been published already. Several magazines have taken my stories."

He regarded me with narrowed eyes for several seconds. "What sort of stories do you write?"

"Oh, all sorts."

"Such as?"

I struggled to think of words to describe my unsophisticated efforts.

"Are they all about the sweet mystery of life?"

"Yes," I said, "more or less."

He poured himself a second glass of port. "D'you like animals?" he asked.

The question took me by surprise. "Animals? Yes. Very much."

"Cats?"

"Yes, we've got a cat."

"Cats are my favourites," he said. "Very proud creatures. Independent. In fact there's only one thing I dislike about them. D'you know what that is?"

I shook my head.

"They always show their bottoms. Have you noticed that?"

"Yes, I suppose you're right. I'd never thought of that."

"I've thought about it a great deal. They always show their

bottoms," he repeated with slow relish. "Apart from that they're fastidious creatures, much cleaner than dogs. They bury their excreta."

His words came to me through a haze brought about by the unaccustomed port, but I was sufficiently aware of the situation to think he was insane.

"As a matter of fact they're much cleaner than human beings. We wash our faces and our hands, do we not? but most of us never wash our arses. Most of us in this country, that is. The French, who leave a lot to be desired in other directions, do at least employ the bidet. Ask the average plumber in this country to install a bidet and he doesn't know what you're talking about. Most of them can't even pronounce it. Now that would be a good subject for you to write about. Why don't people wash their arses when they've been to the toilet?"

He stared at me.

"The paper I write for doesn't really go in for that . . . that sort of article."

"But it is an interesting comment on our society don't you think?"

Mad, I thought, stark staring mad.

"I have a bidet installed in my own bathroom. Imported from the Continent, at no little expense. I use it every day. Every day. Because I know how to live."

He seemed to leave me at that point and we sat in silence until, mercifully, Theo came in search of me and I was able to make my escape.

"You'll never guess what he told me," I said, the moment we were safely out of earshot.

"What? Something about me?"

"No. He talked about cats and their arses, and then he talked about his own. How he washes it every day."

The revelation did not have the anticipated effect on Theo.

"Oh, yes," he said. "Conversation normal. I've had that for years. It's his favourite topic. Anything scatological. I think he's off his chop. You know he's on the Board of the local naughty girls school. Well . . . he doesn't give up his spare time to improve their wayward minds. He just likes to see them punished. Have their little bottoms whacked. All legal. It has to be carried out in front of witnesses, you see. So, he witnesses."

"What d'you think he gets out of it?"

"The mind boggles," Theo said. "You know those knickers we found in his desk? Well, we were both so bloody naive in those days. I mean, we both thought they belonged to Mother, didn't we? Not a bit of it. Know where they came from? The girls' reform school. He brings their dirty knickers home."

"Christ!" I said.

"I'll tell you what my dear father is. He's a filthy old sod."

I suppose what impressed me as much as the secret itself was Theo's calmness in the telling of it. Occasionally my paper ran heavily censored accounts of some sex deviant who had been caught committing an act of public indecency in the local swimming baths, but I had no idea that such aberrations could apply to a man of Harry Gittings's standing.

"How did you find out?" I asked.

"I put two and two together. And of course like most perverts he can't resist dropping hints. That's their kick, of course. Shocking other people. He's always coming out with some new piece of sexual wisdom."

"Like what?"

"Oh, what was his latest? Yes, when I went up to Cambridge he warned about the dangers of promiscuity. 'Always remember,' he said, 'an upright phallus has no conscience.'"

"My father's never ever mentioned anything like that to me."

"No, well, your old man's normal. Dull, but normal."

"He can't help being dull," I said. "He was gassed."

"Gassed on the Somme and gassed at home by your mother's boring conversation – a lethal combination."

"Yes, well, it's sad rather than dull."

"But you mustn't get like them. If you want to be a writer, then you've got to broaden the old horizons, say goodbyeeee, turn your back on all that."

I noticed that even in the short time he had been at Trinity his way of speaking had changed. He was much more self-assertive, perhaps even a little pompous.

"It's easy for you," I said. "You've done it, you've got away."

"Listen, Tony, dear boy. Never envy people. This is never going to be a land fit for heroes to live in, so face up to it early on. Envy is corrosive. It'll destroy your writing and it'll destroy you. By all means try and change this piddling society, but don't base your whole philosophy on envy. It's a dead end. You should hear Kim's views on the subject."

"Who's Kim?"

"Oh, somebody I know."

I felt a sense of apartness. There was Theo, the epitome of the 'Rupert Brooke' undergraduate, in his expensive flannel bags and tweed jacket, his Hawes and Curtis shirt monogrammed on the pocket, that casual elegance that sits easily on the privileged few – in strict contrast to my own appearance, usually classified as neat but undistinguished. Try as I might I could not stifle those shameful feelings of envy, for I wanted what he was able to take for granted. I wanted Cambridge's beauty and freedom – that cushioned, intoxicating life, a mixture of quiet scholarship and hilarious social conventions. It was a period in British history that will never come again, for the old order had changed – the Great War had seen to that – and on both sides of the Atlantic those who had survived were determined to enjoy themselves whatever the cost. But the flamboyant pleasures, the pleasures that were reported, belonged to those who, buttressed by private incomes and by admiration of the masses, tried to perpetuate the security and opulence of the pre-war society by grafting on the sexual emancipation of the Twenties. It was not a Jazz Age for the majority, but a time for survival, a time of dreary cynicism as the brave experiment of the League of Nations rotted at the roots, a time of drift – the tide bearing us all towards the next holocaust.

I used to visit Theo in Cambridge and on one occasion managed to persuade my editor to let me cover the university scene in depth over a series of three articles which, for the first time, carried my by-line. I remember thinking it was strange for a man in his position to be so impressed with my contacts in the outside world and was amazed that I had sold him the idea so easily. Perhaps he was persuaded by the fact that it wasn't going to cost him anything extra, for I roomed with Theo in Trinity during my stay, Theo having bribed his scout to turn a blind eye. The ease with which the rules could be bent impressed me in turn.

It would be satisfying to be able to relate that I had an immediate perception of what was happening behind the scenes in the Cambridge of 1931, but I saw only the surface; and whether by design or accident, Theo, while acting the perfect host, never took me backstage. In many ways it was the turning point in my own life, for I felt that I had been given a glimpse of paradise. If that seems an over-statement it can be excused by my adolescent lack of sophistication: I was so anxious to be welcomed even on the fringe that all critical faculties were cheerfully abandoned.

I imagine I behaved like the tourist I was, punting on the Cam for the obligatory pilgrimage to Granchester, enjoying strawberry teas, joining in the earnest but shallow conversations which Theo and his set continued far into the night. I turned in three articles of acute banality, which revealed nothing new about Cambridge or its undergraduate population, but presumably I wrote what the public wanted to read and even got a modest rise in salary.

I recall that the main topic for debate was a copy of the privately printed *Seven Pillars of Wisdom* which Theo had acquired. He was greatly attracted to the enigmatic personality of Lawrence – the double and indeed treble life he led.

"It's amazing what he got away with, right under everybody's noses. 'Course, he enjoyed all that other stuff in the desert, I'm convinced of that. It was like the Greeks, you know. He went to battle with his boy mistresses. So he had to be brave in order to impress them."

The detailed and exhaustive discussions concerning Lawrence's sexual proclivities bored me. I was far more interested in discovering whether any of the Cambridge girls, dismissively referred to as 'blue-stockings' or 'bottled snakes'

51

(I am not quite sure whether I fully understand Julian Bell's much quoted remark), shared the freedom enjoyed by their male counterparts. My attempts to draw Theo on the subject met with little success.

"Boring. The whole lot of them are boring. Without exception. One doesn't even acknowledge their presence."

It was not a view I could share. If the sight of Theo and his set induced a feeling of envy, then the girls of Girton and Newnham inspired positive worship. I indulged in intellectual and sexual fantasies about them, convinced that somewhere in their midst was my ideal companion – a mixture of passion and purity of thought. More than once I walked the three miles down the Huntington Road to where Girton had been sited beyond the male citadel walls. In an effort to belong I borrowed a silk shirt of Theo's for these trips, convinced that this would give me the necessary poetic look so vital in the early stages of a seduction. Alas, the girls of Girton were not on the look out for poets that season, and I drew a series of blanks. Hope, like tumescence, sprang up afresh every morning, but I never even got to first base.

5

M Y FIRST SUCCESS when it came was of a totally different order, for I struck up an acquaintance with a
chocolate-box-pretty young waitress in a café close to
Trinity. I often went there to spin out a coffee and sticky bun
for a couple of hours while waiting for Theo to join me after
one of the few lectures he attended. I used the time to make
notes for my articles and for future stories, since it was
inevitable that the next novel I attempted would be set in
Cambridge.

Her name was Judy. She was a year or so older than me,
refreshingly aware of her sexual attractions and, more
astonishing, quite happy to discuss them. She had one of
those pert, slightly exaggerated figures, prominent, conical
breasts and a delicious bum. I had never met anybody quite
like her, for the confines of Little Venice had not harboured
such teenage sirens. I was immediately enamoured, my
appetite sharpened by my Girton failures. It is surprising how
easily, at that age, one can renounce intellectual ambitions.

Poor Judy had little or no stimulating conversation, a fact
that Theo criticised the first time I made my intentions known
to him.

"But she can't utter, dear boy. It's all she can do to repeat
the orders. Now, we know that in the dark all cats are grey,
albeit some greyer than others, but even allowing for the
poverty of your tastes, I really think you should aim a little
higher."

"But don't you think she's pretty?"

He stared at her across the café.

"Very. Slightly bovine, but I'll allow you, pretty. Over-
developed, of course."

"Nothing wrong with that, is there?"

"Too pneumatic. I hate sleeping on feather beds."

"You're just jealous."

"My dear Tony, that's the last thing I am. I mean, don't let me put you off. If your thrill of the chase lies in that direction, go to it."

"Well, easier said than done."

"Have you asked her?"

"Asked her what?"

"What? he says! Is she prepared to surrender what Frank Harris terms her box of delights?"

"It's too early for that," I said.

"How can it be too early? Tony, dear, you mustn't ask me for advice. She doesn't happen to be my type, which is of no consequence; after all, that's what makes the world go round. I think she's a very pretty little piece and knowing her class I'm sure she fucks."

"That's a bloody snobbish remark."

It was the closest we had ever been to falling out.

"Well, I'm sorry," Theo said. "I didn't mean it to be. Just stating what I take to be the facts. But don't get upset. It isn't as if you're intending to marry her."

"I might," I said, since sexual convictions are the easiest to defend.

"Well, fine. Congratulations."

"I suppose like your beloved Lawrence you're looking for an Arab boy?"

"Not Arab. They're too unwashed. But you're warm."

He got up from the table as Judy approached. "Look, I've got to cut. Don't take offence. It really doesn't matter one way or the other. You do what you want."

"You're always in here together," Judy said, looking after Theo. "Are you at the same college?"

"I'm not at college," I said. "I'm just here working, on a visit. He's my cousin."

"Very good looking."

"He said the same about you."

"Did he? What did he say?"

"He said I ought to ask you for a date."

"Cheeky!"

"So I'm asking you."

She stared at me, wrinkling her full mouth. "Don't know about that. How old are you?"

"Old enough."

"Oh, we know all the answers, don't we?"

The manageress was staring in our direction. From long training Judy seemed to have eyes in the back of her head. "Another cup of coffee, right, sir," she said loudly, then added for my benefit alone: "I'll see if the other's on my menu," and winked.

Having taken this first step I found her more desirable than ever. Watching her swing away from me through the crowded tables I felt those first pangs of a hunger that is never satisfied when one is young and the sap is rising. I envied Theo for other reasons, envied him his self-assurance and his money. I could not help comparing my appearance with those all around: how could she possibly prefer me when she had such superior choices?

By the time she returned I had prepared myself for the expected rebuff. She poured the coffee with maddening slowness, glancing at me as she added sugar and milk. Then she made out another bill, licking a stub of pencil in a particularly provocative manner.

"I don't get off 'til eight," she said. "I'll meet you by the bus stop round the corner."

"You mean tonight?"

"Yes."

She had a trayful of other orders to serve and I had no opportunity of prolonging the conversation. I could not believe my good fortune. It was as if I had just been awarded a First after an examination I was certain I had failed.

Something warned me not to rush and tell Theo the good news. I went to the public baths and spruced myself, then had a haircut. There my courage left me, for I must admit that my visit to the barber's was not without ulterior motives. When I was asked if I wanted anything 'extra', I could only stammer a request for a little pomade. It was lavender scented and slightly nauseated me.

I took up my position by the bus stop half an hour ahead of time. She arrived promptly. Doubtless she was always ready to escape from her twelve-hour shift.

"Where are we going?" she asked.

I hadn't thought of that.

"You smell nice," she said, waiting for my answer.

"It's something I use on my hair," I said. I was desperately seeking not to make any mistakes. "I didn't know whether you'd want to eat," I went on. "Having been in that place all day."

"Oh, I like my grub. Especially when I'm being taken out."

Instinctively my hand went to my trouser pocket. I tried to count the coins without jingling them.

"Fine," I said. "Anywhere you prefer? I don't know the best places, being a stranger."

"All right, I'll take you somewhere. But let's get out of here, shall we?"

She put her arm through mine as we walked off. I could feel her warmth as our bodies touched.

"Did you say you're from London?"

"Yes."

"Is it like they say?"

"Haven't you ever been?"

"I've never been outside Cambridge. Oh, that's a lie. We did go to Hunstanton once. That's the seaside. We went there when me dad was alive."

"Your father's dead, is he?"

"Yes," she said. "He come back from the war with half his face shot away. There wasn't much to live for. He had a lovely face when it was all there." She tightened her grip on my arm. "Tell me more about London. Did you ever see the King and Queen?"

"Yes, several times."

"Really?"

"Yes. At the Trooping of the Colour and on Armistice Day."

"Is it true what they say about the King?"

"What do they say?"

"That he wears make-up when he goes out."

"Who says that?"

"I don't know. Some friend at work told me. She reckons they all do. Prince of Wales and all."

"Well, not that I've noticed," I said airily.

She stopped outside a small restaurant. It had a menu stuck in the window and to my dismay I saw that the set dinner was priced at one and sixpence.

"This is nice," Judy said. "I ate here once before on me last birthday. And don't ask how old I am, because I shan't tell you."

I wasn't able to concentrate at that moment, being too busy working out complicated sums in my head. Without actually counting my money in front of her, I could only guess at the exact state of my finances.

"We'll go dutch, of course. I made quite a bit in tips today. It was one of the good days."

"But I'm taking you out," I said bravely.

"Yes, so what? You always go dutch the first time, otherwise it isn't fair. I mean, I know you haven't got any money."

"How?"

"Look, I wasn't born yesterday, you know. Anybody who makes a sticky bun and a cup of coffee last two hours isn't exactly flush. Come on."

She more or less pushed me inside. I couldn't get over her. The fact that she had accepted my invitation had been wonder enough, but she continued to amaze me. Her conversation as she prattled on through the simple meal was mostly gossip based on famous people she had read about. I learnt that she lived alone with an invalid mother on the outskirts of Cambridge. Several times during the course of the meal she made reference to the fact that her one recurring dream was to escape from her present environment and go to London. I confess it did cross my mind that perhaps I was being used, but I misjudged her. More than any other woman I have ever known she was devoid of guile; she just said what she meant, and there were no strings attached. She enjoyed her food and I was content to watch her eat, for the anticipation of what might lie beyond the meal had destroyed my own appetite.

"Hey, aren't you going to eat that?" she said. When I shook

my head she speared my lamb chop and took it to her own plate. "Can't waste it. I love lamb. Don't like to think about all them little sheep jumping about, but you've got to live, haven't you? D'you think they know?"

"Maybe."

"I don't think they do. Same with everything really, isn't it? If you thought about it, you'd never do anything. You've got to enjoy it while you can. That was what my dad always used to say. I'll show you his photo when we get back."

"Back?" I said. "Back where?"

"Well, you're taking me home, aren't you?"

"Yes. Yes, if you want me to."

"Aren't you funny? You've gone all white. Little white patches on both cheeks." She smiled at me across the table.

"Won't your mother mind?" I asked.

"She's an invalid, I told you. She's been in bed for six years. Rheumatoid arthritis. We haven't had much luck, our family."

"Who looks after her when you're at work?"

"Oh, neighbours come in. She's great, my mum. Never complains. She always says, you have a good time while you're young, because it ain't going to last."

"Six years. That's awful."

"Yes. Doctors say she could go on for another six, or it could all be over next week. They don't really know, do they? They're all about the same." She laughed. "Bloody useless."

We caught the last bus and the journey to her home took twenty minutes. We sat close together and she felt for my hand and squeezed it. "Hope you brought your pyjamas," she said.

I looked around quickly to see if any of the other passengers had overheard, and this made her laugh again.

"Perhaps you don't wear pyjamas."

"Depends," I said, in what I hoped was a calm voice.

"Only teasing you."

It was a short walk from the last bus stop to the house where she lived. It was in the middle of a terraced row, red bricked, with a small bay window in front. I hesitated at the gate.

"I wasn't really teasing on the bus. You can come in if you want."

"But your mother . . ."

"Listen, I'll tell you something about my mum. She ain't religious, 'cos she's got bloody little to be religious about, and she ain't narrow-minded. So she don't worry about me going in fear of mortal sin. When you lie on your back for years like she has, you don't think too much about the bleeding life hereafter. You say sod it!"

I was beginning to have second thoughts. Marriage, I thought ignobly. That's what she's looking for; she wants to trap me into marriage. She and her sick mother have probably worked it all out.

Judy had her key in the front door. "Come on, nobody's going to eat you."

I cast a glance down the deserted street. She opened the door and went inside to light a gas bracket in the small hall-way.

"I tell you what, I'll borrow a couple of pennies if you've got them. For the meter."

I stepped into the hallway and closed the door behind me. She came to me and kissed me on the lips, her mouth opening as we touched. I felt her breasts against me.

"I'll just see me mum," she said when the kiss was over. "Go in the back room and make yourself comfortable. The meter's under the sink." She started upstairs.

I walked with some difficulty into the kitchen-cum-parlour at the back of the house. Striking a match, I found the gas jet and lit it. Then I put two pennies in the meter. The room was spotlessly clean. There were two armchairs on either side of the iron range, a scrubbed pine table and a dresser. On the tall mantelpiece above the range was a photograph of a Tommy, stiffly posed in an ill-fitting uniform. I took this to be her dead father, for there was a distinct resemblance about the eyes and mouth. A cat appeared, uncurling from behind the coal scuttle, back arched, suddenly purring loudly as though somebody had switched it on. I bent to stroke it and it threaded in and out of my legs, frenzied with affection.

"That's Kitchener," Judy said.

I looked up to see her standing in the doorway.

"He's one of the old contemptibles usually. You're very favoured." She had taken her coat off upstairs.

"Like a cup of tea?"

"If you're having one."

"I always make one for Mum when I come in." She moved to the sink and filled a heavy kettle, blackened from standing on the open grate. "You can help me. Cups and saucers on the dresser there."

"How is your mother?"

"How is she ever? She's a bloody miracle, she is. Lies up there all day, sometimes she can't even brush a fly from her nose. Sometimes it's worse than others, you see. But we've got good neighbours either side. They come in and out all day. She can't do anything for herself."

"Does she know I'm here?"

"Yes, I told you. We don't have secrets, Mum and me."

She brewed the tea, having warmed the pot in traditional fashion, moving about the kitchen in bare feet, the cat following her everywhere, its purr like a motor.

"Give him a saucer of milk while I take this up, otherwise he'll give us no peace."

She left me again and in the quietness I could hear her talking to the sick woman upstairs, chattering on as she had with me in the restaurant. I tried to imagine what it would be like to be bedridden, then I poured some milk into a saucer and the cat jumped up on to the table and tried to lap it there.

"Don't be so ruddy anxious," I said, as much to myself as to the cat.

"Didn't you pour yourself a cup?" Judy said when she returned. "You're a daft one. Be stewed by now. My dad used to like strong tea. You could skate mice across his cup."

She poured two cups, adding at least four spoons of sugar to her own, then sat opposite me in the other armchair, lifting her legs and placing them in my lap.

"Oh, that's a relief. Best part of the day, this." She blew the steam off her cup and smiled at me over it.

"Are all London boys like you?"

60

"How d'you mean?"

"Quiet."

"I'm not always quiet. I was just enjoying this, being with you."

She stared at me. "Do you want to stay the night, sleep with me?"

I didn't answer at once. Her frankness utterly amazed me. "If you want me to," I said, not looking at her.

"Wouldn't ask you if I didn't, would I? I'm not a tart, you know. Is that what you're thinking?"

"No, 'course not."

"I haven't slept with anybody in, oh, over six months. I'm very choosy. I have to . . . like somebody, I don't mean love them, 'cos that, well, that's something else, but I have to like them. I like you. You're so serious."

"I like you too," I said.

"So you'll stay, will you?"

"If you want me to."

"There! You've said it again. It's not just what I want. I know what I want, it's you we're talking about. Look at me. I know what's worrying you. You've never done it before, have you?"

"It's not that," I said.

"What is it, then? You got a girl in London? Because if you have just say, I won't get mardy. But look at me and tell me straight."

I raised my eyes to hers. There was no malice in her face: it was as devoid of malice as it was of make-up. There was a bloom about her, a kind of innocence, the look of somebody who would never betray you.

"No, I haven't got anybody like that."

"I was right first time then. You haven't been to bed before?"

"Not all the way."

"Well, you either have or you haven't. Nothing to be scared of, you know. It's lovely, better than you've ever imagined." She put her cup down and came and sat in my lap. "You are a silly. Sitting here all buttoned up. You look like our vicar. Give me a kiss, and open your lips this time."

We kissed, then she said, "Give me your hand. Put it there."

She took my hand and placed it on her right breast. I could feel the nipple beneath the cheap fabric of her waitress's blouse.

"Is that what you ordered, sir?"

She kissed my eyes, the corners of my mouth, the side of my neck, my ear. "I wasn't lying," she said. "What I told you. I'm not a tart, don't think that. Oh, I've done it before, but that's a good thing, because it's morbid if neither of you have a clue. I've only done it three times, all with boys I liked, and never for money. I've just got the taste for it, you see, and I'll make it all lovely for you, you just wait. Look, I'll show you, I'm proud of these and I know you've been looking at them in the shop. I always know when boys are looking."

She unbuttoned her blouse. She was wearing only a vest underneath. "Slip it over my head," she whispered. "Two buttons at the back."

I did as I was told. "My hands are cold," I said.

"They won't be for long."

I lifted the vest over her head. Nothing I had ever seen could compare with the beauty of her young breasts. The gas-light seemed to bathe them in a golden haze. They were bigger than I had imagined and I was scared to touch them.

"Kiss them," she said. "I like having them kissed."

I bent my head and put my mouth to one nipple. It seemed to jump at my first touch and she pressed herself into my face as I tasted her.

"Oh, that's it, that's it, I love that."

Her head was thrown back and I lifted my face from her breasts to kiss her neck, seeking to trace the patterns she had recently taught me.

"No, kiss them again, kiss the other one, I love to feel your mouth on them."

It was no hardship to satisfy her. I felt as though I was suspended in time. I put my hands under her breasts and lifted them as I kissed them. I dare say I would have been content to please her in that fashion the whole night through, but the mood was suddenly shattered by the cat jumping on to our laps.

"Jealous, you see," Judy said. "Like all men. Will you be jealous?"

"Don't know, do I?" I said. "Will I have anything to be jealous about?"

She didn't answer that, but took my face in her two hands and stared into my eyes for several seconds. "Don't think badly about me, will you? I can't help myself."

Then, a moment later, "I fancied you, you see. I know girls aren't supposed to say that, but if they waited for the right man to ask them, they'd die old maids most of the time. I like fucking. Does that shock you?"

It did, but I pretended otherwise. I had never heard a woman say the word before; in some stupid chauvinistic fashion I doubted whether women even knew of it. It didn't come out as a swearword when she said it, that was the biggest surprise. It sounded gentle from her lips and after all, I thought, it is only a *word* – why do we attach so much importance to it?

"Come on," she said, rising from my lap, her breasts brushing my face. "We mustn't shock Kitchener. Let's go to my room."

"What about . . . ?"

"Don't worry. You worry so much."

She turned out the gas and led the way upstairs. Even then I still couldn't believe it was happening to me. I had imagined the scene a hundred times, conjuring up version after version, but I had never cast myself in the role of the seduced.

Some women have an aptitude for love, and to this day, nearly fifty years after the event, I can still recall the excitement Judy's body gave me.

"Just don't think about it," she said, "because there's nothing to go wrong. You see? There, you see! See how easy it is? Doesn't that feel nice? It's the best feeling in the world, isn't it?"

She was so feminine – clever enough, thank God, not to make me feel I was being used. Because she made everything seem so natural, my nervousness left me, I believed I was the teacher not the taught. We are so conditioned to expect the worst, to think of failure and humiliation. Judy enjoyed me because she enjoyed the very act of sex. Her pleasure was more intense than mine, but then, perhaps she had more need of love than me that night. I was consumed with simple lust, not the frenzy that destroys us in later years when our bodies need to be goaded to triumph, but the trembling urgency of ignorance. I had no idea that pleasures and sorrows were so inexorably mixed, and her tears dismayed me, for when I eased out of her body that first time she cried uncontrollably. It was as if the act of loving had released all her hidden fears. She lay in my arms, her nudeness touching every part of me, her tears running between us. I can put explanations to it now, since the whole business of living seems an endless preparation for sorrow, but that night I had no such perceptions. I was too dazed with the wonder of it all.

Afterwards, it was like watching somebody come round after an anaesthetic. "Oh, I needed that," she said. She pushed wet strands of hair from her forehead and lifted herself above me. Her breasts quivered a few inches from my mouth and I could not resist suckling them again. Many future choices were made in that small back bedroom, for I judged the women who came after by Judy's nubile body.

"When shall I see you again?" I said.

"You're seeing me now. All of me."

She raised herself higher before sitting down on my legs. "Was it like what you imagined?"

"Better."

"Well, I take that as a compliment."

"But shall I?"

"Yes, if you want to. But don't get soft on me, will you? I don't mean this sort of soft either."

"Why not?"

"Because I won't make old bones."

"That's a dreadful thing to say."

"Is it? Not really."

"I want to be with you for ever."

"Now you do, and that's nice, that's how it should be, but you don't have to make any promises. I'm not looking to catch you. I bet you thought that, didn't you? Be honest now."

64

"No," I said.

"I wouldn't blame you. I mean, I'm very brazen when I want to be. I knew I'd have you from the first moment you walked in. You couldn't take your eyes off my titties, could you? I like that. They are pretty, aren't they?" She cupped and held them, stroking them as she would smooth a piece of velvet. "Pretty for now, anyway. Won't last, of course. They're too big, they'll be down past me waist by the time I'm thirty, so you'd better enjoy them while you can. Why're you laughing?"

"You say such funny things."

"I face up to the truth. My dad taught me that. He used to make me look at his face. See, I never could, not when he first came home. I used to run away and hide. You won't *really* want me, not for life. You think so now, because I've just made you happy. And we can go on doing that, but don't make promises you won't be able to keep, because then you'll feel guilty and it'll all be spoilt."

She lay across me, her head on my stomach.

"Talk to me about London."

"It's just bigger than Cambridge, that's about all. I live in a place called Little Venice. There are canals, but they're not as pretty as the Cam. I'll take you on the Cam."

"Have to be a Sunday, then. I work the rest of the week."

"Yes, well I have to work too, you know. But I'll save my money and come and see you at weekends."

We talked far into that night. She was curious about Theo and asked me what our relationship was. "I thought you were his fancy boy until you looked at me," she said. "We get them all in there, you know. You can always tell. Or I can. Makes you laugh, don't it? I mean, I'd rather have me than some boy, wouldn't you?"

"Well, I've shown I would. Theo's not like that."

"Want to bet? If he's not, he ought to be. And he's stuck up."

"Really?" The thought had never occurred to me.

"Oh, yes, I'm always made to know my place when I serve him."

I told her about Harry Gittings and his peculiarities,

relating the story of how Theo and I uncovered the secrets of his desk that afternoon.

"Dirty pictures are for dirty old men," Judy said. "I've seen some – one of the girls at work had a boy friend who was always showing them to her. I mean they don't shock me. You can't be worried by pictures, can you? Just boring, I think, especially when you can have the real thing. Your friend's father sounds like he just needs a good fuck."

"But some of the pictures were very odd. I mean, really odd."

"What way?"

I told her of the nun and the legionnaire.

"You mean like this?" She slid her head down to my groin. "Nothing odd if you love somebody. 'Course, you don't have to dress up like a bleeding nun to do it. You just do it, like this." And to my further amazement, she did it.

"You said 'if you love somebody'," I whispered when the sweet agony was finished. "Did you mean that?"

"This is love, isn't it? What we've been doing."

"But I want you to love me, not anybody else."

"I can't promise that," she said. "You have to take me as I am. Don't be so serious. Look, that's serious, in that room next door. And there's plenty of that around. Too much. Half the people don't know they're alive, and the other half wish they were dead. We're both lucky, you and me, for the time being anyway, and that's all you've got to think about. You start thinking about for ever, and you're in trouble."

We slept in each other's arms and the following day I had to return home. I saw her every other week for the best part of that year, using Theo as my excuse to the family – an easy enough lie to carry off, for anything to do with Theo met with my mother's immediate approval. Judy never changed. She didn't seem to have moods, and could always laugh me out of my sombreness. I began another novel, leaning heavily on the affair for my plot with somewhat transparent attempts to disguise the personal experience as fiction. For the first time in my life I didn't consult Theo, or show him work in progress. He knew the real reason for my frequent visits and adopted a lofty tolerance towards me. But some instinct for self-preservation held me from telling him the whole truth, and of course the whole truth was that I loved with an intensity that amounted to a sickness. I could think of nothing else but Judy between visits, my existence at home and at work a necessary interval of pain that could only be relieved when I was once again in her arms.

I was so proud of her. She seemed without fault. I kept trying to convince her that nothing she could ever say or do would weaken my resolve. We seldom quarrelled, nor did she ever give me cause for jealousy; our only differences sprang from my insistence that I would one day marry her. I made elaborate plans, saved what little money I could and when apart from her wrote endless letters protesting my intentions. The only sorrow she ever brought me stemmed from her reluctance to put pen to paper in return.

"You wouldn't want my letters," she said. "I don't know how. I'm not educated like you; my letters would be proper tripe."

"No, they wouldn't, and in any case I don't care. I just want you to write that you love me."

"You're like the government, you are. You want a Means Test before you'll believe anything. I do love you, you great stupid."

"Well, just write that. You could write that."

I gave her pen and paper and sat over her while she wrote to my direction in large, curling letters. Then I put the sheet into an envelope and addressed it to myself.

"Now post it," I said.

"You're daft. Waste of money, that is. Take it with you."

"That wouldn't be the same."

In the end I posted it myself. Obsessive love leads us all into traps of our own making. From pride we become careless. I made the mistake of forcing Theo to invite Judy to join one of his boating parties.

"But it'll embarrass her," he said. "It always embarrasses those sort of people to move outside their own circle."

"What a toffee-nosed bloody attitude. I go to bed with her, for Christ's sake!"

"Well, we know that. What's that got to do with it? Unless of course you discuss Proust in bed."

"You'll like her. She's funny and amusing. And I want her to come."

"Then be it on your head, Tony dear. I assure you I'm not thinking of myself, I'm only warning you for your own sake."

Judy bought a new hat for the outing, spending what to her was a sizeable amount of money in order, as she put it, 'not to let you down'. If Theo had raised doubts in my mind, I was forced to keep them to myself. For the first time in our relationship I had the feeling that she was vulnerable, something which had never occurred to me before.

I travelled up on a night train, arriving at Cambridge with the milk churns on the morning of the trip, and called for her before she was up. She greeted me in her shift, her eyes and face blurred with sleep. I had never found her so attractive, and we made love in one of the armchairs with Kitchener looking on with bland indifference.

"Let's have breakfast in the nude," I said. "I want this to be a day to remember."

"What's got into you?"

"I just feel very good. And you look marvellous – you always do immediately after we've done it."

"Just as well, isn't it? You didn't give me much option. What d'you want for breakfast?"

"A lot. I need to replenish my strength."

"I'm not eating a lot. I want to save room for all the posh food you say we're going to have."

We set off in high spirits, arriving at the riverside rendez-vous before the others. "Are there going to be many of them?" Judy asked. "You know I'm not very good with names. I can only remember faces and orders. Like, I think to myself, the poached eggs were for the red face in the corner, and the cheese sandwiches were for the one with spots by the window."

"Oh, tell them that, they'll love that."

"I shall do no such thing. I want to put it on today."

"You don't have to put it on," I said. "Just be yourself and they'll love you as much as I do."

Theo and several companions arrived with the picnic hampers. I was slightly disconcerted that there was only one other girl in the party, the sister of a rather reedy undergraduate called Flesch. Her name was Rachel. She had the arrogant, spoilt manner of a Jewish princess. Theo introduced everybody by their first names, but hesitated when he got to Judy.

"And this is Miss . . ."

"This is Judy," I said.

"Judy," Theo repeated. "A friend of Tony's."

"Are you up here?" Rachel asked. She was wearing expensive clothes and rather too much perfume.

"No, I live here," Judy said.

"Oh, a local girl. How interesting."

I looked around at the rest of the party. In varying degrees all the young men had that easy manner, bordering on insolence, that comes with total acceptance of their social lot. Theo caught my eye and gave me a knowing smile, as if to say, Well, I did warn you. I took Judy's hand and helped her into the boat.

"Are you going to row?" Judy asked me.

"No, I think we'll leave that to the experts," Theo said. "It's too early for falling in."

"It won't sink, will it?" she said.

"No, dear. The only thing that will sink today are my principles."

This came from a young man who had been introduced as Guy. He had epicene good looks and I immediately singled him out as a potential rival. He took one of the oars and sat facing Judy and me. I had to admit he rowed extremely well and I was still so unsure of myself that I imagined this would impress Judy. Another young man called Stephen took the other oar and we set out in great style. It was one of those perfect days in early spring, just hot enough for comfort. Judy trailed one hand in the limpid water as we glided past the bright greenery of trees that had just burst their buds.

Rachel and her brother sat in the prow smoking Balkan Sobranie Russian cigarettes in long holders, while Theo announced he would read selected passages from *The Ancient*

Mariner to encourage, as he put it, 'the galley slaves'. This suggestion was immediately shouted down, and Guy began to sing an obscene version of the Eton Boating Song which began, 'Jolly old homo sailors' and went on in similar vein.

"Did you know," Theo said, when the song was finished, "that Dennis has gone to see Freud in Vienna to seek a cure?"

"Ah, a clear example of don't be afreud," Guy said.

The rest of them found this funnier than the retelling of it suggests.

"Who's Freud?" Judy whispered, and Theo immediately pounced.

"Now, can somebody explain to our charming guest? Guy, how would you describe Freud?"

"B.B.B."

"Let me translate," Theo said. "Professor Burgess, world-renowned authority on the sexual habits of policemen and engine drivers . . ."

"And postmen," Guy shouted. "Don't leave out the postmen."

". . . Professor Burgess is of the opinion that the Viennese saga can best be described under the heading Bums Before Butter. Am I right, Professor?"

"Absolutely."

"Personally, I would challenge the Professor's finding. As we all know he is somewhat blatant in his view of human nature, having been frightened by his nanny who had a moustache bigger than Lloyd George. In fact some people firmly believe that his nanny *was* Lloyd George, which perhaps explains all."

If Judy was disconcerted by this exchange at her expense, she gave no sign other than to squeeze my hand. She kept a smile on her face and pretended to enjoy the joke as much as the others.

"How long before we sight land and break open the champers?" Stephen said.

"We shall shortly be entering the erogenous zone, Stephen dear, so just continue doing your impersonation of a hearty Blue. Take the stroke."

They decided to moor at a suitably deserted spot another

two miles up river, and as the boat slid under the alders lining the bank one of the overhanging branches swept Judy's new hat from her head. It started to float out towards the opposite bank.

"Oh, no!" she screamed.

"Hat overboard!"

"Well, come on, Tony, do the decent thing and swim for it."

I started to take off my jacket.

"No, don't," Judy said. "It's not worth it."

"'Course, it's worth it," Theo said. "And we all want to see Tony do his stuff."

"No, the sight of naked flesh this early would be too much for me," Guy said. "Come on, Stephen, pull her round. We'll get it."

We went chasing after the elusive hat, bobbing like some red buoy on the current, and Flesch eventually fished it out. It was completely ruined.

"What a shame," I said.

"Doesn't matter."

"You must buy her a new one," Rachel said. "There are so many pretty new colours this season."

"It'll probably dry out," I said, trying to be helpful.

"Talking of which, let us wet ourselves with a little bubbly. Break out the hampers, men! Guy, dear, apply your well-known muscular strength and remove the first cork."

We scrambled on to the bank and with the boat tied off prepared the picnic. I took fresh heart, stifling my fears that the whole trip had been a mistake as far as Judy and I were concerned. The first bottle of champagne was quickly disposed of and a second opened. Theo took the empty bottle and strode down to the water's edge.

"Attention, please! Quiet, please! I call upon Dame Nellie Burgess to launch this ship."

The others applauded as Guy got to his feet and joined Theo by the boat. Taking the bottle and assuming a high-pitched voice he proclaimed: "I name this ship, *Repulsive*. God Bless All Who Sail in Her." Then he smashed the empty bottle against the hull.

"Not a good year," he said in his normal voice, while the rest of us applauded loudly.

"Aren't they funny?" Judy said. She was slightly flushed from the unaccustomed champagne, which I noticed she had drunk rather too quickly.

"Those who go down to seamen shall not perish from the face of the earth. There is some corner of a foreign whatsit, as we all know, where England's sons dropped their trousers while gentlemen now abed thought themselves accurst they were not there." Guy put on another voice for this recital, a sort of Church of England gothic. "I now call upon Father Gittings to give the Blessing."

"Thank you," Theo said. He put his hands together. "Let us pray. Oh, Lord, who has seen fit to let us buy this food on tick, grant us now the courage to eat it without a conscience. Look down, O Lord, upon this humble sod – green sod, I mean – and give us the strength to stay sober. In the name of our fathers, our mothers, or anybody else misguided enough to let us dissipate our lives in this holy place, for ever and ever, Amen."

"Amen," we all intoned.

There was caviar, and smoked salmon, and strawberries out of season which Rachel had brought with her. Judy eyed the caviar suspiciously to begin with, but was easily persuaded to try it.

"It's the start of a lifetime's romance," Stephen said. "If only people ate more caviar there'd be less unrest in the world. Don't you agree, Theo?"

"I not only agree, I intend to take positive steps to spread the good word. I'm going to start a new political movement – The Workers for Caviar Party. We shall march on Downing Street and hurl whole sturgeons through the windows."

I suppose I was somewhat of a prude in those days, a secret prude to boot, because although I found their dialogue too arch and not really funny, I lacked the courage to say so. In an effort to convince Judy that it was all terrific fun, I joined in the general merriment, occasionally making my own vapid comments. I couldn't make up my mind whether Judy was enjoying it or not. She seemed to be, but of course she had no

72

idea what they were talking about most of the time, and they for their part made no real effort to include her. She had to take them or leave them.

The lunch over, Theo suggested one of those elaborate word games, so beloved by my generation. His choice had very complicated rules, almost impossible to follow, which he refused to repeat when Judy asked for guidance. The game consisted of one member of the party choosing a famous historical figure while the others had to seek the identity by a series of oblique questions, such as 'If I was a piece of music, what would I be?' or 'If I was a flower what sort of flower would I be?' I have suffered such after-dinner games all my life and they never fail to irritate me.

The whole thing was over Judy's head, of course. When I tried, tactfully, to guide her, they shouted me down.

"No helping! Unfair! Disqualified. You've lost your turn. Next."

They played at least six rounds before the effect of the champagne wore off. Then, with the spring air turning chill, we re-embarked for the journey home. Judy was very quiet and sat fingering the ribbon on her ruined hat. It had dried, but was patently beyond saving.

"I'll buy you a new one," I whispered.

"Don't bother," she said.

Flesch and Theo rowed home, while Guy sat with his arm around Stephen. I thought I saw Guy's hand fondle Stephen's groin, but in the fading light I couldn't be sure. When we said our goodbyes Theo was the only one who troubled to be politely effusive to Judy – the others, intent on their own further pleasures, could hardly be bothered to acknowledge her presence. It was made quite obvious to both of us that we were not welcome to continue the day's festivities over dinner.

Judy made light of the snub on the way home. "Do you really enjoy that sort of company?" she said.

"I don't know. I haven't been exposed to them that much. What did you think of Theo?"

"He was the nicest. I didn't know what they were talking about most of the time."

"What did you think of Rachel?"

"I'll ask you that question."

"Well, I didn't fancy her, if that's what you mean. I fancy you. I'm so sorry about your hat."

"Teach me, won't it? Shouldn't waste me money. That Guy, he was a card, wasn't he? Full of himself. Wouldn't trust him with anything."

"I gather he prefers the boys."

"What about your cousin?"

"I don't know about Theo," I said. "He's changed a lot since he came to Cambridge. He didn't used to be like that. He's sort of brittle now. As though he's putting on an act to impress people."

"I think he likes a bit of the other."

"I don't really think he's made up his mind," I said.

"You're so nice about everybody, that's your trouble. You don't see through people. If you want to know the truth, I thought they were a snotty lot. Taking the piss out of us all the time."

I defended them, not for my own sake, but for hers. I knew she was right, but I tried to steer her away from the obvious hurt. We walked hand in hand in the sharp evening air, and I could scent the dangers ahead. I had a premonition of losing her, for even in love we are none of us so constant as totally to ignore the opinion of others. My defence was half-hearted and I doubted if she was taken in by it.

When we reached her home she turned at the door and kissed me on the lips.

"Don't come in tonight," she said. "I don't feel like it, and I must spend some time with me mum."

"Nothing wrong, is there?"

"No."

"I mean, nothing I've done?"

"'Course not. Just that I'm tired."

"I'm sorry it wasn't a nicer day."

"That's all right. Wasn't your fault."

"Shall I see you next weekend?"

"If you want to."

"You know I want to. We'll spend it on our own."

"We were on our own today," she said.

74

6

THAT SUNDAY ON the river marked the beginning of the
end between us, though I was too blinded by my own
romanticism to see it at the time; at nineteen it is
difficult to perceive we are equipped to love more than once. I
was doing well on the newspaper, being now entrusted with
the occasional book review, a minor leg-up which eventually
led to my appointment as 'Literary Editor' the following year.
This was a grandiose title for a humble occupation, but
which carried with it certain perks, since it has always been an
unwritten tradition that book critics can supplement their
meagre wages by selling their review copies at half the
published price. I was required to plough my way through
innumerable historical novels, since our readership was
pointedly 'down-market' and non-fiction seldom came my
way, unless by mistake. I tried my best when judging these
worthy efforts, and laboured in the belief that I was meant to
take them seriously. I was swiftly corrected by my editor.

"You're not here to bury them," he shouted. "You're
supposed to praise the bloody things. Look, let me show you.
Take out all this rubbish" – the blue pencil went to work on
my polished prose – "and concentrate on three things. Tell
them the plot without comment, add the odd description like
'masterly' or 'seldom have I read a more compelling account',
that sort of thing, and then, most important, put the name of
the publisher and the price. You don't have to be bloody
Bernard Shaw. You're just giving information, that's all. See,
let me give you a tip. The more you praise, the more they'll
send us, and you'll make a few more bob. Plus the fact we
might be able to twist the bloody publishers' arms to take a
few ads. It's a cynical business, lad."

I did as instructed, but was able to slip in the odd serious

75

review when the page needed making up. I can claim to have been one of the first to recognise the worth of H. E. Bates who arrived on my desk like a breath of fresh air, dispelling the heady pollution of my average fare. Unless one is drawn to the role of critic, sitting in judgment of one's fellows is a dispiriting business, making executioners of us all, since it is easy to fell a tree in a matter of seconds without giving thought to how long it has taken to grow. I was glad of the extra money while hating how I had to earn it.

Armed with what was then a decent living wage, I tried to convince Judy that my repeated offers of marriage could be taken seriously.

"No," she said. "It wouldn't last."

"But, why? Why do you keep saying that?"

"Because it wouldn't. I'm not the marrying sort. It isn't all having your oats in bed, you know."

I used every argument I could think of to make her change her mind. I thought the main reason for her reluctance to contemplate marriage was her mother. "If we got married," I said, "we could do more for her. You never know, they keep finding new cures for these things, and at least she'd feel happier knowing there was somebody to take care of you."

I used to sit and read to her mother, who was like a print made from an under-exposed negative. The only thing about her that the disease had not touched was her hair: it was still thick and glossy, not unlike Judy's – a young girl's halo surrounding the wasted face of a prematurely aged woman. I used to help Judy turn her in the bed and one weekend I made a window box which we planted with flowers, moving the bed so that she could see them without effort. Her body was grotesquely thin; years later when the first photographs of Belsen were released I was reminded of Nature's imitation, seeing again that pitiful frame in the iron bedstead, the skeleton hands lying motionless on the white counterpane, the outline of the body like a twisted log. I think she knew what I was trying to accomplish with Judy and approved, but she hadn't the energy to influence her daughter. What little religious belief I still retained was obliterated in her presence: I could not contemplate the sort of God who condoned such a living death. Yet it was to the same God I pleaded, away from Judy, asking Him to help me change her mind.

I continued to take Theo partly into my confidence, but although he listened politely he found it more and more difficult to conceal his irritation.

"Why do you cling to your middle-class origins? That's what baffles me. Here you are with apparently every young man's dream – a nubile mistress who fucks like a stoat, who doesn't want marriage. So accept it! The boot's usually on the other foot. You don't know how lucky you are."

"I do, really I do, it's just that I can't bear the thought of ever losing her."

"Well, you're going the right way about it. From what you tell me her mind's quite made up. If you force her into marriage just to satisfy your morbid taste for respectability you'll end up the loser. Her very obvious charms will swiftly be ruined by the arrival of a puking son and heir – since I'm sure you'll want to go the whole hog once the ring's on her finger – and you'll be sitting by the conjugal hearth wondering how the hell your Juliet became the Duchess of Malfi."

"It doesn't have to end up like that."

"Tony, dear, if you want to be a writer then read the writing on the wall. It's staring you in the face. In words of fire. Marry young and your creative balls shrivel."

"If I don't marry her I shall lose her."

"Yes, probably. Not lose her exactly. She'll always be a shining memory. You'll just move on, that's all. There's a great deal to be said for the thrill of the chase, you know."

"You speak from experience, of course?"

"I speak from a certain kind of experience."

"I don't think you've ever had a woman."

"Now don't get personal."

"Oh, I see, it's all right for you to dish out the advice, but no one's allowed to give you some."

"But I'm not asking for advice."

"Okay. But you still haven't given an answer. You haven't, have you?"

"Yes, as a matter of fact."

"Who with?"

"You really shouldn't ask me. Gentlemen don't kiss and tell."

"I don't believe you."

"As you choose. I can assure you that I'm telling the truth."

"Well, all right. How was it?"

"Different, shall we say?"

"Was she a tart?"

"You're such a stickler for detail, Tony. If by that you mean, did I have to pay for the experience? no, not in the accepted sense. No money changed hands."

"Well, why didn't you tell me before?"

"In the first place you never asked me, and secondly, whenever we meet it's difficult to get beyond your endless saga of love amongst the ruins."

He refused to be pressed further, and since he could usually get the better of me in any argument I was forced to let the matter drop. I sometimes found his pose of bored superiority very hard to take, yet I still yearned for our relationship to continue on the old, intimate footing. The fact that I had to earn my living and he didn't drove a thickening wedge between us, but I clung to the sacred and profane fragments of our childhood friendship. I suppose I always wanted to impress him in those days.

Judy was right when she said that I was still an innocent about so many things. I had no idea that the pattern of Theo's life was forming there, in Cambridge, on the loom of youth. If I gave any real thought to his hedonistic way of life, it was just ordinary curiosity, the fascination we have when a close friend shocks, or dares to stand aside from the mainstream. While not flaunting his homosexuality like Guy Burgess (transparently bogus when talking of his 'two nephews'), Theo was at no great pains to conceal it. I suppose I was square enough at that time to believe that, in Theo's case, it was just a passing phase, something he would discard the moment he left Cambridge. He was not a peacock queer or a member of the green carnation set, nor did he ever make the slightest attempt to convert me to the cause. Burgess did make one pass at me, a blatant one, easy to block, but then I gather he groped at anything that moved. It's even possible that Theo put him up to it, as a sort of double get-even ploy, the kind of joke he greatly enjoyed. Knowing what I do now, anything seems possible.

There were so many deceits, all interwoven, dovetailing together like the components of a Chinese puzzle box. Now I can immediately find the pressure points: the box opens at a touch and has no power to surprise. We were saving money in 1931, not souls. Being the outsider, I saw only the surface currents of that Cambridge generation, the obvious whirl-pools of discontent. Politically, I had no awareness. I dare say my all-consuming passion for Judy left little room for any-thing else: people in love make poor revolutionaries. I was conscious of the changes taking place all over Europe, but they seemed so remote, so tedious when set against the day-to-day realities of my own struggles for identity. If I listened at all to political voices, I preferred Ramsay Mac-Donald's soothing lullabies to the siren songs of the doomsday crowd. In that respect Theo and I appeared to be as one. He, too, professed a total disinterest for the political arena. He was sardonically amusing, at his vitriolic best when discuss-ing the middle-class Marxism that attracted so many of his contemporaries. "They say they want to use the same bath water as the hunger marchers, yet the poor dears protest they can't get though life without two dressing gowns." On another occasion he described the Cambridge political scene as 'the flight to the herd', quoting, without due credit, what I later learnt was one of the better remarks of Professor Joad.

Obviously it wasn't difficult to fool me, but as subsequent events have shown, he managed to hoodwink the authorities as well. He was a Pitt Club man and was also elected to the Apostles, a fraternity so exalted that it was known as The Society. Modesty became nobody in those days. But having arrived he was content to remain anonymous. I saw him standing on the fringe, quizzical, faintly condescending, the face nobody can remember when looking at old wedding photographs.

He always knew how to slip the blade into my back when I was least expecting it, drawing blood but never touching any

79

vital organs. He pricked away where Judy was concerned, always careful to give the impression that he was doing it for my own good.

What disconcerted me most was his casual admission one day that he had written a novel.

"It's my dusty answer to *Chrome Yellow*," he said. "I decided that all the smart young men want putting in their places, so I've written a novel that is so old-fashioned it practically screams to be remaindered on publication day."

"What's it about?" I said.

"It's a stroll through the past, a tender look at the age of illusion."

"Has anybody seen it?"

"Yes," Theo said, with that casualness that always conceals triumph. "Yes, I've really had the most amazing luck. The first publisher I sent it to must want his head examined, because he accepted it."

"Just like that?"

"Just like that. A contract, advance, the lot."

"How much?"

"Seventy-five pounds, would you believe?"

"Well, that's fantastic," I said, trying hard to keep the pack-ice out of my voice. "Congratulations. I never knew you wanted to be a writer."

"Nor did I. It just sort of happened."

"When are they going to publish it?"

"They're rushing it through for their autumn list."

"What have you called it?"

"*Burnt Umber*. A bit self-conscious, don't you think?"

"No, I think it's good. I shall have to try and review it," I said, in a pathetic attempt to get on to the score board. "Can I have the first copy?"

"It's dedicated to you," Theo said, and the salt really burnt into my wounds. "I won't sign it, though."

"Why not?"

"I have the feeling the unsigned copies will be the rare ones."

Nothing upset me more. I thought about my own abortive efforts, the long hours I had struggled to arrive at that point which Theo had achieved first time out. Friendship demanded that I conceal my bitter sense of the injustice of it all, but alone in my room that night, staring at the thick pile of manuscript representing all my hopes, I gave way to a bout of self-pity. I had been so open with Theo about my own work in progress, discussing the chronic lack of interest shown by publishers, asking his advice, soliciting his help, reading selected passages in expectation of his blessing – and all the time he had been working in secret. Maliciously I hoped his debut would be ignored by the literary world. I even entertained the idea of giving him a bad review myself, but in the event he confounded us all. When eventually I read *Burnt Umber*, I was forced to admit that he came fully equipped to the novel form. His narrative had a disarming elegance, as though no effort had been required in the writing, technique concealing the technique as it were, so that the reader was carried forward with lulling ease.

I had to admire his cleverness. There was I trying to ape the current literary darlings, borrowing from all and sundry – the starkness of Hemingway, the tightrope daring of Huxley, the cynicism of Aldington – with the inevitable result that what finally found its way on to paper was a hopeless jumble. Theo, on the other hand, had spurned all previous map references and struck out on his own. His timing was impeccable: most young writers of the period were desperate to parade their disenchantment, and yet here was a new novelist with the courage to say goodbye to all that, cock a snook at current trends and write about the old values without irony. He had somehow chosen a theme that his contemporaries had ignored, rightly judging that the older generation provided a wider readership, one that felt out of touch with the innovators – out of touch and perhaps threatened by them. The present, he told his readers, is always chaos, its morals always false. Only the past has any meaning for us if we are to survive.

I had no trouble persuading my editor to let me give *Burnt Umber* due prominence on my weekly page, since my more exalted colleagues had already prepared the way. Mr. Howard Spring found it 'impossible to lay down', Mr.

81

Swinnerton pronounced it a 'minor masterpiece', Mr. Godfrey Wynn found it an experience 'to make your heart sing' and Mr. Ralph Strauss capped it all by stating 'a work of genius'. My own review, my first exercise in back-scratching, followed the example set by my peers. It was an act of considerable generosity in the circumstances.

Thus was laid the first deceit, bearing no resemblance to the rest of his life, but the foundation stone, solid, respectable, on which he built the entire edifice. To operate as Theo did for so many years without detection requires relentless dedication. I followed as closely as anybody the flight and exposure of Burgess and Maclean, closing ranks with the rest of that motley band of armchair critics who never fail to appear in the wake of such a scandal. How could those in authority have failed so miserably in their duty? we asked. I even went into print with my own meagre contribution and asked Theo to check my copy for any obvious mistakes of memory. Theo was approached by the *Sunday Times* to give his version of the origins of such species, but declined on the grounds that it would interfere with his more serious work in progress. I remember admiring him for that.

Later, when the Third Man theory was finally exploded with Philby's appearance and canonisation in Moscow, we met over dinner and shook heads in common bewilderment.

"It's the most extraordinary thing one could possibly imagine," Theo said. "First Guy, then Donald and now Kim. It's like suddenly discovering that Oscar Wilde, Bosie and Frank Harris were all founders of the T.U.C."

"Did you have any inkling at Cambridge?"

"I can't have had. I mean, I always thought Guy would end up on the front page of the *News of The World*, but for normal reasons, like buggering a whole boys' choir at evensong during Wimbledon. I suppose I vaguely knew they were taken up with all that communist hysteria in the Thirties. They were always urging me to support some lost cause. But Kim, you see, he supported Franco. What was it he said in his statement? 'Many of us who made the choice in those days changed sides . . . I stayed the course.' Well, that doesn't add up, does it?"

"Nothing adds up as far as I can see, except that we've been made to look ridiculous. I feel sorry for poor old Macmillan."

"One must never feel sorry for politicians. In opposition they are just tolerable, in office insufferable."

Theo never joined any political party. He was much too careful for that. He layered his many deceits like a master pastry chef. To achieve their maximum purpose spies must either live totally in the shadows or else openly appear to be what they are not. It still seems incredible to me that Theo could have mapped out the rest of his life while writing *Burnt Umber*, for although the-writer-as-secret-agent is a familiar figure, embracing such distinguished names as Maugham, Buchan, Greene and Fleming, from their own accounts their recruitment appears to have been by accident rather than design. I was vaguely caught up in intelligence myself during the last war and there again my own involvement stemmed from a typical War Office bog-up rather than an inspired piece of planning. What came first in Theo's case – the literary chicken or the deceptive egg? Now that he is dead I doubt if we shall ever trace the truth to its source, but from a careful study of his journals all the evidence would seem to point to a conscious, meticulously plotted synopsis from which he never deviated. The only thing that could have gone wrong from the beginning was his own writing talent. Had he failed to convince the world at large that he was a literary force to be reckoned with, becoming almost overnight a respected Establishment figure, then it is possible that the rest of the story would have been different. He might have joined Guy and Donald, forming an unholy trio, lost pensioners of that 'élite force' Philby was so proud to serve. It is doubtful whether his Russian masters would have done him the further honour of keeping his books in print, for he wrote glowingly of a way of life that Lenin so ruthlessly destroyed. The chances are, given his sexual tastes, he might have been granted Burgess's last, sad prize: the accommodating factory hand playing the accordion to the drunk with the Eton tie.

As a writer of fiction I am at a disadvantage in setting down this story. Long service at the typewriter has trained me to give my public what it wants: characters with sharply defined motives, heroes with heroic qualities, villains who pay the price. Real life is not so tidy. Today the murderers are literally in our midst, just as the foxes now scavenge in urban dustbins. The village policeman can be armed, Miss Marple is hardly a match for the Baader–Meinhof gang. It is only in films that the Bonnies and Clydes look more glamorous than the boy and girl next door and set next season's fashions in the pages of *Vogue*. The realities are more terrifying than our fictions, for we can live with what we invent. It's the truth that scares.

7

Guy began the day with an argument. He had brought one of his latest 'nephews' with him. This one was called Stephen and he apparently met him on a train and boasts that he masturbated the youth twice in the W.C. "You do that with gun dogs, too, you know," he told me in that boring tone he always adopts when he sets out to shock people. "Always take a new gun dog into the woods and play with it. It's yours for life after that." I asked him whether, in that case, he wanted Stephen for life. He really annoys me when he's so brazen in public.

Despite my prior warnings Tony insisted on bringing his little Nippy along. I have to admit that she is attractive in a bovine sort of way. If she didn't have such large tits I could actually fancy her myself. She was wearing a ridiculous hat, as though dressed for a wedding rather than a trip on the river. Tony should have told her the form, but he probably doesn't know any better himself. He hasn't developed at all and his attempts to appear sophisticated are embarrassing. He's actually convinced himself he wants to marry his Judy, which of course would be a disaster and put a full stop to any hope he has of breaking out of the rut. The moment her looks have gone, as go they will, he'll start to loathe her for ruining his life. The inevitable result of marrying beneath one's class. Writers need to be utterly free.

I suppose the trip itself was quite a success, and the weather stayed good. Leon ('The Flesch is weak,' as Guy describes him) and his sister make such a point of being Jewish. She has obviously been spoilt from the cradle and is determined to be spoilt all the way to the grave. Still, like most Jews, they feel compelled to flaunt their wealth amongst the Gentiles, which worked to our advantage today, because she brought strawberries out of season. I don't think Tony's Judy had ever tasted caviar before – she ate it like fish paste.

We got back reasonably early but I couldn't face another meal with Leon and Rachel, so excused myself on the grounds of tiredness. Came back here and changed into my shop assistant's outfit to go cruising. Got lucky almost immediately. Went to one of my favourite haunts, the lavatory on the green behind the church. Sunday evenings are usually fruitful, probably because there is such a direct relationship between religious fervour and sin. There was a man standing there as I walked in. Late thirties, I would imagine, quite well built and a little shy at first. We stood side by side in silence for a few minutes to make sure the coast was clear, then he put his hand across and felt me. "I only suck," he said. I noticed he had very bad teeth when he smiled, but by then I was too excited to call it off. He was quite good at it and extremely grateful, as they say. I would have returned the favour, but we heard people outside and only just got ourselves together before they walked in. I really must avoid that place for a few weeks. Familiarity breeds danger.

One curious thing. All the way back to college I kept thinking about Tony's Judy and whether I could get her to perform. The idea intrigues.

There were several other entries for the same month (he didn't always make daily notes) and most of them were graphic descriptions of his sexual anarchy. There is of course a pathetic sameness to all pornography, endless repetition being required to sustain the reader's interest, and Theo was no exception. He collected and tabulated his nightly conquests with the industry of a dedicated lepidopterist, pinning them to his pages before they had stopped fluttering in his memory. Never less than explicit, he used the journals to rid his imagination of those carnal descriptions he so religiously excluded from his published novels. There was a kind of exaltation in the written confessions, a spitting in the face of cosy, conventional British life.

I had been prepared for the pornography; it was the rational passages that curiously had the power to confound and wound. So much so I could not continue reading, but had to pour myself a much stiffer brandy than my heart specialist permits these days. It took me a good half an hour to collect myself and be sufficiently calm to read on.

July 20, 1930

I don't know what got into me today. Perhaps my father's letter started the ball rolling. He gave me his usual boring lecture about

86

over-spending, followed by his even more boring lecture about the importance of personal hygiene. I really think that stupid old fart is going off his head. I can't bear to think what Mother goes through day after day, because she must know what he's up to. Curiously enough he doesn't frighten me any more. Getting away from home at long last has changed all that. He frightens Mother, though. I noticed the last time I saw them that she has totally withdrawn into her shell. All that pious stuff he spouts about the sacrifices he has to make to fulfil his social obligations. I think he suspects I see through him and is worried about this; that's why he tries to probe me. What I'd really like to do would be to shock him, and maybe that'll come. He's such a hypocritical snob, churching himself twice every Sunday and then going straight to the Reform School for his mental wank.

His letter put me in a bad mood and I skipped old Dawlish's lecture and instead went out and bought myself an expensive pair of shoes. I wore them out of the shop and then walked to Bright's where the bosomy Judy works. I sat at one of her tables and chatted to her until the Gorgon at the cash desk glared at us. She's exactly the sort of girl who would drive my father over the brink. That's what gave me the idea. It'll take time and effort to work out, of course, and I shall have to tread carefully where Tony is concerned. But I think it could be done. We shall see.

July 23, 1930

The more I think about the idea the more it appeals to my doubtless perverted sense of humour. The first thing is to gain her confidence. She mustn't feel rushed – that would be a big mistake. I'm convinced that the best approach with girls like her is to make them believe they are performing an act of charity. The first moves are very critical. I must say the plan intrigues more and more, and at the same time excites. I felt so keyed up last night that I had to find what is laughingly known as relief. It was willingly granted by a very engaging postman that Guy obligingly passed on. Too old for him, but very acceptable to yours truly. Had a sense of humour too, because I was quicker than usual. "Oh, special delivery," he said. Which I thought was reasonably witty, given the circumstances.

July 30, 1930

Tony was here at the weekend, so it was impossible to progress matters. But I laid some more groundwork. We went out into the country for tea on Sunday at my suggestion and I deliberately went out of my way to charm Judy. At the same time I presented a picture of quiet melancholy. She noticed this and asked if there was anything worrying me. I said no in such a way as to imply yes, but it doesn't matter. Women are always intrigued by sorrow and always jump to the conclusion that they are the cause. (It's a theme I could usefully employ in the novel. I want to create an English Bovary if I can, but set at the end of the last century in a large country house. Grander than Flaubert and turning his plot inside out.)

But Madame Judy. I feel more and more confident that I can pull this off. One can't really feel sorry for Tony. He's so slavishly devoted to her that even I can see he gets on her nerves at times. I'm sure women really prefer a touch of the cad. That is what is wrong with his writing. All the women he writes about are impossibly perfect and consequently incredibly boring. His trouble is that he thinks Hemingway has discovered the secret of the universe. I'd like to write a parody called *A Farewell to Nurses*, a sort of literary enema. Taking the longer view, if I can carry through my plan I might be doing Tony a favour, not that I would expect him to appreciate the fact at the moment, but it might shake him out of his suffocating complacency and be the making of him as a writer.

When we said goodbye I kissed Judy on the cheek. The first kiss between us. Tony looked approving and in a whispered aside thanked me for being so nice to her.

August 3, 1930

Changed my tactics today, and went to Bright's with Kim. Made a point of not sitting at one of her tables, but smiled and waved to her. Always the perfect gentleman. Kim was breaking in a new pipe. I thought it made him look faintly ridiculous, too much the prototype earnest student. We were joined by David Haden Guest wearing his hammer and sickle badge – defiantly, I surmise – and only too anxious to bore us with another repeat performance about his recent experiences in a German clink. Politics bore me, especially foreign politics. Our own lot are tedious enough, with Ramsay Mac and his cloth cap choir singing hymns of praise for The British Working Man. Have to be careful what I say since Guest's father is of that breed, and gets very touchy. From what he tells us about the workings of the Nazis they sound the ideal party for my aged father. Very much up his street. Guest is all for recruiting people for the cause. Kim infected to a lesser degree, and with his pipe gives the impression he would rather be a spectator than a participator. I tried to stifle my yawns and kept a watching eye for Judy. Whenever she looked my way I tried to convey I was sorry not to be served by her.

August 4, 1930

Started to apply a gentle pressure today. Went to Bright's alone and was lucky enough to find one of her tables empty. Told her how disappointed I had been yesterday. While she was making out my bill I asked her whether she'd ever consider coming out to dinner. I said I wanted to ask her advice about something. "That is, if you don't think Tony would object," I said.

"Why should he?" she replied. "You're his best friend."

"It's just that he's very possessive where you're concerned."

"No harm in going out to dinner, is there?" she said.

It was all too easy. We made a date for Friday night when she gets off work an hour earlier. So far so good. But I mustn't rush things. Before people betray they have to have total trust.

August 6, 1930

Could hardly wait to get back here and write it all down. Without undue modesty I must record that I was absolutely brilliant tonight. Left nothing to chance in the preparations. Booked a table for two at the Cloche Hat, a discreet restaurant about six miles out of town which serves passable food. Hired a car and picked her up at her home on the dot. Gave her full marks for being ready. Didn't say much on the way there and made sure that we sat apart in the back seat of the car. Merely said how grateful I was she had accepted my invitation.

She seemed amazed by the menu. Funny how, like most pretentious establishments around here, they feel compelled to disguise average British cooking by describing it in French. After translating I ordered for us both, and chose a bottle of claret to have with the main course. Talked glowingly of Tony for a great deal of the time which had the desired effect, for by the time we reached the dessert (she had the sickliest concoction on the trolley) she could hardly contain her curiosity. What was the advice I wanted?

"Oh, I've thought better of it," I said. "You'll think it stupid."

"No, I won't. Tell me."

We were sitting opposite each other and I put out my hand and let it rest on hers briefly. "I don't really know how to put it," I

89

said. "But if you promise you won't laugh, I know I try and give the impression of being somebody who knows his way around, but I had a somewhat strict upbringing. I suffered from ill health as a child and never really mixed with other children. Tony was my closest, my only friend really. So when I came to Cambridge, I really wanted to make up for lost time and find other friends. Well, I've done that to a point. I mean I've got lots of male companions, some of them very nice, and some of them . . . well, you've met a few, and how shall I put it? They're . . . they've got a different attitude to me. I'm not sure what I am really, that's what worries me. I'm not really very good with girls." I paused there for effect. I had her complete attention. "You see, I envy Tony having somebody like you. You don't have any sisters, do you?"

She shook her head.

"Well, there it is," I said. "I've managed to tell somebody at last. Got it off my chest."

"It shouldn't be difficult for you to get a girl."

"Easier said than done. You can't have girls in your room, and anyway most of the girls I meet are so stand-offish. Not like you. I don't mean that rudely, please don't think that. I just mean that you're easy to talk to."

"Have you talked to Tony about it?"

"No," I said. "I don't really think he'd understand, to tell the truth. Or else he'd turn it into a joke. Which it isn't."

"It's awful for you," she said.

"Well, thank you for listening. It's just such a relief to find somebody who will listen sympathetically."

I didn't press it after that, and I must say that she surprised me. I hadn't expected her to have that sort of sophistication. I knew I'd planted the seed. I changed the subject then, and over coffee I asked about her mother and told her what a good daughter she must be. We didn't linger and I drove her home, only reaching for her hand as the car pulled up. "I can't thank you enough, Judy," I said.

"Nothing to thank me for," she said. "I've had a lovely evening."

I saw her to the door, but made no attempt to kiss her.

"I'm spoilt," she said. "Coming home in a posh car."

I said I would try and look in for morning coffee later in the week and thanked her once again. I could hardly have wished for the evening to have gone better. I was so pleased with myself I nearly made a pass at the chauffeur, but rightly thought better of it.

There was a three-week gap in the narrative at this point and I can only assume (having no diaries of my own for the same period) that I was too much in evidence for Theo to progress his scheme. I wish I could look back and state that I had premonitions, but I had none. That much I do remember. My relationship with Judy continued smoothly. We made love as frequently as possible and I proposed at least once a week. Suspecting nothing, I had nothing to fear. I seem to remember that all three of us spent more time together than before, and that Theo no longer tried to score points where Judy was concerned. I attributed this to her personality rather than his sudden change of heart, because alone with me he was as caustic as ever.

It was a time of national turmoil, of course. The country was boiling up for the inevitable collapse of the Labour Government, though few envisaged their total annihilation and MacDonald's inglorious defection. Without much enthusiasm or political awareness I was forced to play my part on the fringe, for there were political meetings going on all over London and I was required to cover my quota. We were in the third year of the Depression and there was a general feeling of disillusion, heightened by the Japanese invasion of Manchuria and the shattering strike in the Royal Navy at Invergordon, an event thought by many to herald the approach of civil war.

Harry Gittings paid a visit to Cambridge during the autumn, inviting me to have lunch with him and Theo at The George. He spoke darkly of revolutionary forces on the march and warned us both of the dire consequences should Europe's madness cross the Channel. I think merely to goad and display his new-found courage to me, Theo deliberately opposed his father's argument. Harry Gittings was not accustomed to being crossed, especially by his son, and the meal was a disaster. It astonished me to see Theo stand his ground, for his father was formidable when aroused, his voice growing ever lower and more intense as his fury increased.

"Father, don't take it all so seriously," Theo said. "You'll have a stroke. We're merely having a friendly argument."

"It is not an argument. There is nothing to argue about. I am telling you the plain facts of the situation and you are contradicting me. You're supposed to be here to educate yourself, not live in some ivory tower. When the war comes you'll have to fight."

"Not necessarily."

"What're you talking about?"

"I could be a conscientious objector."

"I'll tell you something," Harry Gittings said. He leant across the table, knocking over a cup of coffee. "If you ever refused to fight for king and country, I'd take a gun to you myself."

"Well, I dare say you'll be spared such a display of paternal love, Father, because there isn't going to be a war."

I was amazed at Theo's self-control. "I'm sure Tony here is as disgusted as I am," his father said. He summoned a waiter to bring him a fresh cup and a napkin to cover the coffee stain. "Unlike some people he has to work for his living, not live off the fat of the land at other people's expense. You don't know how bloody privileged you are."

"If I don't I'm sure you'll remind me. You're very good at that, aren't you, Father? Reminding people how grateful they should be. If you don't want to pay for my education, just say so. I'd be quite happy to leave."

"Then what would you do? You'd be lost."

"I should earn my own living."

"What as?"

"I might surprise you."

"The only time you ever surprised me was when you were born. You weren't expected to live, you know."

They seemed to have forgotten that I was present. I welcomed the return of the waiter, hoping this would calm matters, but Harry Gittings was not the sort of man to worry about staff. He really was one of the grossest men I have ever come across.

"I take the trouble to come up here," he said, "and I'm treated like this. I shall have no hesitation in telling your mother *exactly* the sort of son she brought into the world."

"Of course she did have help. Unless you're trying to tell me I was an immaculate conception."

Blood rushed into Gittings's face, rather like the cat in some of the early *Tom and Jerry* cartoons.

"You bloody little blasphemer," he hissed. "If we weren't in a public place I'd smash you down."

Still Theo held his ground, though I noticed that he did ease his chair a little further from the table.

"Then I'm glad we're in a public place," he said. "Because you might not have it all your own way. The time has passed, Father, when you can threaten me. I hate to ruin your day totally, but the only person you frighten is yourself. You're awfully red in the neck, which is never a good sign in a man of your age."

Gittings jumped up from the table. There was a second or two when time seemed to be suspended. I was conscious that the rest of the diners were looking in our direction and that the head waiter was approaching. Gittings fumbled for his wallet, extracted a few notes and flung them down in front of me. "Pay the bill," he said.

"Is anything wrong, sir?" the head waiter asked with a total lack of spirit. Gittings ignored him and left the dining room.

"Nothing wrong," Theo said. "The meal was excellent. But we'd like some brandy, I think."

"Well," I said, when heads had turned away. "That was quite something."

"Now you know. I don't suppose you ever believed me before. He's mad, of course. Let's hope it doesn't run in the family."

He poured two very stiff brandies. "Did I ever tell you he once held me out of my nursery window? When I was about two."

"What did he do that for?"

"I'd been crying. I had tummy ache or something. Kept him awake, so he held me by the legs, face downwards until my mother fainted. He's the genuine article, my dear father. He makes Mr. Barratt look like Pickwick."

"Christ!" I said. "I'd no idea it was as bad as that."

93

"Oh, I could tell you more, but it's too boring. The twist is, I think he wanted a girl. Somebody he could dominate or worse when Mother's gone."

"Do you think he will cut you off?"

Theo shrugged. "Yes, probably. Except he's such a pious snob, he wouldn't want to lose face with his fellow Masons. He's the absolutely perfect one-man reason for a revolution."

I came away from that lunch with increased respect for Theo. Having never been exposed to such family traumas I found it hard to imagine how people survived them. Added to which, the fact that the whole episode had taken place in the stately surroundings of The George's main dining room on a Sunday gave it a surrealist flavour. The row had flared up so quickly. One moment we had all been eating our roast beef, the next moment the table had been struck by lightning. I didn't want to think about what was in store for Theo's poor mother.

I saw Judy later the same day and gave her a fairly graphic reconstruction. She was amazed, of course, but perhaps not as shocked as I had anticipated. I remember being surprised by her reaction.

I didn't see Judy or Theo for three weeks after that. The General Election meant I was kept busy in London. I won't pretend that the paper I worked for made any vital contribution towards a greater understanding of the political morass, or that my reporting of the local scene heralded the debut of another Stephen King Hall, but I did get exposed to the seamier side of democracy in action. It was a dirty election, and I had a ringside seat for some of the minor bouts. It was illuminating stuff to somebody of my tender years, conditioned to the belief that by some mysterious process unknown to ordinary mortals the electorate is blessed with choosing from the cream. All I saw was a succession of dreary little men making dreary little speeches, generating less passion than a sackful of dead mice.

There was a spurious excitement, to be sure, mostly generated by hot air, but Ramsay MacDonald's eventual betrayal of his previous convictions in the name of patriotism introduced me to a cynicism about the political scene I have never had cause to renounce. Over the succeeding decades success has brought me into social contact with many of our leading politicians and I am inclined to Turgot's dictum that 'scrupulous people are not suited to great affairs'. Most of those who have come within my passing orbit have easily persuaded me of their mediocrity.

In the hiatus caused by the General Election I was touched to receive a note from Theo saying he missed seeing me and that in my enforced absence he would try and give Judy a night out. I thought it very noble of him and wrote back and said so. Of such is the Kingdom of Heaven.

October 19, 1931

I think I shall go mad if I attend another political meeting. I would rather look at Comic Cuts than read a single line of any of the manifestos. The King is dead so let's re-elect the King. Land of Hope and Glory. I have resisted all calls to join in the campaigning. The only discernible advantage of this election from my own point of view is that the public lavatories seem to be frequented by a better class of queer. Have cast my vote three times in two days with three separate parties. One was a labour of love, one was extremely liberal and the third a shade too conservative. But I was the good time had by all.

Such activities left me with little opportunity to pursue The Great Plan. Wrote to Tony. A subtle touch, this. Received his enthusiastic blessing by return of post. This morning took my place at the coffee table and was gratified by her obvious pleasure at seeing me again. She asked if I was feeling any better and I told her that she had been a great help. We talked about Tony and I let slip that he was delighted she and I were now such good friends. Asked her to accompany me to the cinema on Saturday. Invitation accepted.

October 23, 1931

On reflection the choice of *The Blue Angel* was a lucky one. Heavy Germanic romanticism, but just what the shopgirls ordered. She loved it. Clutched at my hand during the sad parts and I lent her my handkerchief when the lights went up. Said she had never seen a film like it, which I suppose is true enough, because none of us has. We managed to get a drink before closing time and then I

95

walked with her for what seemed like ten miles to her depressing little house. She linked arms part of the way and talked mainly about Hollywood stars and were they really as wicked as they were made out. It was obvious that she wanted to believe they were, and I did my best to hint at erotic delights. "Don't they kiss beautifully?" she said. This as we reached the street where she lived. "I suppose they do," I said. "I haven't got much personal experience to go by." She asked me in for a late night cup of tea and after a show of reluctance I accepted.

Inside, the house lived up to its depressing exterior. Large and friendly cat which immediately proved dotty Father's favourite theory. She made the tea and took a cup upstairs to crippled mother. Everything seemed familiar, as though I had been there before, a criminal revisiting the scene of the crime, as it were. Decided that this was because Tony has described it all in such detail many times over. We sat on either side of the fire with Kitchener the inscrutable Sphinx between us. Conversation soon returned to earlier discussion about the sex life of the stars. I invented lurid stories of orgies which she swallowed without question. Dialogue bordered on the explicit and I detected that it was exciting her. Funny how dirty talk levels us all. Gradually worked around to my alleged dilemma.

"But you must have had girl friends," she said. "Good looking chap like you. Didn't you ever smooch?"

"Well, I know it sounds ridiculous, but I honestly didn't. My father wouldn't let me bring a girl near the house. Tony's very lucky, having somebody like you. I expect you'll get married one day."

"What makes you think that?"

"Well, I assume you will. You're both in love."

I must say she surprised me with her next remark. Tony has always given me the impression that she is as keen as he is.

"He wants to," she said, "but I shan't let him." I didn't have to fake my reaction. "I like him too much to wish that on him. It wouldn't last, you see. I can't make him see it now, because his head's full of nothing else, and in any case I don't want to hurt him. There's probably something wrong with me. Well, I know there is. I keep telling him not to get too fond of me, but it goes in one ear and out the other."

"Perhaps he'll find a way to make you change your mind?"

She shook her head.

"Why're you so sure?" I pressed.

"Because I am. Because I know me too well. I know what I'm

like. I couldn't promise to be faithful, you see. I like variety. I know girls aren't supposed to say that, but I can't help it."

I often read that one of the solaces of growing old is that we can look back without anger. The sorrows and mistakes of our youth, whether misspent or not, are supposed to fade with the passing of time, but I have discovered that I must be one of the exceptions to the rule. I find that whereas I am often hard put to remember who I dined with a week ago and frequently forget my own telephone number, my recollections of distant events remain unbearably vivid. In particular I seem to have retained every detail of my time with Judy: none of those who came after her has ever effaced her memory. The fever and the fret of those days and nights in Cambridge still have the power to disturb. Reading these sections of Theo's journals became too painful at times. I can understand Judy – she was at least consistent – but Theo's role is harder to take. It is not necessary to trust to stay in love, but friendship is more fragile than love.

I have edited some of Theo's eroticism from the remainder of this episode, not for reasons of prudery – it's too late for that – but because it is not a pain I wish to share.

I judged the moment ripe to advance more boldly. As Guy always says, 'One can always apologise, the important thing is to have something to apologise for.' I knew that she and I were talking in a kind of shorthand. We stared at each other and she smiled.

"What're you thinking? How awful I am?"

"No," I said. "If you must know, I was wondering what it's like to kiss somebody like you."

"Only one way to find out, isn't there?"

She came and sat in my lap. Her lips were more pliant than I had imagined. I missed the accustomed roughness of my usual partners and the fact that her breath was untainted by tobacco. Altogether very curious. I was careful not to appear too anxious.

"Just relax," she said. We tried again.

"I don't think I'm very good at it," I said.

"Never mind about that. You're all tense, that's why. Did you enjoy it? Was it nice?"

97

"Yes," I said. "But I don't think we ought to take the lesson any further, do you?"

"Why not? You mean because of Tony?"

"Yes, I suppose so."

"What about my feelings?" she said. "Don't I have a say in it?" She wriggled about on my lap. "You know what they say, you can't get off the train while it's moving. You men are all alike, all such babies, crying for the bottle and then when it's given to you pretending you don't want it. You're not really worried about Tony, are you? You wouldn't be here if you were."

I must say I gave her ten out of ten for that.

"If you're not going to buy," she said, "you shouldn't have fingered the goods."

"But aren't you worried about Tony?"

"Yes and no. I would be if he found out, because I wouldn't like to hurt him. But he won't find out from me."

I decided that my bogus show of resistance had gone far enough, because rather to my surprise I was by now more excited than I had thought possible. Visibly so, which she was not slow to notice. We undressed with what is known as unseemly haste and the last of life's great mysteries was revealed to me. Definitely a sight to gladden the aged father's heart, in fact probably a sight to put paid to it. I did have certain preconceptions, but photographs don't really prepare one for the living flesh. Tony had described her breasts, of course, but even so at first glance quite alarming. The nipples intrigued me, and remembering her remark about the baby's bottle I closed my eyes and thought of Nanny. I think what struck me most was the overall softness.

At the time I dare say Judy felt she had struck a blow for the cause, since women can make a virtue out of adultery more easily than men. Whether they ever repeated the experiment is nowhere recorded. There are a few further references to her in the journals, but nothing that elaborates on the joint deception. It is even possible that for once Theo felt some guilt, though it is more likely he became bored once he had achieved his original objective.

I've thought about it a great deal. I even went back to Theo's first novel the other day, since few writers can resist the temptation to make use of their own secrets. And I was right. There as aspects of Judy in his character of Masie

Price, the first love of the hero of *Burnt Umber*, but Theo turned her inside out, like one of those reversible jackets. He was nothing if not a consummate technician. None of us creates entirely from the imagination: there is always a starting point. Alone at our desks we dredge forgotten pools, searching like a murder squad for bodies that disappeared long ago. When eventually they rise to the surface, time may have bloated them and distorted the features, but we can still make use of the corpses.

8

I HAVE NOTICED THAT when people begin to suspect, rightly or wrongly, that the framework of their society is disintegrating they are seldom over-particular in the conduct of their own lives. We were all careless, it seems, during the late summer of 1931 and the months following the election. There was a feeling of hopelessness in the air that contaminated everybody. It reminded me of those pyramid letters one sometimes receives, unsolicited, through the post. You know the sort of thing: you must either send six copies immediately or else the chain will be broken and misfortune will be heaped upon you. As a child I was terrified of them and followed the dire instructions explicitly, though I never received the post-bags full of bounty that were supposed to flow in return.

Certainly there seemed to be such a chain of ill luck. My mother died in the spring of 1932, surprising everybody. Mercifully there was no lingering illness, as had been the case with Judy's mother. The diagnosis was made and within three weeks she was buried. The word 'cancer' was only slightly more socially permissible than 'syphillis' in those days, and my father asked me and the twins to keep the cause of her death a secret. "Just say she passed away," he told us. "We don't want people talking about it." He showed little emotion at the graveside and in truth I had to force myself to shed tears, for we had never been close, a fact borne out by her Will, since she left her small personal estate, amounting to a few hundred pounds, to be divided equally between my two brothers.

Harry Gittings and his wife made the journey down to London for the funeral, but he spoilt the sympathetic gesture by telling us that it had proved quite convenient since he had to consult Counsel in chambers. He invited me to have lunch with him at the Strand Palace, a hotel he favoured because of its proximity to the Law Courts. On arrival, I found we were dining alone. He ordered for me, briskly, choosing from the set, and therefore cheapest, menu of the day.

"You don't drink at lunch, I hope."

I did, given the chance, but his question demanded a refusal.

"We'll have Malvern water. Good for the bowels, flushes out all the toxins. Regular bowel movements are the secret of good health. Your mother would have been alive today if she'd only followed my advice. But women don't, you know. The only time you can get a woman to take advice is when she's concerned about money. Then they're all ears. People think it's only doctors who see human nature in the raw. Quite wrong. It's we lawyers who see people with their trousers down. How's your father taken it?"

The non-sequitur took me off balance.

"Not too badly."

"Will he marry again?"

"I don't know."

"They weren't happy, you know. Never got on. Did you know that?"

"They seemed to get on all right," I said.

"Children never notice these things. Unless there's actual violence in the house. Your father ought to get out more, broaden his horizons, meet people. Find himself somebody young and marry again."

I wasn't shocked by his reference to my parents' relation-ship, but I found his talk of remarriage so soon after the funeral in poor taste.

"You got a girl, have you?"

"Yes. Sort of."

"I'd like to meet her."

The idea filled me with horror, and I bent low over my grilled mackerel.

"Has Theo got a girl?"

"I'm not sure," I said.

"Really? I'm sure he confides in you."

"I think he's got a lot of friends in college."

"My son is a great disappointment to me, did you know

101

that?" He leant across the table to emphasise the point. "Great disappointment. You saw the way he behaved to me that Sunday. Didn't that disgust you? Let me tell you something, something for your further education . . . Theo is well on his way to becoming a bloody nancy boy. D'you know what I mean by that?"

"I think so," I said.

"Somebody who goes to bed with men instead of girls. They perform unnatural acts, do disgusting things to each other. I'm not going to spell it out for you over a meal, but I'm sure you get my drift. And if I'm right, if what I suspect is true, then God help him. You tell him that next time you see him. Will you tell him?"

"I'm not sure it's my place to tell him," I said with a sudden surge of courage. The conversation was turning into a nightmare.

"Well, you try. If you're his real friend, you try. Because I'll tell you something, Tony. This country we live in is morally bankrupt . . . *morally* bankrupt as well as down the drain financially. All the decent chaps, the men of my generation, were killed in the trenches. You wouldn't be here, any of you, if we hadn't fought and died for you. And what is happening now, what's happened since? We've got a lot of namby-pamby politicians running round in circles wetting themselves when they should be cracking the whip. And we've got a generation, your generation, who think life is a joke that parents pay for. They don't know the meaning of the word patriotism. They're all nancies, nancy boys. I *know*. I don't read about it like most people. I see it, every day, in the courts, face to face. People behaving like animals. Animals. Having sex like animals. Gratifying their perverted desires like dogs in the street. D'you understand what I'm saying?"

"But not everybody's like that," I said.

"We're not talking about everybody. I'm telling you about people who should know better, who've been given all the advantages in life. We know the lower classes can't help being what they are, but the real people, the people born to govern who should be setting an example, they're the ones who are letting the side down. You mark my words, you're going to see blood run in the streets before very long. Anarchy. Yids and communists and nancy boys, inflaming the British working man, giving him ideas. It'll be the end of England as we know it."

The sheer volume of gloom bordered on the ridiculous. Harry Gittings was such a bogus character, reminding me of something out of a third-rate touring melodrama. He affected smart clothes, always wore a buttonhole and a silk pocket handkerchief. When he talked he nodded his head downwards, like a chicken taking water. As he warmed to a favourite subject he closed his lips tightly at the end of each sentence in a curiously prissy manner. I found him repulsive – all my childhood fears had been replaced by loathing. I don't think I have ever disliked any man so much before or since.

Over coffee he continued the monologue, telling me of his dedication to public service, how things would be different if everybody followed his shining example. "Duty! That's a word this generation's never heard of. D'you think I want to spend my spare time making sure that a lot of sluttish little girls are set on the right path? Of course I don't. But I consider it my duty. We've got girls in that reform school who were pregnant by the time they were fourteen." He put his head on one side to emphasise his disgust. "Fourteen!" They'd had carnal knowledge of their fathers, some of them. The sin of incest. You can't deal in ordinary terms with those sort of people. They're degenerate. But you have to *try*, that's the point I'm making. People like me *have to try*, we consider it our duty. And for no personal benefit, you understand? We get no thanks in return."

He had made himself red in the face. By now I was desperate to escape. I realised I had been used. He had no interest in me, but his estrangement from Theo meant that I was his only contact and he had elected me the go-between, a role that carried no rewards whatsoever. I think even then I saw through him. Even though I lacked any clinical comparisons, my instincts alone made me aware that the origins of Theo's revolt were to be found in his monstrous father's intolerance. Now, of course, I can be persuaded to draw some parallels with Philby's father, an eccentric of other dimensions from Harry Gittings, but both dominant personalities with a burning sense of their own importance.

I left the hotel feeling vaguely sick. He had extracted a final promise from me that I would convey his displeasure and threat to Theo. I gave it with fingers crossed beneath the table. The after-taste of his dialogue added to my queasiness, and I nipped into the nearest pub for a quick beer before closing time. I found myself looking with new curiosity at the people around me, seeing them through Gittings's suspicious eyes, wondering what hidden vices their sullen faces concealed. The trouble with the Harry Gittings of this world is not that they have the power to disturb us, but that they are capable of infecting us with their prejudices.

It would have been unthinkable, of course, to have relayed his message to Theo verbatim. The young seldom betray each other in such bald terms. I would sooner have shattered the smug virginity of my twin brothers than voice any criticism of Theo to his face. Our arguments, and we had many, were never on that personal level. There were many aspects of Theo's way of life that I did not understand, but I did not try to analyse them. Even after Gittings had forced me to recognise the true nature of Theo's sexuality, I still did not actively relate the physical details to Theo. If I thought about it at all, it was still in the abstract. Since I was totally ignorant of his seduction of Judy at that time, I felt no personal threat. If Theo preferred the company of men to women, then if anything it gave me a feeling of superiority, a certain pity for him at the thought of what he was missing. Had Gittings directed all his venom towards Burgess, then I might have reacted differently. In his blundering, offensive way Gittings had stumbled on the truth – his definition of duty was light years away from Theo's and I dare say he was disturbed enough to have committed violence had he ever discovered the real facts of Theo's life.

None of these thoughts was uppermost in my mind at the time. I had dared to challenge my own luck and the tide had turned against me. Now that my mother was dead I could no longer keep up the pretence of enjoying the family hearth. The smugness of my brothers was all-embracing. They even treated mourning like a form of holy orders, silently reproachful of me like two prematurely-old spinsters. I made up my mind to leave home as soon as possible.

I was still convinced that Judy could be persuaded to marry. My first plans embraced the fantasy of moving to Cambridge, claiming Judy for my own, finding a job there and living a life of pastoral bliss while I laboured to become a published writer. The fact that Theo had done it was the added spur I needed, for nothing provokes like the success of a close friend.

It all seemed cut and dried for twenty-four hours. Then I was sacked from my job on the paper. Following the election, I suppose the demand for local newspapers slackened as people tightened their belts, and all such minor luxuries were dispensed with. The editor was apologetic and gave me a generous testimonial letter, but the good old maxim of 'last in, first out' applied and I added one more statistic to the growing ranks of the unemployed. I had no money saved; all I had was my final week's wages and a new sense of injustice.

I was too proud to reveal the news to my father or the twins. My job had always demanded erratic hours and for two weeks, until my money gave out, I tramped the streets following up every lead I could. Having no special qualifications I usually got passed over, and at the end of the fortnight all I had to show for my efforts was an evening's casual labour washing dishes à la Orwell in a Soho restaurant. In my ineptness I dropped a whole pile of plates, the cost of which wiped out my meagre earnings. I returned home defeated and confessed the true situation to my father.

"I really think it would be best if I left home and tried for work elsewhere. It would be one less mouth for you to feed and less of a wrangle."

"Where would you go?"

"I haven't really decided," I lied. "Maybe Cambridge. Lodgings are cheaper there and I've made some contacts through Theo."

"Well, you'll need something to tide you over." Although we had never discussed it my father was well aware of my hurt at having been completely excluded from my mother's bequests.

"I can't give you much, as you know." His own salary had been cut along with many others, but he drew fifty pounds out of his Post Office Savings – an enormous sum of money to my eyes. I protested it was too much.

"No," he said. "I'll give you a tip. When you lend people money, always make sure you lend them enough to sustain their dignity. If you give them too little they resent you for it and have no compunction about forgetting it."

"I won't forget."

"I'm sure you won't. That's why I'm giving it to you. Just take care of it and don't waste it. I've got no worries; I know you're going to make it. We're just all going through a bad patch. I was thinking of selling this place anyway, getting somewhere smaller. We don't need all the space now that your mother's gone."

"She wasn't a very happy person, was she?" I said.

"No, I don't think she was. Life didn't give her what she wanted. I didn't have enough ambition for her, you see. I often wondered why she married me."

It was the first intimate conversation we had ever had, and it came too late for me to be able to be of any comfort to him.

"Perhaps," I said, "perhaps she changed."

"No, I don't think so. I think she was always the same person. A lot of people marry just to escape, you know. They don't quite know what they're escaping from, or to. It's just the idea that appeals to them."

"At least she didn't suffer when she died."

"No, that's true. She did most of her suffering before."

I felt a stab of remorse for my selfish lack of perception, and when I said goodbye, kissing my father awkwardly – the first time in many years we had allowed ourselves any outward show of affection – I found I was crying.

I took a coach to Cambridge, beginning my economies, and went straight to Judy's place of work on arrival. Much to my surprise she wasn't there. I made enquiries of the woman at the cash desk.

"She's left," the woman said.

"Left? You mean left for good?"

"I don't know. You'll have to ask the manageress."

I went in search, but that lady was busy and couldn't see me. I asked one of the other waitresses.

"They fired three last week," the girl whispered. "They said food was missing from the kitchens, and since nobody owned up, they fired three girls to make an example."

I lugged my suitcases all the way to Judy's home. She greeted me warmly enough, but I immediately sensed a subtle change in her. I put this down to her recent misfortune.

"Well, that makes two of us," I said. I told her of my parallel experience, trying to conjure up the courage to talk of it lightly, but the suddenness of our change of fortune had chilled us. I said nothing of my wilder plans for our joint future.

"I suppose you want to move in?" Judy said.

"Is that all right? I haven't had a chance to look for anywhere else."

"'Neighbours are funny," she said. "They turn a blind eye as long as it isn't stuck under their noses. It's easier while you're able to pay the rent regular, but the agent doesn't miss a trick."

"I've got some money my father lent me, and two can live as cheaply as one."

"Three can't," she said.

"You'd rather I didn't, then?"

"I'm not going to kick you out tonight. All I'm saying is, things are different. Moving in is different from just sleeping with me. You don't know how narrow-minded people are around here. And I've got me mum to think of."

"Yes, I see."

"We're a pair, aren't we, you and me? I haven't got over what that mean old sod said to me at work. Wish I had nicked stuff from the kitchens now, but I never even brought scraps home. None of us did. It was the bloody chef; he's been at it for ages. We all knew."

"I've got an idea. They probably need help at the college. We can ask Theo to make enquiries. He'd vouch for you."

"No, I wouldn't want to put on him."

"Have you seen him recently?"

"Not for a bit. What're you going to do?"

"Oh, I'll try the obvious, have a go at getting on the local paper. And if that doesn't work, I'll take anything. Just 'til I get my head above water. And whatever I've got, or get, is yours. That goes without saying."

"You're sweet," she said. "Too good for me."

"Balls," I said. "Double balls, in fact. It's the other way round from where I'm sitting."

"Oh, sure. I'm a great catch. All tits and no prospects," she said with a flash of her old humour. "Go and talk to Mum while I get us a meal. But don't let on that I've got the boot. I haven't told her."

I kissed her. Her lips were colder than usual. "It'll all work out, darling," I said. "You'll see."

I sat and chatted with her mother until Judy had prepared the meal. As I looked at her frail, motionless figure in that condemned cell of a bed, the remainder of my courage drained away. I realised I had no idea where to begin.

After a sparse meal of soup Judy left me alone while she prepared her mother for the night. I took out the pages of the new novel I had been working on, rereading them by the dead fire with Kitchener on my lap. I had made a better start, but I forced myself to recognise my work still lacked any form of passion; it was all half-digested experience bought second hand. I put the pages in the grate and set a match to them.

"What're you burning?" Judy said as she returned.

"My past," I said dramatically.

"Your writing, wasn't that your writing? Why're you doing that?"

"Because it's no good."

"But last time you told me you were pleased with it."

"Well, I was wrong," I said.

She made love with a kind of quiet desperation that night, as though trying to make up for her lukewarm welcome earlier. There is something about lying in the dark with the girl you love, the warmth of her soft belly pressed against you, legs entwined, the damp hair against your cheek – the rest of the world shut out completely. There is something primitive about it, a throwback to childhood nights when a storm is raging outside and only the warmth of the blankets pulled high gives any hope for survival.

"I must try and see Theo tomorrow," I said.

"You set great store by him, don't you?"

"He's my best friend."

"It's funny that, really. You're both so different," she said.

9

"Is that what the old merde actually said? Did he actually use those words?"

Theo seemed far more interested in his father's threats of future action than in my own present dilemma. He was nothing if not consistent.

"Yes," I said. I had prefaced the tale of my own misfortunes with a colourful account of my lunch at the Strand Palace.

"God, he's so pathetically bourgeois! One really should choose one's parents more carefully. They're such an embarrassment in later life. I suppose you had some of the usual, did you? A clean bowel is a clean mind *et cetera*. Well, we mustn't disappoint him. I shall have to think of something quite conclusive. I don't want him to spend the rest of his life being constipated by doubt."

Theo's evocative phrase is an accurate description of my present state of mind. Even now, with all the evidence so neatly set out in those schoolroom exercise books he used to record his treasons, I still have doubts. They are mostly doubts about my own intelligence. My own horizons were so narrow in those days that I was totally unaware of the outside forces which were even then shaping the lives of Theo, Guy Burgess, Maclean and Philby. I suppose I can be excused where the other three are concerned, for they were never intimates, but I am amazed at my own cupidity with Theo. Did I overlook all the clues, or did he share with Philby and the others such a consummate and natural talent for the double-life that there was none to overlook? This must have been the period when they were all recruited and it would be a savage exaggeration to imagine that any of them were master spies overnight. They were undergraduates, with no influence, no access to State secrets; they were not familiar with the corridors of power . . . And yet they were part of a long-term strategy, quick frozen in a manner of speaking for future consumption.

In order to illustrate how innocent our lives seemed on the surface, mine genuinely so, and Theo's judged not by the knowledge I now possess but by the events I witnessed, it is necessary to set down the various stages of our emotional development. If I anticipate later knowledge for the sake of convenience I shall be cheating on myself, pretending intuitions I never had. If that presents me in an unflattering light, well, I must take that risk. In writing of betrayals one should always guard against becoming too apt a pupil.

Theo did change around this time, but like many others I misread the plausible explanations for such changes. The publication of *Burnt Umber* had not only given him the means to withstand his father's financial blackmail (his first novel earned him £1,000, a not inconsiderable sum in 1932, plus the Findlater Memorial Prize for Fiction) but also immeasurably strengthened his public self-confidence. With that brand of modesty which makes sure that one's friends are aware they are rubbing shoulders with success, he had subtly informed me that he was now the centre of attraction, lionised by the literary set, his mantelpiece festooned with invitations from those members of society who cannot resist claiming every new hero as their own special property. "Such a bore," he said, "but I suppose one has to suffer them; it's good for sales. I doubt if a third of them have actually *read* the book, but at least they've bought it. The really amusing thing is quite a few think I've written about them, their family and way of life."

"Still, it must be terrific," I said, "to see yourself in print."

"I must admit it is a bit of a giggle. And getting a prize as well. My publisher's tickled pink."

He seemed to have gathered a whole new set of friends, names unfamiliar to me, and while he had not abandoned his previous cronies he was disinclined to talk about them. "Guy?" he said when I enquired. "Fine as far as I know.

He's become so rabidly political, that's his trouble. Proper little revolutionary. One should never take politics *that* seriously."

Listening between the lines I had the impression that part of Theo's disenchantment stemmed from the fact that Burgess and his set disapproved of Theo's choice of subject matter in *Burnt Umber*. It was not fashionable to write a nostalgic view of the upper classes, and smacked of betrayal. "The heart of England," Kim Philby had said in an election speech for a Trinity contemporary, "does not beat in stately homes and castles. It beats in the factories and on the farms." Despite such fighting words, I did not notice that many of them wore cloth caps. Whatever their personal habits, sexual or otherwise, it was the adultery of the soul that claimed most of their spare time.

It had taken me a week to get Theo on his own and explain my predicament. He listened sympathetically enough, but volunteered no immediate solution.

"I can quite see Judy's point of view," he said, when I explained her reluctance to let me move in with her on a semi-permanent basis. "An outward display of morals is the hallmark of the poor." It was not the answer I wanted to hear.

Having spent the first night with Judy I had done the honourable thing and sought lodgings elsewhere, eventually landing up with a Mrs. Pike, a widow in her late fifties who had lost both her husband and only son in the war, the son being killed a few hours before the Armistice. Their pictures were everywhere in the small house. I had the dead son's bedroom at the back of the house, overlooking a distant view of the colleges like a constant reminder of Xanadu. Of necessity her conversation was coloured by the joint tragedy, but she was a kindly soul and within a strictly limited scope cooked me ample meals for the two pounds and five shillings a week I paid her for full board. She fussed over my laundry and I didn't have the heart to tell her to use less starch on my shirts: she seemed to dip them in concrete and I had a permanent rash on my neck where the razor-like collars chafed. There was no electric light, only gas in the downstairs rooms, and I went to bed with a candle, a comforting source of illumination before sleep, but a strain to work by. I wrote every night until the candle gutted, and when inspiration faltered, as it frequently did, I made copious financial calculations in an effort to stretch my dwindling capital for as long as possible. All luxuries were out. I attempted to grow a beard, not only to save the cost of shaving but in the hope that it would make me look older, since I convinced myself that what few jobs there were going would first be offered to more mature men. The effect, alas, hovered between the ludicrous and the unsightly: my beard grew in patches, giving me the appearance of a demented gypsy. I allowed myself five Woodbines a day in the beginning, and bought a cheap holder to prolong their thin delights to the last centimetre. Alcohol was forbidden, save for the occasional half pint of bitter if I treated Judy at the weekends.

As soon as I had finished Mrs. Pike's breakfast of fried bread and fatty bacon washed down with strong cups of tea – her panacea for all ills – I started the day's search for work. My early efforts to get back into local journalism were quickly smothered. The editor's letter didn't even produce a personal interview; dog didn't help dog in those days. I applied at the local library, who directed me to the labour exchange, who in turn directed me to the back of the queue. My only success in the first month was a chance encounter in a workmen's café, where an elderly sage let slip that there was a chance of employment in what he described as 'a high quality butchers'. I ran all the way to the address he gave me, only to find it was an establishment specialising in horse meat, ostensibly for consumption by cats and dogs. The sight of slabs of horse, with their curious yellow fat being attacked by swarms of large flies, was enough to quench my thirst for security at any cost. Beggars, I decided there and then, sometimes had to be choosers.

In an effort to cheer us up, I took Judy to the cinema one night. Cinemas gave better value for money in those days: there were always two full-length feature films, a newsreel, or two cartoons and a trailer for forthcoming attractions. For the princely sum of sixpence (in the old coinage) one could escape reality for three hours or more. We chose a comedy bill – Will Hay and gang, and Ernie Lotinga in another of his Josser roles. I noticed that the somewhat hangdog manager was jack of all trades, taking the money at the box office, then rushing up to the projection booth when, as often happened, the film broke down. Feeling lighter of heart when the programme finished, and emboldened by previous humiliations, I stopped by his tatty little office and asked if he was looking for any assistance. He proved to be practically stone deaf and I had to repeat my enquiry before it penetrated.

"Haven't got an assistant," he said. "I'm the manager, so if you've got any complaints you tell me. I can't do anything about the toilets until next week."

"No, I was enquiring whether you wanted any extra staff."

"Staff? I am the staff."

Judy had to walk away at that point. "Yes," I persevered, "I just thought that possibly you might be looking for some help. I-am-seeking-employment."

"Seeking what?"

"Employment. I-am-looking-for-a-job."

"Oh, I see. Thought it was a complaint. What sort of job?"

"Any. I'll tackle anything."

"Do what?"

"I don't mind what I do. I'm very keen. I'll work very hard."

"Yes, well, I can't help that. It's the war. Burst my eardrum. Exploded right next to me. Say it slowly."

I gave every word the same deliberate emphasis. "I-would-be-very-grateful-if-you-would-consider-giving-me-a-job."

He stared at me for a long time. "Here?"

I nodded.

He seemed surprised that anybody would wish to join his tottering organisation. He shifted some papers from under a stained tea mug. "I'll show you something. Just so you don't think I'm making it up. It's my own business, you see. I'm not in with any of the big boys. What am I looking for? Oh, yes, here it is. Look at that. That's last week's take. Makes you bloody cry. See what they left me after charging rental? I'm being ground into dust, I am."

He thrust a piece of paper under my nose. I looked at the figures on it. "Look at the last figure. That's what I was left with." I forget the exact amount but it was less than twenty pounds. "That's why the toilet's not mended, you see. And I've got to buy a new lamp. Nearly had a fire tonight."

"I'll work for very little."

"You can say that again. What d'you call little? People have different ideas."

"Anything you say."

"Well, I could say three quid."

"I'll take it," I said.

"You what?"

"I accept."

"Haven't offered it yet, have I? I was just talking aloud. How do I know you're any good? Do you know anything about running a cinema?"

"No, but I could soon learn."

"I see. I've got to teach you, have I? Might as well carry on as I am."

"All right," I said. "I'll make a bargain with you. You don't have to pay me at all for the first week. If you think I'm useless at the end of the week you owe me nothing. But if you keep me on, it's three pounds a week."

He looked at me and then at Judy. "That your wife?"

"No, I'm not married."

He stared at his pieces of paper again, then back to me. "Are you any good at mending toilets? Because that's likely to be your first job. You have to wear a tie, you know. When the public comes in. I like to see people neat."

He was wearing a crumpled dress suit and black tie, giving him the appearance of somebody playing a waiter in an early Hal Roach comedy.

"Don't have one of these monkey suits, I suppose?"

"No, I'm afraid not."

"Well, can't have everything, can I? All right, it's a deal then. Eight o'clock tomorrow. I'll be here. What's your name?"

"Tony. Anthony Stern."

"Stirr?"

115

"No, Stern."

"Tony, is it? Mine's Clifford Pinkwater."

That sent Judy off again, but fortunately he didn't hear. I kept a straight face.

"Very nice of you, Mr. Pinkwater."

"I'm the manager and the owner. The whole works."

"Yes, well, I'm very grateful. I'll be here at eight o'clock sharp."

I shook his hand, which surprised him. "Thank you very much indeed. You won't regret it."

I backed out of his office, grabbed Judy's arm and rushed her outside, just in case he had second thoughts.

"There, you see! I did it. Isn't that fantastic? I mean, that's a real bit of luck."

"Pinkwater," Judy said, and was off again.

"Clifford," I said.

We both fell against each other in an excess of hysteria.

"Do you know anything about toilets?" Judy said.

"They flush with success. Like me."

Arms entwined, exchanging snatches of Mr. Pinkwater's dialogue, we walked home discussing my new fortune, stopping en route for a fish and chip supper, an extravagance I felt I could now afford.

I presented myself for work the following morning, taking care to arrive a quarter of an hour before the allotted time. Clifford arrived on an ancient bicycle, still wearing the trousers of his evening suit well hoisted with cycling clips.

"Tony, isn't it?"

"Yes," I said anxiously. For one awful moment I thought he had forgotten our arrangement.

"I'm not good on names."

He removed his clips and hung them on a nail behind his desk. Then he took a small mirror from one drawer and, propping it against some cans of film, carefully arranged his sparse hair. I was to discover that he was very vain about his appearance.

I waited for his instructions.

"Can you boil a kettle?"

"Yes."

"Over there. Gas ring. Needs something in the meter. Here." He gave me a couple of pennies. "When you get paid, we'll share that. But I don't mind treating you this week. Take your coat off."

He brewed us both a cup of tea.

"Listen . . . what's your name?"

"Tony, sir."

"I'll get it in time. Listen, Tony, what you've got to learn about the general public, is they've got no respect for other people's property. Take that broom, and go in the auditorium and sweep up. I've given you a cup of tea, because you'll need a strong stomach. You'll find a bucket of sawdust over in that corner. Put some of that down first, it helps mop up the mess. They spit, you know. All over the floor. It's not a pretty sight. If there's anything worse, use the disinfectant. Any lost property, bring to me. When you've done that we'll get cracking on the toilet."

It took me the best part of two hours to sweep between the rows of seats. I noticed that most of the consumptives seemed to sit in the first five rows. Mr. Pinkwater looked in several times to see how I was progressing. He spent his morning rewinding the films for the first performance. The cinema opened at noon, the programme commencing fifteen minutes later.

"Never many here for first house," he said. "Usually out of works and old age pensioners. They get in half price, you see, until two thirty. Sit anywhere they like. Oh, and any ex-soldiers wearing a badge. Just take the money, you don't give them tickets. Give them tickets and half of them'll try it on the following day. Swear blind they've paid already. And watch out for kids sneaking in through the fire exit once the lights are down. Just sling 'em out, don't argue."

Our efforts to repair the men's toilet were unsuccessful, since it was obvious even to my untrained eye that his clients had totally wrecked it. "Put a notice on the door," he said. "Don't put 'Out of Order', because they'll ignore that. Write 'Keep Out, Danger of Infection'. That might do the trick for those of them that can read. And wipe some of that filth off the walls."

I removed as many of the obscenities as I could. They had a depressing sameness about them, being mostly crude drawings of the male and female sexual organs and accompanied by pencilled samples of the artists' poetic wit, such as *Stand on your arse, not on your feet, shit down the hole, not on the seat* – a piece of advice that appeared to have been ignored by many. I could not help comparing my lot with the life led by Hollywood stars. Norma Shearer seemed a far cry from the lives led by her Cambridge admirers.

I spent the rest of the day supervising the patrons to their seats and acting as policeman for the small boys attempting to effect free entry. Mr. Pinkwater seemed reasonably pleased with my progress and there were odd moments when I could slip into the auditorium and enjoy snatches of *Will Hay*. I made up my mind to survive, come what may. There was only one other person on the staff, George the projectionist, a borderline maniac whom I was rightly warned to avoid at all costs. He spent most of his time reading Bible tracts and as a result frequently missed the changeovers. When this happened the audiences went wild, hurling debris towards the screen and whistling loudly until normal service was resumed. I noticed that this behaviour was not confined to any one section or age group, nor were the frequent interruptions resented by our audiences. On the contrary, they seemed to welcome an opportunity to let off steam. In the case of a major breakdown, Mr. Pinkwater would advance to the front of the auditorium and crave their indulgence. He was greeted with even wilder applause. These episodes had a ritual all of their own and were considered part of the entertainment.

On Saturdays Mrs. Pinkwater put in an appearance to help cope with the most popular matinée of the week. The programme times were altered and customers were given an extra short film to prolong the value for money. Half the house was given over to children and was known as The Tuppenny Rush – with good cause. The entire programme was changed twice a week, with special films on a Sunday. This meant that cans of film were constantly arriving and being collected, and the paperwork drove Clifford into short sharp furies – from time to time he would sweep all from his desk.

Mrs. Pinkwater confided to me that she had been on the boards, a claim which later boiled down to one appearance in the chorus during the war, her career being curtailed the moment Clifford spotted her. "I think it can be said, I swept Clifford off his feet. Not all the nice girls love a sailor, you know, and the moment I clapped eyes on him, I said, Ruby, it's going to be a khaki wedding. He's a very passionate man, Clifford. Hidden depths."

Certainly he was a pleasant man to work for, and not un-generous. Despite our arrangement he insisted on paying me for the first week and never asked me to contribute to the cost of my twice daily cup of tea. Together we managed to spruce up the entrance and I impressed him by finding a brand-new toilet at cut price in a bankrupt builder's yard. We made some simple frames to display the still photographs that the film companies provided, and I persuaded him that there was extra profit to be made by selling bags of peanuts and sherbert dabs. I can't pretend that The Splendide, as it was proudly named, was anything but a flea-pit, but we did try and the business gradually improved. I was able to take over a lot of the paperwork for him, and since the flirtatious Ruby had also given me her seal of approval, my future seemed reasonably secure.

Judy's situation was not as happy. She was still without a regular job, and had been forced to accept a few mornings charring in the larger houses on the fashionable side of town. She was paid a few pence an hour and her efforts hardly kept her and her mother in the bare essentials. I tried to get her to accept part of my wages, but all she would allow was to let me buy the occasional cheap joint of meat which she cooked and which she and her mother shared with me.

Although I had little spare time to spend with Theo, to his credit he was most solicitous whenever we did meet and generous with his hospitality. His favourite topic of con-versation was ways and means of getting even with his father.

"I think I've finally got it," he announced one day. "The

master plan, and it requires your presence."

"Mine?"

"Yes, I don't want to waste it. I have to have a committed audience. Can you get a Sunday off?"

"Doubtful."

"Well, try. You must try because this is going to be too good to miss."

"What're you going to do?"

"Well, for several weeks now I've been writing home to Mother and dropping certain calculated hints. Very subtly, and since he reads all her mail as a matter of course he's bound to be intrigued. I've told Mother that I've met a very nice girl. In the last letter I put my tongue firmly in my cheek and said that I'm getting rather serious with this girl and that I hope Father will approve."

"But what girl? Have I ever met her?"

"There isn't a girl. That's the whole point. She doesn't exist, as such. But what I'm angling for is an invitation to take her home to meet the aged parents." He paused for effect. "And when that happens, you've got to be there."

"If she doesn't exist, how can you take her home?"

"*She* doesn't exist, but *he* does. Have you ever met a character called Raymond Blake? No, you didn't come to the last revue, did you? Well, the amazing Raymond happens to be extremely presentable, and when done up looks more like a girl than most girls. He does a fantastic impersonation of Jessie Mathews, high kicks and all. So, we've been rehearsing. Raymond is going to become Miss Angela Pritchett, only daughter of Sir Charles and Lady Prichett, who live abroad of course. Sir Charles retired to Bermuda for his health. I mean, we've really worked it out in great detail. We rehearse all the time."

"You'll never get away with it."

"Yes, we will. I promise you, made up and dressed, Raymond is the real McCoy. We've had a couple of trial runs. I've taken her out to restaurants and you'd be amazed how many heads turn. He's got marvellous legs and an absolutely flawless complexion. Don't think it's going to be your average female impersonator. Raymond is an artist."

"And you are actually going to try and pass him off as this Angela to your parents?"

"Yes. Don't you think it's a marvellous idea? I can't wait. Now listen, you can help. I've thought about it a lot. I want you to write to Mummy, just a chatty letter telling her all your news, and somewhere in the middle slip in the odd sentence about meeting Theo's Angela and what a charming girl she is, you know. That's all. Nothing too pointed."

"Gosh," I said. "Well, okay, but I hope you know what you're doing. Your old man will have a heart attack if he ever finds out."

"He won't. I know him too well. He won't be able to resist taking a look at the lady of my choice. That's quite beyond his powers of resistance. All I hope is Raymond isn't too much of a hit and Daddy tries to slip a hand up her skirt."

"Oh, God, that would really be a corker."

"And when the great day comes, you've got to be there. I'll make sure it's a Sunday, and we'll all arrive together. So speak to your improbable Mr. Pinkwater and write that letter."

Despite considerable misgivings I managed to compose a casual reference to Angela in writing to Mrs. Gittings, and I broached the subject of a day off with Clifford. Adding my own fantasy to Theo's, I explained that my closest friend was getting engaged and had invited me to the engagement party. I chose a time when Ruby Pinkwater was present, knowing that anything vaguely sentimental always made her eye-black glisten. I was entitled to half a day off a week and said that I would work two whole days to make up for the Sunday. Ruby did all the work for me.

"Of course he must go, mustn't he, Cliffy?"

"Yes, I suppose so."

"'Course he must. You go, my duck. We never had an engagement party. Wasn't time, you see, what with the war on and that. 'Bout time you got yourself a girl, too. Give you ideas, this will. Nothing like a wedding to get things rolling."

"Well, they're not getting married just yet."

"Nice girl, is she?"

"Very," I said. "Her parents are titled."

"Titled! Fancy that. My, you do move in posh circles, don't you? Did you hear that, Cliffy? She's titled."

"What title?"

"No, the girl, love. The girl's titled."

"What girl?"

"His friend's, Tony's friend, the one we've just been talking about. He's so deaf, poor love. Never mind, I'll tell you later."

I reported back to Theo, who related that he thought my letter had done the trick.

"Let me read you this," he said. He produced the latest letter from his mother. "Blah . . .blah . . .blah . . . where is it? Here it is, yes. 'Your father and I are very pleased with your news, although it did come as something of a surprise. Tony wrote to say what a nice girl Angela is, and as you know, I go a lot by Tony's opinion. I've discussed the matter with your father who thinks we ought to be allowed to meet her before things become too serious. So why don't you bring her over for lunch one day?' You see! Hooked! I shall write back immediately of course, very excited and thanking them for being so understanding. I might even humour the silly old sod by saying how relieved I am to have Father's approval at long last. It's all working out quite beautifully."

"Listen," I said. "I'd better meet Raymond before the actual day, otherwise I could quite easily put my foot in it right off and ruin everything."

"Yes, you're right. That's a good point. Well, we'll arrange that. You're in for a very big surprise, you know."

"I'm not the only one. I still don't know how you've got the nerve."

"It isn't nerve. I just have a malicious urge to get even."

It was arranged that Theo and Raymond would organise a dress rehearsal for me in Raymond's rooms. I went there after work the following week and the door was opened by a very good-looking girl in her early twenties. She was very trim, with a slightly angular face, hair cut fashionably short, and wearing the regulation blouse and skirt. I was completely taken in.

"You must be Tony," she said. "Do come in, we were expecting you." She put out a well-manicured hand and then suddenly jerked me across the threshold with more than feminine strength.

I half fell into the room and looked around as Theo gave a shriek of triumph from his hiding place behind the door.

"You see! I told you! Now admit it, he fooled you. This, dear Tony, allow me to introduce, is Miss Angela Pritchett."

"Hello, Tony," Raymond said, reverting to his normal voice.

I had to admit that the deception had been perfect. It was all the more impressive for the fact that I had gone forewarned. Over a bottle of very good sherry, we spent the rest of the evening planning strategy for the promised luncheon. Theo and Raymond instructed me in various aspects of Angela's character, where she had been brought up, what her interests were, and so forth. I became as involved as they were, and we had to restrict our inventions which were always in danger of becoming too farcical.

The date of the luncheon had been fixed for the Sunday following, and it was agreed that we would travel to Norwich by hired limousine.

"In for a penny, in for a Rolls," Theo said.

It was arranged that Raymond would change and make up in my lodgings since we didn't want to risk exposure before we had left the college precincts. Our explanation to the good Mrs. Pike was that the impersonation was in aid of a charity Rag, something she accepted without question having long been familiar with university pranks of this nature. We used her as a final guinea-pig before setting off in the chauffeur-driven Rolls.

"Don't cross your legs," was Theo's last instruction. We all three noticed that the chauffeur gave 'Angela' the eye as he opened the rear door for her, and we took this to be a good omen.

As Theo had predicted his parents had made a real effort for the occasion. Genuine last-minute alarm doused our inner hysteria and the formal introductions were accomplished without mishap. Harry Gittings produced his special sherry.

"Angela doesn't drink," Theo said quickly. Raymond picked up his first cue.

"No, I don't thank you. Daddy doesn't approve of women drinking."

"Very sensible," Gittings said. "I gather your parents live abroad now."

"Yes. Poor Daddy's got a gammy leg."

"The war, I take it?"

"Yes. The doctors said that he had to live in a warm climate. Of course, he misses the old country."

The rest of us had our drinks by now. I saw Raymond lick his lips. There were beads of perspiration pushing through his make-up.

"D'you think I could be very rude and ask for a glass of lemonade?" he said.

"Yes, how remiss of us," Theo's mother said. "I'll get it. We don't have lemonade, but I've got some barley water."

"Lovely. I get a little car sick on a long journey."

"Just like me," Mrs. Gittings said.

"Well, I must say, this is a very pleasant surprise, Angela. We're delighted to welcome you to our humble home. I often wondered what sort of girl Theo would eventually land up with."

"Now don't embarrass Angela, Father."

"I have no intention of embarrassing Angela. I was going to say, if you'd allowed me to finish, that you don't know how lucky you are."

"Oh, I do, Father."

"Are you at college, too, Angela? This Girton place?"

"No. I'm taking languages privately."

"Languages, eh?"

"Yes. Daddy's a great linguist. He speaks eleven Indian dialects. Of course, I shall never be as good as him. But I think French is useful, don't you?"

"Yes, I suppose it is. Can't say that I'm overfond of the French. Very unreliable as a nation."

"But I love French things, don't you? French knickers especially."

There was a long pause before Harry Gittings spoke again. I buried my face in my glass of sherry, Theo looked out of the window, and Raymond kept an absolutely straight face.

"That barley water to your liking, is it?"

"Very refreshing."

"I was telling Angela, Father, of your keen interest in young people. The work you do at the Reform School."

"Yes, I do my bit."

"It's a girls' school, I believe?" Raymond said.

"Yes."

"What do they get sent there for, exactly?"

"Oh, well, all manner of things. Stealing and stuff like that. 'Course, there's a lot of talk about social causes these days, but personally I think that's all claptrap. We give them discipline and a sense of moral values."

"Very important, I'm sure."

"What're you up to, Tony?" Mrs. Gittings asked me.

"I'm still working in the cinema."

"I don't approve of the films they show these days," Gittings said.

"You don't go to the cinema, Father."

"I sit on the local Watch Committee, that's enough."

"What do you watch, Mr. Gittings?" Raymond asked sweetly.

"Well, we have to decide what's good for people to see, young people that is. There's so much licentious stuff around. Semi-nudity and the rest of it. That's what fills the reform schools."

"But they don't see the films, Father."

"I don't want to go into it, Theo. It's not a suitable conversation for a Sunday, or in the presence of ladies."

"We'll have lunch in a minute," Mrs. Gittings said. "Perhaps you'd like to wash your hands, Angela. I'll show you." She led Raymond away. We watched him leave the room. He gave the slightest wriggle of his bottom as he left.

"Well, Father," Theo said when we were alone, "do you approve?"

"Seems a charming gel. I hope you respect her."

"I'm so relieved you think I've made a wise choice. I know we haven't always seen eye to eye lately."

"How serious is it?"

"Between Angela and me? I think she's very fond of me."

"Well, I'll tell you something for your own good. For your good too, Tony. I don't mind admitting that I've had grave suspicions about you, Theo. I don't want to spell it out, but it seemed to me you were mixing with quite the wrong set."

"I don't quite follow."

"I think you do. Tony knows what I'm talking about. I think Angela's arrived on the scene just in time. We'll leave it at that, shall we?"

Theo and I nudged ourselves as we went into lunch. The first part of the meal passed off without incident. Raymond kept up amusing small talk and laughed at Harry Gittings's more banal jokes, which obviously charmed him. Mrs. Gittings, I could see, was not quite so charmed. From time to time she stared at Raymond as though something was puzzling her.

"Must be so interesting to be a lawyer," Raymond said.

"Yes, I suppose it is."

"You must see human nature in the raw."

"In a manner of speaking, yes."

"Daddy always says human nature is basically animal. Would you agree with that, Mr. Gittings?"

"Well, I think most criminals, er, people with criminal instincts, are, yes, closer to animals than, er, human beings."

"Daddy used to tell awful tales about what went on in India?"

"Really? Did he, yes."

"What sort of things?" Theo asked.

"Well, I hesitate to say. I mean they weren't very nice things."

"They have different customs out there."

"Oh, it wasn't the Indians' customs. He was talking about ours, the British. Some of the young officers didn't always behave as they should."

Once again I intercepted a look from Mrs. Gittings at the other end of the table. I folded and refolded my napkin, unable to contain my mounting tension.

"Yes, well, I suppose some of them did cut loose, being in a foreign country," Harry Gittings said. "What about coffee, Lucy?"

Mrs. Gittings rang a small china bell.

"Perhaps I shouldn't tell tales out of school," Raymond continued.

The scene had started to take on the appearance of something out of *Pygmalion*. A fuse had been lit, as pre-arranged, and it was slowly burning towards the charge.

"Oh, do," Theo urged. "I love hearing you tell about the old Khyber Pass and life in the hills."

"Well, of course, I was too young to appreciate what was going on. But sometimes when Daddy got, well, shall we say, the teeniest weeniest bit pissed, he did let his hair down." Raymond pulled himself up and looked at Mrs. Gittings in wide-eyed innocence. "Oh, dear, perhaps I shouldn't have said that. I don't know what came over me. I've given myself quite a hot flush."

Coffee was served at that point and we had a merciful interval of silence until the housekeeper had left the room. It was difficult to decide what Harry Gittings was feeling. His neck had coloured when Raymond uttered the word 'pissed' and I noticed his hand tighten on the stem of his wine glass. Surprisingly enough I didn't think Mrs. Gittings had reacted at all.

"I think perhaps I should apologise," Raymond continued.

"That's all right, Angela."

"If I hadn't been drinking barley water I would have said I was pissed myself. Oh, there I go again."

"Is this some sort of joke?" Gittings said.

"No, of course not, Mr. Gittings."

"We're not used to that sort of talk at our table, young lady."

He could sense that something was wrong, but still hadn't put his finger on it.

"I think it's just the excitement of meeting you all."

Theo exploded at that point. He tried to turn his hysteria into a fit of coughing, but without much success.

"It's not funny, Theo," his father said.

"Oh, I just feel so awful," Raymond continued. "I mean I so wanted to make a good impression, and I've absolutely fucked it, haven't I?"

Theo fell backwards off his chair, unable to restrain himself any longer. Gittings's face, which I was studying behind my napkin, seemed to break into pieces. I had never seen a man so astounded. It was obvious that the final climax was at hand and I prepared myself for escape. Raymond rose to his feet, fluttering a hand around his pearls in a show of nervousness.

"Always a bridesmaid, never a bride, that's me. I never learn. Daddy always said he wanted a nice, well mannered girl and instead he got me."

"Oh, God!" Theo choked. "No more, Raymond. Don't go on!"

The penny finally dropped for Gittings. He pushed his own chair back and, shoving Raymond aside, strode out of the room.

Using his normal voice Raymond called after him. "No offence, Mr. Gittings, sir. Just harmless undergraduate fun."

I suddenly became conscious that Theo's mother was laughing. I turned to her and the tears were rolling down her cheeks. I had never seen her laugh like that before.

"I'm sorry, Mother, really. But we just couldn't resist it. Did you see his face?"

Mrs. Gittings had her handkerchief to her mouth.

"Oh, it was worth it," she said. "It's the best joke I've ever heard. Serves him right."

"I hope I didn't really go too far?" Raymond said. He started to wipe off his lipstick.

"Yes, you did, you did go too far," Theo said. "I thought you'd gone mad. That wasn't what we rehearsed."

"No, well, I mean I just got carried away."

"You'd better all get out of the way," Mrs. Gittings said. "Oh, it's been such a lovely day. I've waited for a day like this. Just to see the look on his face." She started to laugh again. "Go on, off you go."

"Will you be all right with him?" Theo asked.

"Yes, of course I shall. Goodbye Tony."

I kissed her.

"Goodbye . . . it's Raymond, isn't it? You didn't really fool me, you know, but you make a very good girl."

"A rather rude one," Raymond said.

"Well, that was the joke, wasn't it?"

She kissed Theo and bundled us outside to the waiting car. "You're sure you'll be able to handle him?" Theo asked anxiously.

"Quite sure. After all, he can't blame me. But I don't suppose he'll be too keen to talk about it, anyway. Write to me, dear. I do so look forward to your letters. And take care."

She waved us out of sight. We collapsed into the back of the Rolls and went over the entire scene line for line all the way back to Cambridge.

10

THE FAMILY BOAT burnt at last. The success of Sunday's inspired
adventure exceeded wildest expectations. Raymond was incredible, even though he deviated from the set plan, carried away, no
doubt, by his own cleverness. I never knew revenge could be so
sweet. *Vindicta docili quia patet sollertiae* or perhaps it was better
expressed by dear old Seneca – *Ultio doloris confessio.* Certainly my
long-awaited revenge was a confession of many past pains. I feel
absolutely no remorse. On the contrary, for the first time in my
life I have a sense of complete freedom. He had it coming, as they
say in the gangster movies, the dirty rat.

I think Tony was as amazed as anybody. Still unable to break
loose from his suburban chains. I probably shocked him as much
as the aged father, although he would never admit it. But
shocking people is a rewarding pastime, I've found. Not in the
sense that Guy shocks; that's too crude and obvious. One has to
conceal motives if one is to survive. That is where I part company
with them all. K, for instance, is becoming too openly vehement. I
warned him against this the other day. Apparently he has
received approaches from the same source. I haven't made up my
mind yet, but as and when I do, I certainly intend to be more
circumspect. Otherwise, I think the groundwork has been carefully prepared. Have removed all incriminating fingerprints. The
biggest mistake is to admit to any beliefs. One must appear to be
an atheist in all things bright and beautiful. Give us this day our
daily dose of subterfuge and lead us not into public temptations.

Reverting back to Sunday's joyous episode, I was interested to
note my own reactions to Raymond. As himself he attracts me
greatly, although we have never laid hands on each other. But his
impersonation which, according to popular belief, should have
made him that much more attractive in my eyes, totally failed to
excite me. I could admire the sheer beauty of it, but 'Angela' left
me cold. I have tried to analyse why this is so. Why am I only
attracted to the other end of the scale? Is it that I can never take
what is there for the asking? I have to put myself in a position of

danger; the real excitement comes when I am at risk. Another reason, I suppose, why I am drawn to K's philosophy. That seems to me to hold promise of a lifetime's romance. But I must approach it in quite a different way.

June 27, 1933

Guy's behaviour gives increasing cause for concern. He has just announced that as soon as he has finished here he intends to go to Russia and help further the Revolution. A typically crass idea, since it is doubtful whether he would be welcomed with open arms, given his basic personality. It's also second hand, borrowing from Donald, whom he is infatuated with, though professing otherwise. Methinks Miss Burgess protesteth too much. I refuse to be drawn into their mesh. If I proceed at all, and it is by no means certain that I shall, I shall proceed at my own pace and in my own way. There is no one to betray us but ourselves. That is my constant reminder. Write nothing, join nothing, make no speeches. Time is always on our side. Let the Klugmans* and the like take all the outward glory, since this serves another purpose, necessary to sustain the public image. But that isn't our purpose. Our aim must be long-term, a slow accumulation which, if properly carried out, will never be recognised. That is the attraction for me, since it is entirely in character.

June 29, 1933

Burnt Umber now in its third edition and still collecting bravos, which is satisfying on two levels. Tony, who I saw yesterday, is guarded in his praise. This was predictable, since his own efforts to scrabble into print have so far been abortive. He came round last night and read me work in progress from his current opus. Could hardly conceal my irritation because he arrived unannounced and wrecked what I had hoped would be a night on the town. Recent events have left me with little time for pleasures.

I encouraged him with false words, and then he proceeded to bore the arse off me with more talk of Judy. He still clings to his pathetic idea of everlasting happiness, and it was all I could do to stop myself blurting out a few home truths about the young lady. He also kept dropping hints that I should write to Chatto and Windus on his behalf and put in a good word, but I don't want to

---

*James Klugman, eminent historian and member of the British Communist executive. A.S.

spoil my own market. We can't have too many geniuses in the family.

July 2, 1933

Celebrated my birthday with three assignations in three different locations within three hours – blowing out several candles, so to speak. Have had no contact with aged father since the great day, so wasn't expecting any birthday greetings from that quarter. Did have a card from Mother, but assume he now censors her outgoing mail as well because there was no letter with it. I miss seeing her, but one has to be resolute.

I chose today to commit myself irrevocably. Apparently I passed the initial tests with honours, and have convinced my masters that their trust will not be misplaced. Can't say that I am greatly attracted to them as people; squalid, ordinary, dull creatures devoid of humour, but perhaps this is normal in their vocation. They have set me another problem to solve – far more complicated than before and one that will need a great deal of thought. It is the problems within the problem that fascinate me. And of course everyday life has to go on since it is vital to give the appearance of total respectability. They don't mind my extra-curricular activities since they are devious enough to see that these can lead to useful contacts in the future, but they have urged discretion. I hardly followed the advice tonight, but I had promised myself a birthday fling and don't think I took any undue chances. I went to London for my birthday dinner, since Lilly Law has been having a purge locally. My trouble is that permanence bores me. I can't bear the thought of a lasting relationship. Those loyalties are promised elsewhere.

July 15, 1933

Have made good progress on the second novel, despite having to finish my thesis. I find that one stimulates the other. Have now worked out the plot in some detail and committed five chapters to paper. Have taken fragments of the aged father and grafted them on to the character of Lord Brandel, and this works a treat. I shall leave in just enough clues to satisfy my own sense of humour, and if the final result comes out as anticipated I have the thought of dedicating it to him, which I know will infuriate. So much hard work has made Theo a dull boy sexually and I doubt whether I shall be able to sustain good intentions much longer. Nocturnal dreams hardly compensate.

132

Still on the subject of the new novel, I find that I am also making use of Tony's character. Brandel's eldest son who brings disgrace on the family by running off with the local whore was subconsciously based on Tony. I recognised this last night and can see ways and means of improving it now that the truth has surfaced.

He did use me as the model for his character, giving me the only title I am ever likely to have. With the benefit of hindsight, having read his journals, I can discern traces of my early self in young Lord Brandel scattered through the pages of *The Gilded Aviary*. It is not a flattering portrait. I can now also detect the moral change in the area closest to him at that time, for his second novel is a story of deception. Perhaps failure is always closer to the human condition than triumph.

I remained besotted with Judy. Our relationship seemed on the surface as secure and content as I imagined marriage to be. My romantic pride dictated that I continue to pursue that goal, and I was confident that my insistence would one day wear her down. I was totally unprepared for the blow she dealt me.

She met me outside the cinema one night. I had not been expecting her, but was overjoyed to see her.

"Nothing wrong, is there?"

"No, not wrong. I've just got something to tell you."

"Your mother's all right?"

"Yes, it's nothing like that."

I linked my arm through hers as we started to walk. "I know what it is," I said. "You've finally changed your mind and you couldn't wait to tell me."

"Well, I've changed my mind, that's for sure. I am going to get married."

"Say that again."

"I never wanted to hurt you, you know that."

I stopped her under a street lamp and for the first time I could see her face clearly. There was no good news in her expression.

"I'm going to marry Mr. Fraser."

"What're you talking about? Who's Mr. Fraser?"

"He's one of the people I work for. A widower, and he's

asked me to marry him and I've decided to say yes. But I wanted to tell you before I told him."

"That was big of you."

"Don't be like that."

"Well, what am I supposed to be? How can you just say it like that? You always told me you never wanted to get married. God, I asked you often enough."

"I didn't say that. I said I wouldn't marry you. Because you're different."

I felt sick and angry. I couldn't believe what she was telling me.

"I suppose he's got money, this Mr. Fraser."

"Yes."

"Yes, he would have. But you don't love him; you *can't* love him."

"No, you're right, I don't love him. I could never marry anybody I loved."

"What sort of answer is that?"

"It's the truth. Why d'you think I always said no to you? I'd only hurt you more."

"But he's different?"

"Yes. He's just lonely."

"How old is he?"

"Oh, I don't know. Fifty maybe."

"It's disgusting. How could you think of marrying an old man like that?"

I paced up and down the street, anguished and totally at a loss to know how to deal with the situation. Coming back to her I returned to the attack.

"It can only be his money," I shouted. "Why don't you come out and admit it?"

"But I do admit it," she said calmly. "Of course that's the main reason. I thought you'd understand that."

"Why should I understand? I don't have to understand anything."

"You think we should just go on as we are?"

"Yes."

"You know how it'd end, don't you? You'd hate me."

"How d'you know I don't hate you now?"

134

"I just hope you don't. Listen, Tony, you have to try and understand. What else have I got? There's me mum, I've got to think of her. He promised to take care of her, get her proper treatment. He's not a dirty old man, and he's not getting a great bargain in me. He's just lonely and want's company."

"You won't ever sleep with him, I suppose?"

I had a sudden vision of her body pressed against the unknown Mr. Fraser and it blinded me to everything else. "You'll just take his money, is that what I'm supposed to believe?"

"Well, I've told you," she said. "If you can't understand, there's nothing more to say." And with that she started to walk away.

I ran after her and caught her by the arm, pulling her round, searching for her lips. I had the arrogance to think that I could kiss her into changing her mind.

"But you love me? How can you do it with anybody else?"

She made no attempt to move out of my embrace, but she was passive, all passion spent. It was like kissing a stranger.

"You'll only make it worse for yourself," she said. "I never pretended, did I? You can't say that I ever pretended with you. I always told you the truth, and I didn't look for this to happen. It just did. People like me don't have much choice."

"But I could take care of you, if you'd let me. All right, look, we won't get married, I won't ask you again, I promise. But let's just go on as we are. I'll earn more money soon. I can ask for a rise in a month or so, and maybe my book'll be published. But don't go with this old man; I couldn't bear that. I'll do anything else you ask me, but just don't marry him."

My sudden jealousy of the unknown Mr. Fraser rose in my throat like bile, distorting my voice. Some lovers are only jealous of the past, of the years they didn't share, yet I have always felt the worst pain stems from the unknown. We can sometimes come to terms with the rivals we know, but future lovers have an advantage we can never smother. It is difficult to believe that love can ever take any other form than one's own, that those bodies we have worshipped can mould them-selves against a stranger, that those cries of loving pain that

135

we produced can be conjured up by others. I had no weapons to fight her with.

"I have to marry him," she said. "It's my only chance."

I dropped my arms. We stood like statues. I couldn't find the right words to repay her for the hurt she had done me. It was like the nightmare within a nightmare, when one part of the subconscious fights to convince us that we shall shortly wake and find everything normal – then the horrors take command again and the headlong fall into the pit continues. I tried to believe that we had never met that night, that before long my eyes would open and I could reach out to touch the gutted candle in my familiar bedroom and face a day suffused with the old happiness.

"I know you hate me now," she was saying, "but later you'll see I was right."

"You and your right," I blurted. Pain had made me stupid. I had no idea what I was saying, what I wanted to say. "Well, go to him then! Go and crawl into bed with that fucking old man, take his money, be safe, be what you want to be, you little whore, do anything you bloody well like. Go on – what're you waiting for?"

She stared at me for a few moments and then walked away. The pubs were closed; it was too late to get drunk, too late for everything. I walked the streets aimlessly, first going to Theo's college, and then circling back, past the cinema again, coming back to the very spot where we parted, like some mad traveller lost in the desert. Then of course, I wanted to apologise and I ran all the way to her house. There were no lights showing and I hammered on the door and called her name. A neighbour opened a window and told me to shut up. I went to the back of the house, but everywhere was dark. The window of the room where she slept had the curtains drawn. I threw gravel up to it and pleaded with her, but nothing happened. I imagined her lying in the bed we had shared so many times, as motionless as her mother, listening to me, hearing me without pity. I stayed there in the weed-wet garden, staring up at the blank window, telling myself I would always remember, wondering how much more there was to discover about hate.

For a period I went slightly mad. I became unable to converse normally, taking refuge in fantasy and lies, saying the first thing that came into my mind whether it made sense or not.

I wrote Judy long, passionate letters, sometimes taking them round by hand at night and slipping them under her door, fearful they might go astray if trusted to the post. She never answered them. I even wrote to Fraser, finding his whereabouts from the Electoral Register. My letter was returned unopened, readdressed in Judy's childish hand-writing. I scanned the local newspapers for any announcement of the marriage, intending to make a dramatic appearance at the ceremony. Whenever I was not at work I hung about at the corner of the street where Fraser lived, hoping to catch sight of her, but he seemed to have spirited her away. A 'For Sale' notice went up at her old address and I could see straight through the empty house. Alone in my bedroom at night I found I was talking to myself, carrying on two-way conversations with her.

I debated whether to give notice and leave Cambridge, disappear from everybody who had ever seen us together. I longed for some violence in my life. The mushy, romantic films I was compelled to watch day after day intensified my sense of loss, for I was reminded that whereas the love scenes on screen would be repeated at the next performance without change, my own were gone for ever.

11

WHILE MY LOVE affair came to an end, Theo's was just beginning. Being so obsessed with my own loss I failed to discern any change in him, but it was then, during his last year at Cambridge, at a time when he was least able to hide what was happening to him, that the commitment was made. It was all going on under my very nose, and I saw nothing.

During that crucial year he made a conscious decision and never again allowed self-doubt to put a foot in the door. He must have believed, like Auden,

> To be young means
> To be all on edge, to be held waiting in
> A packed lounge for a Personal Call
> From Long Distance, for the low voice that
> Defines one's future.

At some point during those Cambridge years the fatal connection was made, the low voice from a distance gave him the definition he had been seeking and he accepted the call. Perhaps, given the slightest leaning towards religious belief he might have turned towards Roman Catholicism, for he was ripe for some form of paternalistic dogmatism, and the concept of sin was important to him. Yet that would probably have been too simplistic for Theo; he needed something beyond mere faith – he needed danger.

I repeat, I saw nothing, I suspected nothing, I challenged nothing, I lacked all perceptions. Now I can savour the various ironies, salt them away for future use, but that does not make my present task any easier. I can only set down this story as an act of contrition, my own rather than Theo's, for apparently the God he worshipped never failed him. While others wavered, Theo, like Philby, held the faith. Such stead-fastness provokes a grudging admiration, especially when set against his other career. Even the comparison with Philby has holes in it, because Philby could take refuge in other things when the going was rough – his marriages, his socialising, drink, the companionship of the bed and the bottle. Even an unsuccessful marriage is better than none when other deceits make the mind a celibate. Theo denied himself such mundane comforts, for there he was at the end of his days hidden away uncomforted, comfortless, only able to communicate with total strangers.

It is all in such contrast to those steamy Cambridge years. He soared then, a daring young man on a literary trapeze, sufficiently outrageous to attract the attention of the authori-ties without incurring their outright condemnation. He was early marked as a coming force, and because his novels deliberately went against the tide they partially excused his public excesses.

If it was all plotted, as I am now forced to believe it was, then it was a campaign of diabolical cleverness. Theo was the only variant in the group, an isolated figure from the rest, but again this was entirely in character: he loathed officialdom and would have scorned to take the Establishment route mapped out for the others. Once trapped into service he must have convinced his Russian masters that his own individual form of cover was the only one with which he could survive. He enjoyed being recognised as a literary figure, and as his reputation increased so his cover became more and more secure. It enabled him to travel widely without arousing comment, it gave him an income in half a dozen countries, and the opportunity to mix with and study all classes of society. His writing was so far removed from current political thought as to totally disarm suspicion, and he never allowed himself to be grouped with the literary set of fellow travellers. Nobody ever suspected that a writer regularly recommended by The Book Society could ever be a threat to its members. It would have been as unthinkable as the previous generation accusing Galsworthy of being a child molester. None of his fellow defectors enjoyed such a safety valve, and although it failed him in the end he outlasted them all. Just as his novels were plotted with impeccable care, so he applied the same technique to the pattern of his secret life. Ultimately, like any spy, he became the prisoner of his own convictions, but until those last lonely years he made sure that the cell he willingly inhabited was comfortably furnished and to his own taste. The world of the one-night stand, the casual pick-up, the quick impersonal gratification, was sufficient for his sexual needs – or at least one hopes that it was – and I am sure he reasoned that the additional risk of betrayal that any permanent relationship brings might have proved his undoing.

I know little of the inner workings of the Communist Party, though I suspect that its officers are as rigidly conventional in their own way as any Empire Loyalist. Theo's individuality must sometimes have alarmed them as well as impressed. They could only have tolerated his eccentricities in the belief that he could deliver the goods. Every political creed acts from expediency and Theo was a risk they judged worth taking. All the same, he must have given them their share of anxious moments. He ignored the baneful repressions forced upon most people, just as his sense of the ridiculous rejected the jaunty Marxism openly practised by those who jumped on the passing revolutionary bandwagon. The use of the word 'comrade' appalled him: it was only in the sexual act that he felt any urge to identify with the so-called masses. He could take 'the people' into his bed, but not into his heart – though, again, I don't know why I am so emphatic. Perhaps that philosophy was just another sleight of hand he fooled me with; perhaps in his shadowy relationships I find so difficult to comprehend, he deceived neither himself nor others; perhaps they were his only acts of unselfish honesty.

Theo and the Cambridge cell traded on that enduring trait, British 'reserve' – used it, perfected it. They played the game, spoke the official language, knew the umpires on first-name terms. Spies are supposed to be figures who live in a twilight world, semi-fictional creatures existing in that hinterland that lies between le Carré and Fleming. They are not supposed to wear Savile Row suits in real life, talk to Ministers as equals, write novels that can be obtained from Boots' lending libraries.

I recall the furore that swept England when Guy Burgess and Maclean defected, the sense of personal violation that so many people felt. Squalid little figures like Blake are considered ideally cast for their roles, but not symbols like Guy and Donald. As a nation we are seldom so ridiculous as when we surrender to one of our periodic bouts of outraged moral indignation; and when questions of so-called national security are coupled with a measure of sexual innuendo outsiders might be forgiven for thinking that the Martians have finally landed. In trying to determine why this should be so, I am reminded of something Orwell once wrote – 'the *privateness* of English life'. Appearances may not be everything, but by God they count for a lot.

Certainly the outward appearance that Theo presented to me in those far-off days aroused no suspicions. I merely thought of him as lucky – lucky not to be in love, lucky not to have loved and lost. Following Judy's departure out of my life, I had avoided him for several weeks and finally he sent a note round to the cinema asking if I was ill. I forced myself to make the effort and went to his rooms on my day off.

I found him with Guy and the man he called Kim, to whom I had never been formally introduced. Kim regarded me critically as we shook hands, a pipe clenched awkwardly between his teeth, like a stage prop that an actor hasn't fully rehearsed with.

"Sorry. Kim Philby," Theo said. "Cambridge's answer to Stanley Baldwin. So: where have you been hiding? I was worried about you. Tony works at the splendid La Splendide, did you know?"

"No," Philby said. There was a pause. "But then, I'm not . . . not a great film fan." He had a pronounced stammer which I will not attempt to reproduce here; it gave the immediate impression that he considered every word before committing himself. "Films don't reflect ordinary life. I like newsreels, though. 'Course, they're all slanted, just like the capitalist press."

He seemed to use quantities of matches to keep his pipe alight.

"Christ, why don't you have a gasper like everybody else and give up that hearty stuff?" Guy said.

Philby just stared at him.

"I'm sorry if I interrupted something," I said, as the conversation sagged.

"No, we were just having a drink," Theo said. I was suddenly conscious of my own shabbiness in their midst, for since Judy's departure I had neglected my appearance.

Extinguishing yet another match, Philby turned to me and with that same agonising slowness, giving each word equal value, he asked if I was a genuine member of the working class. The question took me off guard.

"Working middle-class," Theo volunteered for me. "Don't let his Jarrow outfit fool you. He only hires that."

"What do they pay you at your cinema?" Philby asked.

"I get three quid at the moment."

"Bloody . . . exploitation."

"Oh, I don't know. I suppose I'm lucky to have a job at all."

"Nobody's lucky. It's your right," Philby said. He seemed touchy and aggressive about something. His pipe had gone out again and he searched for a fresh box of matches.

"What the masses want," Guy said, "is free beer, free fucks and freedom. That's rather good, isn't it? Should have used that in the last election. Our candidate would have romped home. Voting for free fucks, dear? Yes, well, put your cross just there. Kim, why don't you throw that pipe away? You really do look like Baldwin."

I could see no way of entering their world. In their company Theo took an unaccustomed back seat. He sat with his legs across the arm of a battered easy chair, sipping his sherry, slightly quizzical, raising the occasional eyebrow to me behind their backs.

"I must say," Guy continued, "changing the subject, or rather not changing the subject, I heard a marvellous story about Mrs. Baldwin the other day. Apparently she was opening some girls' school for Tory virgins and somebody asked her about married life. She said, 'Whenever sex rears its ugly head in Stanley, I close my eyes and think of England.' Don't you think that's good?"

"You made it up," Theo said.

"No, I didn't."

"What do you think about when it raises its ugly head in you?"

"Yes, that's a good one. Let's invent a new game. We all have to say what we think about at the moment of truth. You can first."

"I don't want to go first," Theo said. "In fact I don't want to play the game."

"All right, well, I'll start. What do I think about? Certainly not England. I mean, it's absolutely true, though, isn't it? Half the time one has to think of something else, otherwise the whole process is too boring."

"Speak for yourself," Philby said.

"I am speaking for myself, dear. Never the one to relinquish my favourite topic. Lenin. I think of Lenin. D'you think he did it often? Be a marvellous conversation piece, wouldn't it? A real stopper. You know, you're with some boring little thing and doing all the work, and you suddenly stop and say, 'You're not half as good as Lenin. He was just amazing on that train.'"

I looked quickly at Philby to see if he found it as amusing as Theo. He was pressing the ash in his pipe with a dampened finger and appeared not to have heard any of it.

"Now you, Kim."

"I don't do it that often," he said. "And when I do I happen to enjoy it."

"Do the girls talk as much as the chaps? I was at it the other night with quite a pretty little thing, just over the age of consent, and it never drew breath. I said to it, 'Don't talk with your mouth full, dear.'"

Then he turned to me. "Tony, you must be an expert on the ladies. I remember that bosomy little whatsit you brought on the boat. D'you still see her?"

"Not very often," I said.

"We were all very taken with her, weren't we, Theo?"

143

"Very."

"Was she very good at it? I'm told they don't move about much. You have to do it all for them; is that so?"

"Not that I've found."

"Oh, I'm relieved to hear it. It's a closed book to me, you see. Never having done it with the fair sex. God, is that the time? I said I'd meet Lady Maclean an hour ago. Nice to meet you again, Tony."

He kissed Theo goodbye, but happily was more formal with me.

"I wish he wasn't so bloody one-track," Philby said as the door closed. "You can't have any conversation with Guy without him turning it around to his favourite topic."

"Oh, I don't know," Theo said. "At least it's more amusing than his political drivel. The spectre of our Guy as champion of the downtrodden masses is hardly one of the most convincing performances."

"You must have found it very boring, Tony."

"Well, I haven't met many like him," I said.

"No, Tony leads such a sheltered life by comparison. And strictly moral, too. Tony believes in the institution of marriage."

"Marriage is a lunatic institution," Philby said.

"Actually, I agree," I said.

"Oh, we've changed our minds, have we?" Theo eased himself out of the armchair to pour liberal replenishments of sherry. "What happened?"

"Nothing. I just decided to concentrate on my writing."

"Well, I'll drink to that. I must say, being published does lead to the most extraordinary encounters. The mail one gets – mail as in Royal, that is. Some of the letters I receive are quite bizarre. I had one yesterday from a vicar in Cornwall. He'd read *Burnt Umber*. Hadn't bought it, of course, borrowed it from the library, but one has to be grateful for small mercies. Went on and on, pages of it, saying I was the new Trollope, which I hope was not a veiled nudge in the wrong direction. But he ended up asking if he could have a lock of my hair. What d'you make of that?"

"Hair today and gone tomorrow," Philby said. He smiled at his own atrocious pun.

"Oh God!" Theo moaned. "I shan't quote you."

"What're you writing, Tony?"

"A novel."

"Everybody I meet seems to be writing novels. It's an epidemic. Life isn't a fiction. All the smart young men trying to be Firbank or Huxley, completely out of touch with what is really happening in the world. What's happening is that the world is changing. People endlessly writing about unimportant issues, delving back into our boring past, as if any of it mattered." He turned away suddenly, as though he had not meant to be caught out in such vehemence.

I wanted to answer him, to justify my own efforts, but somehow the words did not come. I was the interloper in their society. Part of me admired them, part of me found their attitudes tiresome. I realise now that they were a new breed of revolutionaries, not the traditional student anarchist, shabby and bearded, but drawn from well-to-do families, in Philby's case the son of a distinguished Civil Servant, who shouldered the white man's burden as his birthright. This is what made them so hard to detect. They were like the murderer in Chesterton's story, who turned out to be the postman: everybody saw him, nobody saw him. Because of their backgrounds, because of the ease with which they moved through society and exploited their connections and inner knowledge, they appeared to pose no lasting threat. Early flirtations with the Communist Party were excused – undergraduates had always had a radical destiny to perform. While our politicians were mooning about Europe gathering the flowers of appeasement, bringing home the wilted blooms like wedding bouquets, all serious-thinking young people were up in arms.

In this climate the Philbys and the Burgesses and the Macleans could operate without attracting undue attention, their own future designs easily concealed. The real threat was thought to come from Germany, not Russia. Heroes and villains were scrambled together, distant figures in a foreign landscape, our island mentality ensuring that we did not heed the warning signs in our own midst. The poets were ignored, preaching only to the already converted – *Evolution the dance, revolution the steps*, in Day Lewis's clarion slogan. The general hope among my generation was that revolution and pacifism could go hand in hand, the religion of non-intervention, Gandhi the Father, the Son and the Holy Ghost. Any sort of protest was acceptable, the important thing was to join the universal club. Even Theo's homosexuality was, I believe, more a part of this movement than the more Freudian explanation – a tradition inherited from the 'Apostles' – because to be queer was to be on the inside, a privileged, if sometimes fearful, member of an élite group, knowing what the public at large seldom suspected, having free access to a sexual speakeasy. It is a natural progression for the sexual fugitive to gravitate to undercover political activities, and those who were looking to recruit found no shortage of willing disciples.

Of course it has all been so faithfully documented since and seems so obvious in retrospect, but at the time the real clues were well hidden. We were the young seeking to be old, youth having its fling belonged to the Twenties. Previous literary giants were dying, and only Wells from the old guard remained to give us his great dream of the future. Perhaps betrayals have become too commonplace, they no longer have the power to shock. Yet it was with a feeling of shock that, a few days ago, I came across Theo's membership card to the Communist Party. It fluttered from, of all things, a copy of Virginia Woolf's *The Waves*, when I was deciding how best to dispose of his effects. It was dated October 1932, something of a vintage year, it would appear for the Cambridge cell. I don't know why I was quite so shocked – perhaps it was the final confirmation of my own naivety. Seeing his name written on the faded card took me straight back to his room in Trinity all those years ago, and the true significance of his mocking smile when Burgess and Philby were sounding off. I compared the casual elegance of his life then to the way in which he spent his last years and for the first time I could trace the connection. Only death released him from deceit, and he passed it on to me – the last joker, as it were, in his pack. In many ways he took greater risks than his more notorious contemporaries, for the journals might have exposed him at any time, yet he carried his secrets to the grave.

When my affair with Judy came to such an abrupt end, I made serious attempts to transform my personal anguish into fiction. The results were banal and fortunately I retained enough common sense to recognise the fact. Even though I knew I had lost her for ever, I was still driven by the need to justify myself in her eyes. I wanted to show her evidence of material success. So I abandoned my Scott Fitzgerald efforts, turning instead to more immediately saleable plots. I embarked on a spy novel, heavily influenced by Buchan and to my surprise (since the writing of fiction is always a surprise) I found that the writing came easily. Naturally Theo was the first person to be taken into my confidence.

"But what an extraordinary choice," he said. "Spy stories are dreadfully old hat, aren't they?"

"Why should they be?"

"I don't know. Perhaps I'm wrong. It just seems a strange decision on your part. Why don't you write about something you know?"

"I tried that. It didn't work."

"Detective stories, yes. But not spies, I would have thought. I mean, does that sort of think really go on now?"

His replies disappointed, but did not flatten me as had often been the case in the past. I was slowly finding my own feet again, and the creative adrenalin was flowing back – even Theo's critical tourniquet could not stem it. Every night after I had finished at the cinema I could not wait to get back to my room and pick up where I had left off. I became a virtual hermit for months on end, my energies unfettered by sexual demands. I spent little money and was happily able to repay my father the fifty pounds he had loaned me. He had sold our old home by now and was living in a flat overlooking the zoo in Regent's Park. My twin brothers had gone their separate ways at the time of the removal and he confessed to me that it was a great relief to live on his own. We were drawn closer to each other by virtue of this common isolation. He hinted that he had formed a liaison with another woman, 'nothing permanent, but quite good for the old ego, I've found,' and seemed anxious to earn my approval for such an arrange-ment.

When I had finished the new novel something made me cautious where Theo was concerned. I still wanted his praise, but I was not prepared to risk his condemnation. I had saved enough money to have the manuscript professionally typed, but when I received the pristine pages, stapled, the title and my name pasted on the front cover, I might have been looking at a work written in a foreign language. I stared at the neatly typed pages, reading words that seemed to have come from a stranger. After living with a book for months on end a writer often feels such a sense of alienation.

I parcelled it up and sent it by registered post to the first publisher of my choice, having spent some time in the local public library deciding which list was most likely to accom-modate my new style of writing. Then followed a six-week agony of waiting that will be familiar to anyone who has ever attempted to earn their living by the pen. Outsiders never realise the extent of an author's misgivings.

I went through the whole gamut, sometimes racing back to my lodgings during my brief lunch break to see if the second post had brought the long-awaited reply. It was the longest six weeks of my life. Then, suddenly, one morning, the letter was there on the doormat. I carried it up to my room and propped it against my dressing table mirror while I shaved. I could not bring myself to open it at once for fear that it contained yet another rejection. Symbolically, I shaved my throat first, preparing for the tumbril. I dried my face, put on my one good suit, polished my shoes and flattened my hair with water and Brylcream. Only then did I feel calm enough to open the typewritten envelope. I sat on the edge of the bed and extracted the crisp, single sheet of headed paper.

Dear Mr. Stern,
My partner and I have now had an opportunity to consider your unsolicited manuscript entitled *The Death of Innocence*. We think it shows sufficient promise to ask you to be good

enough to come and see us. Perhaps you will be so kind as to telephone this office for a convenient appointment.

Yours sincerely,

Nicholas Brogan

I must have read it ten times before I became aware that Mrs. Pike was shouting for me to come and have my breakfast while it was still hot. I studied every word. 'Sufficient promise' had to mean something. Guarded, yes. But then that was to be expected from a business man. Still, he would hardly ask to see me if he was going to reject it. That would be a waste of his valuable time. Or perhaps it was his way of letting people down gently. 'Yes, I meant what I said, Mr. Stern. It does show sufficient promise for the future if not this time. Go away and stick at it, and show us your next.'

I had difficulty in swallowing my tepid boiled egg, causing the motherly Mrs. Pike to enquire whether I was under the weather. I had decided to withhold all information from my circle of friends until success was confirmed.

I went to a public call box during my coffee break and telephoned Mr. Brogan's office. My stammered introduction was translated by a friendly female voice and an appointment made for the following week. Without giving too much away I asked Clifford for time off, a request readily granted since our relationship was now secure.

During the days that followed I rehearsed several speeches designed to accommodate anything Mr. Brogan might put to me. In the event, of course, all such careful preparations went by the board.

Brogan's offices were in Bedford Square, that still elegant oasis of Georgian splendour, surrounded as it now is by the concrete building bricks and tourist flotsam of Oxford Street and Tottenham Court Road. I had been away from London a long time and the contrast between the quiet of Cambridge and the packed pavements of the capital unnerved me still further. I was treated as an expected guest by the receptionist and shown up to the first floor without further ado. Brogan rose from behind his book-cluttered desk to greet me.

"This can't be Mr. Stern?" he said.

"Yes."

"The Mr. Stern, author of *The Death of Innocence*?"

"Yes."

"Amazing."

He went to a side door and called into the next office. "Arthur, come and meet our new author."

He was joined by another man who was later introduced to me as Arthur Skilton, Brogan's partner. They both regarded me with amusement.

"How old are you?" Skilton said. His manner, though brusque, was not unfriendly. I told him.

"Well, now, I'd never have guessed. We were expecting a much older man. You know, university don, dabbles in writing spy stories; tricky customers most of them – hate changing a line and very good on contracts. I think this calls for celebration."

"What d'you think?" Brogan asked. "Wait a minute, before you tell me, let's see what we've got."

He went to a cupboard and fished out two or three bottles from behind a mass of books.

"I don't know why we live in such chaos," he said. "Who was it said 'a cluttered desk is a sign of genius'? Well, whoever it was I wouldn't have published him. We'll get organised and down to business in a minute. To you, Mr. Stern."

The neat whisky went straight to my head. I had eaten nothing since breakfast and this, combined with my nerves and the unexpected manner in which I had been greeted by the two men, rendered me immediately tipsy.

"Do you mind if I sit down?"

"'Course not, how rude of us. Shift those manuscripts off that chair."

Brogan searched amongst the debris of his desk and pulled out what I recognised as my own manuscript. It looked well-thumbed.

"Now, then. Let's talk about this. First effort?"

"No."

"No, couldn't be. How long have you been at it?"

"Oh, I wrote three, no four novels before that."

"No good?"

"Rubbish."

"This isn't rubbish, you know. Well, you know that, don't you? Authors always know. They may pretend they don't. We like this, don't we, Arthur?"

"Yes, we're very taken with it."

"We're even thinking of publishing it."

I tried to clear my head.

"Got a few rough edges, the odd split infinitive, but I don't mind those. Critics do, though. The lazy ones. They always pick them out, makes it look as though they've read it from cover to cover. You want another whisky?"

"No, thank you."

"Yes, we've discussed it, Arthur and me. Never publish anything we don't both like. House rule. If we go down, we go down together. No women and children first. Now, who else has seen it?"

"Nobody," I said.

"Got an agent?"

"No."

"Oh, it gets better and better, doesn't it, Arthur? And it's all your own unaided work?"

"Yes, of course."

"Have to ask it, because we've been caught out once or twice. I mean, nothing personal. Well now, think I've exhausted all the usual excuses. That's just my warped sense of humour." He consulted the title page of my manuscript. "Anthony – can I call you Anthony? Why did you choose us?"

"I don't know. Yours seemed the best bet. I studied some of your other publications."

"Well, I can see why you don't need an agent. But let's be serious for a moment. If you want to go away and get yourself an agent, I'll recommend one. I'd send you to Peters. He's as tough as they come and he'll look after you. I don't want you to think we're taking advantage of you, you see. Don't want that, do we, Arthur?"

"We certainly don't."

"We like to keep our authors. Start off as we mean to go on.

I mean, Peters won't better your terms on this one, but he might in the future. If you sell, that is."

He picked up some papers and waved them at me. "Now this frightening document – have you seen one before? – is what is known as a publisher's contract. Drawn up by the best legal brains to ensure that authors are kept in a state of abject slavery. This one's got your name on it. I suggest you read it very carefully, and when you've recovered from the shock, let us know if you want to sign it."

"Oh, I want to sign it," I said.

"You haven't read it yet."

"I'll sign it anyway."

"Arthur, are you and I men of integrity?"

"Average integrity."

"Well, I'll tell you what we'll do, Anthony." He took out a fountain pen, crossed out something on the contract and wrote something else. "Because we happen to like your book, and because we happen to have got you a bit on the ropes, I've crossed out the first advance I thought of, and put this."

He pushed the open contract under my nose. I dimly made out the figure of seventy-five pounds which had been substituted for the original fifty pounds. "Now, that's slightly above average. Plus the usual scale of royalties. Now I'm not saying you couldn't get a bit more elsewhere. Not saying that, are we, Arthur?"

"No. 'Course, he could get a bit less."

"True. No names, no pack drill. But what you'll get from us is dedication. See, we're not too big that we can't give your book our individual attention. I'm the brains and Arthur here's the salesman. Or is it the other way round?"

"I'll go and look it up," Arthur said.

I watched them like a spectator at a tennis match. They seemed to me two of the wittiest and most perceptive men I had ever met, or was ever likely to meet. The whisky had penetrated to my feet by now.

"We think a lot of your book," Brogan continued. "Looking at you I don't know how you came to write it, but then I've never understood authors. I can't predict what'll happen to this, you know. We shall publish it, I hope, and do our best, but don't expect the moon, will you? It might go out there and sink like the proverbial stone. There's no justice."

He drained his own glass. "I'll tell you what we're going to do. We're going to go out and have a bite of lunch, and if you still want to sign after a couple more hours of Arthur and me, I won't stop you. How's that?"

"Sounds great," I said.

"We'll walk down to the Garrick and you can tell us all about yourself."

"I have to be back in Cambridge by six o'clock."

"Six o'clock? Oh, I think we'll be through with lunch before then, don't you, Arthur?"

"Yes, we'll make it a quick lunch."

Over lunch they introduced me to several well-known actors and authors as their new find. My head, already swimming from the previous experience in their office, now seemed likely to burst. When I got to know them better in the years ahead I realised that their double-act was not entirely spontaneous. They knew how to flatter, which is half the game, I suppose, since writers desperately need the assurance that they are not alone. They could also be tough when the occasion demanded, as it often did in their cut-throat business, for despite publishing being an occupation for gentlemen, survival went to the fittest.

I shook hands on their contract over coffee in the Garrick, had a double brandy on the strength of it, and was bundled into a taxi just in time to catch my train back to Cambridge. I slept the entire way and was lucky not to go past my station.

It was the beginning of a long association. They remained my publishers until Brogan died. After his death the firm was taken over by a conglomerate and the relationship was never the same. By then I could name my price, but that first seventy-five pounds always remained the most important sum I ever earned.

12

OR SOME ODD reason Theo seemed irritated by the modest success that *The Death of Innocence* achieved. I had dedicated it to him and the thought did occur that perhaps he suspected some personal innuendo in my pretentious title. He had no real cause to feel jealous, for the sales of the book were hardly stupendous. It was ignored by most of the 'heavies', the only reviews of any note appearing in the provincial papers. My royalties just exceeded the advance and although I was downcast at the time, Brogan and his partner seemed pleased enough, and gave me a hundred pounds for my second.

I sensibly resisted the temptation to chuck in my job at The Splendide, some inner voice urging caution instead of euphoria. In many ways the life was ideal: I met a variety of people, the actual work was not onerous and Clifford seldom bothered me. I was well cared for by Mrs. Pike and had adopted a routine well suited to a writer's needs. The only think lacking in my life during this period was romance. Unlike Theo I was not claimed by the smart set, and indeed, apart from a few isolated fan letters, mostly from readers who felt they could write just as well as me given my luck, the publication of my first novel caused not a ripple.

"You should count yourself lucky," Theo said with the air of a man who has the generosity to pay a beggar fourpence for a penny box of matches. "I'd love to live like an ostrich, but I seem to spend most of my time answering mail from dotty old spinsters of both sexes who imagine they can recognise themselves in my books. It's too boring."

I excused some of his behaviour at the time, first because I was in awe of his greater experience, and also because his mother was dying. Unlike my own mother, Lucy Gittings's terminal illness was protracted and ghastly. She endured three major operations, becoming in the process little more than a shell. I went once to the hospital with Theo, but found the experience too distressing to repeat. Theo was remarkable, for although he found his regular visits just as horrifying, he never allowed his mother to see his anguish. It was only when he came away from the hospital that the mask slipped. He sometimes cried bitterly when we were alone together, reviling his father for past and present wrongs.

"Why did it have to be her?" he said. "Why couldn't it have been that evil sod instead?"

When eventually she died he went on a monumental binge. I like to think that I was closer to him at that period than I had ever been, but who knows? Perhaps I was just the nearest shoulder to cry on – or should the word be 'safest'? In tracing back over the memories of those years I seem to have become infected with the virus of doubt, as though the pages of his journals are still the carriers of his particular disease, making me wary of pronouncing any certainties.

He came round to my lodgings late one night to break the news of his mother's death, bringing with him two bottles of brandy which he solemnly consumed until he passed out. I undressed him and put him to bed in my room and he slept for the best part of a day. I had never witnessed grief on such a scale and I contrasted his behaviour with mine when my own mother had died. Perhaps I envied him – real grief only comes with love.

I sobered him up for the funeral and supported him at the graveside. It was a large funeral – Harry Gittings had seen to that, though the majority of the mourners were his friends. It was touch and go whether Theo's smouldering hatred of his father blazed into a public confrontation, but he managed to keep himself under control. The principal mourners went back to Westfield after the burial and it did not escape my notice that Gittings had already installed a much younger housekeeper. He mingled amongst the guests making pious statements about his late wife. Knowing what I did, it was sickening to watch. As soon as was socially acceptable Theo made his mumbled excuses and left. Gittings followed us to the waiting car.

155

"Well, a very sad day," he said. "But I think your dear mother would have been gratified by the turn-out."

"Yes, people always look forward to their funerals," Theo said.

"What does that mean? You can't resist it, can you? You have to be bloody snide and clever, even on a day like this."

I tightened my grip on Theo's arm.

"I don't suppose I shall see much of you now, shall I?" Gittings went on. "Well, I can't say I shall be too sorry about that. I'm not too keen to have a pervert in my house, even though he is my own son."

"No, one under one roof is enough, isn't it, Father? You can really go to town now."

"What're you talking about?"

"What am I talking about? You, Father. All those lovely treasures you keep in your desk. You can bring those out now, can't you? Have cosy evenings showing them to your new housekeeper. What will you do, dress her up in a gymslip and give her a smacked bottom when she breaks your best cups?"

"I'm warning you, Theo!"

"Oh, you can do better than that – that's very cliché, almost East Lynne. I tumbled you years ago. You're the one who needs warning. One or two hints from me in the right quarters and you'd be right in the shit. Don't you ever threaten me, Father, not ever, because I wouldn't hesitate to drop you in it."

We left him there, his mouth wide open, outrage staining his features brick red.

"I've waited a long time to do that," Theo said as we drove away. "My only regret is I never did it while mother was still alive . . . though I suppose the truth is, incredibly enough, she must have loved him once."

"Takes all sorts," I said lamely. "But don't make yourself ill. She's out of it now, he can't hurt her any more. Nobody can." I heard myself saying all the things others had once said to me.

"You're my best friend," Theo said. "You know that, don't you? I couldn't have gone through it alone."

His guard seemed to drop for those moments, but in

156

writing of that incident I find it puzzling that he makes no reference to his mother's death in his journals. It's almost as if he had to blot it out completely. He wanted love as much as the rest of us, but with Theo love was something he had to buy under the counter; he didn't trust the genuine article.

Whoever recruited him must have traded on this, have known him as well as he knew himself. They picked carefully and they picked well, since the four we know of could hardly be considered failures. I feel it was no accident that their four most successful recruits were all taken from the ranks of those who considered themselves unloved. Yet it would be a mistake to think of Theo as some wistful victim of his own lonely abnormality. That would be too pat. I think the mentality of a traitor must be more complex than that. When caught, the majority of them plead a love of humanity as a whole, that convenient blanket that has smothered so many freedoms. The secrets they steal are always for the benefit of all, it seems, and fellow travellers are much taken with this outwardly persuasive argument, finding it easy to stomach the basic flaw – namely that the love of humanity is curiously selective, since few spies seem disposed to share their thefts with anybody but the Soviet Union.

Time was on their side, time is always on their side. The democracies seldom galvanise themselves except in times of crisis; for the most part they remain sleeping clergymen while their enemies shunt backwards and forwards, exploring every branch line of human fallibility, deliberately taking the longest route, but always in motion, in the sure knowledge that the vital element is not the journey but the ultimate destination.

They found Theo and they salted him away, adding him to the collection. One has to admire their foresight. It must take a particular kind of patience, alien to the Western character, to recruit a number of undergraduates (and there could well be more than the four we know of) at a time when most eyes were lowered over the Bingo cards of appeasement, and prepare them for a war that nobody had thought of. And why Cambridge? That is the other enigma.

There are some of us who are drawn to violence and at this

157

distance I can't be sure whether Theo was a total innocent who was trapped, or somebody who deliberately placed himself in a position of danger. Sometimes the motives of murderer and victim coincide, which perhaps explains why so many crimes of violence go undetected. From the incomplete account he gives in his journals, Theo had premonitions of disaster, yet he still felt compelled to keep his appointment in Samarra. The year was 1934. A vintage year, it would appear.

I don't know what to make of last night's episode. I had misgivings about going in the first place, but he was so persuasive that I finally couldn't help myself. Part of me suspected that he wasn't quite what he seemed, but I fancied him. (No, let's be honest, I didn't fancy him, he excited me beyond belief.) Thirty-ish, and a fascinating mixture. He dressed like a labourer, but was obviously intelligent. Wouldn't let me touch him the first time we met, said he never gave himself to total strangers. I showed myself to him but got nothing in return, which of course only increased my excitement. He let me meet him again, and we had a few drinks together, but he refused to let me buy him a meal. He said he had to very sure before he allowed intimacy. He actually used the word 'intimacy', which I found odd because it seemed out of character. Told me he had been hurt on several occasions and this had made him wary. I told him that he had a terrible effect on me, but was careful not to reveal too much of myself. We talked about love and pain and compared tastes, finding many common interests. He says his name is John, and I allowed him to know me as Ken.

Saw J. again last night. Met him by chance in that pub by the Catholic church. Had the feeling, I don't quite know why, that he knew I would be there. He insisted on buying me a drink and said that he had been thinking a lot about my proposition. "If we're going to have intimacy," he said, using that word again, "it has to be right, in the right surroundings. I can't bear a quick gobble in some sordid cottage. That isn't my cup of tea at all."

There were one or two rugby hearties in the pub who started to make snide remarks in our hearing, so we drank up and went for a walk. I found out that he drifts around a lot, seldom staying long in any one place, but takes labouring work where he can find it.

At the moment he is working on the Appleby Estate, digging drains, and has been given the use of one of the bungalows on the estate while the job lasts. He suggested that I come there Saturday night. "I'll give myself to you then," he said. "I can be very loving with the right person."

He let me kiss him when we said goodbye. I can't remember feeling like this about anybody, but the way he put it and the expectation of Saturday made me quite light-headed. I slept soundly all night and woke this morning still feeling elated.

Sunday

Followed J.'s directions and found the bungalow without too much difficulty. It is about a mile from the main house and fairly isolated, being away from the road and surrounded by a spinney. He is only occupying two of the rooms since the rest of the place is unfurnished. Not much in the way of creature comforts, but he had done what he could and was touchingly houseproud. I took drink with me and some food. "You shouldn't have done that," he said. "This is my treat." I helped him gather some firewood and we lit the fire and drew the curtains. I had made up my mind not to hurry things and we ate the meal he had prepared. I can't say that his cooking impressed me, but I made all the polite noises and pretended that it was to my liking. I suddenly had a glimpse of the the sort of domesticity that Tony longs for and for the first time could see what he means.

We chatted about a number of things and he surprised me with his awareness of world affairs. We decided the bedroom was too cold, so after we had cleared away the remains of the meal we brought the mattress and laid it in front of the fire. It was like one of those Warner Brothers movies where the boy and the girl are trapped in the mountain lodge in a snow storm, the world outside completely cut off. I told him this and it made him laugh. "What a romantic you are," he said. "I like that." He liked a lot of things. I have never known anybody quite so passionate. I usually find that people of his class have a sort of brute aggressiveness.

At one point, when we had finished the first bout and we were having a drink, I asked him, "Is that what you call intimacy? Don't you ever call it something else?" I wanted to draw him out. Dirty talk always excites me. We were totally naked in front of the fire and instead of answering me he started to play with mine again. I noticed his hands were surprisingly soft for a labourer

159

and I was driven by unreasoning desires. We did things to each other I have only previously dreamed about. I stayed all night, and over breakfast he told me that he had fallen in love with me. I am besotted about him.

Wednesday

We have now fallen into an old married couple's routine, though J. quite properly cautioned me about falling into any pattern that might arouse suspicion. We have already had one narrow escape when one of the gamekeepers knocked at the door the other night we were bathing each other in an old hip bath in front of the fire. I hid in one of the empty rooms and the man apparently went away unsuspecting. I agree with J. we have to be careful, because if he was chucked out of his job all this would have to end. For the first time in my life I don't feel the need for anybody else. We satisfy each other in a way I didn't think possible. My work is going well because I have no frustrations.

When I saw Tony at college today he remarked on the change in me.

"What sort of change?" I asked.

"You just seem very relaxed."

I gave him my Gioconda smile and went out of my way to praise his latest novel when he read me a chapter. I felt very generous, though what he read seemed terribly mundane. He is what he writes – well meaning and dull.

Friday

Don't know how to describe my feelings at the moment. J. has been very moody of late and last night after we had slaked each other he said he had a confession to make. "An old friend has turned up out of the blue," he said. "Somebody out of my past. It's all over, it was over years ago, but he won't take no for an answer. I told him about you and me, but he thinks I'm just making it up to get rid of him. Would you be willing to meet him? It's the only way he'll be convinced."

I was torn. This is something I have always been at pains to avoid, some ghastly triangle situation, especially if this friend is the possessive type. They get so hysterical. J. says he's already threatened suicide in the past. I had a sudden vision of this bliss ending. J. went on protesting that the other was a burnt-out case, but was obviously still under some sort of compulsion, because otherwise why would he be so insistent? I suggested we bought this character off, but he was adamant that this wouldn't work.

"I know him too well," he said. "He's a very determined one is Harry. I mean, don't misunderstand me, I've nothing really against him, it's just that I'm so happy with you and I don't want anything to spoil it."

I couldn't put up much of an argument after that and we finally agreed a plan of campaign. We'd invite Harry to have supper with us, treat him kindly, but make him see that his cause is lost. I can't say that I'm altogether happy about it, but there seems no alternative.

Tuesday

Harry, cry God for Harry. Totally, but totally different from anything I had imagined. First impressions not favourable. Skin rather yellow and unhealthy looking. Older than expected, and indeed looks older than J. described him. Would guess in his late thirties, well mannered and with just a trace of an accent. Not a foreign accent exactly, but something grafted on as sometimes happens when people have lived abroad. Was perfectly polite to me, though somewhat removed for the first hour or so. I had made up my mind to charm him, feeling that charm in this case the better part of valour.

We had quite a pleasant dinner, roast chicken which I provided and J. cooked rather well. Plenty to drink. Conversation skirted round the problem but couldn't be avoided for ever so I broached it when I judged the atmosphere sufficiently thawed. He listened in silence to my statement of the defence and didn't seem too disturbed when I explained that although I knew J. still had great affection for him, our present situation could not be attacked.

Then he said a rather sad thing, I thought. He told me his whole life had been made miserable by passion. "I can't remember a time," he said, "when I was free of it."

He didn't only mean J., it was something deeper than that. I was relieved to see that he would accept defeat so gracefully, because although he several times repeated that J. was the one decent episode in his life, he was very unemotional. I suspect he might have been somewhat in his cups by then, for we had all drunk a great deal. I drank to calm my nerves in the first place and could hear myself slurring my words. I didn't see any traces of the hysteria that J. had spoken of. On the contrary he seemed flat and ordinary, and I warmed to him.

Looking back, I don't quite know how the rest of the evening developed, but I suppose that confession time breeds a certain relaxation. Perhaps J. and I were anxious to show there was no

161

hard feelings, or perhaps the underlying eroticism of the occasion, heightened by the drink, took over at a certain point. All I know is that we were suddenly all three naked – an absurd, bizarre scene in that stifling little room, the firelight playing on our entwined bodies. Harry and I were both rivals for J.'s attentions. I have never minded sharing in any case, and it was a time for extra generosity. In other circumstances I might have found it farcically sordid, but we were all swept up into a collective madness, a frenzied saturnalia. Then Harry produced a camera, saying that he wanted something to remember us by. He took a series of photographs of J. and me in the act – again a new experience. Variations on scenes from a nunnery. I played nun to J.'s Legionnaire, a conscious echo of the discovery Tony and I made all those years ago. There is something very special about making one's own pornography. It's the ultimate in narcissism. All in all a unique evening.

Tuesday

I spoke too soon. J. has disappeared. We had arranged to meet as usual at the bungalow, but when I arrived the place was dark. No sign of him anywhere. I tried to break in, fearing something might have happened to him, and although I broke a pane of glass in one of the back windows I still couldn't open it. I waited around for over an hour, then spotted the gamekeeper in the distance and thought it wise to keep out of sight. I have a feeling of panic.

Thursday

Still no sign of him. Have been back to the bungalow twice more, and today I was so distraught I went in daylight. Was able to look in the windows and could see none of his things. Have no idea what to do next. Can't go to the police for obvious reasons. The only· clue I have is that he once told me his parents lived in Liverpool. The whole thing is inexplicable. I can't believe that there is any connection between his disappearance and the evening we spent with Harry. That would be unthinkable. Unthinkable, but something I have thought about.

Friday

Took my courage in my hands today and called at the Appleby Estate Office. Had rehearsed what I was going to say, inventing some distant relationship with J. I was going to tell them that I

162

had to break some bad news to him. Just in time I remembered I had no idea whether John was his real name. It was too late to turn back, because I was inside the office by then, so I quickly changed my story. I said that I had heard that some of the bungalows on the estate were for rent and could they tell me which ones were available. They were rather shirty and said that it was not their policy to rent any property, that the bungalows were reserved for staff. I was forced to admit defeat. Came back here and was violently sick.

Monday

Stayed in bed over the weekend, unable to think straight. The whole thing is a nightmare. I feel unreal. I am one long nerve-end.

Tuesday

Forced myself to get up and went back to the bungalow. I don't know whether it was horror or relief that I found it was occupied. Smoke was coming from the chimney and I rushed to knock on the door. The door was opened by a gypsy-like woman with a baby at the breast. Had to pretend I had lost my way and asked for directions to the main house. It is obvious that J. has gone for ever. I keep hoping that I shall have some word from him, some explanation. Anything would be better than this vacuum.

Thursday

Another week and still nothing. Can't concentrate on anything. When Tony came round last night I was abrupt to the point of rudeness and had to apologise, saying I had neglected my thesis and needed to placate my tutor. No idea whether he believed me or not, nor do I care. My writing has gone to bits. After Tony left I dressed in old clothes and went looking for some sex, I didn't mind what. Picked up a stockbroker in The George and we did it in the back of his Morris Oxford. It was like cold mutton, as Oscar said to Yeats. Felt worse afterwards and got away as soon as it was finished.

Monday

News at last! Received a letter from Harry this morning, post-marked London. Brief and to the point. In it he said he was sure I was worried about J. He apparently knows his present where-abouts and hinted that J. has had some sort of breakdown. Asked me if I could meet him in London this Friday when he will explain all. There was no address on the letter, but he gave me a time and a place. I shall go.

Saturday

How polite he was. He might have been inviting me to join the Salvation Army. Polite but straight to the point. I thought it was just blackmail at first, alarming enough in itself, but something I could have come to terms with. Nothing was an accident, I realise that now. Meeting J. was not the happy chance I once imagined. Everything had been planned; they had had me in their sights for a long time. Guy was the pimp, a willing convert who had suggested I might like to join the club.

I asked him why they felt they had to go to such lengths, that perhaps the direct approach would have been simpler.

"We like to be sure," he said. He told me that J. was too enthusiastic in my case. "One can't afford to be emotional in this job, as I hope you appreciate. Just as there's nothing personal in my proposition to you. It's just a matter of business, a commercial transaction if you like." All said like a salesman trying to hawk his samples. Nothing overt.

He greatly regretted the necessity of reminding me of the existence of the photographs. The negatives had been lodged with his superiors who would not hesitate to make use of them should my answer be other than the one they were looking for. "Think of them as an insurance policy for loyalty," he said.

His superiors had the greatest respect for my talents. This was merely a preliminary talk, a clearing of the ground as it were. I would be contacted at a later date and given more detailed briefings. They just wanted an answer in principle. I could take my time, because time was on their side. They just felt from what Guy had told them that I was sympathetic material. "Would you disagree with that?" he asked. "Could I say that much?"

I suppose I was too amazed by the whole scene to put up much of a counter-argument. His politeness was somehow more threatening than anything else. He even apologised on J.'s behalf. "He wanted to write you a goodbye letter," he said, "but we don't encourage a lot of written evidence." When I asked him if I would be allowed to see J. again, assuming I agreed to their terms, he said he thought this might be arranged. "But give it a while," he said. "He's not in the country at the moment. We felt he needed a holiday. He takes his work so seriously. Such a conscientious young man."

I asked how long I had got to make up my mind.

164

"Shall we say two weeks?" he said. "We don't want to leave it too long, things go off the boil. I'm sure we haven't made the wrong choice. You'll find that once you've taken the decision everything falls into place. We look after our own."

I found a little of my old self-confidence and complimented him on his tact and the choice of venue (Lyons Corner House in Coventry Street). We shook hands when we parted.

I stayed in town overnight. Was propositioned twice in Leicester Square, but declined.

Tuesday

Having thought of nothing else, I finally took the plunge and talked to Guy today. He couldn't resist smirking of course, when I told him some of the history of my case.

"Crude, I suppose, but effective," he said. "I had no idea I was letting you in for all that. I thought it would be straightforward, like it was with me. I dare say they thought it wasn't worth wasting film on me. Mind you, I wouldn't have said no to a little liaison, a little icing on the cake. I'm all for that."

He must have known what I wanted to talk about because he insisted we took a punt out. It was bloody cold on the river, but poetically the right setting for what we were about. And so it begins.

Sunday

They have contacted me again. I shall go and I shall agree. What Guy says makes sense. It's comforting to feel part of a family. Funny how quickly one learns and adapts. I have already taken certain precautions with these journals. After all, it's a game that two can play.

13

THE THIRTIES WERE years when we all did our fair share of crystal-gazing, predicting, arguing, violently disagreeing as to which way the world was going. I used to envy those who had no doubts, some to whom *The Times* leader was gospel, others to whom anything printed in the *Worker* was immediately Holy Writ. Lacking the courage of anybody's convictions, I fluctuated daily. I once consulted a fortune teller at a local fair, since we all need that necessary flirtation with the unknown from time to time. It turned out to be a farcical encounter, for the advertised medium had slipped out for a cup of tea when my turn came, her place being taken by her daughter.

"But are you qualified?" I asked.

"Oh, yes. It runs in the family. Do you want the large ball or the small one?"

"What's the difference?"

"Five bob."

"I'll take the small one."

We sat opposite each other across a rickety card-table covered with a tablecloth patterned with the signs of the zodiac. She produced the economy-sized crystal ball from under the table and placed it between us with nicotine-stained hands. It immediately rolled off, which I took to be a discouraging sign.

"That's never happened before."

She examined it for damage, then wiped it with a piece of velvet before going into the statutory 'trance', passing her grubby hands over the ball in series of ludicrous gestures. I became more interested in her behaviour than in my own future. Once the preliminaries were over she bent forward and stared into the crystal.

"Concentrate," she said.

I stared fixedly at her cleavage.

She suddenly staggered back from the table. "Oh, my gawd!" she exclaimed. "Oh, my gawd, I've seen something. I've never seen anything before."

The experience unnerved her so much she was unable to continue and after a wrangle she gave me my money back and left the tent in search of her mother, desperate to share the revelation. I never did find out what she saw.

The episode seemed to sum up my own life at the time. I was conscious that I had embarked on a journey without maps, in a state of mind that could best be described as muddled. I had some sympathy with the unknown author – the only non-pornographer amongst the clientele of the male lavatories in The Splendide – who scrawled the despairing question, IS THERE A LIFE AFTER BREAKFAST? on our walls. Breakfast in my case had been the publication of my first novel; what had followed had been anticlimax. I suppose the truth of the matter was I was still living in the emotional vacuum that the end of the affair with Judy had bequeathed. A state of grace without religious beliefs is difficult to sustain, and in cutting myself off from all normal social intercourse during the period when the novel was being written I seemed to have lost the knack of making new friends. The solitary life can lead us into areas of quiet madness, and for a brief period I embarked on a strange quest. I chanced upon a photograph of an unknown girl in a magazine which inflamed my imagination. I convinced myself that here was somebody to whom I could entrust my affections and wrote to the editor of the magazine stating that I was convinced the girl was my dead sister's child I had lost touch with for ten years, and could he kindly supply an address for her. My enquiry was treated with the contempt it deserved, though I was to make use of the idea a decade later in one of my novels.

My own loneliness prevented me from perceiving Theo's dilemma. I had no inkling of his affair with the *agent provocateur* called J. – that secret lay buried for forty years until the squalid bedroom in Englefield Green gave up its treasures.

Time and time again over the past few months I have puzzled over the contradiction of the journals. It seems such an extraordinary risk for him to have taken – after Burgess, Maclean and Kim Philby were exposed he could not have been that confident of his own safety: there must have been many moments when he listened for the tread on the stairs in the early hours. And yet he never destroyed them, he ignored even the elementary precaution of depositing them elsewhere. We all like to be amateur psychologists, and never more so than when we are judging our friends. I am as guilty as anyone, applying a little knowledge in dangerous doses. Where Theo is concerned I am driven to believe that the only explanation worth entertaining is that he tempted his own fate, but lacked the conceit which finally makes criminals boast of their secret life. He needed to leave some record of his guilt, and a lifetime's devotion to the written word dictated the form it would take.

Theo's day-to-day existence was so different to mine. He worked amongst noble buildings, conjuring his plots in Wren's great library while I slaved away in Mrs. Pike's mundane back bedroom. He was surrounded by contemporaries intent on like hedonistic pleasures; I met only those concerned with buying a few hours respite from the drab repetitions of their everyday lives. I noticed that whenever parties of under-graduates came 'slumming' to The Splendide they frequently mocked what the rest of our audiences found romantic. But they saved their real malice for the bourgeois traditions of the middle-class; they channelled their anger into pacifism. For the first time in their lives most of them came face to face with actual poverty, not some classical exercise in historical neglect but the poverty that marched with brave songs through the streets of Cambridge. The bleak reality of the Depression suddenly had a human face, and for many of Theo's con-temporaries this was the moment of political awakening. Coupled with the growing awareness of what was happening on the Continent, this was the culminating disillusion with the old order. It was as if, as was the case with the substitute medium I encountered in the fairground, they had suddenly seen the future for the first time, and the collective shock frag-mented, driving many of Theo's generation to the four points of the political compass.

I wish I could record that I was part of that awareness, but my life continued to be made up of fictions: the realities passed by. I know now that people like Burgess and Philby went to see for themselves – Burgess to Russia and Philby to Austria. Whether their journeys were part of a master plan or merely prompted by wanderlust I shall never know. Theo stayed at home, never openly associated with any cause, the detached observer, the rising young novelist who took the longer view, giving the appearance of being a liberal democrat too involved in his vocation to descend into the sawdust of the arena.

After he had taken his Tripos in 1934 (a few months after the affair with J. came to an abrupt end) he announced that he had made a decision for both of us.

"It's absurd to waste your life cleaning out cinema toilets," he said. "I've got enough for us both to live on. We should move to London. I've found a little place behind Flask Walk in Hampstead. It's just big enough for us to live together and apart, if you know what I mean. We can both write and lead separate lives under the same roof. You can pay me what you can afford, but there are no conditions. What d'you say?"

His gesture took me completely by surprise. Until that moment I had formed the impression that Theo had outgrown our childhood friendship – that he still tolerated me out of family loyalty, but that the old intimacy of our relationship had gone for ever. Whether by chance or design, he had timed his offer well. I was increasingly dissatisfied with my lot. I found Clifford and Ruby stultifying; they were kindly and well meaning people, but totally content with what life had offered them. I would always remember them with gratitude, but I had all but smothered myself under their blanketing complacency.

Yet I hesitated. "You've really thought it through, have you? I mean, I don't want to seem ungracious or ungrateful, but the arrangement could present problems."

"What problems?"

"Well, can't you guess? We do have different tastes, after all."

"Oh, that! Tony, dear, as far as I'm concerned you can bring anything home. And I shall extend the same courtesy to myself. We'll sign a non-aggression pact, strict neutrality. The only favour I shall demand as landlord is first claim on the bathroom."

I travelled to London with him on my first free day to inspect our new home. It was a charming, three-storied house tucked away in a mews and had obviously once formed part of a stable-block. It was unfurnished, and although Theo suggested that he be responsible for the entire decor, I insisted that I made my own contribution and furnish my own two rooms. I had saved the odd fifty pounds, and by scouring the second-hand shops I managed to purchase the essentials for just over twenty pounds, acquiring a solid mahogany bed, a simple pine desk, an armchair and a collection of odd pieces of china together with a roll of carpet salvaged from a warehouse fire.

Clifford and Ruby received my news with genuine dismay. I kept in touch with them for a few years but the best of intentions are whittled away and it wasn't until near the end of the war that I learnt that the old Splendide had been gutted by a freak accident involving a Home Guard exercise. Apparently the cinema had been used for a lecture to demonstrate the best way of dealing with incendiary bombs during the Blitz; the demonstration had gone disastrously wrong.

It was with the same mixed feelings that I departed from Mrs. Pike. Clearing my things from that bedroom I remembered the pain of my time with Judy, the long hours spent writing my novel by candlelight – it was like a monk leaving his cell to venture into the real world. There are some places one never forgets and others where memories are erased immediately.

To compensate, of course, there was the excitement of moving into Hampstead – the feeling of accomplishment, never to be repeated exactly, at having achieved a place of one's own for the first time. The fact that I could now close the door and look around at my own possessions was a pleasure that stoked my creative energies. Out of necessity I had to get to work quickly, for I was determined not to sponge on Theo, but pay my own way through my writing. I began as

I meant to continue, keeping to a strict, spartan regime, cutting out all luxuries except my daily quota of Player's Navy Cut, since this was the age when lung cancer was scarcely spoken of and young and old were assailed from every hoarding to accept the pleasures of nicotine as part of life's rich harvest.

Our arrangement seemed to work perfectly. We kept ourselves to ourselves for the most part, and I was at some pains to let Theo see that I respected his privacy. It was usually Theo who disturbed the peace, for he could never resist relating the latest gossip. I was aware that he entertained a variety of 'midnight callers' but they were seldom in evidence during our working hours. "The captains and the queens have all departed," was one of Theo's most repeated remarks if ever we met at breakfast. Perhaps because writing is such a lonely pursuit, one that only a fellow writer can respect and understand for long periods, we need to have a sympathetic companion on tap without the complications of an emotional relationship. Theo and I were able to discuss our works in progress, and the fact that our two styles were so different rendered the criticism we offered each other that much more valuable: we were not in competition except to have the last word on occasions. Being the more successful at that time, Theo was already showing signs of a magnificent disdain for the critics, an attitude I was not confident enough to imitate.

I could not help admiring his self-confidence, for he blossomed as never before the moment we came to London.

"So much to choose from, my dear. There are sections of this fair city positively swarming with talent. As you know, I prefer rough trade to the more obvious queens."

"Aren't you ever scared at the risks you take?"

"Yes."

"Why do you do it then?"

"Because I like being scared, dear. Your trouble is you don't get about enough. You don't meet anybody. This whole literary thing is a game, dear. If you want to get on you've got to join in, dip your toes in the muddy waters and splash a few people. I shall take you around."

He was as good as his word and the following week I went with him to a cocktail party given by the wife of an elderly and extremely rich art dealer, a Mrs. Steel. "We call her Madame de Steel, dear," Theo said, "if you'll excuse the pun. All the money in the world. Her aged husband made a mint selling quite frightful pictures to war profiteers. The point is, she knows everybody, and it'll be very good for you."

I was taken to an elegant house in Eaton Square where we were received by a butler in livery.

"T.B.H., dear," Theo whispered as we waited to be announced.

"What's that mean?"

"To be had," he said, with a nod in the direction of the butler.

Mrs. Steel wasn't at all what I had been led to expect. I guessed her to be in her middle thirties, possibly half the age of her husband. From Theo's description I had imagined her to be vulgarly obvious, but she was soft spoken and gave the impression of being somewhat shy. She had that pampered look of the very rich, and I felt like Gatsby seeing Daisy for the first time.

It was a crowded party with a strong literary emphasis and I knew nobody, though I was able to recognise several famous faces. Sensing my discomfort Diana Steel took me in hand and introduced me to a group. Nerves blurred my perceptions at the time and I confess I have no accurate recall, though I seem to remember that during the course of the evening I exchanged a few pleasantries with the young H. E. Bates, a fellow lost soul. For the most part I stood on the fringe of conversations, never quick enough to catch up with the constantly changing threads, so that by the time I had thought of a witty contribution the dialogue had moved on to another subject. Eveybody gave the impression of being very successful and at the same time indifferent to that success. But the food was good and the drinks plentiful.

After the meal I wandered off to look at Steel's personal art collection which, contrary to Theo's earlier verdict, I found exciting. Perhaps Steel only sold the rubbish to his *nouveau riche* clients and kept the best for himself. He had several

172

exquisite Marie Laurencins, a Picasso of the Blue Period, one huge van Dongen, a Marquet, a whole collection of Bakst (whom I later found he had known intimately before settling in England before the First World War), a little-known contemporary of Renoir, Marval, and two or three superb Braques. But what caught and held my attention was a large female nude hanging above the fireplace in Steel's study. It was done in the style of Boldini, the model depicted as just stepping from her bath, the head turned away, one arm outstretched to pick up a towel so that the breasts were taut and prominent.

"You like that, do you?"

I turned to see my host standing behind me.

"It's very disturbing," I said.

"Do you know anything about painting?"

"Not a great deal."

"I was lucky. I knew most of them at a time when they were either unknown or unwanted. I was lucky. Very lucky. Of course, now they say I had an eye. Well, they were looking at the same things, but they didn't buy them. I did. But I'm glad you like this one. It happens to be one of my favourites, that's why it hangs in my study." He smiled at me. "It's very comforting to be reminded of youth and beauty, don't you think? No, of course you don't, because you are still young. But it will be comforting, take my word for it. I'm sorry, forgive me, I don't think we were ever introduced?"

"Tony Stern."

"Ah, yes. You're the friend of . . . Oh, I'm hopeless on names."

"Theo."

"Of course, the amazing Theo, our rising star. And what do you do, Mr. Stern?"

"I write too."

"Novels?"

"Spy stories. Well, I've only had one published."

"I'm not very up on the literary world. That's Diana's province. I only steal from the rich. And I never dissuade them from their own mistakes. I learnt that lesson a long time ago. If money wants to speak with a common voice, then why

173

try and change it? All artists have to live, even the bad ones. Of course if people really want my opinion, I give it, but I don't volunteer it any more. I'm not a Duveen, that seems like too much hard work."

At that time I had never heard of Duveen, but I nodded politely. He seemed as though he wanted to talk. He was fascinatingly ugly, reminding me of photographs of Frank Harris, and I could detect traces of a mid-European accent when he became animated about his favourite subject. His descriptions of life in Paris at the turn of the century which he decorated with highly personal anecdotes held me spellbound.

"I was a painter myself for a time. At least I called myself a painter, but I laboured under one great disadvantage. I had no talent. A facility, yes, but the spark was missing. One should always be aware of one's limitations, don't you agree? There is nothing sadder than a competent artist. I remember the real moment of truth. It was many years ago, when I still entertained some hope for my own career. I was taken to Matisse's studio and when I looked for the first time at what he was doing, I felt that my whole life was a sham. It seemed impossible for me ever to pick up a brush again. So I never did. I became the next best thing. I started to sell the works of people I admired. It wasn't easy. Nobody accepts original art in the beginning. Nobody. I don't care what it is, people are frightened of what they can't immediately comprehend. Sometimes it's a book, a poem, sometimes a piece of sculpture, or a painting, or a symphony . . . on occasions it's a woman. A woman like that perhaps." He stared up at the nude. "I'm glad you find it disturbing. Beauty should be. She's still beautiful, don't you agree?"

"I'm sorry?"

"My wife. I thought you recognised her. That's a painting of my wife."

I have the feeling that I blushed.

"It's a curious thing. The artist who painted that had a great future, in my opinion. But he never lived to fulfil the promise. He was killed at Verdun. I've tried for a long time to discover more of his work, but with no success. I bought it for very little money and then I set about discovering the model."

"What a romantic story," I said.

"Yes, I suppose it is."

We were interrupted by Theo and his wife at that point. "There you are," she said. "We thought Tony had taken fright and disappeared. What's Anton been telling you?"

"I've been admiring your portrait."

"Hardly a portrait."

Again I felt the blood rush to my face.

She turned to Theo. "You wouldn't call it a portrait, would you, Theo?"

"No. I like my portraits to be realistic, and you're much more beautiful than that, Diana."

"Oh, such flattery."

"Don't misunderstand me, Anton, I'm not speaking from memory."

The sophistication of the exchange only added to my embarrassment. I found it odd to be discussing a woman's nudity in front of her husband. To be standing next to Diana Steel in the flesh, both literally and figuratively, was unnerving.

"Why don't we all have dinner?" she said. "Are you two doing anything?"

"Free as the wind," Theo said, answering for both of us.

"Well, then that's settled."

"I can't," her husband said. "I have to have dinner with those Americans."

"Oh, that's right. Well, don't suggest we join you. Right, well give me time to powder my nose. Theo, ring up the Savoy and get us a table. The Grill, I think." She kissed her husband. "Poor darling, you're going to have such a dull evening."

Mr. Steel excused himself a few moments later and Theo and I were left alone.

"What d'you make of them?" Theo asked when we were on our own.

"They're both very nice. He's a fascinating character."

"In small doses. Don't you like her?"

175

"Yes."

"I saw you colour up when we were discussing that." He pointed to the nude painting. "She's T.B.H., too, you know."

"How d'you know? You just say that about everybody."

"Theo knows, dear. Take his word for it. Poor Anton isn't up to it any more. She's very discreet, though. I mean, she's not about to say goodbye to all this for the sake of a little bunk up. You should cultivate her."

"How could I do that?"

"Do you mean, how could I do that from a moral point of view, or *how* could I do that? If it's the latter, quite simple. Don't rush it, just let things take their course. I know she's got the eye for you."

"You're absurd," I said.

"Okay, have it your way, but I'm never wrong about these things. Why d'you think she invited us to dinner?"

"Well, it's not going to happen, so the whole conversation is academic."

"Did you meet anybody else interesting?"

"Not really. They all seemed very full of themselves."

"Writers always are, dear. And always a disappointment to meet, present company excepted. Were you introduced to Arnold Bennett?"

"Arnold Bennett? He's dead."

"Did I say Bennett? I meant Walpole. Hugh Walpole."

"No, I hardly met anybody."

"Oh, you ought to have met him. He's very kind to up and comings. It's no good me trying to widen your horizons if you behave like some shrinking wallflower."

Diana Steel rejoined us before Theo could expand on his favourite topic of the moment. The Steels' Rolls was waiting outside to whisk us through the evening traffic to the Strand. I sat next to Diana while Theo occupied the jump seat and kept up an endless stream of chatter, for which I was grateful, since it absolved me from making a fool of myself. Diana seemed to have drenched herself in a particularly heavy perfume and from time to time the soft suspension of the Rolls nudged us together.

Dinner was an equally heady experience. Diana insisted

that I order oysters once I had stupidly revealed that I was a stranger to their oily charms. She seemed to know all the waiters on first-name terms and I was suitably impressed by the impeccable service and atmosphere of The Grill. Noel Coward came in with a party after the theatre and stopped by our table.

"Isn't it awful about poor Lottie," Diana said when Theo and I had been introduced.

"What's happend to her now?" Coward said.

"She was playing tennis, fell down and broke her leg in two places."

"Are there two places?" Coward said in his most clipped of mandarin voices.

"Do you think he rehearses those sort of lines?" Theo said maliciously when Coward had gone.

"No, I'm sure he doesn't."

The conversation then turned to the current theatre, another topic about which I was abysmally ignorant. I became more and more conscious that I had done nothing with my life, seen nothing, met nobody of consequence. There I was sitting next to a beautiful and witty woman, drinking champagne in close proximity to the famous, and without a word to say for myself. I thought, how dull she must think me, what a clumsy bore. She and Theo monopolised the conversation, for they talked the same language while I could only interpret the occasional word. What had begun as an evening of enchantment rapidly became an agony. I drank too much and allowed myself to be guided towards a series of over-rich courses, so that by the time coffee was served I was feeling distinctly queasy.

To my horror I heard Diana say, "Shall we go on somewhere?"

"Oh, what a lovely idea," Theo said. "Unfortunately, I can't. I have a certain assignation which I daren't break. But why don't you and Tony go somewhere? He's dying to live it up, aren't you, Tony?"

I had no opportunity to head him off.

"Then Tony and I will enjoy ourselves. Where would you like to go, Tony?"

I had no idea other than to find my way to the nearest men's room.

"You choose," I said. "But don't think you have to just for my sake."

"Oh, Diana never goes to bed," Theo said. He ignored the look I gave him.

"Will you excuse me for a moment," I said. I picked my way through the tables very carefully, only making a bolt for it when I was out of their range. The Savoy's cuisine was wasted on me that night, for I gave back what I had received. After splashing my face with cold water I felt just able to face the world again.

By the time I returned to our table Theo had disappeared. I wondered whether I should make a token effort to offer to pay for the meal, but no bill was presented.

We drove to a night club in the vicinity of Berkeley Square, subsequently closed down during the war for its black market activities. I was grateful for the semi-darkness. Diana ordered more champagne. "Can I ask you a very rude question?" she said. "Are you and Theo a twosome?"

"How d'you mean?"

"Well, you live together, don't you?"

"Yes, we share a house."

"Do you share anything else?"

"Oh, I see what you mean. No. No, we don't. Theo's my best, my oldest friend; we're related, second cousins."

"Then it was rude of me. But perhaps forgivable in view of Theo's reputation."

"Does he have a reputation?"

"Amongst those in the know."

"I think I should tell you, if it isn't already obvious, that I'm not in the know."

"Do you want to be?"

"I'm not sure. Theo says that it's important if you want to make your name quickly."

"I haven't read your book, but I shall get it tomorrow. That's two things you have to forgive me for. Do you?"

"Of course," I said.

"Would you like to dance?"

178

"Look," I said, "I may as well be honest. I'm not in the know and I can't dance. I'd probably cripple you."

"Oh, I doubt that. Take your shoes off. Nobody'll notice here. And there isn't room to dance on this floor, you can only shuffle together."

I was relieved to find that my socks had no holes in them; since leaving Mrs. Pike my limited wardrobe had suffered from neglect. I lead Diana Steel on to the crowded dance floor where most of the couples seemed to be joined together with glue. Diana took my right arm and placed it firmly in the middle of her bare back. "Just relax," she said. It seemed to me that every woman I met gave me the same advice. I had only taken a few tentative steps before she nestled her cheek against mine.

"It's such a relief to find somebody who isn't queer these days," she said.

The band was playing Vivian Ellis's 'Faster, Faster!' from Cochran's new revue and the words seemed particularly appropriate for the occasion – 'step on the gas, boys, and let's save some time' – for the pace of the evening had suddenly accelerated: I was not so naive as to mistake the pressure of her body against mine as we swayed together.

"What're you thinking about?" she said. "You're very quiet."

"I was concentrating, otherwise I should fall over. I'm not very good, am I?"

"You don't have to be good, you're young," she said. "Did Theo tell you much about me?"

"No."

"Unusually discreet of him, and totally out of character. I can't believe he said nothing."

She spoke close to my ear and to my amazement she suddenly closed her teeth on the lobe.

"But you admired the painting, didn't you? You're in the know to that extent."

"Can we go and sit down?" I said. "I've an idea I'm going to pass out."

"Oh, well, we can't have that."

179

We went back to our seat in the corner. She poured herself another drink.

"What is it – the wine, the food, or me?"

"A combination."

"How sweet. I'm being very wicked, aren't I? Teasing you. I don't usually cradle snatch, but I might make an exception where you're concerned."

"What about your husband?"

"Is that what's bothering you? We have an arrangement. Does that shock you?"

"But he's so nice."

"Yes," she said, drawing out the word. "Yes, he is. He's also thirty years older than me."

She emptied her glass of champagne and picked up her handbag.

"It's past your bedtime," she said.

"I'm sorry. I didn't mean to offend you."

"I'm not in the least offended."

She took took two five pound notes from her bag and placed them under her glass. "Let's go, shall we?"

Once outside she shook my hand. "You don't mind getting a taxi, do you? It's been such a pleasant evening."

She got into the waiting Rolls, the chauffeur nodded to me with just the hint of a smile, and then she was gone. I walked to Trafalgar Square, then down Whitehall and on to the Embankment. Derelicts were dossing down for the night, like characters from a Chaplin movie. I stood looking down into the sluggish waters of the Thames until my head cleared, angry with myself for lacking the courage to take what had so obviously been mine for the asking. I thought about her nude body in the painting, then I thought about her husband and felt sorry for both of us.

Perrins Walk, NW3
Wednesday

I must guard against becoming 'camp'. I hate it in others, yet find myself sliding down the same slope. Last night, having dinner with Diana and Tony at the Savoy I heard myself being falsetto. In enjoying the wider freedoms of London I must be careful not to overdo it. I led myself into the trap, too anxious to impress Tony with my social contacts. Work suffers, everything suffers.

Excused myself after dinner and left Tony to Diana's tender mercies. She will eat him given half an opportunity. Met with Harry who again refused to disclose J.'s whereabouts or pass on any message. He also mentioned that I was drawing too much attention to myself, which suggests that I am being watched. I will play their game, but not necessarily strictly according to their rules. When I asked him exactly what is required of me, he was vague to the point of irritation. It is my belief they are just collecting people in a haphazard fashion with no concise plan in mind. Most of the literature he has given me (which I read and destroyed) is banal, written by idiots parrot style and patently handed to them from afar. They believe they can step straight into the vacuum created by the collapse of the Labour Party as a political force, but again they completely misread the character of this country. Strangely enough both opposing extremes are flirting with the intellectuals at the moment, while the Continental pot is coming slowly to the boil. But any attempt to have a rational argument with Harry is a waste of time – he goes by the book rather in the manner of a sergeant major who has displaced his brains by too much foot stamping. Not a pleasant little man, eaten up with class hatred and determined to impose his will on anybody he senses has any intellectual advantage. He cannot understand that whereas I am attracted to the concept in its purest form, I have no illusions about the basic squalid nature of the human race. People *en masse* are repellent. He is concerned with abstracts. I am fascinated by realities.

Perrins Walk
Friday

When pressed, Tony revealed that his evening with Diana ended abruptly and unconsummated. He was non-committal about his feelings towards her. I have turned over a new leaf, no longer seeking endless social diversions and have cancelled all future engagements. I have been putting in six or seven hours a day at the new novel and now feel that I have it by the throat. It will be my most ambitious book to date, a hideously complicated plot which I am struggling to simplify. Like James I am drawn to 'the wasting of life', with passions that might have been. Two people groping for each other in the darkness. The idea of love that is formed too late. It's all there in my head, but needs digging for.

Perrins Walk
Friday

The idea that my every movement is being watched is both fascinating and alarming. I may have misjudged their application, which since it is basically small-time civil service in essence, hideously concerned with ephemera – the kind of details that the average person forgets in a day – is that much more dangerous. I was contacted yesterday and ordered to make certain social excursions, thus negating all my good resolutions. Knowing of my friendship with Diana, they want me to cultivate some of her political friends. In particular Mosley. He is going to dinner with her next week and my brief is to get myself invited. This is bound to irritate Diana since, being a single man, I always present a seating problem. She has a fetish about odd numbers.

Saturday

Finally got Diana to come to the telephone and flattered her into an invitation. She says that I will have to escort old Lady Howarth to make up the numbers. Better than I could have hoped for, since she is stone deaf, dotty but pleasant with it. Always has some scandal to impart, which will come in useful for the new novel since I am short on incident. I can't imagine that such an occasion will yield much for the cause, but they are convinced that we must infiltrate at all levels.

Perrins Walk
Thursday

There was no danger, not the slightest chance of being suspected, and yet I found the experience of sitting at Diana's dinner table last night very frightening. At one point old Lady Howarth asked me whether I was feeling all right. Since she is deaf she tends to shout her questions and the whole table stopped talking. I hastily explained that I found the room somewhat hot and her conversation too stimulating, turning the whole thing into a vague joke. Fortunately Diana agreed with me, blaming the temperature on Anton's compulsion to have the heat at tropical level.

Mosley I found fascinating, a brilliant speaker, with all his facts at his fingertips and very persuasive. He is much better looking in the flesh, a somewhat dashing figure, reminding me of Douglas Fairbanks. He was at his best when describing his vision of the next few years. His convictions seemed to carry weight and were listened to with respect around the table. I sat across from Harold Nicolson who was most complimentary about my last novel.

I enjoyed myself on an intellectual plane because it is the first time I have ever been exposed to political talk on this level, face to face with people who actually have the power to change our lives. But at the same time the inner feeling, the knowledge that, however circumspect, I am actively committed at last, gave me butterflies. If this sort of social occasion can bring such a reaction, I wonder how I will react when put to stronger tests? Forget nothing, I was told. We will decide what is important, not you. Deception gives a curious feeling of superiority – I hadn't realised that before.

Perrins Walk
Sunday

I went to church today for the first time in years. Why? I wonder. The mumbo-jumbo still nauseates me, and I totally reject the idea of Christ as a divine. I can embrace the conception of a unique man totally possessed, but then belief comes to a full stop. Perhaps the petulance and spite of the Old Testament arrested my faith during Sunday School days. I was terrified of those stories, with their endless wrath and wailing and gnashing of teeth, the smiting and the ritual murders – they gave me nightmares, I remember. I would try and creep into Mother's and Father's bed, only he would never have it. I suspend judgment on anybody who set themselves up as God. So why today's return to the fold? Am I testing myself? Religion always wears my father's face. I saw him today in the pulpit.

Wednesday

They appear satisfied with my report. I used the opportunity to make another enquiry about J., but drew the usual blank. They are playing cat and mouse with me. The time is not yet ripe to take a stand. I must choose that moment carefully, and at a higher level than Harry. I am convinced that he is very much the office boy. He takes a sadistic pleasure in reminding me how much damage the photographs could do. Retold last week's Old Bailey trial of the stockbroker and the guardsmen with great relish, insisting that they had a hand in the exposure and that this is only the tip of the iceberg. I suspect he is lying and that the boast has no real substance, but one can't be sure.

I have picked up the threads of the novel once again, but feel that I have made a mistake in cutting myself off from all socialising. I have been very good lately, yet like Proust I need to seek contacts – the vanity that comes from being admired fires my creative energies in the same way that sex provokes a surge. A curious paradox this, that a roll in the gutter and the stimulation of intellectual conversation produce the same results.

The arrangement with Tony still holding together. I find it amusing to think that he sits downstairs manipulating his fictional spies, blissfully ignorant that the real-life counterpart uses the same bath. I sometimes have to make a concentrated effort not to spill the beans, the urge to shock him is so strong.

14

Looking back on the novels I wrote during the years 1935-1939, I am astounded at the contradictions that leap from my pages. There I was churning out thrillers which dealt with the assassination of mid-European dictators, civil wars and international spy rings, consolidating my reputation as an author who anticipated history, and yet the full implication of what was happening in the world never seemed to penetrate. I am not only think of Theo – he was a separate issue – I am referring to my share of the collective myopia. I saw the newsreels, had all the right feelings about Abyssinia, applauded Eden, was shocked by Guernica, admired Hemingway, laughed at Mussolini, read Geoffrey Dawson's pontifications on disarmament, rearmament, pacificsm, public morality and the rest, listened to Baldwin's 'appallingly frank' speeches, was disturbed by Mosley's excursions into the East End, joined the Left Book Club for a period, allowed Churchill my qualified admiration, welcomed Einstein in our midst, found Hitler grotesquely fascinating, Goering merely grotesque, was fanatical about Len Hutton, attempted to read *Mathematics for the Million*, felt comforted by the proliferation of Odeon cinemas, adored Our Gracie and *Quiet Weekend*, fell in love with Jane Baxter in *George and Margaret*, sent flowers to Kay Hammond in *French Without Tears* – in fact behaved like any other young man about town who should have known better, analysed more deeply, cared more passionately, wasted less time.

My books began to sell, the third novel going into several editions. I bought some hideously uncomfortable modern furniture for my part of the house, had a small Augustus John on my wall, acquired the beginnings of a library, ordered my suits from Sackville Street and had my hair cut at Trumpers. I joined the Garrick and the Savile, smoked Balkan Sobranie cigarettes, paid income tax for the first time in my life and spent the rest.

The house in Perrins Walk seemed to bring both of us luck. Theo was equally prolific and wrote with apparently effortless grace, reaching a different audience than mine; smaller, more selective, less middle-brow. Critics now spoke of his 'matchless virtuosity', he was applauded for his 'strange, haunting fermentations from the past'. ("They'll put me down like port," he said.) And we were told that 'Of all the writers of the younger generation, it is Gittings who arouses our boldest hopes.' It would be wrong to suggest that all this acclaim went to his head. He enjoyed his success, but was not unduly impressed by it. Whereas I was interviewed by the Beaverbrook Press, his views of the literary scene were solicited by rather more august publications.

It was about this time that he became noticeably pro-German and we had several non-conclusive arguments about the purity of German youth. This appeared to be his main attraction to the emerging Nazi ideal. He inclined, like so many of us, to dismiss as mere propaganda the increasing number of disturbing reports of German militancy, since it was generally agreed that the Treaty of Versailles had been self-defeating in its punitive clauses. The French, with their constant changes of government, seemed the more suspect, unreliable, a nation without backbone and arrogant to boot. There was a curious undercurrent of sympathy for the Germans, perhaps because they had cast themselves in the role of the underdog, always an irresistible challenge to political punters.

"I thought of joining the Anglo–German Fellowship," Theo said one morning.

"Why?"

"Why? Well, for one thing I like to repay a debt, and my German publishers are quite the nicest people I have to deal with. So generous with their advances. And secondly I think we ought to do something to counteract all this anti-German hysteria."

"Well, which is it, money or conscience?"

"You know me too well. Mostly money. But I do think that

everybody is going lulu at the moment. A lot of scrubby little Reds rushing about stoking up the hate. Anyway, I'm told the Fellowship holds very good dinners."

A few weeks later he asked me if I would like to be his guest at one such dinner.

"You joined, then?"

"Yes. I think it's worth while."

It was a formal, black tie affair at the Savoy and the guest list was formidable. I confess I was impressed, especially as the first person I was introduced to proved to be a fan: there is nothing like flattery to appease a conscience.

"Well, look who's here!" Theo said.

He raised an arm to somebody in the distance. I turned and saw Kim Philby sauntering towards us.

"You remember Tony?"

He stared at me while struggling to make his lips form the right words, finally managing to say that he remembered me very well, his stammer seeming, if anything, more pronounced than I remembered.

"What are you up to these days?"

"I've been doing a little journalism, so called, nothing very spectacular and now I've been asked to edit the Fellowship magazine. I constantly read about your success." He turned to include me. "And yours, of course. Seems a long time since Sundays on the river."

"Who's the guest of honour tonight? I did know, but I've forgotten."

"It's on the invitation," Philby said. "The Kaiser's daughter, the Duchess of Brunswick."

"Just as well we didn't hang him, then. Might have cast a gloom on the evening. It's quite a turn-out."

"Have you seen Guy recently?"

"Not recently, no. He rang me some time ago and said he was off to Berlin for the Olympics. He's probably still there. After all, it must be his idea of wish-fulfilment."

We were separated after that and took our places for dinner. I found myself seated opposite Diana Steel. After our previous encounter I fully expected her to ignore me, but she seemed to have forgotten, or perhaps forgiven, my refusal to get to know her better. There was no sign of her husband.

The food was excellent, the speeches predictably boring, though I remarked that most of the guests received them as tablets handed down from the mountain. I got a spurious pleasure from being amongst the famous and near-famous, since I was still of an age when titles impressed.

When the dinner broke up we found an angry demonstration had formed outside the riverside exit, and the guests were jostled by a mixed bag of Jews and communists as they made their way to the waiting cars. Although the police were in evidence, and some arrests made, there were a few ugly moments. Theo and I got separated in the crush and I found myself pushed against Diana Steel.

"Have you got transport?" she said.

"No, we were going to get a taxi."

"Well, you won't get one now. Come and share with me."

I hesitated, but she took my arm firmly and we elbowed our way to the outskirts of the crowd and spotted Diana's chauffeur who had sensibly parked on the Embankment. As we drove away more police reinforcements were arriving.

"Such excitement," Diana said. "I must say it makes some of the speeches very apt. Bloody Reds. I hope the police wade in. I'm all for that."

"I didn't see Theo, did you?"

"No, I didn't. Are you worried about him? I wouldn't be, he can take care of himself. I must say I never expected to see you here tonight."

"I'm not a member," I said. "I came as Theo's guest."

"Do I detect a note of disapproval?"

"No, not really. I'm neutral."

"You can't afford to be neutral these days. Surely you were impressed with the speeches?"

"The faces change, but the actual words seem remarkably similar."

"I disagree."

"Are we going to have another row?"

"Another one?"

"Well, I got the impression that out last meeting wasn't exactly cause for celebration."

"Really? I can't honestly remember."

"Oh, dear. And there was I thinking I had made a memorable impression with my Fred Astaire impersonation. I can actually get through a fox-trot now without crippling my partner."

"I thought you were very young, that's all. I've read your novels, by the way."

"I'm flattered. Did you enjoy them?"

"Oh, I enjoy most things. I read everything that comes out. Mostly in bed. It's my only bedtime activity these days."

"How is your husband?"

"You're right on cue, aren't you? He's well. Boring, but well."

I glanced to see if the glass division of the Rolls was closed.

"Why do you stay married to him, then?"

"Because it suits me."

The chauffeur slid the glass partition open. "Where to, madam?"

Diana turned to me. "Where would I like to go?"

"I've no idea."

"Didn't you want to show me where you and Theo hibernate?"

"Yes, if you like."

"Could we have a little more enthusiasm?"

"It's not up to your standard," I said. "But you're very welcome to take pot luck."

I gave the chauffeur the instructions and we headed for Swiss Cottage.

"What I like about the Germans," Diana said, "is they're positive. We're such a nation of drifters. I'm also mad about the uniforms. They're so theatrical. I mean, what have we got? Boring old Lloyd George."

"I thought he approved of Hitler?"

"Doesn't make him any less of a bore."

"You seem to find most men boring."

"Well, you are. You have very few uses."

"You charm them into your bed, I take it?"

"Am I going to charm you?"

"Well, not into your bed," I said. "On the other hand,

providing I'm not too boring, I might let you charm me into mine. It's rather narrow, like my mind."

"You haven't forgiven me, have you?"

"Yes, I think so. You were very aggressive."

"That put you off?"

"I like my women to be pliable."

"What a ghastly word."

"Soft, then. Look," I said, "I may as well ask you once more, because I'm not an experienced adulterer. What is the position between you and your husband?"

"Darling, you do harp on it, don't you? Does he know, is that what you're asking? Yes, I think so. He doesn't know names, nor do I give them. I mean, you won't suddenly be hauled through the courts, if that's what you mean. You aren't rich enough for me."

"Fine," I said. "At least I know where I stand."

The Rolls was too large to manoeuvre into the narrow entrance to Perrins Walk.

"Kenton, why don't you drop us here and come back later."

"Any specific time, madam?"

He avoided looking at me, and there was a certain intimate insolence in his manner. One day, I thought, you're going to have trouble with Kenton.

"Oh, three hours," Diana said carelessly.

There were no lights on, indicating that Theo had not yet returned.

"Do you think he's all right?"

"Yes, I'm sure. He met an old friend at the dinner, from his Cambridge days. Well, this is it," I said, turning on the lights in my study. "Not what you're used to, I'm afraid, but as the saying goes, it's home."

"How d'you know what I'm used to?"

She flung her coat down with that lack of concern that often distinguishes the haves from the have-nots. "I take it there is a bedroom?"

"Oh, yes, all mod. cons."

"I was never a great one for sofas."

I poured us both a drink.

"Did you really enjoy this evening?" I said.

"I met you again, didn't I?"

"Well, that may not prove a blessing. Seriously did you?"

"Yes, those sort of functions amuse me. You obviously didn't."

"I don't know enough about them. It seemed a strange sort of evening, really. Gave me an uneasy feeling."

"But we're closer to the Germans than any of the others. After all the royal family is related. You have to prefer them to the French."

"I don't know the French. Or the Germans for that matter. I've never travelled, you see."

"Well, we must remedy that. I'll take you with me next time I go."

"My only impression of Paris is Orwell's."

"Oh, I couldn't read it. Who wants to know what goes on in kitchens? I've never set foot in my kitchen, and I certainly don't want to set foot in anybody else's."

"If you like Germany and the Germans so much, why don't you go there?"

"I've been, several times. One goes to Paris for the clothes and the food. One goes to Germany for something else."

"What's that?"

"Sex. Decadence."

"Sex is very important to you, obviously."

"Why obviously?"

"You talk about it all the time."

"It's the first time I've mentioned it."

"By name, yes."

"Oh, darling, I love that little boy look. I bet I can guess about you. You think a lot about it, but you don't do it often. Had maybe a couple of affairs, not very happy and think that it should all be romantic. Yes? Am I close?"

"You're a bitch, aren't you?" I said.

"Yes, darling. I don't want romancing. You don't have to make any effort in that direction. No ties either side. I can't bear being anybody's private possession."

"That's not so unique. I've been through all that."

"Oh, was that your little Nippy? Theo told me about her."

"Did he? That was loyal of him. Then he probably told you she was much younger than you, or perhaps he left that bit out."

"We're wasting an awful lot of time, you know. Why don't you show me the rest of this mansion. Take me into the west wing."

"I might have changed my mind."

"I don't think so."

She stood up and kissed me full on the lips. We went into the bedroom.

"Oh, it's like a *wagon-lit*," Diana said. "I love having it in sleeping cars. We'll take the night train to Paris when we go. Undress me. You can tear the dress if you like. Tear it, go on, be impatient, pretend you can't wait, pretend we've just met."

I tried to follow her instructions, but she had judged me correctly, I was too romantic to enjoy her playacting and in the end, impatient with me, she ripped her own clothes. I found her behaviour slightly ludicrous and became icy cold, detached, looking at her naked body writhing about on my single bed with the eyes of a voyeur rather than a lover. She fascinated me because I had never come across a woman like her. I was excited by her, since she knew how to excite. Part of me was repelled by her, and that too is a form of excitement that we may not always wish to acknowledge. Diana had needs that were alien to me, and the fact that I was able to satisfy them did not signify that I shared them. During our spasmodic affair I came to use her in the same way as, in the beginning, she so obviously used me. I have no illusions that I was ever her only lover. After that first night we spent together (the unfortunate Kenton had a longer wait than three hours) we met whenever the mood took her. It is not so difficult to accommodate lust when one is young.

I can see now how nearly I was drawn into the net. Had it not been for my sexual romanticism I might have followed a parallel route to Theo, for the seduction of the gullible is more easily accomplished in bed than in the classroom, and Diana was a persuasive teacher. It was such a patient process where Theo, Philby and the rest were concerned. They were told it didn't matter how long it took to penetrate British

Intelligence, and in a way outside events smoothed their paths. The inexorable progress towards a second world war provided the necessary self-justifications as well as the necessary cover. There were complimentary tickets to be had for the dress-rehearsal in Spain, a chance to see if all the war toys worked when wound up. It was a time when heroism could wear many disguises. The real nature of the struggle was obscured by the propagandists of both sides, for the age of compromise was upon us.

When Theo announced that he was going as a freelance journalist accredited to Reuters to cover the Spanish civil war, I greeted the surprise statement with awe rather than suspicion. Again he had been provided with an external alibi which I accepted without question. Some time earlier he had shown me an item in the Personal columns of *The Times* with a fine display of disgust.

"God, how sickening!"

"What's that?" I said.

"The aged bloody father. He's marrying that teenage, so-called 'housekeeper'. Fucking old hypocrite."

"Well, what does it matter? You don't see him any more."

But even I had to share his disgust when Gittings actually had the lack of taste to send us both a wedding invitation.

As the date for the wedding approached he suddenly mentioned his plans for going to Spain.

"Get out of the country altogether," he said. "That's what I want to do. Do you think it's a good idea?"

"Well, yes, but not for that reason alone, surely?"

"No, it was just coincidence, but it's come at the right time. I want to go anyway. And I can make him squirm a little, because I shall write and tell him that I intend to put some distance between us."

"How long will you go for?"

"I don't know. It's a fairly loose arrangement, and everybody thinks it'll be over very quickly. I happened to be having lunch with my publisher and he mentioned he'd been asked to suggest an impartial observer, and could he put my name forward. Apparently they jumped at the idea."

"Well, it's certainly a new departure for you."

"Yes. I thought that. I'm a bit bogged down with the new novel and this thing has unsettled me so much, I thought I'd give it a whirl."

"How do those things work?"

"What d'you mean?"

"Do you rove around? I mean are you accredited to one side, or both, or what?"

"I shall be with Franco's lot," he said. Perhaps he felt it necessary to explain the choice in more mundane terms. "You know me, I'm not one of Nature's heroes. According to Diana that's going to be the winning side." He smiled. "Lacking any strong convictions of my own, I thought I'd take the safest bet."

Despite his self-denigration, there was an element of heroism in his decision which I applauded. The role of foreign correspondent had long been one of my fantasies, and I certainly did not suspect him of any sinister ulterior motive in selecting to report on the Franco campaign. The whole Spanish civil war seemed to me a strange mixture of good and evil on both sides, the issues being far too complex to be judged in black and white terms.

Theo departed without fanfare. He showed me the letter he had finally written to his father and I was relieved that he had omitted most of the actionable abuse. He promised to write to me, but it was a promise he did not keep. I certainly had no idea of his experiences in Spain until the journals came to light, and reading them I can see why.

Salamanca
March 15, 1937

The most surprising thing about this war is the politeness. Everybody I have met so far is full of old-world courtesy – doubtless a characteristic of the Spanish race which strikes a newcomer more forcibly than the old hands, but I had a preconceived notion of conflict which has been knocked sideways. Not that I have seen any fighting so far; only the distant rumble of guns and ambulances bringing back wounded from the front lines. I must learn a whole new vocabulary. War creates new words, new ways of describing old horrors, and most of my fellow correspondents speak the language with irritating superiority. They also seem to treat the whole thing as a gigantic binge interrupted by bouts at the typewriter when they file their stories. I haven't got the hang of it yet.

I am living in a semi-derelict hotel with half a dozen others. The service is primitive and the food strangely unappetising to my taste, though I am beginning to live with it. Spent most of the first week on the toilet, which gave me plenty of time to think about what lies ahead.

Although official sources give us daily bulletins, I gather the form is to ignore these unless one is desperate. Most of the hardened journalists rely on rumours – either rumours they exchange in the bars, or else those they invent and circulate. The actual war itself is so totally confused at the moment, and it is surprising how many of the rumours eventually become true in the end. I suppose a war of this kind, where – excepting the foreigners who have joined in – Spaniard is killing Spaniard is the purest form of conflict. Like a family who systematically set about destroying each other. It would be unacceptable to write this for public consumption, but in a way civil war is more excusable than one where you fight total strangers.

The natives are not only polite, but extremely friendly. I don't know who first pronounced Latins are lousy lovers (are Spaniards Latins?) but they couldn't have done any extensive homework on the subject. No field trials, as it were. I have already experienced a variation of death in the afternoon, though far from the bullring.

Because most of the big names are reporting the other side, we are treated very well indeed. It is a far cry from Perrins Walk, and I have been mildly surprised at my ability to adapt to the changed circumstances. I am still not entirely clear exactly what is required of me, but have been told to be patient. Contact will be made when they are ready, and more explicit instructions issued. They are thorough, very cautious indeed. I live in expectation.

Salamanca
April 28, 1937

I feel like a criminal. Today I looted a single book from a ruined house. I must be curiously unfitted for such everyday tasks, since nobody else pays any attention, but I found myself shaking as I walked away. Having stolen it, I felt compelled to read it. It was a book of French aphorisms; odd to find it here – bygone culture stained with brick dust, fond memories of a world that will never come again. Much taken with a saying of Bjion's that I had never come across before: "Although small boys kill frogs in sport, yet the frogs do not die in sport, but in earnest" I will now add to that with a pompous on-the-spot observation – I can state with the utmost authority that there is very little difference between a dead communist and a dead fascist. They both died not in sport, but in earnest.

Of course Guernica is the only thing being talked about at the present time. Opinions sharply divided. The official line is that the town was blown up by Basque communists as a propaganda exercise, though it seems fairly obvious that this is not a version that will be swallowed by many. Unofficially there is great satisfaction that the Germans have at last flexed their muscles in no uncertain fashion. I have filed a factual dispatch, including both stories and leaving the reader to form his own opinion as to the truth. I doubt whether it will be printed intact, but there it is.

Contact was made last week. The sheer cynicism of the operation takes one's breath away, but I listened and was finally convinced of the long-term strategy. I appreciate that initial sacrifices have to be made here in order to prepare for the inevitable. I am given to understand that this is already regarded as a lost cause, to be kept alive for the sake of appearances only. The lethal rain in Spain is to be endured only to test the umbrellas. My present job is to establish a subtle leaning towards the Right which, I am assured, will stand me in good stead in times to come. I was warned about being too brash and complimented on progress made. My informant also gave me news of Kim who is out here too. We haven't bumped into each other and I was advised not to attempt to make contact. This proved difficult, because the moment my German departed I walked into the bar here to find Kim with his mistress propping up the counter. He gave himself airs, as befits a correspondent for the London *Times*. Perhaps the surprise of seeing me accentuated his stutter, but at times he was almost incoherent, waving his hands in the air as though trying to clutch the words and cram them into his mouth. The lady I found somewhat tiresome. When he got his words together K. was vehement on the subject of world communism as the real threat to civilisation. He convinced me, though I dare say he was putting on a show for the benefit of the others in the crowded bar. Some of his stuff didn't go down too well, but he appeared not to notice. He is much more adept than I shall ever be.

May 17, 1937

I don't know how to put my present thoughts down on paper, yet I must make the effort, otherwise I shall go mad. I think perhaps I am slightly mad already. In the past two hours I have drunk a whole bottle of Scotch, for which I paid through the nose, and it hasn't had the slightest effect. I wish to God it had, for then I might be spared these nightmare images. I went to the hospital today intending to file a story on the wounded, since London has asked for more personal stories. I was shown around the wards and, using an interpreter, got some useful human interest stuff. The suffering of the wounded takes a stronger stomach than mine – I had no idea how obscene gaping wounds can be, and I am amazed that the human body can be blown half to pieces and yet deny the soul release.

Just as I was preparing to leave, a new batch was brought in from the front. The journey had been a long one and many of them were dead on arrival. I stood as the stretchers were passing close enought to touch and blood dripped over my shoes on more than one occasion. I have never seen anything like it and never want to again. Most of the wards are full and as more and more ambulances arrived they were forced to put the bodies down in the corridors. I had to step over them in order to get out and as I reached the last stretcher, which was half in and half out of the building, I had a sudden premonition of my own death. I looked down at this last stretcher – the shattered head of the young man lying on it was turned away from me and pressed close to the wall. The body was partially covered with a piece of blanket and from the twisted outline it was obvious that there wasn't much left below the trunk. I don't know why, but I felt compelled to bend and look at the face. I think I knew what I was going to see, but I could not stop myself. It was J. Half of the jaw had been shot away, that beautiful mouth I kissed was like something seen on a butcher's slab, the flesh whitened, the gums exposed, only his top teeth showing. The shock was so terrifying I actually fell across the body and his blood stained my clothes. My interpreter helped my up and I was led outside to vomit.

I hardly know what I am writing, I can't get that last image out of my mind, or what remains of my mind. I wish I could die myself, drink and drink until a black curtain of nothingness descends, but I am stone cold sober and nothing comes between that poor lovely face. I wish to God I could pray, or smash this room, or had the courage to end it all, anything but this agony, anything.

15

MY OWN LIFE was not coloured by such momentous events. While Theo went to Spain, I went to Denham. Out of the blue I was suddenly summoned to meet Sir Alexander Korda, that flamboyant messiah of the emerging British film industry who brought his Hungarian panache, two brothers and considerable charm to bear upon the confused scene. One of his acolytes telephoned me to say that Alex had read my novels and would like to discuss the possibility of me writing a film script for him. I knew nothing whatsoever of the intricacies of film-making, but could not resist the flattery. I duly presented myself outside his office in Denham Studios.

In those days Denham was an oasis of concrete in the unspoilt countryside of Buckinghamshire, situated close to a picture-postcard village where many of the stars took up temporary residence. I was greeted by an attractive secretary, given coffee and asked if I wouldn't mind waiting, as Alex had been forced to take a meeting with a group of City financiers. The explanation was hardly necessary as I could, without straining, overhear the shouting match coming from the inner sanctum. It sounded as though the participants would shortly come to blows, and I was impressed that the secretary and others bustling in and out of the office paid no attention. It was quite obviously a commonplace happening. I drank my coffee and leafed through some film trade papers. I thought, what have I let myself in for? The row in Korda's office continued unabated, rising now to a new crescendo. Then a lull and the buzzer sounded on the secretary's desk. She picked up the intercom phone and listened briefly. Then she took in an unopened box of Havana cigars. As the door to Korda's office was opened I glimpsed the great man pacing, and in front of him a group of City gents, nattily attired in the standard bankers' uniform. The door closed again.

Left to myself I studied the photographs on the walls. Here were many of the screen greats smiling down, the women heavily re-touched, their mouths outlined like the slots in pillar-boxes, the men looking like the famous Brylcream advertisements. All were signed with messages of undying affection for Korda.

"Is it still going on?" a voice said.

I looked round to find a somewhat wild young man in baggy trousers and moth-eaten sweater.

"You mean in there? Yes, I think so."

"Oh, Christ! Well, look, as soon as you can, try and get word to Alex that Carol wants him on Stage Four. Betty's refusing to shoot that additional scene. She says the dialogue is fucking awful. Tell him, will you?"

"Er, yes, if I can."

"Well, it's absolutely vital. I mean, we can't shoot."

"Betty?" I said.

"Yes. The stupid cow, she should be grateful she's even in work. But she's already phoned her poncey little agent, so the shit is flying."

"Right. Well, I'll do my best."

"Thanks," he said and left.

The row had died down in Korda's office and much to my surprise I heard the pop of a champagne cork and afterwards laughter. I waited for another twenty minutes, during which time the frantic young man returned.

"Any luck?"

"Not yet."

"Oh, well. There's been a new development. She's taken all her clothes off and gone to her dressing room. Alex is the only person who can do any good now."

He seemed much more cheerful than before.

"You're not the bloke from the insurance company, are you?"

"No."

"Oh, thank Christ for that. Just occurred to me, you might have been. I'm not supposed to talk to him, you see."

He disappeared again, having helped himself to some

cigarettes from a packet on the secretary's desk. Finally the meeting came to an end, and the deputation was ushered out by Korda. They all seemed in a remarkably good mood, several of them were smoking the cigars and there were handshakes and smiles all round. When they had been shown to the door, Korda turned to me.

"My dear Mr. Stern, please forgive me for keeping you waiting, but I had to deal with a certain urgent situation. Such a bore, but there it is, these things are sent to try us. Please come in. Would you like some champagne? Darling, open another bottle."

His secretary did the honours.

"They were bankers, as you could see. Lovely people, but no comprehension of what we creative people have to live with. I mean, they should feel privileged to lend me their money, don't you think?"

"Yes," I said.

"Of course. But one always has to start from the very beginning every time. See, they don't understand how we have to spend the money. They don't appreciate that one isn't making pots and pans. They think everything is a balance sheet. Films aren't balance sheets."

"I suppose they only think in one way."

"Well, it happens to be the wrong way, dear Mr. Stern. Is that cold enough? Warm champagne is hideous."

"I have a message for you," I said, as soon as I could get a word in. "About Betty. On Stage Four."

"Such a talented artist. You know her?"

"Er, no. It was just that this young man came by while you were engaged and asked me to relate an urgent message about her. She's apparently refusing to say the lines, shoot the scene or something, and has taken all her clothes off."

"She does that every day. Such an exhibitionist. And she really should keep her clothes on, because what is revealed is not, shall we say, God's gift to the British film industry. Her face is her fortune. How long ago was this?"

"About twenty minutes, at least."

"My dear, excuse me again." He turned to his secretary. "Get me Carol on Stage Four."

I had time to admire the paintings on his walls while the secretary dialled. They were very impressive even to my inexpert eye. The whole office reeked of affluent good taste.

"Carol, dear, I understand we have another little problem? . . . Yes, so tiresome. Is she still there? . . . And there's nothing else you can shoot round her? No, good, you did the right thing. I'll come over."

He turned to me. "Mr. Stern, how can you ever forgive me for such bad manners? Unfortunately the situation requires my presence. Listen, my dear, it's quite simple. You are a great writer. I'd like you to write for me. Have you an agent?"

"No."

"Oh, that's good. They always make problems between creative people. Don't worry, we'll send you a contract, and you write for me. It's all very pleasant; you join the family and we make lovely films together. So kind of you to come. Next time we have a real talk."

He shook my hand and wandered out. I swallowed some more of his vintage champagne.

"What did all that mean?" I asked the secretary.

"It means you're hired. We'll send you a contract."

"Just like that?"

"Yes, Alex never wastes words. He liked you."

"But what am I supposed to do when I get the contract?"

"Well, if you've got any sense you'll sign it."

"I meant, after that."

"Then you'll write us a script."

"Any script?"

"It depends. Alex gets an idea and he just follows his nose. You'll love working for him."

"Is it always like this?"

"Always."

"Well," I said. "It's been a pleasure, as they say. I hope I see you again."

"I'm sure you will, Mr. Stern. Alex never breaks his word where artistic people are concerned. Do you smoke cigars?"

"Not those," I said, "but I'm willing to learn."

I took one. I never smoked it. It remained on my desk for the best part of two years until it dried and flaked away to dust, like so much of the film industry.

In due course a fat contract arrived through the post. I read it carefully, but was unable to understand more than a few paragraphs. It appeared that London Films Ltd, would own all my vital organs for a period of twelve months, during which time I might be required to write an original film script of not less than eighty pages, three copies of which had to be delivered in bound form, and for which I would receive the amazing sum of two thousand pounds, payable in fifty-two equal instalments. There were options to retain me in this elegant slavery for a further two years at the discretion of the said London Films Ltd. I didn't hesitate. I signed it before anybody had second thoughts. Then I heard nothing. Three weeks went by and, amazingly, the cheques started to arrive. Still I heard nothing. Having deposited the first two cheques, I rang Korda's office. He was abroad, I was told.

"What d'you think I should do, then?"

"About what, Mr. Stern?"

"Shouldn't I start writing something?"

"Oh, you've got an idea, have you? Alex will be pleased."

"No. I'm not quite sure what he would like. I mean, is there any particular sort of story he's looking for?"

"Not really."

I got the distinct impression that she found my questions amusing.

"Well, I hate to take money under false pretences."

"Oh, nobody would think that of you, Mr. Stern. We don't work like that."

"When will he be back, d'you think?"

"His plans are a little vague at the moment, but as soon as I have any news I'll let you know. Don't worry, Mr. Stern."

I put the phone down and stared at the latest cheque. It was the beginning of a lifelong romance with the idiocies of the film industry.

In the midst of all this I finally heard from Theo. A post-card arrived, stamped in Berlin. It gave only the briefest of details. He had left Spain and was researching a new book. I was to expect him when he arrived. He was well and hoped I was, too. It was the sort of duty postcard one writes on holiday and then forgets to mail, so that it arrives after one has returned home.

Korda was back in England and I had a further audience with him, only slightly less baffling than the first. He hoped I could come up with an original idea that might serve as a star vehicle for Robert Donat. Arrangements were made for me to have dinner with Donat, but I was denied that pleasure, since Donat was an asthma sufferer and had to cancel at the last moment. I set to work with enormous enthusiasm and the vaguest of guidelines, because in those days I was embarrassed to take money under false pretences.

I continued to see Diana at odd intervals and although the relationship left much to be desired, she did pump the sexual adrenalin along my veins – a necessary relief from my daily stints at the typewriter. She was as good as her word, though, and took me to Paris, a trip I justified as being useful for my work. I found that I behaved like any other tourist set loose in that enchanted city for the first time and was immediately enslaved, reviling myself for what I had missed.

I suppose it was a time when we wanted to cling to some form of permanence, for the clock was moving towards Munich. Looking back, I can see a bitter irony in our activities: there was I bent over a typewriter inventing a spy plot for Korda's celluloid dream factory and there was Theo in Berlin already leading the double-life he sustained to the end of his days. Word filtered through that he was being fêted by the Nazi hierarchy since he was one of the few literary figures of any consequence who seemed sympathetic towards the German problem. He was careful not to burn his boats in every direction, and unlike the Duchess of Roxburghe did not go so far as to suggest that the peace of Europe could be stabilised if only Goering were invited to England for the grouse season, but he allowed his name to be associated with a plea for closer understanding between the two countries. He had asked me to deal with his mail during his absence and I opened several abusive letters from friends as well as strangers who were appalled by his behaviour. I confess that as time went by I became more and more perplexed by his apparent disregard for the changing climate of opinion.

At home we were just beginning to come to terms with the gilded amateurism of Chamberlain as he pushed everybody's darling from the centre of the stage and assumed the star role for himself. The soon-to-be-familiar initials of A.R.P. entered our lives and the spectre of war, far from being a foreigner's distant game, became almost overnight a familiar in our midst.

Autumn in Paris notwithstanding, there was something basically squalid about Diana, and our relationship came to an end the night she took me to hear Mosley speak.

"He's divine," she said. "The only man who makes any sense at all."

What I witnessed that evening depressed me unutterably. We left her Rolls a few streets away from the location of the meeting, and despite my increasing misgivings joined the throng milling around on the Whitechapel pavements. There was a good turn-out on both sides: hand-picked bully boys sporting black shirts, and an equal number of the Jewish Brigade, while in the side streets the mounted police waited with staves drawn. It was quite obvious that the evening had to end in a near riot and I tried to dissuade her from going any further.

"There's going to be a fight. You know that, don't you?"

"But that's half the fun."

"How can you call it fun?"

"Oh, don't be so dreary. Go home if you're scared. I can take care of myself."

I should have accepted the offer – there was never any need to act the gentleman with Diana, and I was scared. Perhaps I was more scared of showing I was scared, and I stayed. Predictably, the moment Mosley started to speak the bottles started flying and there was soon a pitched battle taking place in front of the platform. The police moved in on cue, the crowd breaking into chunks as the horses appeared and we were lucky not to be crushed against the boarded shop windows.

"Satisfied?" I shouted. "Now come on, for God's sake,

while we're still in one piece." I dragged her to safety in a side street and we made a circular detour back to the parked Rolls.

"You bloody wet," she said, as soon as we were inside the car. "What are you, a Jew lover?"

I didn't answer her.

"I wonder you're not circumcised, go the whole hog, you boring little fart."

"One thing I shall always remember about you, Diana, is your amazing command of language. Now, do you mind if I get out?" I rapped on the glass partition. "Let me out here." The chauffeur pulled over to the kerb and stopped the car.

"Yes, get out and piss off. You'll feel at home here, this is Yid country."

I have always wished I could carry off such scenes with dignity, have some brilliantly witty and cutting remark to hand, but somehow it never happens. I just walked away quickly as the Rolls continued towards the City. I never saw Diana again.

That evening made me more conscious of the growing crisis and the fact that we were patently all living on borrowed time. I attended some Civil Defence lectures given in Hampstead, a futile gesture since it was fairly obvious that when the war came I was the perfect age for cannon fodder and hardly likely to be classified in a reserved occupation. But it was better than doing nothing.

There was an element of farce about those early days of Civil Defence. The class barriers hadn't yet fallen, and the strangers who gathered together in drill halls all over the country were linked by a potent mixture of patriotism and fear. I think we were all convinced that within hours of any declaration of war the whole of England would be blanketed by a cloud of mustard gas – for some reason death by gas topped the horror poll; it was as if everybody chose to forget that death from a bullet or high explosive bomb is equally final. The farcical aspect was supplied by our well-meaning and dedicated instructors, for many of them treated the subject as something akin to religious knowledge. Lacking any practical experience themselves, reading from govern-ment pamphlets which in retrospect often resembled Dead

Sea Scrolls, they were often the blind leading the blind. I remember with particular pleasure the lecture on fire drill. Our instructor found it almost impossible to get past the procedure of how to couple the hose to the pump without his own face becoming a conflagration of embarrassment. "One takes the, er, how shall I put it, male element and, er, in accordance with standard practice, er, inserts it into the, er, well the, er, female counterpart." This invariably earned him a round of applause and was eagerly awaited by the old hands.

There was no general exuberance such as my father had described to me when recounting the outbreak of the 1914 war, but in contrast the general mood seemed to me to be one of grim resignation.

On my third visit to the course of lectures I noticed a particularly attractive girl of my own age sitting by herself against the lukewarm radiators that barely took the chill off that draughty Hampstead schoolroom. With that casual air that most men assume when they are on the make, I took the vacant chair next to her.

"First time?" I asked.

She nodded.

"All sounds fairly horrific, doesn't it?"

"Horrible. Do you think it'll happen?"

"Well, the way things are going."

I offered her a cigarette which she accepted. I noticed she was not wearing any rings on her wedding finger. During the tea interval (the war never interrupted that, and we started as we meant to continue) I found out more about her. I had already decided that the national emergency would have to take second place to personal need.

"What d'you think you'll do if it comes to the crunch?"

"I don't know. I suppose women will be called up as well this time. That's what all the papers say."

"What accent is that?" I said. "Not London, is it?"

"No, I come from Lancashire. I thought I'd lost it."

"You work in London, do you?"

"When I'm working. I'm an actress."

"Really? What a coincidence! I work in films myself," I said.

She was gratifyingly impressed. I introduced myself and discovered that her name was Jill Perry. I think what first attracted me to her were her eyes; they were extraordinarily pale, and violet rather than blue. Actresses in those days made no attempt to look like the girl next door, for glamour rather than an assumed dowdiness was considered a necessary adjunct to talent, and Miss Perry had obviously taken some pains to make the most of her physical attractions. I thought she was one of the most stunning girls I had ever seen and could hardly believe my good fortune that we had been brought together by a shared curiosity about the male and female functions of a fire hose.

"Why do you think there has to be a war?" she said.

"I don't know."

"Everybody's telling everybody they don't want it, but here we all are getting used to the idea."

"There's still a chance, I suppose. Are you in a play now?"

"No. I've just done a tour, but they ran out of money. I had quite a good part, too. Still, that's the way it is with this profession."

"I can't think somebody like you will be out of work for long."

"Oh, there's no shortage of me. You should come to some of the auditions."

As fast as I tried to turn the conversation, she just as skilfully reversed back into the topic that obsessed her. "It's the gas attacks that frighten me. I can't even sleep in a room where there's a gas fire. Do you think the Germans will use gas?"

"I suppose they might," I said, thinking of my own father. I could recall his hawking cough that had disturbed so many of my childhood nights.

"I mean, they're going to issue gas masks. They wouldn't do that, go to all that trouble and expense, if they didn't believe it's going to happen."

"Well, they have to take precautions."

"I think I'm a terrible coward," she said. "Even coming here and listening to this frightens me."

"I don't suppose any of us feel very brave. I don't. But is not knowing better than knowing?"

"I think so. I wish I hadn't come."

"I can't agree there," I said, plunging. "If you hadn't come, I wouldn't have met you. So at least Hitler's done something good."

She gave no indication that my awkward flattery had registered.

"D'you think Germans feel the same as we do?"

"Well, I expect they believe what they're told, just as we do."

"It all seems so futile," she said. "We're helpless, aren't we?"

We went back to our seats for the remainder of the lecture. This consisted of illustrating ways and means of making a room gas proof, and in listening to the instructor's voice tabulating the coming horrors in officialese, I caught something of Jill's fear. Panic spurred me to take risks, so that when the lecture ended I was prepared to shed my previous personality and become just a man on the make.

"I don't live far from here," I said. "Perhaps you'd like to come back for a drink or a coffee?"

She looked understandably dubious.

"I couldn't stay long. I share a flat with another girl and it's my turn to cook. She's a dancer, and luckily she's working. What do you do in films?" she said, and doubtless the non sequitur sprang from previous encounters with predatory casting directors.

"I'm a screenwriter. I'm working for Korda at the moment."

My reply seemed to allay her worst fears and after another token hesitation she accepted the invitation. I can't say that I blamed her – she was, after all, absolutely correct in her assumption. My intentions were never honourable.

The sight of Theo's luggage in the hallway pulled me up short. I had deliberately omitted to tell the delectable Miss Perry that I, too, shared a residence, and my surprise at his sudden reappearance confused not only my plans but also my powers of speech.

"How extraordinary. He must be back."

"Who?"

"The friend, my cousin, who . . . we share this house, but he's been away. In Berlin."

"Berlin?"

"Yes. He didn't let me know he was coming back."

Hearing our voices, Theo came out of his study. Perhaps because I was so unreasonably shattered by his return, I found the physical change in him more pronounced. He was much thinner, his clothes seemed to hang on him, and his hair, usually so carefully groomed, seemed to have been cut inexpertly, giving him the look of a shaggy, overgrown schoolboy.

"Well, thanks for letting me know," I said. "This is Miss Perry. We just met at the school, and . . . well, how are you, for Christ's sake?"

"Fine. What d'you mean, school?"

We were talking across her and he suddenly remembered his manners and put out his hand.

"Tony didn't introduce me. I'm Theo Gittings."

"Sorry. Yes, Jill this is Theo."

His name obviously meant nothing to her. Not a great reader, I thought.

"What school did you meet at?"

"School?" I said. "Oh, yes. Civil Defence lecture. They hold the meetings in the local infants school, and we just met there."

"Did Tony say you've just come back from Berlin?"

"I have been in Berlin, yes. Today I came across from France."

"Is it the same over there?" Jill asked.

"Is what the same?"

"The war scare."

"Yes, I suppose so. I don't know what it's like here."

I noticed Theo seemed very uneasy. He seemed reluctant to answer her questions in any detail.

"I don't understand politics," Jill said. "But what do ordinary people think in Germany?"

"They're very pro-British," Theo said. He took a cigarette

from his case and tapped it at both ends before putting it in his mouth. Again I noticed something different about him. His hands, formerly so well manicured, were stained with nicotine.

"Do you think that's a good sign?"

"Look, don't let's have a discussion in the hall," I said. "I invited you back for a cup of coffee."

"Now that your cousin's back you probably want to talk. I'll get off," she said.

The thought appalled me. "Well, stay and have a cup of coffee."

"No, I think I'll get back. It's quite late."

"Can I walk you home, then?"

"No, don't bother. You stay and talk to your cousin. I'm sure you've got lots to talk about."

"There's another lecture on Friday," I said. "Will I see you there?"

"Probably. Depends."

"Let me see you home," I was behaving like an overgrown schoolboy myself, and very conscious that I had lost control of the situation. I felt an unreasonable irritation towards Theo.

"No, really, I'm fine."

She said goodbye to Theo and I walked with her to the end of the road. It's now or never, I thought. I was well aware that I was pressing my luck in the circumstances, but I needed to have one vital piece of information.

"I'd like to see you again," I said, "and if you don't come on Friday, how will I ever find you again? Are you on the telephone?"

"Not really. There is a telephone, but the landlady doesn't like us having calls. Unless it's an emergency."

"This is an emergency." I smiled as I said this, because I had the sudden thought that she must be staring into the face of a sex maniac.

"I'd better not give it you, but I live in Mount Vernon. Number four. You have to go past the graveyard to get to it."

"Doesn't that bother you at night?"

"Not really. Not when you've been in as many flops as I have," she said with a flash of humour. She returned my smile. "I would like to see you again, but I think you should go and talk to your cousin tonight. He doesn't look very well."

I watched her walk off, thinking what pretty legs she had. She moved like an actress.

I thought about her last remark when I got back to the house. Theo was sitting at his desk looking through the pile of mail I had collected for him.

"You're not ill, are you?" I said.

There was a pause before he answered. "No. Just tired from travelling. Why, do I look ill?"

"Not to me, but then I'm not very perceptive. That girl thought you didn't look very well."

"I'm sorry if I ruined your plans for the evening."

"Oh, just wishful thinking. I doubt whether I would have bedded her tonight. I don't think she's the type for immediate seduction."

"Is there anything to eat?"

"Not much, I'm afraid. I wasn't expecting you."

"No, well, I decided on the spur of the moment. I should have let you know."

"We could probably go out to eat. There might be somewhere open."

"It doesn't matter. A boiled egg or something will do."

We went into the kitchen to scrounge around.

"You know me," I said, holding up some very curled bacon. "The perfect housekeeper. I never seem to bother about food when I'm on my own."

"Have you been doing a lot of work?"

I told him about my screenwriting debut and he seemed suitably impressed, especially when I told him what they were paying me.

"How about you? Did you get some useful material in Berlin?"

"What d'you mean?" he said sharply.

"The new book. I thought you were out there researching a new book. That's what you said on the only postcard I got from you."

"Oh, that. Yes. Yes, I did get a few ideas."

212

"What's it like in Berlin?"

"You can't tell, really. Nobody wants to talk. They're very polite to us, very anxious to convince us we're their natural ally."

"But . . .?"

"Well, it's like meeting a lot of people at a wedding party. You get very friendly while it's all going on, and exchange addresses, and yet you know that the invitations will never come to anything."

"You seem very on edge."

"Do I?"

"How many minutes?"

He stared at me blankly.

"The eggs, how d'you like them?"

"Oh, four minutes, four and a half."

"I suppose it will happen sooner or later, and that means us. If we have any choice, what would you go in? Army or what?"

"You have to pass a medical, don't you? I might not pass."

"Assuming you did."

I served his eggs on toast and he sat at the kitchen table to eat them while I made some coffee.

"I've tried not to think that far," he said.

"I think it's all fairly gloomy, though. I mean, pathetic old Chamberlain is bleating around. He always looks like something out of Madame Tussaud's to me. Of course Eden's gone, you knew that?"

"Yes. The Germans were pleased about that."

"You keep saying Germans, but you mean the Nazis?"

"There's not that much difference," Theo said. "I'd say that most of them think the sun shines out of Hitler's arse."

"But all these stories we hear; is it as fearful as they make out?"

He stared down at his half-eaten egg. "I met him, you know. Hitler. I was introduced at some official reception."

I stopped what I was doing. "Well, go on! What was he like?"

"Impressive," Theo said. "I could see why they follow him."

"Did you meet any of the others?"

"Only Goebbels – repellent, face like one of those awful lap dogs, which I suppose he is – and a man called Bormann. They all think the real enemy is Russia, you know. It's not the Jews they're after, it's the Reds."

"But they're kicking the Jews out."

"Put it this way, they're not encouraging them to stay. There's a lot of talk about the purity of the race. Most of the young men are very handsome, hand-picked, I'd say, for the benefit of tourists like me."

"But you weren't tempted?"

"I didn't say that."

"And Spain," I said. "I want to know all about Spain too. I read some of your pieces, of course."

We drank coffee and talked for the next two hours. I kept noticing how nervous he had become. He wasn't very forth-coming about the Spanish experience and at one point I almost thought he had tears in his eyes, but I could have been mistaken. He seemed to be waiting for something, and when the doorbell went he was on his feet before me.

"That's probably somebody for me."

"For you? But nobody knows you're home."

"Yes. It's somebody I met on the boat."

"Oh, I see. I thought you were a bit on edge. Why didn't you say?"

"I'm not on edge."

"Fine. I can take a hint. You can do the same thing for me when eventually I get Miss Perry to nibble at the bait. See you in the morning."

I went to my own room to plan future strategy where Jill was concerned. I heard Theo admit his visitor, but curiously the conversation between them was held at the front door. It seemed to me that they were both talking in a foreign language, and I heard my own name mentioned once. Then the door slammed and all was quiet. I listened and it became obvious that Theo had gone out with his visitor. I went to the bathroom to brush my teeth, amazed he had the energy even

214

to contemplate whatever he was contemplating, and slightly
miffed that everything always seemed so cut and dried
between Theo and his lovers. If only Miss Perry could be so
easily persuaded, I thought.

16

DURING ALL THAT unreal summer of 1938 we made a conscious effort to push outside events to the back of our minds. Theo seemed to become more his old self in the weeks following his return from Berlin, though he still couldn't be drawn into any serious discussion of his foreign experiences. He started work on a new novel, the one eventually published under the title of *The Burnt Heart*, and in all probability when the time comes for a definitive biography whoever undertakes the task will discern traces of his Spanish episode and the death of the boy he loved. We writers often think we cover our tracks completely, but some words force themselves on to the page.

My affair with Jill progressed slowly. She was not another Judy or Diana, prepared to tumble into bed just like that. I enjoyed her company because she cared about so many things. She wanted to be something more than just a decorative piece of scenery and I respected her for that. God knows she could have taken a far easier route to further her career in the pre-war theatre. Girls as pretty as she was could usually find a couch with a contract under the cushions, and she often came back from an interview to relate some narrow escape from the fate that was commonly thought to be worse than death. Of course, she might have been exaggerating to keep me in line, since it is always more difficult to play the cad when you are listening to an account of somebody else's seduction attempt. Not that I felt caddish towards her. I was anxious to get her into bed, but at the same time I felt protective. She had none of the conceits usually associated with young actresses who have repeatedly been told they are beautiful. I went to see her act on a couple of occasions – Sunday try-outs, I think they were called – and although I was predisposed in her favour, I had to admit that she was hardly likely to challenge Peggy Ashcroft. What she had was a presence. She knew how to place her body under the lights: it's a sort of instinct that some actresses have which has nothing to do with acting talent, and careers have been made with less. But in Jill's case the timing was all wrong. Wrong for her, wrong for all of us. It was difficult to think of permanence in 1938.

When Munich happened I shared that general, shaming relief – like getting away with cheating in an exam – that gripped us all. I didn't go to Downing Street, or stand outside Buckingham Palace to cheer, but inwardly my heart sang. I have little memory for dates, but September 30th, 1938 is likely to be the Calais on my heart – not for the right reasons, but because that night in celebration of the snatched peace, I finally persuaded Jill to share my bed.

The landscape of our lives changed drastically after Munich. There were trial 'blackouts' and preparations for war were increasingly in evidence. The garden at Perrins Walk wasn't large enough to accommodate an Anderson Shelter, so we fortified an area under the stairwell, really nothing more than a glorified cupboard, which we reinforced with corrugated iron and sandbags. We also laid in a store of emergency supplies, going about such inherently terrifying preparations with that typical British mixture of mock seriousness and black humour that has so often confounded our enemies.

Theo and I discussed the inevitability of war on many occasions. It was the only time he ever referred to his Spanish experience, describing the effects of aerial bombing in graphic detail. Like everybody else we fully expected London to be devastated within the first few days of the commencement of hostilities. It was entirely characteristic of us that we both, independently, packed our most valuable books and manuscripts before thinking of anything else. We also gave consideration to the desirability of volunteering ahead of time rather than wait to be directed since it was obvious that conscription would come.

With this in mind I took myself off for an interview with the Board of an outfit called The Officers' Emergency Reserve.

There my sparse qualifications were noted with an embarrassed lack of enthusiasm by an elderly gentleman who looked as though he had spent the greater part of his life passing the port.

"Can't hold out much hope of a decent regiment," he muttered. "Present occupation writer, is it?"

"Yes."

"Yes." He stared at me, fingering his buttonhole. "Not likely to change, I suppose?"

"I don't think so."

"Difficult to see where you'd fit in. You are British, I take it?"

"Yes."

"That helps, of course. Well, Mr. Stern, we must just wait and see. 'Course, it may not happen. The Hun is no man's fool, and there's always a chance the old balloon won't go up."

I came away with a keener appreciation of the encounters Jill had to suffer and even more convinced that our days were numbered. It was in this depressed state of mind that Jill and I made plans to take what we rightly surmised would be our last holiday for many years to come. We decided to rent a houseboat and explore the Norfolk Broads. ("My aged and disgusting father has been exploring them all his adult life," Theo told Jill.) It's funny how one can plot pleasures in an atmosphere of fear, but it seemed the only route to sanity at the time.

Towards the middle of August and just before Jill and I took off, Theo confided that he was going to accept a government job.

"What sort of job?" I asked him.

"Oh, well, it's all a bit vague, but I gather they're going to set up some sort of propaganda department in anticipation of Armageddon, and they've asked me to be part of it."

"You crafty sod! Didn't row me in, I suppose? When was this decided?"

"They've been pestering me for some time," he said.

"And it'll be classified as a reserved occupation, of course?"

"Probably, yes. Yes, I imagine so."

"You double-dealer," I said. "So while I'm fighting for you, you'll be here in some cushy office with a willing secretary on your knee."

"As long as it's a male secretary. Anyway, who's to say London won't be the most dangerous place?"

"Don't you believe it. Propaganda departments will be buried under ten feet of concrete reinforced with steely lies. When do you start?"

"I suppose I've sort of started already."

"Well," I said, "you've ruined my holiday. You crafty sod, I repeat. I shall never trust a single government communique."

In retrospect, that last August of peace seems the best holiday I ever had. Jill and I cut ourselves off from everything and everybody. We didn't take a radio with us and we didn't buy a single newspaper. Most days we ambled along in our rented houseboat, reminding ourselves of Kenneth Grahame-land, the calming feeling of drifting on water in glorious contrast to what was happening in the outside world. I have never slept so well or made love so often. To be in love and cut off from the rest of suffering humanity is to sample the age of illusion. Those hot summer days seemed to consist of nothing but gentle bouts of love-making in the curtained cabin, watching the green, ever-moving light play across Jill's nude body – an Ondine borrowed for a few brief weeks. I remember her tumbled hair and the breakfasts we took on deck when everything was still, the sun just starting to burn through the drifting patches of river mist, while birds flew low over the water to snatch at our thrown crumbs.

We were still there, innocent, uncaring, on September 3rd when a small boy suddenly appeared on the far bank, running for dear life. We waved to him and he waved back, his face pink with excitement. "We're at war," he shouted. "We've declared war, on the wireless!"

Then he was gone, desperate to spread the good news. Instinctively we looked up into the wide skies, hearing the drone of a single-engined aircraft appearing on cue. We watched it out of sight and then we went down into the cabin, and made love for the last time. All the holidays were over.

*

The implacable darkness of the blackout was the hardest thing to get used to – the rest was anticlimax. We had been expecting immediate horror and wholesale carnage, clouds of lethal gas blanketing the rubble of our ruined cities: what we got was minor officialdom shouting at us to seal the cracks of light. If we had been hoping for a new sense of urgency and purpose after the long years of drift, we were disappointed. Chamberlain was still there, his features set in a hurt expression as though Hitler had cheated him at the bridge table. After that first morning the sirens remained silent; it was business as usual, the only outward indication that anything untoward had happened, the appearance of Polish soldiers in our streets – sad reminders of our good intentions – with their slightly musical comedy hats and heel-clicking good manners, giving rise to the first generation of Polish jokes. We spent our time listening for the clarion call to duty and all we heard was the leaden voices of our masters who gave the impression that it was their collective intention to bore Germany into submission. The only acts of attrition were a series of R.A.F. leaflet raids, a war strategy of such benevolence it might have been devised by the Salvation Army.

I tackled Theo on this subject, accusing him of writing the actual leaflets. He denied all knowledge.

"Well, what exactly is your exalted department doing, then?"

"My lips are sealed."

"The whole thing is pathetic. Does anybody seriously believe that the Germans read what we drop? Apart from providing them with free toilet paper, what bloody good is it doing?"

"Greater minds than ours are at work," Theo said.

"Name one."

"Goebbels."

"At least Lord Haw Haw makes the occasional joke."

"Yes, but we're not supposed to listen to him," Jill said. "Personally, I love Alvar Lidell. Do you think he still puts on a black tie to read the nine o'clock news?"

"When that goes," Theo said, "we shall really be at war."

Apart from such frivolous exchanges, he was seldom forthcoming about his new occupation. He kept odd hours and often disappeared for days on end without explanation. I found it difficult to settle to anything. I had finished the Korda commission and sent the script to Denham and that was the last I heard of it. I tried to start a new novel but my fictions seemed to belong to a bygone age and I abandoned it after a few chapters. Jill moved in with us when her flat-mate went to join the Women's Land Army – a piece of war effort that provided a good proportion of the jokes that B.B.C. comedians beamed at us. There was little work going in the theatre, despite the fact that most of them had reopened after the early panic closures. She was as restless as I was and told me that she was seriously thinking of joining E.N.S.A. – that much-maligned entertainment organisation which did little to enhance its launching with posters that proclaimed: COME THE FOUR CORNERS OF THE EARTH IN ARMS, AND WE SHALL SHOCK THEM.

My own future was resolved for me. I received notification to present myself at a barracks on the outskirts of Chelmsford in Essex. Obviously the interview with The Officers' Emergency Reserve had been the dismal failure I had imagined. After a farewell dinner at Perrins Walk, during which we killed the last three bottles of decent Burgundy we were to see for the next six years, I took my Beau Geste exit and journeyed to Chelmsford.

There any remaining illusions about the Army were swiftly dispelled. I learnt to survive, to endure the brutalised camaraderie of my fellow sufferers, to shave in three minutes flat in cold water and run all the way to the open latrines and back in order not to be last in line for the congealed breakfast. I was given a rifle manufactured in 1915 that kicked like a mule, and a uniform that brought me up in a rash wherever it touched bare skin. I looked as dashing as an Old Bill cartoon and believed I was on the verge of a major heart attack whenever we went on a forced route march. As far as I could gather, the British infantry was still being trained to fend off Napoleon's Old Guard, the philosophy of most of our officers being that, although Hitler had broken the rules in Poland, once he came face to face with seven inches of blunt bayonet he would settle for a more civilised form of warfare. We were allowed five rounds of live ammunition on the firing ranges, since bullets were in short supply: those of us who actually hit any part of the targets were regarded as potential sniper material.

After eight weeks of such enlightened instruction I was posted to the Somerset Light Infantry which the barrack-room wit suggested was due to the fact I had once got drunk on draught cider. Much to my surprise I felt physically stronger, walked with a pronounced swagger and behaved as though a member of an élite force.

Granted a brief forty-eight hour leave, I went back to Perrins Walk with a lean and hungry look and fell upon the admiring Jill with the ardour of a man who has served a long term in the Foreign Legion. I also commandeered the bath-room for hours on end, much to Theo's annoyance.

"It's your privilege to take second place to we brave boys in khaki," I said. "How are things in the rumour factory?"

"Dull by comparison to your own exciting life."

"Written any good leaflets lately?"

"We also serve," he said, "who only sit and ponder."

I had no sooner joined the Somersets when my Company was posted overseas. We embarked for France as part of the ill-fated British Expeditionary Force – fully prepared, in the words of the then popular song, to do laundry service on the Siegfried Line.

In thinking of those extraordinary, far-off days, and trying to piece together Theo's parallel story, I wish I could provide myself with a rational explanation for everything. But every-where I look there are loose ends. The spoor marks have been mostly obliterated, some by time, some by deliberate acts by persons as yet unknown.

This much seems obvious: at some point during the period he spent in Spain and Berlin, Theo received the instructions that were to shape the rest of his life. It must have been then that his relationship with the Comintern moved from the shallows of an undergraduate playpool to the deeper waters where one either sank or swam. There is a definite gap in the journals after Spain. When the entries resumed they had a different, almost Kafka-like quality. Perhaps he was under orders, or perhaps he merely adapted his technique to suit the changed circumstances, but I can find no evidence of a code being employed. Instead, I believe he hit upon the idea of setting down fact as fiction, changing names and localities and employing the third person instead of the more dangerous, betraying 'I' of the earlier years. If so it was entirely in character, for he always maintained that British officialdom could never come to terms with literature. Doubtless pride in his craft as a serious novelist played an important role as he painfully doctored the entries in those identical exercise books. Even when he was deceiving others he could not resist trying to write well, and perhaps he knew that this final conceit was the one that would save him. The passages I am about to quote are Theo's version of hell – his Gilbert Pinfold's ordeal, if you like, the actions of a man who was a writer first and last. This was his war, the one he fought with himself.

If for 'Alec' you read 'Theo' then the whole thing starts to make sense.

17

. . . WHAT WOULD BE most painful to him, Alec thought? For the world to discover his worthlessness, or to remain dependent on those he no longer loved?

He woke covered in sweat, his mind immediately alert to the danger he carried within him like malaria. For a few moments he had no idea where he was.

"Wakey, wakey, sir," a voice said very close to his ear. He turned in panic and pitched on to the floor. In the act of falling he was conscious of a hot liquid stinging the hand he thrust out to save himself.

"Sorry, sir, very sorry. Didn't mean to startle you like that."

He was helped to his feet and found himself staring at a stranger in uniform. Memories of the country he had recently left came crowding back, and once again his instinct was to try and escape, but the room was moving and he lost balance again.

"Woke you up with a start, didn't I? That's a black mark, can't have that. Here, just sit down on the edge of the bed, sir, and get your bearings. You were in a real deep sleep."

Alec sat on the hard edge of the bunk, his eyes gradually becoming accustomed to the dim overhead light as he remembered where he was. The stranger in uniform had a Cockney accent and was smiling.

"Be in Victoria in under the half hour, sir. So I usually call my gentlemen in good time, in case they want to have a sluice and a shave. All right now, are you? My mistake but we'll put it to rights. I'll get you fresh cup of Rosy; we seem to have spilt this one."

He backed out of the sleeping compartment and Alec had an impression of a pitted landscape flashing by.

"Thank you," he said, as the door closed. "Thank you, stupid of me," talking to himself. He pulled himself upright and stared at his reflection in the mirror over the handbasin. Home, he thought, I'm nearly home and then he started to shake involuntarily, like a man suddenly struck with a virulent fever. He reached for a cigarette and had to strike three matches before he could get it

224

alight. Why am I fully dressed? he thought, looking down at the rumpled bed. Why not pyjamas? The cigarette calmed him, but he still had to struggle to find the answers. He pressed the cigarette into the serrated edge of the fixed ashtray and returned to the washbasin, splashing his face with cold water that tasted of iron on his lips. As he straightened he found himself reading a notice which said, *In Case of Emergency Pull The Chain Downwards. Penalty for Wrongful Use £5.* The words helped him focus on reality. He drew deeply on the cigarette again, his mouth full of the bitter taste of betrayal. I shall have to get used to that, he thought. It was like an alcoholic telling himself to become accustomed to an endless hangover. I'll give up smoking, he thought. To compensate, one addiction in exchange for another. But it was a further promise to keep and he had made too many in recent weeks.

There was a knock on the door, barely audible over the noise of the boat train travelling at speed over the suburban points. Alec opened the door with a hand that had stopped trembling.

"Here we are, sir. I made a fresh pot. Least I could do after that little episode. No offence taken, I hope?"

"No, it was my fault," Alec said, taking the fresh cup of tea. "I'm a very heavy sleeper."

"Now then, sir, have we got all we want? Razor, shaving soap? I always carry some just in case any of my gentlemen come unprepared."

"I think I have everything, thank you."

The man leaned across and turned on the hot water tap. "Watch this, sir. Scald you this would. Still, better hot than cold."

The strong tea completed the process of revival and when he had sipped half of it, he scraped a razor over his stubble, performing the routine actions like man under hypnosis. Why am I doing this? he thought. Just because that man suggested it, and it suddenly struck him that he had obeyed without question. They did a good job, he thought. I'm already conditioned. It seemed to him then that his whole life had been a preparation for betrayal, that he was going home to an old familiarity.

(This must refer to the night he arrived back unexpectedly and surprised me with Jill. Although writing with aplomb in a style hitherto foreign to him, I can detect a certain unease. A writer can never completely hide an element of self-destruction.)

They didn't waste any time. Alec wanted space to breathe, a chance to gather up old threads, make quite certain that none of the patches on his previous personality gave him away, but he was not allowed such luxuries. He realised that this would be the pattern of his life from now on, that his every act would be watched and judged. What had they told him? Things will happen that you won't understand, but accept our word that the right decisions are being taken in the right order. You are important to us and that carries heavy responsibilities.

The whole structure of his life had become a hideous novelty overnight. Until this point he had only half-believed in the existence of a malignant force operating from afar, but his recent journey abroad had robbed him of this last comfort. So much of his life had been a walk with fantasy and now the fantasy had been crowded out. Even so, the speed with which they worked took him by surprise. It was like being hauled back to school a few hours after the last term had finished, to begin again the education of himself. Forget everything you have learnt, begin again, discard the old values, trample on the honour code, it's all right to split, you have our permission. The new curriculum begins now.

Part of him was offended by the company he was now forced to keep. Although he had never thought of himself as a snob, he was appalled by his new set of friends. He had the feeling that the distaste was returned and this added to his sense of uneasiness, that no matter how hard he tried to please, his papers would never be marked ten out of ten. His previous circle were not slow to remark the change in him; it was as if he had come home scarred, a Dorian Gray denied a mirror that gave any true reflection.

(Sections of the narrative are heavily crossed out at this point, as though Theo had grown tired with the effort of disguising his plot with such a heavy layer of literary grease paint. To ghost one's own work is heavy labour. When he resumed, his prose became much more direct.)

"You must be patient with me," Alec said. "I don't come fully equipped to this sort of thing."

The man sitting across the table in the all-night Corner shop picked his nose with grave concentration. There were four cups of half-drunk tea between them and the remnants of a cheese sandwich sharing a plateful of cigarette ends.

226

"We have been patient," the man said. He took the result of his diligent search and rolled it into a ball between his fingers before carefully depositing it on the underside of the table. "You can't say we've hurried you, but now events are overtaking us. I think Berlin explained how quickly things are going. We don't want to be the ones who let the side down."

The voice was right but the appearance, the mannerisms suggested failure – a doctor who had been struck off the register and was determined to get his own back.

"Therefore we have to play our part in good time. Certain arrangements have been made to receive you." – again the suggestion of a medical opinion, as though I'm being admitted to an isolation ward, Alec thought. "You will be contacted quite legitimately. That's already been set in motion. It's a question of patriotism, you see. Don't be too anxious, too keen, that's always taken as a bad sign. You have to learn to understand the Establishment mentality; it's just another branch of the civil service moving in more mysterious ways."

It all sounded so plausible put that way, yet the thrill of staring into the abyss was only exciting until it became contemptible. How have I reached this point? Alec thought. A few months ago I was set in my rut, a respected Oxford don steeped in the classics, dull, ordinary, conditioned by an academic routine I thought would last me out my days. I could number my vices on three fingers, endowed with limited imagination and feeling, a passable analytical intelligence, a reliable memory. Now I am here, my world exploded. "Here" was the outskirts of treason, the unknown bourn, face to face with a stranger who picked his nose while peace receded.

"How will they contact me?" he asked.

"Normal channels. It's another form of income tax, in a way. They want you to pay your dues, that's all."

"And then?"

"Just take things as they come. It's all very methodical, not at all like the thriller writers. That's just a smokescreen to fool the majority. The real thing is all routine, paperwork, something you're used to."

"I'm not used to any of it," Alec said.

"You should have thought about that earlier," his companion said. He opened a fresh packet of cigarettes, extracted one and replaced it with what looked like an identical paper cylinder he took from his jacket pocket.

"These are your brand, I believe?"

"There's a number you can call written on the inside. Memorise it, then destroy it. Call me when you've been accepted, but only when you've been accepted. You should hear within the next two weeks."

He slid the packet across the table.

"We've every confidence in you," he said. "Every confidence. You're going to be a feather in our cap."

Then he got up, leaning across the table to shake hands formally, saying in a somewhat louder voice: "Very pleasant to see you again. Good luck with the project" – though there was nobody to hear but a drunk sitting a few tables away, and a tired waitress clearing the debris of forgotten meals. Then he walked swiftly away.

He's left me to pay the bill, Alec thought. It was the only gesture he fully understood. From that moment onwards he would always be paying.

If he was honest with himself, the actual initiation had been easy. And quite different from anything he had imagined. He had moved from one extreme to the other. From the squalid absurdity of secret telephone numbers hidden in cigarette packets, to the cloistered calm of his club. Some ten days later he was enjoying an after-lunch cigar and leafing through the pages of *Country Life* (he had long nurtured a hankering for a thatched cottage in which to spend his retirement) when he was approached by a fellow member who settled down in the armchair next to him. Alec was aware that he was something to do with the War Office, though the main attraction of his club was that few of the members intruded upon others; it was considered bad form to talk too much personal shop.

"Chilly today. Should have thought they'd have lit the fire," his companion said.

"Yes."

"'Course the news is chilly enough without the weather adding to it."

"Yes."

"You take *Country Life*, do you? Some damn good articles in there, I always think. Better than the *Tatler*. Can't stand all that social chit-chat."

Having made the effort to appear unsociable, Alec resigned himself to the fact that he would have to enter into a conversation.

"I was looking at the prices of cottages," he said. "Thinking of my old age."

228

"Dorset. That's the county. Though I don't know that most of us will see old age, the way things are going."

"You don't think so?"

"I'm damn sure of it. We've bought a few months credit with that Munich job, but it's not going to last. He's not going to be satisfied with just that, not if I read it correctly. It's going to come and we won't be able to wriggle out of it next time. Nor should we."

"No, I suppose not. It seems a terrible prospect."

"Run out of options, you see. Should have called his bluff when he walked into the Rhineland."

"Yes. I'm not very well up in these matters, I'm afraid."

"Why should you be? You dons live in your ivory towers and very necessary, too. Always regret I never walked amongst the dreaming spires. Been Army all my life. You're not on the Reserve, are you?"

"No."

"I think we'll all be in it, of course, one way or the other. Going to be a different kind of war from the last one."

It suddenly struck Alec that the conversation was a probe. He felt a sense of enormous relief, like a man who has been consulting several specialists and is finally given a diagnosis – even bad news is sometimes preferable to the unknown.

"They're going to be looking for chaps like you. Chaps with brains. Not going to be six inches of cold steel when you get over the top boys. There's still a lot of that sort of thinking around, of course. Mistaken, in my opinion. It's going to be a war of nerves."

"Are we as unprepared as they say?"

"We're thin on the ground. Very thin. Need everybody we can muster."

I mustn't seem curious or anxious, Alec thought. If this is the approach I was told to expect, the important thing is to be totally ignorant. He stared down at the cover of *Country Life*, at a picture of an England that was destined to disappear for ever, an England he was just about to betray.

"I hear you travel quite a bit?"

"Yes. I try to. It broadens the mind, I find. Teaching the classics year in and year out is apt to solidify the old intellectual arteries."

There was a pause. How curious, Alec thought, I really believe that he's embarrassed, he can't quite bring himself to discuss what he's really here for. Not for the first time he was amazed by the comparison between the two organisations. His contempt for the class his companion represented was tempered by a sort of awe – they have a purpose, he thought, and we muddle through, inhibited, half-articulate, desperate to observe the social conventions whatever the circumstances. The whole country was governed in the same way, strictly adhering to a set of Queensberry Rules that everybody else disregarded. Chamberlain waving that piece of paper, a bookie's slip for a horse that was never going to run.

"I'm sure that somebody like yourself has a role to play," his companion continued. He had the studied manner of a West End actor. "Not necessarily in uniform. If you were interested I could put somebody in touch."

"You mean some sort of propaganda work?"

"Yes, that kind of thing."

"I doubt if I'd be any good."

"Well, these people seem to think you might."

It was the first reference to third parties. I don't suppose he meant to say that, Alec thought. Still playing the innocent, he gave no sign he had detected anything untoward.

"Yes," he said, "by all means, then, if you think I could be of some value."

"Good. I've got one or two contacts and I'll pass your name along." He brightened a little, as though he had just discharged an awkward chore. "Be a relief in many ways when the old balloon goes up. Can't bear all this hanging around. Hope you find your cottage. Useful to have a funk hole, comes in handy."

(Theo is not straying far from reality in his fictional account. Reading various authenticated memoirs, one gathers that recruitment was often conducted in this gentlemanly, oblique fashion. Approaches were made in all directions, to academics, scientists, mathematicians, actors, lawyers, writers and even the criminal classes. There was doubtless an element of desperation in the beginning, with a few enlightened men casting the net wide in order to make up for lost time.

Inevitably one comes back to the apparent recklessness of Theo's journals-cum-notebooks, this overriding compulsion he had to document his own treasons. They give me the feeling that he might have welcomed being exposed, that the layers of deceit were his way of testing himself. He was not alone, of course: many of his fellow travellers could not resist the conceit, for there must be many moments in a double-agent's life when the burden becomes intolerable. There is always the early precedent of Casement's *Black Diaries*.)

Alec had never anticipated that his next contact would be a woman – an elderly woman at that, one of those brusque, capable ladies that the British seem to have invented as a third race. One couldn't imagine the French or German counterparts operating in the same way or at the same level. The British seem to accept such things, he thought. After all, the most popular woman writer of detective stories had actually got her readers to accept a female detective, a preposterous idea on the face of it, but swallowed wholesale and with every sign of relish. The lady who interviewed him might well have been the model for Miss Marple. Sensibly dressed, smart without being showy, the sort of woman you would expect to be in charge of a village jumble sale. Perhaps the faintest suggestion of a moustache on the upper lip, but powdered out. A hint of 4711 Cologne whenever she took her handkerchief from the sleeve of her jacket, and a no-nonsense manner of smoking her Kensitas.

She had greeted him as she might have welcomed a nephew she had not seen for several years. The telephoned appointment had been for four o'clock sharp at Brown's Hotel and she was waiting at a reserved table when Alec walked in at five to four.

"How very nice of you to spare the time, Mr. Morris. I'm Miss Malcolm. What sort of tea do you prefer? I ordered Earl Grey, but if you'd rather have Indian or China, we can soon change it. I believe your usual tipple is Earl Grey."

"Yes. How clever of you to know."

"I wouldn't say clever. Just efficient."

They all sat down and tea was served almost immediately, together with a selection of sandwiches that seemed to have been carved by a miniaturist.

Miss Malcolm got straight to the point. "I think I'm right in saying that you could be looking for some interesting, different employment in the future?"

"That was the idea, yes."

"And the fact that you've taken the trouble to keep this appointment means you're still interested?"

"I'm interested in exploring it further."

"Good. How many lumps?"

"None. I don't take it."

"Oh, you put me to shame. I like mud at the bottom of my cup. It keeps up the energy, or so I tell myself."

She poured with a steady hand, then lit another cigarette.

"Do you mind if I do?" Alec said.

"I can hardly object, can I? Tea, cigarettes and cats, my life revolves around all three."

"You're fond of cats?"

"Fond isn't the word. I am somewhat enslaved by them. Do you like cats, Mr. Morris?"

"Yes, I do. I prefer them to dogs."

"Oh, then we're going to get along. I always feel there's something odd about people who don't like cats. You've travelled quite a lot, I believe? How well do you know Germany?"

"Reasonably well. I studied there for a time and frequently go back for holidays."

"Yes. Well, holidays may be curtailed in the near future."

"I suppose so."

"The sort of employment we had in mind would be political in nature. Does that worry you?"

"I don't think so."

She asked her questions in a chatty, conversational manner and to the rest of the residents in the lounge they must have presented a conventional tableau.

"Very political in fact, involving, shall we say, a certain element of discretion. Do you follow me?"

"Yes."

"Of course it would be work of the highest importance; that is why we are approaching people of your standing."

"Very flattering."

"No, not flattering. Just a sensible precaution. We can't afford to make mistakes."

"Can you give me any more detailed idea of what might be involved?"

"Well, I know it sounds rude, but do you know, I can't. That really isn't my forte. They just think I'm rather useful getting to know people and making recommendations. How's your tea, need topping up?"

"Thank you. So, where do we go from here?"

"I go back to the office, where do you go?"

The sudden dart of humour took him by surprise. For the first time during the interview he became aware of her femininity. Be careful, he thought. She may look like your maiden aunt, but there the resemblance ends.

"The one thing we all have to learn in this line of business," she said, "is that things are never quite what they appear. It's a little confusing at first, but I'm sure you'll soon get the hang of it."

"Have I passed the first test?"

"I've certainly enjoyed our little talk. But could I ask you one last question? It's rather personal, I'm afraid, so please forgive me. Do you have any . . . emotional attachments that might preclude you from taking such employment, assuming it was offered?"

"No," Alec said, looking straight at her as he answered. "No, nothing to speak of. I lead a somewhat solitary life, as I'm sure you know."

"Don't we all?" she said. She gathered up her gloves and handbag. "Forgive me if I have to rush. Do stay and finish some more of those delicious sandwiches. It's all paid for."

Alec got to his feet to say goodbye. "I never thought I'd be a kept man," he said.

"Oh, you're not. I claim it all back on expenses. So nice to have met you. I'm sure we'll meet again."

He watched her walk briskly out of the lounge. Much to his surprise he saw that she had rather shapely legs.

He was asked to make a second meeting less than a week later. He made apologies and declined, pleading a prior engagement that was impossible to break. One mustn't appear too keen, he thought, and already he was training his mind to think one step ahead. An alternative date was agreed and on this occasion he went to an address off Grosvenor Square. This time Miss Malcolm was joined by his original contact from the club, and again he was put through his paces in more detail. He might have been applying for the job of headmaster at some minor public school, the only marked difference being he was offered Scotch instead of Earl Grey. He was told that, subject to his own final decision, an approach had already been made to his college. There would be no objection to his having leave of absence, though for the time being nothing was cut and dried. In the event, the story for general consumption would be that he was having a rest on medical advice. 'A slight patch on the lung, we thought, in view of the fact that you're a heavy smoker.' Alec had further cause to admire their thoroughness. It would be dangerous, he thought, to be fooled by the seemingly amateur approach. Once again the meeting ended with nothing actually resolved, though he came away convinced that he had passed their tests.

This was confirmed a fortnight later when a fellow don enquired about his health. "Heard a rumour and hope it's nothing too serious."

"Well, I have been told to take it easy. But reports of my death are premature."

"Have they told you to give up the weed?"

"Oh, yes. I'm cutting it down."

"Well, sorry to hear it, Alec. Take care of yourself."

Miss Malcolm phoned that evening. His medical report had now been carefully studied and they would like him to come in and discuss the treatment involved. "It would be tidier if we could start from August 1st."

He had a stiff drink before making his own telephone call. The number rang half a dozen times before it was answered. "I've been accepted," he said. "They're taking me in on August 1st."

"Congratulations," the voice said. "We'll be in touch. Don't use this number again." The line went dead.

The following day he attempted to trace it through Directory Enquiries. He was told that it was now a defunct line. It had been used by a firm of toy importers operating from a warehouse in Shoreditch.

18

THERE WAS LITTLE that was heroic about my war. Shortly after our arrival in France I was put in charge of unit intelligence. This mostly consisted of sticking flags in maps to mark the locations of local brothels, and resulted in my being promoted to unpaid sergeant. I was later transferred into the Field Security arm of the Intelligence Corps proper and had my own Section, most of them misfits who, like me, were considered liabilities as infantrymen.

Until the German invasion of the Low Countries, mail reached us without too much delay. Faithful to me in her fashion, Jill wrote regularly. She had managed to get herself into an E.N.S.A. troupe and was touring Army camps in Southern Command, appearing once nightly in a production of Edgar Wallace's vintage thriller, *The Case of The Frightened Lady*. "An apt title for this particular lady," she wrote, "since our coach driver is a monumental drunk and I am nightly amazed that we ever survive in the blackout."

I heard nothing from Theo, although several times I wrote to Perrins Walk and enquired after him through Jill. "I phoned him after I got your last letter," she wrote, "but there was no reply. If and when we get nearer to London I'll try and find time to go home." Her use of the word 'home' struck a comforting note. Then her letters stopped: by then the Allied armies were in full retreat and Dunkirk was upon us.

I was amongst the lucky ones who got out of France before the surrender. I landed at Newhaven in a dangerously over-loaded fishing boat that had already made three trips to the beaches. I lay below decks with a dying man across my legs and another holding my hand as tightly as a scared child. Once we had disembarked it was every man for himself. Willing ladies handed out tea and buns and we were told to make our own ways back to our base units. I had no idea where I was expected to report, and instead took advantage of the general confusion to return to London. Nobody was likely to miss me and my consuming thought was to find Jill. Perrins Walk seemed as good a base as any.

I found the house deserted, looking as though it had been abandoned in a hurry: Theo's bed unmade, the sink full of unwashed crockery, my own room chill and dusty. I had no idea of Theo's whereabouts, but I rang E.N.S.A. headquarters to start my search for Jill. The phone was answered by a weary female voice.

"*The Case of The Frightened Lady* company," I said. "Do you know where they are?"

"The who?"

I repeated the question. "I'm trying to locate a Miss Jill Perry."

"Oh, well, I wouldn't know anything like that. I'm just temporary, just manning the switchboard."

"Is there anybody else? This is an emergency."

"Everything's an emergency," the voice said. "Are you a relative?"

"Yes," I lied. "I'm her husband and I've just got back from Dunkirk."

"Oh. Well, all I can do is take your number."

Without thinking, I started to give my Army number, then corrected myself. I knew that nothing would happen; the woman at the other end had that sort of voice. I took a bath and shaved. My skin was ingrained with grease from the deck of the fishing boat and there was blood from the dying man under my finger nails. I felt like a murder suspect. Even though I scrubbed myself the stink of smoke and death lingered, so I purloined Theo's only bottle of cologne. Then I cooked the only egg in the house. I was sitting at the kitchen table wondering what to do next when the phone went. I rushed to it.

"It's all set," a male voice said. "Exactly as planned."

"Who d'you want?" I said. "Are you calling Mr. Gittings?"

The line went dead immediately. I waited for.the caller to ring again, but nothing happened. There was a calendar pinned to the wall above the phone and as I replaced the receiver I noticed that there was a circle drawn round one date. I'd lost all track of time but when I checked, I found it was that day's date that had been scored.

The quiet of Hampstead was unreal. I went upstairs to my room and sifted through my books and possessions, staring at them as though they belonged to somebody else. It was the same with Theo's room – I felt like an invader scavenging for loot. There was a copy of *Tit Bits* on Theo's bedside table and I remember thinking that was hardly his normal reading matter. There was something missing in the house and for a long time I couldn't think what it might be. Then it came to me: any trace of Jill was missing. She was not the tidiest of people and in the old days my chest of drawers had always been littered with the debris of her several handbags, the surface white with her spilled face powder, my ashtrays holding a collection of hairpins. Eventually I fell asleep on top of my bed, going out as though knocked unconscious and immediately plunged into nightmarish dreams, faces floating past me, drowned men spinning down into a vortex. The bang of the front door wakened me and with newly-acquired instincts for survival I rolled over, falling on to the floor.

"Who's that?" It was Theo's voice.

I appeared, still in shock, at the top of the stairs.

"Christ!" he said. "You made my heart stop."

I went to put on a light and he screamed a warning.

"Don't! I haven't fixed the blackout."

I did nothing to help as he struggled with the home-made shutters. Without any justification I felt the serving soldier's resentment of civilians: Theo's neat appearance contrasted sharply with how I felt and looked.

"Where's Jill?" I asked.

"Give me a chance. Haven't said hello yet. Listen, I'm glad you're back safely. I never expected to see you again. The news has been terrible."

"Well, the news is right. I want to know where Jill is."

"I'll tell you, just let me catch my breath. D'you want something to drink?"

He rummaged around and produced a third of a bottle of

237

gin. "Nothing to go with it, I'm afraid." He rinsed two glasses and poured generous tots.

"Welcome back."

"Tell me."

"God, you're one track. She's at home. She's gone home to her parents. I put her on the train myself."

"When?"

"Today."

"Today? Oh, Christ! you mean I've only just missed her?"

He nodded, and poured the rest of the gin in my glass. I was aware that I had drunk the first tot too quickly.

"She's all right, though?"

"Yes . . . Yes."

"What does that mean?"

"Just that. She's fine."

"But?"

"My God, you've come back in an aggressive mood."

"I'm sorry. I was asleep, and I don't know, I don't mean to be aggressive. I'm just anxious, that's all."

"She's been staying here for the last couple of weeks," Theo said. He seemed to be searching for his words. "She hasn't been too well, you see. But she's all right now. Don't look so worried, I promise you she's all right."

"There is a 'but', though. I can tell."

"Yes . . . Look, now don't get upset, but the fact of the matter is, and I may as well come straight out with it, she had an abortion."

I stared at him. His words meant nothing to me. They were just part of the general nightmare, sounds heard dimly through the increasing gin haze, part of the swaying journey in darkness with a dying man bleeding over my legs, just another aspect of the bloody war. Theo fumbled for a packet of cigarettes and lit one for me. My fingers still had traces of dried blood under the nails.

"Tony, dear, obviously I would have contacted you if I'd been able, but there was no way."

I nodded.

"Just no way."

"When? When did she have it?"

"About a fortnight ago, I believe. She didn't tell me all that much. Difficult things to arrange, so I'm told. I mean, they're not my line of country, and of course they're illegal. Anyway, she got it done somehow, and then it went wrong or something. A friend of hers, a girlfriend, another actress in the same company, rang me one night asking where you were and I couldn't tell her anything, so then she appealed to me, could I help? So I helped. Did the best I could."

I got up and walked around the room.

"The problem was my best was pretty useless, but I did manage to get hold of a reliable doctor – somebody in my out-fit gave me his name and he agreed to come and see her. She was here by then, and not very well at all. I gave her my room. Not every doctor will touch these things, even after the event, but this bloke turned up trumps. Apparently, it hadn't been done too expertly; these back-street jobs never are, I gather. But he patched her up, came in twice a day for the first three days. I slept in the room with her, slept in a chair by the bed because she was delirious for a while and it wasn't safe to leave her. I'm telling you all this because it does have a happy ending. She's all right. I made sure of that. She's fine now. And she's gone home where she'll be properly looked after."

I finally managed to put the only other question that mattered to me.

"Whose child was it, did she say?"

Theo studied my face before answering. "Well, yours I presumed."

"How could it be?" I said. "I haven't seen her in over five months."

He looked away. "Oh. Well, I'm not very up on these things. She didn't tell me, and I didn't ask her."

I had the feeling the room was closing in on all four sides, like the remembered childhood terror of the Edgar Allen Poe story. I sat down again and found I couldn't stop myself crying. "I'm sorry," I said. "It's just reaction. That and the tiredness and the gin."

"Doesn't matter," Theo said.

"I'll be okay in a minute." The many ironies slowly began

239

to penetrate. Theo gave me his handerchief and I had a sudden vision of him playing nurse to Jill: well-meaning, half-embarrassed by the intimacy of it all, probably a little revolted by being confronted with such unfamiliarities, but doing his best.

"I'm really sorry," he said.

"Don't be silly. Thank God you were here. Why the hell didn't she tell me? I wouldn't have cared that it wasn't mine."

"Perhaps she did try. Perhaps the letter never reached you. On the other hand, she might have been too scared to tell you, seeing as . . ."

"Yes," I said, thinking back to those afternoons on the houseboat just before the war started. "I've ruined your handkerchief. Still got grime all over me."

"What's a handkerchief between friends?"

"Oh, God . . . I don't know. D'you have her home address?"

He went to the dresser and took a piece of paper from a jug. "They're not on the phone," he said, "if that's what you're thinking."

I was halfway towards the hall. "Well, I'll go there. Can you lend me some money?"

He gave me nine pounds, all he had on him.

"What's your own situation? I haven't asked you that. Are you supposed to rejoin your unit?"

"Yes, but sod that."

"Well, don't get into trouble. Everybody's very trigger-happy, looking for parachutists disguised as nuns."

"I'll risk it. Just go and change. If anybody stops me I'll say I lost my uniform on the way back."

I started up the stairs, then remembered the telephone call.

"By the way, somebody rang just after I got here."

"For me?"

"Could have been, I don't know. He didn't give a name. Just said something about everything's arranged exactly as planned. Then he got cut off."

"Strange. Did he ask for me?"

"No."

"Probably a wrong number."

240

"Unless you've got a secret lover. How is your love life, by the way?"

"Dull."

"I see you're now reading *Tit Bits*; thought perhaps you're on the turn."

"That must have been Jill's," Theo said. "She must have left it there."

I suddenly became conscious of what he had done for me. I went back to him and put my arms round him. "I'll never forget what you did," I said.

He seemed embarrassed. "I've always liked Jill," he said.

While I was changing he shouted up the stairs to me. "I have to go out again, see I wasn't expecting you. Take care of yourself. When will I see you?"

"I'll ring when I get there."

"I'll leave my office number by the phone."

"What're you up to now? I didn't even ask about you."

"Same old thing. They've given me the rank of major, so next time we meet, salute."

I walked all the way to Euston Station, keeping to the back streets. The station was crowded – a mass of servicemen and civilians milling around in the hope of finding room on those trains still running. There were long queues at all the booking offices and I waited twenty minutes before I got my ticket to Manchester. Then my luck ran out. I was at the barrier before I realised that the platforms were stiff with Military Police. All servicemen were being closely scrutinised, but I still believed I could brazen it out if challenged, forgetting that my army haircut and generally haggard appearance betrayed me. I got on to the platform but was headed off by a Provost Sergeant as I made for the Manchester train.

"Excuse me, soldier," he said.

I kept walking.

"Excuse me, sir." I couldn't ignore that. "D'you have any means of identifying yourself, sir?"

"Not on me. Why are you stopping me? I'm not in the Army."

"Just doing my job, sir. Be easier if you could provide some identification." He was staring at my hair. I was such an amateur at it.

"Okay," I said, bereft of any further inspiration. "You're right. I am in the Army. I'm a sergeant, Intelligence Corps, just back from Dunkirk. I'm trying to get to my girlfriend. She's just lost a baby. It was stupid of me, I know, but I'm desperate, so give me a break."

"Can I have your name and number, Sergeant?"

I gave them.

"No travel warrant?"

"No. I promise you I'm not on the run, and I'll report to my unit as soon as I've seen her. You've got tabs on me now, so turn the other way, will you?"

"Can't," he said.

"Why not? What's it to you?"

"My stripes, that's what it is to me, Serg. Nothing personal, but you should know the rules."

"Fuck the rules," I said. "What difference will it make?"

I might have persuaded him, but he was joined by his officer.

"What's the trouble, Sergeant?"

The sergeant came to attention with shattering, text-book perfection. "This sergeant travelling without a warrant, sah! Lost his uniform at Dunkirk, sah!"

I was grateful to him for that piece of embroidery. The officer looked me up and down.

"What's your unit?"

"Intelligence Corps, sir."

"Oh." We were nobody's favourite. "Well, you'd better rejoin them, hadn't you? Get him over to Chelsea under escort, Sergeant."

He walked away. He had a boil right in the centre of his shaven neck. I heard the guard's whistle herald the departure of my train. The lucky ones scuttled past me to grab at closing doors and swing aboard. The scene suddenly resembled the last reel of a Warner Brothers melodrama.

"Sorry," the Military Police sergeant said. "Did me best, but he's a right pisser."

"That's okay. I know you tried."

242

I followed him to the waiting room being used as a clearing house. It was crowded with a motley collection of dispirited men. I took my place amongst them and after a two-hour wait we were herded into Bedford trucks and taken across London to Chelsea Barracks where I was again interrogated. Resigned to the inevitable by then, I still kept torturing myself with images of Jill, imagining her loneliness and terror going to some squalid, anonymous house in the suburbs to end a life. There were other kinds of war, different betrayals.

After being rekitted I was sent to a holding unit just outside Aldershot. The camp there was under canvas and was crammed with remnants of the B.E.F. who had arrived from all points of the compass. At the first opportunity I persuaded one of the clerks in the adjutant's office to send a telegram to Jill asking her to get in touch. She phoned the following evening and I had to take the call in the Guard House, overheard by a leery group of squadees. The best we could manage was an exchange of pleasantries, all the while skirting the main topic.

"I never thought I'd hear from you again," she said.

"You know me. Indestructible."

"I didn't mean that."

"I know what you meant, and you're wrong. Look, I'm having to share this conversation . . . We're confined to camp, but is there any chance of you coming down here? When you feel up to it, that is."

There was no answer.

"Hello? You still there?"

"Yes," she said, and I realised she was crying.

"Don't," I said. Then the time pips started to go and I hadn't got any more change. "Write," I shouted before the line went dead.

War plays so many tricks. She did write, but the letter never reached me, because by the time it arrived I had been moved elsewhere, having been singled out for an O.T.C. crash course. I found myself billeted in an elegant Lutyens house a few miles inland from Worthing on the Sussex coast. Things had hotted up after Dunkirk. There was a shortage of junior officers with any sort of field experience and my intake included several other N.C.O.s salvaged from the ill-fated French episode. Once again I tried to let Jill know of my changed whereabouts, but since I was now posted inside a restricted area any chance of her visiting me was ruled out.

The German invasion was expected any day and our training was pushed through at speed. It was a remote existence. The house was set amongst rolling farmland and had it not been for the dogfights tracing black and white doodles in the summer sky, I could have believed I was living in a part of England only seen in travel guides. Most of the civilians in the area had been evacuated; those few able-bodied men who remained were members of the Local Defence Volunteers, and marched up and down the lanes armed with a variety of antique and mostly useless weapons. Despite all the brave rhetoric that Churchill broadcast we were aware that, when the Germans came, we wouldn't be doing too much fighting on the beaches.

One can never exaggerate the absurdities brought about by wars. After I was commissioned I was seconded to MI 5 where I was not required to wear my splendid new uniform. The blow was not softened by the fact that a demented old woman pushed a white feather at me during the train journey to Farnham, my next temporary home. This time I found myself in another large country house that had previously been used as a private clinic specialising in colonic irrigation for rich dipsomaniacs. Naturally, we were immediately known as 'The Colonics' and an anonymous wit chalked 'The higher you go, the more you bring down' above the entrance as a unit motto.

I shared a room with an affable major named Miller (and for some inexplicable reason all Millers were called Dusty) who carried out valiant experiments with some of the abandoned medical equipment and managed to construct an efficient still. The moonshine he produced was commendably lethal once one had got beyond the taste.

Dusty was the only regular soldier amongst us and cast himself as the unit philosopher. Like many of the older hands he had seen service with the Indian Police. "Only outfit that would have me," he said. "Never a great one for exams." He was cynical about everything to do with the Army. "Officially, of course, we don't exist," he told us. "There are no secret services. Why? That's the way the Establishment mind works. Can't admit to anything underhand; destroy the whole bloody system that would. Very dodgy. Might lead to questions in the House. So, if we follow it through logically, if we don't exist we aren't here."

"You've been reading Forster," I said.

"What outfit's he in?"

"He's a novelist."

"Never read novels," Dusty said, and that shut me up. "No, I mean, if we're not here, we can do no wrong. Our job is quite simple . . . ." and he slipped, quite unconsciously I'm sure, into a parody of Churchill's voice. "We are in a non-existent organisation, engaged in non-existent acts of deception against non-existent enemies. We should have quite a cushy war."

His cynicism was not too far removed from the truth at that stage of the war. The head of MI 5 at that time was a distinguished servant of the Crown who had received his baptism of fire in the Boxer Rebellion of 1900 and still administered his department with an Edwardian regard for the proprieties. He was renowned for his views on female staff recruitment, requiring his typists to be *Tatler* material and to have a good pair of legs. This admirable philosophy worked wonders for our morale but produced havoc in the filing system. Since the files were the backbone of the entire operation, his prejudices (which to be fair were social rather than sexual) constituted a major threat to the smooth running of his department. Dusty gave his own verdict on the girls of the typing pool, stating that their education had not concentrated on the traditional three 'Rs' but on the three 'Ds' instead. "They rely on being Debby, Dumb and Daddy's," he said with gloomy relish. Most of them were very young and were run by a ferocious dyke who hovered between acute excitement and an angry state of grace, though Dusty maintained that her lick was worse than her bite.

Shortly after I added my inexperience to the collective chaos our headquarters suffered a major disaster. A decision had been taken at the outset of the war to house most of the files in Wormwood Scrubs Prison, the actual prisoners being moved elsewhere. The transfer was not accomplished without mishap. An aged prison chaplain was somehow never informed of the changed circumstances and continued to conduct his weekly services to a congregation of MI 5 cynics in the devout belief that he was still addressing his criminal flock. He confided that, for the first time in his life, he really felt he was 'getting through' and when eventually the top brass discovered he was still operating *in situ*, a decision was taken to preserve his illusions. "Preached a bloody good sermon," Dusty told us. "He'd have made a criminal out of me."

It was generally understood that we could put our fingers on any undesirable political figure in a matter of minutes. Alas, this was a figment of many disordered imaginations, and the reality was quite the reverse. Dusty once made a routine check through the cards and discovered that a maiden aunt of his was listed as an undesirable on the grounds that she paid a yearly pre-war visit to Baden Baden. He added to the incriminating evidence, stating that his aunt kept a dachshund, only went to the Proms when Beethoven was on the programme and used a German bayonet as a fire poker.

A Luftwaffe incendiary bomb put paid to most of these astonishing documents and the gentle hero of the Boxer Rebellion was tactfully retired. Naturally, we of the lower orders based at Colonic Hall only heard faint echoes of such distant thunder. Our life continued to have something of the flavour of a long country weekend. Jill and I finally made contact and I set in motion my own piece of subterfuge, persuading her to come south and join me. I installed her in a small flat over a butcher's shop on the outskirts of Farnham, a move of considerable cunning since a tame butcher in wartime was a friend indeed. There seemed to be a bomber's moon every other night that autumn, and when the Blitz started in earnest Jill and I would often watch the distant battle from a high point on the Common. We were reasonably safe except for the occasional stick of jettisoned bombs, though I daily expected to receive a call telling me that Perrins Walk had been razed.

It was Dusty who discovered what Theo was up to. He had acquired some samples of the work being carried out by the 'Buxton' group, a quasi-propaganda outfit which was tenuously linked to the S.I.S., but more or less operated alone. The Buxton boys' activities supposedly came under Section D, and they had a reputation for dirty tricks which were frowned upon by the older hands.

"What d'you think of these?" Dusty handed me a batch of postcards. They were photographs done with a professional gloss. The first one I turned over depicted Stalin buggering Hitler, their respective heads having been skilfully superimposed on some original pornographic pose.

"It's going to be Buxton's Christmas card this year, I'm told," Dusty said.

I leafed through the rest. There was a set of Goering in the nude, his head superimposed on a gross female body, a gigantic medal hanging between pendulous breasts. The captions were in German, the humour basic. Another set featured Goebbels and Hess. Yet another Bormann, shown naked on all fours, pulling a sleigh with Hitler on board. Later in the war we discovered that a German counterpart to Buxton was producing material in the same vein, depicting Churchill and members of the Royal Family.

"Not really my taste," Dusty said. "Bit too sentimental for me. I prefer the hard stuff. Still, good for morale – Hitler's morale, that is. He's never looked so good."

I didn't think much more about them until a few days later I was handed a memo from the Buxton outfit soliciting our help in accurately identifying the names of certain German divisions believed to be poised for the invasion. The memo was initialled T.G. and the coincidence seemed too strong. According to the fictions we were living amongst, Buxton (which was a cover name) didn't exist anywhere, but Dusty had the number and I called Theo. When he answered the phone I could hear music being played in the background.

"You're obviously having a hard war," I said

"We're putting rude words to the German national anthem. Dangerous work."

"How are you?"

"I'm not quite sure."

"What about Perrins Walk? Has it been hit yet?"

"Still standing at the last count. We've lost some windows, though and some tiles off the roof. Over your bedroom."

"Oh, great! Look, any chance of us meeting for a meal? Jill's down here now and I think I could slip away for a few hours at the weekend."

"Yes. That would be fine."

I thought he sounded slightly guarded, but imagined that he couldn't talk freely.

"Where shall we meet, then? D'you know anywhere good? It's so long since I've been in London."

"There's a place in Berwick Street I've been to. They sometimes have steaks. Can't vouch for them, but they're eatable."

"Okay. What's the name?"

"The Golden Hind."

We arranged to meet there the following Friday evening. He seemed disinclined to prolong the conversation.

"Your memo," I said. "I'm dealing with that. That's how I tracked you down. You'd better be more careful."

It all seemed an absurd game in those days. We blundered about aimlessly, since no cohesive master plan existed. One classic example I remember resulted in our arresting a number of Section D operators in the mistaken belief they were German agents who had been parachuted in. In fact they were trying to set up secret ammunition dumps as a precaution against the expected invasion. Nobody had bothered to tell us they would be working in our area. Those genuine German agents who did manage to land seemed to have been trained in the art of immediate exposure, and most of them were apprehended within hours of coming ashore, not because we were ultra efficient but because they had neglected to memorise the intricacies of British licensing laws: even to this day there are few things more guaranteed to arouse suspicion in these islands than a stranger who attempts to get a drink after hours. I knew of four who were caught in this way. All four were tried and three were executed. It was the only time I believed the game was being played for real.

19

THERE WERE TWO distinct groups in the Blitz: those who lived like moles and those who ignored it. The clientele of The Golden Hind belonged to the latter category. They were mostly rich by the standards of the day, and getting richer, for people who could afford to eat regularly at black-market restaurants were having a good war. There might be a sprinkling of young officers out to impress their girlfriends, but generally the tables were well booked in advance by those who had steered themselves away from the Forces. The food was pretentiously ordinary, the menu unpriced, and the drinks exorbitant.

Theo had booked a table for three in his name. Jill and I arrived first. It was a big night for her and although I took an instant dislike to the place I wasn't going to spoil it for her. Our relationship had changed since the abortion, for few women go through that experience without scars of some sort. She was over-grateful for everything I did, and it had the effect of passing her guilt to me. Not that I blamed her. I didn't blame anybody, but all the same things had changed. One can never go back.

Perhaps it was the atmosphere of the place, or the over-satisfied faces that turned to stare at us as we took our seats, but I had the feeling that the evening wasn't going to live up to expectations. We had a couple of drinks, but when Theo still didn't appear, I made a phone call to Perrins Walk. There was no answer, and by now the Cypriot head waiter was getting edgy so we ordered our meal and started without Theo. The steak when it came could have been horse, but it was so smothered in a nameless sauce that only a pathologist could have given a final verdict.

"What could have happened to him, d'you think?"

"No idea," I said.

The air raid warning had gone at the usual hour, but apart from the odd rumble in the distance it seemed to be a quiet night. I later learnt that the docks at Dagenham had got the brunt of it.

"What sort of work does he do?" Jill asked.

"I don't really know. I think it's something to do with the Ministry of Information."

"He's really a very kind character, isn't he?"

"Yes."

"I never really knew him . . . before. Of course, you've known him all your life."

We sampled that curious British dish known as trifle, eating without enthusiasm. I felt like I sometimes do when I go to the theatre full of expectation only to find that an understudy has been substituted for the star. Jill and I were behaving like an old married couple who had long since exhausted any interesting topic of conversation. Without Theo the whole evening seemed pointless and I found myself staring at the other diners with growing resentment: I didn't want to feel part of them. I had worn my uniform that night to please Jill, and in a way that made me more of a collaborator.

I ordered a last round of drinks and paid the bill, which was a greater outrage that I had prepared myself for. The head waiter returned to the table and for a moment I thought he was going to complain at the paucity of the tip.

"I think there's a phone call for you," he said.

"Oh, right. Must be Theo at last," I said to Jill. "Is it Major Gittings?"

"No," he said. "It's the police." He watched me anxiously as I made my way to the pay-phone which was in the corridor between the restaurant and the kitchens.

"Lieutenant Stern?" a flat voice asked.

"Yes."

"Duty officer Cannon Row here, sir. Sorry to trouble you, but a friend of yours has got himself in a spot of bother, I'm afraid."

"Who?"

"A Major Gittings, sir. He told us you could be contacted

at this number and I wondered if you'd mind coming to the station."

"What sort of trouble?" I said.

"I think it'd be best if we told you that when you get here, sir."

"I'll come right away."

I didn't bother to explain anything to Jill until we were outside. A taxi was out of the question so we trotted through the all-but deserted streets. The air raid was still in progress and the sky behind us was glowing red, the first wave of bombers having come and gone.

"D'you think it's anything serious?" Jill kept saying.

"I don't know, do I? They never tell you anything over the phone."

The front of Cannon Row police station was heavily sand-bagged like all public buildings, and we pushed our way through the gas curtain into the dimly-lit entrance hall. There was a young girl sitting on a bench clutching a bright purple teddy bear, her make-up streaked. I tapped on the glass window of the reception office and after a pause it was opened by an elderly sergeant.

"You contacted me," I said.

"What name would that be, sir?"

"Lieutenant Stern."

"Oh, yes. Yes, well, if you just hang on a minute I'll have somebody take you down."

The window closed again.

"I hate these places," Jill said. "They remind me of hospitals."

The young girl stared at us. "He fucking did nothing," she said blankly. She had teeth missing at both sides of her mouth. Jill reached for my hand.

A plain clothes detective appeared from a doorway and approached us. "If you'd like to come this way, sir."

Jill and I moved forward.

"I think it'd be best if you came on your own, sir. If the young lady would like to wait."

I followed him through a series of doors and we went down one flight. He showed me into what I suppose was an

251

interrogation room. Theo was sitting at a table, his head resting on his arms. He didn't look up when we came in.

"Your friend's arrived," the detective said. He turned to me. "You can identify him, can you, sir?"

"Yes, of course," I said.

I don't know what I had been expecting, but I was shocked by Theo's appearance as he raised his head. One eye was nearly closed and he had blood at the corner of his mouth. He was in civilian clothes and the front of his jacket was stained with dried vomit. He didn't say anything to me. He just looked.

"What's all this about?" I said. "What happened?"

"Well, we'll get to that, sir. I just wanted a formal identification to begin with. Only the gentleman hasn't got any papers on him."

"Yes," I said briskly. "It's my cousin and his name is Theo Gittings and he's a serving officer with the rank of major."

"Fine. Now I'd like a word in private, sir."

"Well, just a minute. Are you holding Major Gittings? I mean, has he been charged with anything?"

"Not at the moment, sir. We're in the process of deciding that and thought you might be able to give us some additional information. Won't take us long, sir."

I addressed Theo directly for the first time. "Are you all right?"

He nodded and mouthed the words 'help me'.

The detective ushered me into an adjoining room and closed the door.

"Now what the hell's going on?"

"Tell me something more about your cousin, sir."

"Well, first of all tell me something. Why have you got him here?"

The detective took out a battered packet of tobacco and a roll of rice papers and began to fashion a ragged cigarette. I suppose it's part of the standard technique for them deliberately to take their time.

"Your cousin could be charged – I'm not saying he will be – on a number of counts. Drunk and disorderly, liable to cause a breach of the peace . . ." He licked the gummed edge of the cigarette paper like a man preparing to play the flute. ". . . and gross indecency, sir. That's the one that concerns me most."

"Must be some mistake," I said.

He lit the cigarette, watching my face all the time. Bits of burning tobacco fell from the end and he ground them out with his heel.

"See, what makes it tricky, sir," he continued, ignoring my remark, "is him being an officer in the Army. We picked him up in civvies, but by rights we have to turn him over. Now I don't want to do that unless it's absolutely necessary, if you get my meaning."

"I still don't understand what you mean about gross indecency."

"He was picked up in a public urinal."

"But how did he get the black eye?"

"I imagine somebody clocked him. That's what usually causes black eyes. Somebody who didn't care for his sort. And I'll tell you something else, off the record. If he wasn't in the Army, I'd black the other bloody eye for him. I'm not too keen on queers."

I decided not to answer that.

"Now you say it's a mistake, and I might, just might, take your word for it."

"He's been under a lot of pressure," I said.

"Is that so?"

"Yes, he's got a very top secret job, a lot of responsibility. It must have got too much for him, and he got drunk and behaved in this totally uncharacteristic way."

"That's how you'd describe it, would you?"

"Absolutely. Believe me."

"Is he married?"

It was then that I took the plunge. "No," I said, "but that's his fiancée upstairs. Now, can I say something off the record?"

"Go ahead."

"She lost a baby recently. Only it wasn't his."

His homemade cigarette was curling upwards, burning unevenly, and he crushed it between his thumb and first

253

finger and put the stub in a tin lid. He made the action look as though he was gathering further evidence.

"Ask her," I said, pushing my luck now, but conscious that I had to convince him.

He looked at me for a long time. "Well, it's late," he said. "And I want to get home. I haven't been home for four nights. Most of that time I've been helping to pick up bits and pieces of people. Not something I enjoy, but I'll tell you something, it doesn't upset me half as much as queers. So you take your cousin off and tell him to stay home with his fiancée. He won't be so lucky if there's a next time."

"Thank you," I said. "That's very decent of you."

"Yes, isn't it? Especially since the whole thing is a mistake."

We went back into the interrogation room. Theo looked worse than before and needed my support as we made our way upstairs, the detective following. It was lucky that, without any signal from me, Jill instinctively put her arms around Theo the moment she saw him. I have no idea whether the detective really believed my explanation and the girl with the purple teddy bear distracted him as we made our exit. "You ought to be in the bleedin' war," she was saying as we made our way out into the street.

"D'you think you can walk?" I asked Theo.

"I'll try. Anything to get away from that place. I'm sorry."

"Well, we'll keep our eyes open for a taxi. We might get lucky, though I doubt it."

"What happened?" Jill asked.

"Theo got in a fight," I said. "You take his other arm."

Together we helped him find his feet as we headed in the direction of Hampstead. He had to rest frequently and was obviously in bad shape, although the cold air gradually sobered him. We didn't talk much on the journey and happily we only had to walk as far as Tottenham Court Road. There we found an empty taxi who was persuaded to take us to Perrins Walk.

We got him upstairs and I undressed him and put him to bed while Jill made us all some strong coffee.

"How did you manage to talk him out of it?" Theo said.

"Oh. Told him a few half-truths. What does it matter?"

"It matters a lot. I'll never be able to thank you."

"You don't have to be grateful. The only thing that concerns me is why the hell you ever got yourself in such a situation. I mean, I'm not going to preach at you, but you must have known there's always the risk you're going to pick up the wrong person."

"You don't have to tell me."

"Well, why tonight of all nights? We were looking forward to seeing you and having a reunion dinner."

"I know," he said. "But something happened."

"I can see that, I just don't understand why."

Jill brought the coffee in and a cold compress for his swollen eye. "Did the police get the man who hit you?" she said. It was typical of her that she didn't question the story I had concocted.

"Apparently not," I said. "He got away in the blackout."

"I think it's terrible. Did he steal any money?"

"It was my own fault," Theo said. "Tony's just trying to be tactful. There's no reason why you shouldn't know the truth since I ruined the evening. I got up to town early and instead of coming here, I went to a bar where I've usually been lucky. Tonight my luck was out. I had too much to drink and picked up the wrong man. Just a normal hazard for queens like me."

"Don't talk like that," Jill said. "You're not a queen."

"Well, I certainly behaved like one tonight," Theo said with a faint attempt at humour. He winced as she applied the compress. "Your turn to look after me. We're a pair, aren't we?"

It was the first time the topic had ever been openly broached between us all and I couldn't help thinking what a strange trio we made. I think, like a lot of women, Jill had the idea that she could somehow change him. There was a certain bond between them that I could never share.

We made him as comfortable as we could and gave him a couple of aspirins, then Jill and I went downstairs to share that curious aftermath of excitement that always attends the misfortunes of a friend. I can't remember that Jill and I had ever discussed Theo's homosexuality in explicit terms, but now

255

that it had been forced into the open she couldn't resist questioning me.

"Is that how they go about it?" she said. "Just picking up strangers in pubs?"

"A lot of them do, I guess."

"But Theo always seemed different. Not obvious. I always imagined that he had a regular boy friend somewhere, if I thought about it at all. When you first brought me back here, I even thought you and he might be a twosome."

"Is that why you held out on me for so long?"

"No, I didn't really think it, but it just occurred to me the first time."

"Understandable I suppose."

"Have you always known?"

"More of less. Not when we were kids, but later when he was up at Cambridge."

"Were you shocked?"

"No. I don't suppose I understood it, perhaps I don't even understand it now, but I wouldn't say I was ever shocked. Does it shock you?"

"Not with Theo. It just seems he's looking for something he'll never find."

"That's true of most of us."

"It must take a very sad person to always love in secret," she said, with more truth than either of us knew at the time.

There was no question of us going back to Farnham that night. I rang the duty officer and sold him some tale of the trains having been cancelled, an excuse which was never questioned in wartime. Theo was sleeping it off by the time we went to bed, but I woke in the middle of the night and heard him groaning. Jill hadn't stirred, so I got up and went into his room to find him coming out of a nightmare. He looked like a broken boxer at the end of a lost fight.

"I was in Spain," he said. "They kept showing me dead bodies."

I made us some tea this time and sat on the end of the bed to keep him company.

"D'you want to talk about tonight?" I said. "Would it help?"

"There's not much to tell . . . I just had a shock and I guess I took the easy route. Or what I thought was the easy route."

"It's just the bloody war," I said. "It gets everybody down."

"Yes, I think you're right."

"Is it anything I can help about?"

"You've helped enough already. I thought I was for the high jump there. He was a real queer-basher."

"Did he give you a hard time?"

"Oh, he didn't use rubber hoses or anything like that. That job had been done for him. D'you think he knew who I was?"

"He knew your name, obviously."

"No I meant, do you think he connected the name?"

"He didn't strike me as a literary man," I said. "I think his education stopped with Oscar Wilde."

"I'm sorry Jilly had to see it."

"She's on your side. I think if you ever wanted to change, she'd make an honest woman of you."

He smiled at that, but the effort made him wince. His eye was completely closed now.

"Would you mind if that happened?"

"We could have a ménage à trois . . . Jill and I won't last for ever, if that's what you're asking. What happened sort of changed things. Nobody's fault. Blame the war again."

"I hate what I'm doing," Theo said. "But none of the alternatives are much better, are they?"

"It all seems madness."

I shall never know whether he was on the brink of a confession that night; perhaps if I had pressed him, albeit in innocence of the true causes, he might have shared the guilt, though what I would have done with the information I have no idea. We all betray each other sooner or later; even the most faithful husband commits adultery in his heart.

He told me all in the end, of course. The mising clues in the crossword are all there in his unpublished novel. He was too good a writer not to be selective, but try as he might he couldn't bury all traces of the personal crime, the guilt he took with him to that underground room in Cannon Row where, without my well-meaning intervention he might have found an escape from the continuing loneliness of the rest of his life. It's ironic, but in prison, he would have been safe.

The sense of unreality grew stronger every day. Alec felt he had entered a world that divided loyalty like portions of a wedding cake: everything neatly boxed, an equal amount of marzipan to each section, just a taste of the cake itself – and stale before you ate it. In the first few months it sometimes seemed to him that he was the victim of some elaborate practical joke, the pay-off for which was never going to be revealed. "Be patient," they had said, "all will be revealed." But nothing was. He was never contacted no instructions reached him. He was doubly anonymous. The war hadn't touched him; he read about it and there were minor inconveniences, but for the most part he had merely exchanged one backwater for another. The only thing he missed was young faces. He seemed to be surrounded by middle-aged strangers talking a foreign language, people who were adept at changing the subject if he ever attempted to have an intellectual conversation. They seemed strangely indifferent to the wider issues he had expected them to be concerned with, and spent most of their time plotting how to enlarge their own empires at the expense of others supposedly on the same side. One of them actually used Alec's simile of the wedding cake. "There's only so much to go round, old boy, and it's my job to see that we get more than our fair share."

He felt like a foreigner in London, just another displaced person in the basement flat they had found for him off Hyde Park Gardens – an area where the tarts patrolled in pairs. He moved some of his possessions down from the college – mostly his books and a few nineteenth-century watercolours to brighten up the sweating walls of the flat. The illusion of being a prisoner was strengthened by the bars let into the brick surrounds on all the windows: he could only glimpse a portion of the world outside – a series of headless bodies parading past, and the occasional dog lifting its leg against the railings. He had to keep the lights burning all day, even when the sun was out. Fear seeped in easier than daylight. He had little contact with the other occupants of the house, though he suspected from the comings and goings that one of the upper floors was being used as a brothel. He found himself remembering a fragment of Plautus – *Mulieri nimio male facere melius est onus, quam bene* 'A woman finds it much easier to do ill than well.' But there was nothing classical about the world he now inhabited and he felt oddly emasculated.

When, finally, contact was made again he had almost forgotten their existence. He was walking home across Hyde Park one evening during the autumn of 1940, hoping to be safely inside before the sirens went. The dying sun glinted on the rippling bellies of the barrage balloon, giving the impression that they would suddenly burst into flames. As he approached the Bayswater Road he noticed that some of the tarts were taking up their positions earlier than usual. Probably as anxious as I am, he thought, and not for the first time he pondered about their lives. He knew quite a few of them by sight and sometimes nodded in passing, confident that he would not be solicited – they didn't waste time on neighbours, the pickings were to be had elsewhere. Some of them operated in the park itself, giving what a randy colleague at work described as 'a quick knee-trembler' – lust against the trees, with one eye open for the police, and he tried to imagine a time when he would find himself that desperate for human contact.

Just before he crossed the road he noticed a potential customer negotiating with a young whore in front of a recently bombed house. As often happened the blast had been selective: half of a first-floor bedroom was still miraculously intact, the bed itself protruding over the edge of the jagged rafters, the bedclothes turned down ready for an occupant who would never sleep in it again. It gave a macabre symbolism to the scene and Alec hurried past with head down, turning the corner into Albion Street. He had only gone a few more yards when he became conscious of footsteps gaining on him from behind, and the same man who had been propositioning the teenage whore passed close to him. He felt something being thrust into his hand and checked the impulse to shout out. He had been given a scrap of paper. He kept it clenched in his palm while the man continued on without looking back. Alec waited until he was safely inside his basement living room with the blackout blinds drawn before examining the message. It was brief and to the point. "St. Giles High Street Tea-rooms. Tonight. 8.30. Look for a copy of *Tit Bits*."

(St. Giles High Street used to run from the unfashionable end of Shaftesbury Avenue to the junction of Tottenham Court Road and Oxford Street. Now most of it lies buried beneath that monument to the property boom known as Centre Point. During the war it had a fairly disreputable appearance, the area alongside St. Giles' Church being somewhere to avoid after dark.)

Alec spotted his contact the moment he stepped through the blackout curtains into the steamy atmosphere of the tearoom. He was sitting at the furthest table from the door, nursing a cup of tea, with the remains of what look like a plate of corned beef and chips. There were perhaps a dozen tables, six to either side of the oblong room, mostly occupied by foreign servicemen. The stench of fried food was almost overpowering.

Alec took a seat opposite the man, having asked if it was free. The copy of *Tit Bits* lay open between them and he found himself staring at an inverted pin-up – an over-developed girl wearing a black negligee. The contact glanced at his wrist-watch and nodded approvingly.

"Have you eaten?"

"No."

A sauce-stained menu was pushed across. "Steer clear of the meat, it's liable to be horse."

"I've never eaten horse," Alec said. "Is it very different? After all, the horse is a clean animal."

"Sweet," the man said. "Hard to chew and sweet."

"I don't know why we're so sentimental about horses," Alec said, studying the depressing alternative choices. "I dare say we'll all have to make concessions if the war continues much longer."

He ordered egg and chips, thinking, they can hardly ruin those, but he was wrong. They seem to have been fried in rifle grease, and the cup of tea included in the price came in a chipped cup.

"I had an eccentric uncle who used to smash cracked cups," he said. The other man's continued silence made him nervous and he took refuge in small-talk. "He claimed they spread diseases, like lavatory seats." The crudeness of the anecdote offended him, but he couldn't help himself. From the kitchen came the sound of Tommy Handley and company. I'm insane, he thought. To be sitting here eating swill with a total stranger.

As if reading this thoughts the man folded the copy of *Tit Bits* and smiled at him.

"Don't look so worried. This is quite safe. When you leave take this with you." He tapped the folded magazine. "I've already done the crossword, but you could check it for me. I think you'll get the answers right."

"Are you ever going to give me anything to do?" Alec said.

"Yes, we want you to discredit somebody. We've got a serious family problem. One of our top agents has crossed the line. He knows enough about out set-up over here to do a lot of damage. Fortunately he doesn't know the names, but he'll talk enough to start a witch-hunt. So we want you to plant material to throw them off the scent. It'll be a good test for you." He smiled again.

"What will I have to do?"

"Nothing violent. Just destroy a man's credibility."

"Who?"

"Chalmers."

"But I know Chalmers."

"Yes. That's why we've picked you."

"But what happens to him afterwards?"

"Do you care?" The voice hardened perceptibly.

"No, of course not," Alec said. "I was just asking."

"It's all been worked out. You're merely the instrument; you needn't feel there's anything personal in it."

"Will he know it's me?"

"You mean will the plant be traced to you? Not if you go about it the right way." He stirred cigarette ash into a black paste in his saucer. "Just follow instructions and you can't go wrong."

"Does it get any easier?" Alec asked. "After the first time, do you get used to it?"

"You have to be a pragmatist."

"Yes," Alec said. "I'm not sure that I've ever quite understood what that means in human terms. It's always seemed to me a politician's excuse for something unforgivable."

"We don't concern ourselves overmuch with forgiveness. If we did everything would grind to a halt, the great revolutionary march forward, etcetera."

Alec thought he detected a note of sarcasm, but he wasn't sure of his ground. Anything might be a trap.

"We have to act quickly in this case," the man said. "So I suggest you start the ball rolling." It was a dismissal.

Alec pushed his sordid plate away and stood up. He took the copy of *Tit Bits*.

"I think you'll enjoy that issue," his companion said in a slightly louder voice. "Some interesting articles and some very saucy pictures."

From the kitchen a parody of a female voice screeched, "Can I do you now, sir?" and the studio audience laughter followed him out into the street.

(It is possible that Theo based this next sequence on the defection to the West in 1940 of a senior Soviet intelligence officer, Walter Krivitsky. Krivitsky told the British authorities that the Foreign Office had been infiltrated by 'somebody of good family and breeding' and from the description he gave, he could well have been referring to Maclean. For reasons that have never been adequately explained this information was never followed through. Maclean continued to operate without undue suspicion for many more years.)

In the end Chalmers's very blandness counted against him. There was nothing in his past, which in itself was a suspicious factor. Happily married with two perfect children and a devoted fluffy wife, dedicated to his work, educated at Winchester and Oxford, a member of Whites, the Carlton and the M.C.C., he epitomised the perfect servant of the State. He held his drink well, seldom gossiped and was well thought of by all his staff – who afterwards derived much pleasure from saying, "Isn't it funny how wrong one can be? He's the very last person one would have thought of."

When Alec returned home that evening he studied the copy of *Tit Bits* and deciphered the code contained in the completed crossword. It occurred to him that the instructions could just as easily have been passed verbally, but he was conditioned to expect the unexpected. Secrecy was a chain reaction, deceit piled upon deceit like layers of garden compost, and underneath truth lay rotting.

During his lunch hour the following day he went to a small stamp dealer's shop off the Strand and asked to see some Edward VII definitives. He was shown into a back room and left alone with a large stock album. From this he extracted a plain manila envelope, made a small purchase of some stamps and asked for a receipt for them. He put the stamps and the manila envelope into his briefcase and after having a hurried sandwich lunch went back to his office.

Later in the afternoon he visited Chalmers on a perfectly legitimate errand, asking for a particular file that only Chalmers had access to. When Chalmers left the room to fetch the file, Alec planted the manila envelope inside Chalmers's briefcase. They chatted about the lack of soap and clean towels in the men's washroom, then Alec checked one of the papers in the file in Chalmers's presence and signed the registry book. They parted on the best of terms with Chalmers insisting that Alec really must come and take pot luck for lunch one Sunday.

"Rosemary was only saying the other day, it's very remiss of us. We've been promising it for ages."

"I'd love to," Alec said. "I must admit Sunday in London on your own is a long day."

He found that he was sweating when he returned to his own office. "I think I'm coming down with a bout of flu," he told his secretary when she expressed concern. She brought him a cup of tea and two aspirins, urging him to go home early. It was almost as if the illness was self-induced, for by the time he got back to his flat he had a slight temperature. The sirens went early that night, but apart from some sporadic explosions in the distance, which he judged to be coming from the East End dock area, it did not seem to be a heavy raid.

After he had made his supper he dressed warmly and went out and walked to Notting Hill Gate Tube station. There he took a roundabout route to the Elephant and Castle and walked to the nearest public call box. He placed a call to a member of the Special Branch who worked closely with his own Section. The number was engaged. Taking no chances he boarded a bus and travelled back across the river, getting off as soon as he had spotted another call box. He rang the same number again and this time he got an answer. After verifying he was speaking to the right man he plunged straight into his rehearsed speech.

"If you want some useful information on the Stupolsky affair, search Chalmers's home."

"Who is that?"

"A very reliable source. Chalmers is your man," he said, and broke the connection. He ran from the call box, almost knocking over an air-raid warden.

"Don't bloody apologise, will you?" the warden shouted after him, but Alec ran on until his lungs started to burn. An ack-ack gun battery opened up quite close to, and he heard the familiar sound of Dornier engines. He leaned up against a wall, pressing his forehead against the cold brickwork until he could breathe normally again.

Shrapnel started to fall on nearby roofs and a voice shouted out

of the darkness, "Get off the street, there's one right overhead."
He turned and took refuge in a street shelter as the noise of the
descending bomb obliterated all previous fears. The shelter was
crammed with regulars, most of them well equipped with blankets
and Thermos flasks. The atmosphere was fetid – a mixture of
human sweat, tobacco smoke and the smell of fish and chips and
vinegar. A dozen faces turned towards him as he slumped into the
nearest space. It was almost as if he was contaminating them with
some new menace.

An old woman wearing a man's flat cap and an overcoat tied
round the middle with string cackled at him, exposing a mouth
devoid of teeth. "The bleeders are at it tonight," she said.
"Dropping them all over the fucking place. That one nearly had
your bleedin' number on it." She laughed again and he could
hear the phlegm rising in her throat. "Ain't got any fags, 'ave
yer? I've done mine in."

Alec fumbled for his cigarettes and offered her one.

"These are fancy," the old woman said. "Ain't come across
these before. What are they? Bit la-di-da, aren't they?"

Alec did not trust himself to answer her. He struck a match for
her and found that his hands were still shaking.

"Gives you a turn, don't it? Fucking old 'Itler."

"Mind your language, you dozy old cow," another voice said
from the opposite benches. "Got children here."

"Piss off!" the old woman said. She coughed herself puce.
"Gor!" she said when she had recovered sufficiently. "What's in
these, then?" She leaned in towards Alec and he was conscious of
the smell of lavender moth balls.

Then there was a lull outside and on an impulse he got to his
feet and blundered through the gas curtains to the fresh air.
Behind him he heard the old woman say, "Now look what you've
done!"

The bomb had landed two streets away and the fire engines
and heavy rescue teams were just arriving. There were confused
shouts all round him and the roadway was suddenly illuminated
as a gas main went up, sending a sheet of flame above the roof-
tops. Fear and shock had robbed him of a sense of direction, but
he hurried away from the incident, hoping that luck would lead
him to the river. He covered a mile before he came to another
Tube station and was able to feel safe.

He had no need to feign sickness the following morning, but he
felt compelled to go into work. If things had gone according to
plan his own absence might look suspicious. He allowed his

secretary the luxury of feeling concerned for him and tried to concentrate on routine correspondence, deliberately avoiding any mention of Chalmers. It wasn't until he went into the canteen at lunchtime that he was able to confirm that Chalmers had not reported in that morning.

"There's a lot of illness going around," Alec said. "Has anybody telephoned to see how he is?"

By the third day, with Chalmers still absent, the first rumours started. Morris, the number two under Chalmers, sent for Alec in the afternoon of the third day. He was with the Special Branch man Alec had telephoned.

"You know Commander Latimer, Alec?"

"Yes, we have met."

"We've got a situation on our hands, Alec, and the commander would like to pick your brains."

"I hate that expression," Latimer said. "Makes us sound like carrion. It's all informal, Alec . . . Can I call you Alec?"

"Of course."

"Just one or two loose ends I'd like to clear up."

He had the easy manner of the trained interrogator. "How well do you know Chalmers?" he said, with a smile that came like an afterthought.

"Reasonably. I mean, we see each other most days."

"In the course of work?"

"Yes."

"Ever meet him socially?"

"We've had the occasional lunch together."

"Never been to his home?"

"No. He's often talked of inviting me. As a matter of fact only the other day he said he wanted to have me back for a meal one Sunday."

"You know about the Stupolsky affair, of course."

"I know he defected, yes. It doesn't actually concern my Section. I have a limited knowledge."

"Did Chalmers ever talk about him?"

"He might have done. We all did when it became known. There was a certain natural curiosity."

"And?"

"I'm sorry?" Alec said. "I'm not quite sure what you're asking."

"The commander's trying to trace certain things to their source," Morris said.

"How exactly did Chalmers talk about Stupolsky?"

"He seemed excited."

"In what way?"

"Well, he felt it was a windfall. He seemed to think Stupolsky might have valuable information."

"That was all?"

"Yes."

"He didn't seem odd in any way?"

"Look," Alec said, "could I ask what all this is about?"

"It could be," the commander said, "that there's a connection between Chalmers and the Russians."

"Chalmers?"

"Certain things have come to light, Alec," Morris said smugly. He's already banking on promotion, Alec thought. "We can't take you completely into the picture, but it would appear that the evidence against Chalmers is fairly conclusive."

"Curiously enough you were one of the last people to see him on Monday afternoon," the commander said. "Did you notice anything different about him?"

"Monday afternoon?"

"You requested a file. It's in the registry book."

"That's right, yes, I did. No, he was the same as usual."

"What did you talk about?"

"Towels," Alec said.

"Towels?"

"Yes, we were both complaining that they're never changed regularly in the washroom."

Morris and the commander exchanged looks.

"Nothing very illuminating, I'm afraid," Alec continued. "To tell you the truth I wasn't feeling too hot. I thought I was coming down with flu, so I went home early. In case I gave it to anybody else. When Chalmers didn't come in the next day, I felt slightly guilty." He looked at the two men. "I say, he's all right, isn't he?"

"He took the top of his head off this morning," Latimer said. "In the garden shed. Not a very pleasant way of doing it. Shotguns never are, especially for those who have to find the remains."

"One of his children found him," Morris said. "Found bits of him, would be more accurate."

Alec groped for a chair and sat down. "Good God!" he said. "Excuse me, but I can't believe it." He had no need to act. The shock of what he had just been told relieved him of all sham emotions.

"Exactly my reaction," Morris said. "Quite incredible."

"Officially he died of a heart attack," Latimer said. "It's important that none of this gets out."

"But why?" Alec said. "Why would he do a thing like that?"

"We had a tip-off and when we searched his house we came up with this." He went to Morris's desk and picked up the manila envelope. He opened it and shook a key into his palm. "In itself nothing much. Just a · key to a locker on Victoria Station. Chalmers couldn't explain it. He was co-operating at that point, and in fact I believed him. What was inside the locker told a different story, however."

He slid the key back into the envelope. "But even that wasn't conclusive in itself. Evidence can always be planted. But when we went back to Stupolsky we used a little more persuasion, and he named Chalmers. Gave us chapter and verse. It seems we all made a mistake about Chalmers. He was in it up to his neck, from Spain onwards."

Alec composed his face before he looked up. "He seemed so . . . well, it's beyond me. I'm somewhat of a newcomer to these things," he said, and the truth of how he had been used was just beginning to seep through. "But killing himself like that."

"No, I think that was in character," Latimer said. "And at least it saved us the trouble."

That night he did something that previously would have been unthinkable. After giving himself some liquid Dutch courage in the local pub, he walked across Bayswater Road and into the park to pick up one of the young whores. There was no attempt at selection; he struck a deal with the first one who approached him. She couldn't have been much more than seventeen and had a strong provincial accent. He was just sober enought to register that she was more concerned about the well-being of her poodle than the business in hand. She tied the dog to a tree and it fretted and whined all the time Alec took his quick, fumbled pleasure. It was the dog that gave them away and he just had time to adjust his clothing and run into the darkened park as the police approached. He could hear the girl shouting abuse at the police as he plunged further into the darkness and when eventually he felt himself to be safe he sat on the ground and cried. He remembered the girl's pinched, adolescent face and self-disgust made him retch. Chalmers's daughter was roughly the same age.

It was two weeks after Chalmers's funeral – an uneasy ceremony at a suburban crematorium attended by representatives

267

from all departments – before Alec was contacted again. He received a single theatre ticket in his mail one morning. It was for a stall seat to the new Herbert Farjeon revue at Wyndham's Theatre. That was it. No message, no instructions. Staring at it, Alec had a transient moment of relief: they don't know everything about me, he thought: I wouldn't have chosen this particular show. An orchestral concert was more his mark – Brahms or Sibelius.

He went to the theatre on the appointed night. The aisle seat next to his remained empty until just after the curtain had risen, and then his contact, whom he now knew as Peter, eased into it. They did not acknowledge each other. Rather to his surprise Alec found himself enjoying the show and it wasn't until the interval that he remembered the true purpose of his visit. Peter made no attempt to join the crush making for the bar.

"Could I borrow your programme, please?" Peter said. "I came in late and didn't get one."

The request was made in a loud voice, presumably for the benefit of anybody who might have been listening. How absurd, Alec thought, to go to such ridiculous lengths, and then he had a sudden vision of poor, dead Chalmers – death in the potting shed, the child at the moment of discovery, seeing what remained of his face amongst the stored daffodil bulbs, the cobwebs flecked with blood.

Peter went through the motions of studying the programme for a few moments, and then Alec saw him insert a small piece of paper between the centre pages before handing it back.

"Very enjoyable first half, didn't you think?"

"Yes," Alec said. He desperately wanted a drink, but by now the audience was coming back.

Peter stood to let some people pass along the row, and when they had cleared Alec found he had disappeared. As the house lights were being lowered he glanced inside the programme. The slip of paper had an address on it: Flat 3, 98, Limerston Street, Chelsea. After memorising it, Alec tore the paper into minute pieces, sprinkling half under his seat and keeping the rest to dispose of in the street. He watched the remainder of the show with scant concentration and left while the cast were taking their first bows.

He was lucky enough to find a taxi, directing the driver to World's End rather than the exact address (it's becoming second nature, he thought) and then walking by a roundabout route to Limerston Street. He flared a match in cupped hands to read the nameplates on a front door that had been boarded up following previous blast damage. He rang the bell alongside the handwritten card for Flat 3 and after a short pause the door was opened by Peter. He followed him upstairs to the second floor of a three storey house, Peter shining a torch to show him the way.

The flat was surprisingly well-furnished and comfortable and this further disconcerted him, for he had prepared himself to accept something squalid, something in keeping with the company he was now forced to keep.

"Scotch?" Peter said.

"Thank you."

"Gin or what-have-you, if you prefer. I've got everything."

"No, Scotch would be fine."

Peter handed him a generous measure and offered soda.

"No, I'll take it neat."

"Well, I think congratulations are in order. You did admirably. Admirably. Everybody's very pleased with you."

"Including Chalmers's widow?"

"You mustn't think of it like that." he said with fake concern.

"How should I think of it?"

"Just as something that had to be done."

"You lied to me," Alec said. He still hadn't touched his drink, since drinking while Peter had his glass raised would have seemed like a toast he did not want to respond to.

"I don't think so. Did I? In what way?"

"You said you only wanted to destroy his credibility."

"But my dear comrade, we didn't kill Chalmers. He put his own gun to his head."

"Yes. Very convenient all round. That's more or less what Latimer said. I didn't come into this to kill people."

"There's a war on, you know. People do get killed in war. It could happen to us, tonight," Peter said as distant sirens began to wail, soon to be echoed by those closer to hand. "The point is our deaths would serve little purpose. Chalmer's suicide was quite a different matter. I wouldn't waste too much sympathy on him. He wasn't what you thought. I'd save your concern for more positive matters. Look upon Chalmers's timely exit as a warning."

"For whom?"

"You. Me. All of us, comrade."

"Do you mind," Alec said, "not calling me comrade? It's not a word that has much meaning for me. You're not a comrade. You're just somebody I'm forced to know." The whisky had given him a spurious courage.

269

"Next time," he said, "If there is a next time, I want to know what the end of the game is before I start." The anti-aircraft batteries opened up across the river at that moment, but he felt curiously detached from the dangers of the outside world: all his faculties were concentrated on the man sitting opposite him. He was reminded of leaner days, facing a bank manager to whom he had just applied for a loan without collateral. He would have welcomed sudden obliteration at that moment – the direct hit, fear and shame wiped out in one last shrieking rush of descending German steel and explosive.

"All right, Alec, whichever you prefer. We'll dispense with the congratulations since they seem to disturb you. There'll be other things in the future, of course You can depend on that. It doesn't end with Chalmers's death. He was just a small cog. Don't waste too much sympathy on him; his widow and children will be taken care of by two grateful governments. They've got a bonus."

"You mean Chalmers wasn't innocent?"

"Now don't grasp at straws too quickly. I didn't say that, did I? Didn't give you that impression? Chalmers had something to hide like everybody else, though maybe it wasn't worth blowing your head off for. That's why we had to add a little more colour. That's where you came in. If you really want a guilty conscience, Chalmers had to go to save you."

Alec stared at him. The words refused to penetrate.

"He'd served his purpose a long time ago. He was burnt out. We never intended lighting him again. It was you. We think you're a coming man. You were one we had to protect. They were getting too close, you see. That bastard Stupolsky had led them very near; he knew most of it, but he didn't have your name. We had to give them a name. Now they're happy. They've buried Chalmers and they can close the file. You know what tidy little minds they've got."

"I killed him," Alec said.

"You're too sensitive, Alec. Doesn't do to take things so personally. I mean, it's admirable in one way, means you care, but at the same time it complicates matters. For you, that is. Once you learn to take the longer view, everything falls into place. Adapt to changing circumstances, Alec, and you stay alive."

He held his smile for longer than the occasion merited. Somewhere in the direction of Hammersmith a flare descended, brightening the room. They stood like figures in a stage tableau. Then they heard a noise impossible to identify, as though somebody had thrown a heavy curtain from a great height and a wind

270

had caught it from below, flapping it like sail on a capsized ship. They looked at each other, and Peter shouted "Get down!" but before he could throw himself to the ground the entire window frame disintegrated, and blast lifted him into the air like a macabre version of Peter Pan. He was flung into a bookcase on the far side of the room and as that collapsed, part of the ceiling fell down on him and he lay there like some crumpled ghost until blood started to spurt, smearing the white plaster and the torn books. Alec crouched, unharmed except for a single cut from broken glass on the hand he had managed to shield his eyes with. Somehow the blast had missed him, adding another story to the various legends of the Blitz.

For a minute or more he lost all power in his limbs and remained there as though posing for a statue. His eardrums suddenly popped and then he heard the cries of confusion from other parts of the house. Somewhere a whistle was blowing, a nearby wall tumbled, shaking the room and he forced himself to a standing position. He picked his way across the debris to where Peter lay motionless. Blood was pumping out of a jagged hole in Peter's neck and a lump of glass from the window stuck out of his forehead giving him the appearance of a human unicorn.

He had never known such fear before, but part of his brain signalled that he had other dangers to face. He not only had to get out alive, but he had to avoid being identified. The door to the landing swung on shattered hinges. He groped his way out, a step at time, into darkness that was thick with choking dust. Somebody below shone a torch and a voice called out: "Is there anybody up there?"

'Yes," he shouted.

"How many?"

"Only one," he answered.

The beam of the torch provided some slight illumination in the dusty gloom, and he picked his way towards it. Some parts of the stair rail were missing, and he hugged the wall as he descended.

"Hurry it up," the voice said, "the whole bloody lot's going to go any minute."

Suddenly he was close to the light source and hands reached out and grasped him under the armpits, lifting him down the last few feet, and guiding him towards the street. He had no sooner reached the pavement when he heard the upper floors collapse. Other hands helped him away from the scene.

"Sure there was nobody else up there?"

"I don't think so," he said, his brain working quicker now that he was safe.

271

"You injured?"

"Just a cut on the hand. Nothing. I was lucky."

"Get his name," another voice shouted. "We're making a check."

"Look, sit down here, sir, until we get an ambulance."

"I'm fine," he said. "You take care of people who need it."

"Can we just have your name?"

"Maybone," Alec said "Charles Maybone," giving the name of a form master he had once had at Prep school, and wondered why that name had suddenly leapt into his mind.

They left him alone, sitting on the kerbstone as a Heavy Rescue Lorry and and Auxiliary Fire Pump roared on to the scene. Fires were starting at the far end of the street, and helmeted figures ran in haphazard patterns. He heard one of them cry, "There's a kid trapped in number 43," and all the figures converged on one particular spot. I must get away, he thought. Now, before they come back and ask other questions. He seemed to have been forgotten for the moment. Shock, delayed until now, shook his limbs as he got to his feet. He found he had to lift his legs unnaturally high before putting them to the ground – they seemed to belong to somebody else, moving independently. He grasped at some railings for support and the wound on his hand began to bleed again.

"Maybone," he said aloud, "dear old Maybone. Why him? He always caned me," talking to himself as he forced his legs to transport him further and further from the scene. He started to laugh, binding a handkerchief round his wounded hand, a feeling of exaltation taking over from fear.

Another pedestrian arriving to give help loomed in front of him. "You all right, mate?"

"Happy," Alec said. "Very lucky, very happy," as though it was the best joke he had heard in ages.

The stranger stared at him uncertainly for a few seconds. "Good," he said, "good, you're happy, are you?"

"Going home now," Alec said. "Going home. To bed."

He walked on while behind him more rubble fell, burying old treacheries.

20

THEO WAS BETRAYED into betraying by an act of love, becoming in the process more dangerous, perhaps, than those who commit treason from a deep sense of political morality. There must have been a 'Chalmers' episode in his life. We all sent men to their deaths – that was par for the course; most of us were lucky; we did not have to put faces to our crimes. I also believe that it is more than possible they left him alone for a while following the fortuitous death of his control, the man he called Peter. They were ultra cautious and they had infinite patience. It's worth recalling that at this point in the war the convenient logicality of the Nazi–Soviet alliance was in the process of being set aside, an added reason for proceeding with care. Plans for the German invasion of Russia were well advanced as early as July 1940 when most informed sources were only looking towards the English Channel. Well documented warnings went out from our intelligence services and were ignored. The Soviets even dismissed their own double-agents' exact and accurate dates for the launching of Barbarossa, paranoically determined to believe that any information originating from the West had to be a plant. Deceit, like religion, has to begin with faith, and once any of us have taken the first step we are committed to the belief that the dogma we live by is shared by others of the same faith. But the double-agent has no priest to confide in, no ritual to comfort: hot chocolate was Theo's last communion wine. And what did his arms enfold as he died? Not a faith, not another body, not even a stranger's warmth, merely a leaking hot water bottle as he returned, full circle, to the nursery.

There is a conceit in deep friendships which allows us to cling to the hope that, given the opportunity, we can change another person's life. Had Theo and I been closer during that

273

last decade, had I made that extra effort to break into his silence, would the end have been any different, I wonder?

Following the episode at the police station we saw each other more frequently. We never discussed our respective roles in any detail, it being an unwritten law that one maintained a front of ignorance. We usually met for a meal at an old established restaurant off the Strand which to this day is still frequented by government officials seeking a discreet venue. I remember one such occasion around that time, just before I was shunted off at short notice to investigate leakages and corruption in Cairo. We drifted into one of those conversations that follow no particular direction – the sort of dialogue that old friends resume when they have been apart for a period and which picks up the threads of their respective lives in a verbal shorthand strangers find unfathomable.

"I see somebody mentioned Auden and Isherwood again," Theo began.

"Some M.P. I suppose? Has to be."

"Yes. Usual stuff. Why are they seeking refuge abroad, being British citizens of military age?"

"Where are they now?"

"Still in America. Isherwood's in Hollywood, I think, working for the movies. Good luck to him. I hope he's eating better than we are today. What is this?"

"It said rabbit on the menu."

"Tastes like Beatrix Potter," Theo said. "Have you done any serious writing lately?"

"Not really. No time. Well, that's a feeble excuse; one can always make time to write something. I keep a sort of diary. Highly illegal, of course."

"Is it?"

"Yes," I said. "Definitely frowned upon in our trade."

"I don't sleep very well these days."

The non-sequitur seemed perfectly natural to me.

"The moment I put my head on the pillow I start to have the strangest sexual fantasies. They keep me awake for hours."

"Can you share them?"

"No, I don't think so. Hardly likely to be your cup of tea."

"Well, my cup of tea doesn't exactly runneth over at the moment."

"How's Jill?"

"That's over. Sad, but perhaps inevitable. She ended it, and I didn't stop her ending it, if I can put it that way. You should read Proust, like I do, if you can't sleep. Very soothing."

"Yes, he's always been the French cure for insomnia I'm told. I can't say I like him, you sometimes need a map to get to the end of some of his sentences, but I envy him. Envy the life style he led. The idea of a writer sacrificing his mortal body to an immortal work. That's a noble thought . . . He consecrated all his strength, you know, lying there in that comfortless cell he called a bedroom, working all night – that race with death – then taking veronal at dawn and sleeping until the afternoon."

"He believed a writer's first duty is to live for his work."

"I ought to like him more, really."

"Why do you say that?"

"Well, I'm likewise obsessed with the past. I think one of the truest things he ever wrote, and let me get it right, I'm always very shaky on quotations . . . He said, 'Love is less dangerous than friendship because . . . because being subjective, it does not turn us from ourselves.'"

"I'll have to work that one out," I said.

As parts of that conversation surface again, I can't help making the comparison with his own death. He found a cell, the isolation, but he had no Celeste at his end (one could hardly cast the predatory Mrs. Davis in that role) and he betrayed his true calling. He also proved his favourite quotation false.

From Proust we turned, incongruously, to his father. I remember suggesting that perhaps Harry Gittings was Theo's equivalent of Baron Charlus.

"No," Theo said. "The aged father doesn't have the imagination to be anything but disgustingly normal. I'll tell you something though, since we're on the subject."

"What subject?"

"Homosexuality. I was talking to a character the other day

275

who advanced an interesting theory. Did you know that before the purges Russian legislation decreed that an individual's sex life was private and therefore outside the law? Which perhaps explains why so many homosexuals turned to communisim."

He elaborated on this for a while, speaking in a detached, unselfconscious way about his own sexual attitudes, eventually bringing the conversation round to certain studies his department had made regarding the connection between sado-masochism and the appeal of Nazism. We exchanged views about the possibility of Hitler turning towards the Eastern front, both of us maintaining the pretence that we had no special knowledge.

"D'you think it has any effect, what we're doing?" I said.

"We'll know if we win. No, let me rephrase that. We'll know if we lose. The victors never give away their secrets; they may want to use them again. It'll be interesting, though, if he does attack Russia. They'll become our allies. Quite a few people will have to do an abrupt about-face."

"Including our mobs."

"Yes, there is that, of course. I don't trust the Russians, do you?"

"It's been drummed into me that we shouldn't trust anybody."

A few days later he rang me to say that Diana had been killed in an air raid. She was amongst the eighty-four dead when the bomb fell on the old Café de Paris. I was told that girls tore their evening dresses to make bandages for the badly wounded, and those waiters still alive poured champagne over wounds to disinfect them. "I imagine she died as she lived," Theo said, "with her tongue in somebody's else's cheek."

That was the last time I spoke to him for two years.

I travelled to Cairo in a converted Stirling bomber the next day and from the moment I landed I hated every moment of that assignment. The appalling comparisons between the luxury of the few and the squalor of the many, the corruption it was my duty to uncover and the corruption that went unheeded, plus the heat and the filth made it one of the most depressing periods in my life. I was engaged on a squalid mission and the man I was hunting tried to kill me, a botched attempt as clumsy as the rest of his life, but it resulted in my spending a month in a military hospital. During that time I fell in love with and proposed to a Scottish nursing sister. We were married on the first afternoon I was allowed out and spent a three-day honeymoon at the rest camp by the shores of Lake Timsah. Her name was Alison and I would like to think that I made her briefly happy. As soon as I was passed fit I was ordered back to London. By the time my troopship docked at Liverpool she was dead – killed during the disastrous campaign in Crete. I don't even know where she is buried, if she was buried.

The official notification didn't reach me until two months later and by the same post the authorities returned all my letters to her unopened. The few weeks we had together are like uncut pages in a book, and now I can't even recall her sweet face; the only memory I have is her voice coming to me sometimes during a dream as it once did in the blue darkness of that hospital ward: the words of comfort she used as she slipped the pain-obliterating needle into the vein. There was no such instant relief in the months following the news of her death. I took refuge in drink for a while, but nothing wiped out that particular pain and I sought my own destruction with an enthusiasm my superiors mistook for commendable bravery. Heroism is so often akin to a gambler's philosophy: if you go to the tables indifferent to your fate the odds of winning seem to increase. I finally persuaded my commanding officer that I was expendable and they parachuted me into Jugoslavia to join up with Tito's partisans. I can remember that dark descent when I would have welcomed the killing tracers from below, but my luck held and for the next eighteen months I lived a life of charmed recklessness; the more I tested Fate, the more I appeared to have been granted immunity and in the end my self-disregard was rewarded with a medal, the final irony, I suppose, of my personal war.

Smuggled back into England by a tortuous route, my first concern was to try and contact Theo. I found London greatly changed. The streets were poxed with bomb craters and people looked shabbier than I had remembered, but there was an atmosphere of hope now. The Yanks had arrived, of course, and were much in evidence, dispensing silk stockings to over-impressionable girls and depositing liberal dollops of chewing gum on the pavements. Nothing else seemed unduly disturbed. Ascot had been reinstated, elderly peers were still being cited in torrid divorce cases, the Russian Ambassador's portrait was hung in the Tate Gallery and Sir Oswald and Lady Mosley released from prison. Much to my surprise Perrins Walk had survived. Despite a few cracks in the brickwork and some missing roof tiles, it had withstood the worst of the Blitz, and my possessions, damp when they were not dusty, were intact. I had a whole month's leave due to me and what then amounted to a small fortune in back pay which I resolved to squander as soon as possible.

Of Theo there was no sign. His part of the house seemed as unlived in as my own. I made some enquiries at the last known address but the man who answered the phone was war-time cagey and, it seemed to me, deliberately vague.

"I'll make enquiries," he said, "and if we can help you I'll have somebody call you back. Can I have your name again?"

"Stern. Major Stern," I said, pulling rank to see if that would stand him to attention at the other end. But he seemed even less impressed than before.

"We'll check through, Major."

I sat down in that empty, dank house totally at a loss. Expectations of home had been so strong while I was living in the Jugoslavian mountains that the feeling of let-down was inevitable. I suddenly realised I had completely lost touch with my old life style. There was no Alison and no immediate substitute for Alison. On an impulse I rang one of my brothers. The phone was answered by his wife – a harassed, slightly common voice snapped at me, and in the background I could hear a child crying.

"Who?" she said. Then, "will you shut up and be quiet! Otherwise you'll get a good smack. Sorry. I didn't get that. Who is it?"

"Tony."

"Tony who?"

"Your brother-in-law."

There was a pause. "Oh, Tony! That Tony. Where are you?"

"In London. I just got back from overseas."

"No letters or anything, we thought you were dead."

My mood was such that I imagined I could detect a note of disappointment. "No," I said. I started to say, "How's . . . er . . ." and then my mind went a complete blank. I couldn't remember which of my brothers I was ringing, nor could I remember her name.

"Oh, so, so. He's doing war-work, of course. Reserved occupation. Had the usual flu he always gets, and of course we've got three now. That's little Martin you can hear."

I had sudden recall – a vivid picture of life at the other end of the phone: the well-meaning but claustrophobic homeliness, its set patterns of conversation, meals, sex. I listened while my sister-in-law gave me chapter and verse of what they had eaten for lunch the previous Sunday (food, I found, was a chronic obsession for many), how well my brother was doing in his job, what she intended to spend the clothing coupons on. She made it sound as though most of the burden of the war had fallen on her shoulders alone, and it wasn't until near the end of the conversation that she casually mentioned my father.

"Of course, we're just getting over that."

"What's that?"

"Oh, God!" she said. "Now what have I said? You don't know, do you?"

But even as she said it, I did know, for many times in the Jugoslavian mountains I had woken wet and cold from a nightmare premonition.

"Is he dead? Is that what you mean?"

"Yes," she said. "I'm sorry. Poor Father passed over two months ago. We had no means of letting you know, you see."

"No. That's all right. Did he have a bad time?"

"Oh, no. Quite peaceful, the doctor said. He was well looked after."

I tried to picture my father's resigned face the last time I had seen him and what troubled me most was the pointlessness of his whole life. It seemed I had been singled out to hear everything second hand, buying my sorrow in the antique market. At the other end of the line there was the sound of something crashing down, and the baby started to howl again.

"Oh, God, now look what he's done! I'll have to ring off, I'm afraid. Shall we see you?"

"Yes," I said, without enthusiasm, "I'll give you another ring." But as the line went dead I knew I had no intention of making good the promise. With the death of my father the last family link had been severed. It seemed hypocritical to pretend to a loyalty I had never enjoyed.

Before I could move away from the phone it rang again. This time it was Theo.

"You're just in time for a whole orange for Christmas," was Theo's greeting. "How are you, dear? All in one piece?"

"Just about."

"And a major to boot. Very impressive. I've always wanted to meet a war hero. Look, stay where you are and I'll come home. Take me about two or three hours, depending on whether I can scrounge a lift."

"Where are you?"

"That's classified."

"You don't seem to have been living here very much."

"Don't I? No, I suppose I haven't."

While I waited for him I spent the time sorting through a motley pile of mail, most of it referring to a life I had all but forgotten. There were polite reminders from my tailor rendering his account for the last suit I had ordered and which I now discovered had been colandered by moths, and a hardly decipherable note from my father, obviously written from his hospital bed, expressing the forlorn hope that he would see me once again before he died. I burnt this and my letters to Alison in the sooted grate, and the fire was still smouldering when Theo walked in. My immediate thought was that he looked older than his years. We were both in our early thirties, but I dare say the war had aged us prematurely.

"Getting rid of the evidence?" he said.

We embraced.

"Burning my past. Did you know about Father?"

"Yes. I happened to come back and there was a telegram. I didn't go to the funeral, I'm afraid."

"Why should you? Funerals are something to avoid."

"I managed to get this," Theo said. "Traded my butter ration for a month." He held up a bottle of champagne. "The widow before butter or guns, is my motto. I thought we ought to celebrate with something vintage."

The cork flew across the room with satisfying force. It wasn't cold enough, but it was still delicious, the best thing I had tasted in years.

"I know you can't give me map references, but are you a town or country mouse?"

"We've just been moved back to the town," Theo said. "The Yanks have moved in with us, which may have something to do with it. Plus something of a palace revolution. I often get the feeling that our boss sees his mission in life as the suppression of intelligence. Not good for morale."

"How are the Yanks?"

"Well, they go about it in a different way from us, of course. There's a slight whiff of Jimmy Cagney about some of them . . . In fact – well, I suppose I can tell you – I met Purvis the other day."

I must have looked blank.

"Melvin Purvis, the F.B.I. agent who killed Dillinger. Quite a glamour boy. The typing pool got very flushed."

"Are you glad to be back in town?"

"It might make my sexual life a little more varied. Bovine village youths pall after a while."

"I'm amazed you get away with it."

"Yes, doesn't say much for our staff security, does it? I'm very discreet, I never do it on my own doorstep. And I sprinkle my dialogue with hearty references to Rita Hayworth and Phyllis Dixey – whoever she is. The only person who might blow the gaff is Kim, but he's loyal to his old college chums."

"Kim?"

"Philby."

"Oh, yes. How is he?"

"Very much the coming man. Highly respected. Puts us all to shame, in fact. Works night and day. A somewhat transparent case of ambition, perhaps."

"Do you ever see any of the others?"

"Oh, they're all about, I believe. Doing their bit. Did you enjoy whatever you were doing?"

"It was different, shall we say?"

"I'm a bit late, but congratulations." He pointed to my medal ribbon.

"Oh, well," I said. "They pick names out of a hat, I think."

"Do we talk about our literary careers?"

"I don't know. Do we? I haven't written much. Collected a few plots, maybe, to store away. How about you?"

"Well, I haven't penned myself into the twentieth century, if that's what you mean. I mean, the characters I meet, they're all frightfully brainy, do *The Times* crossword in seventeen minutes flat and all that, but incredibly dull and uninspiring. The real thing that puts me off finishing a new novel is that ghastly toilet paper everything's printed on nowadays. I mean, I don't want to be published 'in accordance with wartime standards'. It sounds as though one has been instantly remaindered."

I noticed that he had developed several small nervous gestures, most noticeable when he was smoking a cigarette. He seldom used an ashtray, collecting the ash in the palm of his hand, or else standing the butt upright on the nearest flat surface and letting it burn down. I showed him a trick I had learnt in the field – that of placing a penny over the burning tip: it not only extinguished the cigarette immediately but allowed one to resmoke it at a later date.

"I must remember that," Theo said.

"I'll tell you something else I learnt. It's World War One stuff, but still useful in the survival kit. Never light three cigarettes from one match."

"Oh, yes, that's something to do with snipers, isn't it?"

"Yes, they see it the first time, take aim on the second, and kill on the third."

"You sound as though somebody tried it."

"Yes."

"I don't know what I'd be like, actually under fire. We seem to kill people by remote control. I suppose that's easier on the conscience, wouldn't you say?"

"I don't know. Is it?"

"No," Theo said. He stared at the ash in his palm. "And the thing is, who are the friends and who are the foes? Do you know?"

"You mean Russia?"

"Yes, they're so bloody suspicious, don't you find?"

"In a way. Where I've been nobody trusted anybody."

"It's all so frightful," Theo said. "I can't see anybody winning this one."

We talked about the horrifying reports that were then starting to come out of Germany. Like Theo I had been shown smuggled photographs of the concentration camps. They were almost beyond comprehension. What I found as sickening as the monstrous crime itself was the fact that the Germans had actually documented it in detail.

"Can you imagine the mentality of people taking those photographs?"

"Aren't murderers always supposed to return to the scene?"

"But they don't provide their own incriminating evidence, do they?"

Theo didn't answer that. If I had expected to feel elated from the unaccustomed champagne, I was mistaken. It seemed to have no effect on either of us; it was almost as if there was a third man in the room, a stranger, preventing us from enjoying our reunion or talking with our old intimacy. I realised that the war had changed both of us, but that didn't explain the feeling that stood between us at the time – only hindsight provides those answers. Theo didn't have the same resilience as Philby. He couldn't blur his misgivings with alcohol, he just didn't have the iron constitution for it. Philby came perfectly equipped for his mission in life, and of course he believed in what he was doing, which Theo never did. There we all were, literally shifting the dirt, like ants, carting it from one place to another, a human chain of deception. The host feasting on the host. And that year, 1943, was the turning

283

point. By then the defeat of Germany was only a matter of time and future policy – the methods of penetrating Russia – was already being discussed in the stratified regions of our tawdry profession. The infiltrators were well established in our ant hill by then, blocking channels as fast as they were dug, while on the other side of the Atlantic the awesome secrets of Los Alamos were being mined by another set of idealists.

I was so dim, so stupidly innocent, playing my part like some overgrown boy scout, tracking down conventional spies, my villains cast in old moulds, post-William le Queux perhaps, but definitely pre-Bond. I was not alone, my school of old thought was not that rare. I wonder what I would have done had Theo suddenly lowered his mask – would I have given him an escape route? Friends did betray friends. There were so many ways and means, one didn't actually have to plunge the knife in the back. The game had to go on, and we turned people several times, sending them to certain death primed with false information, dispatching them with all the trimmings of honour. If it suited our purpose we could perform the ultimate act of cynicism and recommend them for some posthumous decoration – there were no rules that couldn't be broken, no graves that couldn't be desecrated, no bottoms to the pits we were prepared to dig.

I never suspected Theo. The only doubts that crossed my mind were concerned with his personal safety. In that respect I came close to the truth of the matter, but I approached it from the wrong direction. I always had a fear that his homo-sexuality would one day produce a scandal – the British will sometimes excuse a man's treason, but seldom forgive his sexual aberrations. I was fearful for his reputation as a man of letters, believing that if his true nature was ever revealed his readership would desert him. But as in the childhood game, I pinned the donkey's tail on the wrong part of the body.

The game is still being played, of course. There is Philby telling all and telling nothing in his much-praised autobio-graphy, yet unable to stem the instincts of a lifetime – betraying his wife, betraying Maclean, switching partners just as he switched sides, without conscience. Who knows how deeply the worms have eaten? We all think we sleep safely in our beds, the mortgage payments up to date, the house insured, the burglar alarm operative: but we haven't read the fine print on the policy – our own treasons are excluded, and outside, the Philbys of this world are still at large, observing us from afar, listening to us through brick walls, photographing us with lens that pierce the night, recruiting the next crop of fellow travellers even as they discredit the old, detonating their minds with new lies. Thank God I haven't any children.

I understand now that the sad pattern of Theo's last years was established long before. In a way he is to be pitied. Unlike his Trinity companions he was never granted the catharsis of defection. His Moscow flat was situated in Englefield Green, but who is to say that his forced confinement wasn't just as absolute? The essence of what they all believed in and worked for is beyond the limits of comprehension for most people. We act as though we are not capable of making the effort to understand the *Communist Manifesto*, or penetrate its many disguises. Theo exiled himself in his own country.

He seems to have abandoned the 'Alec' manuscript after the 'Chalmers' episode. I have found some random notes for a continuation of the narrative, but they don't make much sense, being jottings such as writers make to themselves at the end of a day in order to trigger the creative processes the following morning. Knowing Theo as I did, I would imagine that the act of having sent a man to his death would have destroyed the last vestige of self-justification. He had been trapped and blackmailed into making his own commitment, the point of no return had been passed and for the rest of his life he was on his own.

21

I T PROVED TO be Theo's turn to be sent overseas, and he
spent the remainder of the war out of the country, mostly
in America, though for a period he was stationed in the
Caribbean and it was there, when the fake peace came so
suddenly, that he made his next home. He bought an
enchanting house built of powdered coral on the leeward
coast of Barbados. This was long before the tourist trade
exploded, and the island was undefiled. I envied him the
wherewithal to afford such a move and although I stayed on
alone in Perrins Walk for a few years, it never felt the same
and I sampled half a dozen addresses before being fortunate
enough to secure a set of chambers in Albany where, if the
Inland Revenue permits, I hope to end my days.

He was always inviting me to join him in Barbados,
extolling the virtues of its near-perfect climate, the purity of
the water-supply, the absence of mosquitoes and (probably
the deciding factor in his case) the calming influence of the
local youths. Our wartime exploits quickly receded in the
astonishment of the first years of peace, and we were both
very prolific – I had to be, I was very short of money. That
was another piece of sales talk Theo gave me in his letters. He
wrote that he had never found anywhere as conducive to work
and detailed his daily routine. It certainly seemed to suit him
and during those immediate post-war years he produced three
of his best novels: he picked up where he had left off, but with
greater authority, still writing of times past but in a way that
caught the mood of the period. One forgets that rationing
persisted long after VJ Day, the bomb sites remained, there
was an overall feeling of anticlimax and people hankered for
the return of the old values and felt cheated that victory
hadn't brought instant affluence. The Forces vote had swept

Attlee to power but the great social changes that his government promised to bring about overnight didn't happen – the pinched, Bob Cratchit face of Cripps epitomised Christmases past rather than the much-heralded furture.

Although he had removed himself five thousand miles away, Theo seemed to realise the underlying dissatisfactions and, more than with many contemporary, trendy novels, his work caught this mood perfectly and the reading public responded. I must include myself in the rival camp, for the novels I published in the decade following the end of the war, although successful at the time, had no staying power. Perhaps I should have accepted Theo's frequent invitations; a change of scenery might have meant a change of perspective.

In the event, I stayed put, justifying the self-denial with the thought that my brain would addle in such a hot climate. My wartime wanderings had left me with little appetite for travelling; I functioned better in temperate zones, working amongst the cluttered familiarity of my desk, reference books to hand and a good supply of my favourite cigarettes which at long last had reappeared in the shops.

When at last we did meet it was in Hollywood, during the height of the McCarthy era – the early Fifties, in fact. Theo had written to tell me of his seduction.

They finally discovered this particular whore's price, so I have taken the plunge and am willing to lie back with my literary legs wide open. I have no illusions, but certain friends tell me that the place is not without charms, and really what they are offering is too ridiculous. A gentleman rejoicing in the name of Sol. B. Zeidman, though doubtless of sound mind, is suffering from the temporary delusion that 'Harriet's Day' is the perfect vehicle (his word, not mine) for a lady called Maria Montex, who he assures me is perfect casting for my Harriet. I dare say Miss Montez will bring an added dimension to the role of a late Victorian schoolmistress. They want me to go out there and write what you, with your superior experience of these matters, will be familiar with – namely something known as a 'Draft Screenplay'. They have sent me a first class ticket and I am also to be given free accommodation. The whole thing seems highly improbable, but a change of venue won't do me any harm (and in fact will relieve me of a

287

somewhat tiresome emotional involvement that has run its course), so I am taking the boat to New York and then go by train to Los Angeles, on the Super Chief, I believe. Stand by for further news from the front line in due course.

It was a time when the major Hollywood studios were talent spotting all over Europe. They appeared to have money to burn, and I suppose I was somewhat miffed that Theo had been discovered ahead of me. By coincidence, I didn't have long to wait, for the very same day that Theo's letter arrived from Barbados my agent rang to say he had had an enquiry as to my availability from Twentieth Century Fox.

"I played it very cagey," he said with that irritating casualness agents sometimes adopt when changing the course of one's life.

"Not too cagey, I hope."

"Listen, Tony, you must never be keen where the Americans are concerned. Take it from me. The more you play hard to get the more they're desperate to have you. I told them you were considering an offer from M.G.M."

"But I'm not."

"You and I know you're not. You and I know your last novel didn't sell too well," he continued, displaying an honesty he reserved for his clients. "Now is the moment to play it close to the chest."

"But can't they check whether M.G.M. have made me an offer?"

"Tony, if – and it's a remote if – they check with M.G.M., you'll get the offer from M.G.M. That's the way it works. Nobody at M.G.M. is going to admit they're *not* after you, because an enquiry from somebody else will immediately make them wonder what they're missing." Then he spoilt it all. "They're signing anybody these days."

"You make it sound very exclusive."

"Just stay by the phone and trust me."

My pre-war experiences with Korda had conditioned me to accept that film people moved in mysterious ways, but even I was unprepared for the eventual outcome. Theo had written from Hollywood where he was now comfortably housed in the

Beverly Hills Hotel apparently coming to terms with unaccustomed luxury.

The most impressive thing is the laundry service. I resolutely
stick to collar and tie, which clearly impresses the natives, and I
am fascinated by the speed at which my shirts are returned. They
have a special delivery service which gets them back, perfectly
ironed, in three hours. It must be what makes America great.

I have completed the mysterious process known as The First
Draft, which turned out be a précis of the novel that Frau
Zeidman (birds of a feather stick together, dear) insisted need not
exceed twenty-five pages. So I did my prep and they are now
reading it, which would appear to indicate that they never read
the actual novel, although they paid good money for it. I keep
asking if I can meet Miss Montez, but I am told that this is not
the form and might cause her agent to push her price up. I am
invited out for every meal, but I have resolutely steered clear of
Les Anglais – the few expatriots I have met inspire dread; they
appear to have been put to sleep in 1939, and I am not going to be
the one to kiss them awake. The natives, on the other hand, *very*
approachable and friendly, mad for physical exercise of any
description. Drink plentiful and very potent. The sun shines ever
day and so do I.

I was forced to eat humble pie where my agent was concerned
because in due course his predictions came true. I was offered
a contract by M.G.M. at roughly twice as much as the
opening bid from Twentieth Century Fox. I cabled Theo my
impending arrival and sailed on the *Mary*, taking the same
overland route from New York as Theo. I think the train
journey was more of a revelation than the near-Edwardian
atmosphere of the Cunard Line. Nowadays even America
shrinks beneath the Jumbo jets, but to go from the East to
West coasts in those early post-war days was a heady experience. I was totally unprepared for the vastness of America
and the infinite variety of its terrain. I was also disarmed by
the friendliness of my fellow passengers, since England had
swiftly reverted to old and surly habits. Most of the travellers
on the train appeared to be celebrating the end of prohibition,
and I viewed the passing countryside through a 90% proof

haze for most of the four days and was more or less poured off the train and into the waiting M.G.M. limousine when we arrived in Los Angeles. American hospitality may not always be sincere, but it is certainly generous.

I was driven to the Beverly Wilshire Hotel, my chauffeur proudly informing me that it had been the 'official air raid shelter' during the war, a piece of information I am sure he felt would be of great comfort to a Limey. My suite was festooned with unreal flowers and various gifts of liquor and fruit from my hosts at M.G.M. There was even a letter of welcome from Louis B. Mayer himself, though when I examined it closely I discovered that the signature was printed. A card in the bathroom proudly proclaimed: *The Beverly Wilshire stands, and will ever stand, as a monument to the loyalty and love that Walter Mcarty, the builder, bears for his home city.*

I had fully intended to telephone Theo as soon as I had unpacked, but I wasn't given the opportunity. All four telephones in my suite rang simultaneously. I picked up the nearest one and in the classic tradition of the movies a cute female voice immediately said: "Hi! Mr. Stern. This is Betsy. Welcome to Beverly Hills and the Beverly Wilshire. Mr. Wadsworth is on his way up. Have a good day."

Before I could enquire why Mr. Wadsworth was paying me a visit, there was a knock on the door. I was still somewhat unsteady on my feet when I greeted the unexpected Mr. Wadsworth, who turned out to be one of those rarities, a native without a suntan; young, formally dressed with a matching waistcoat to his dark suit and sporting a thin moustache in the style of Douglas Fairbanks. He carried two bottles of champagne, each gift-wrapped with festive bows.

"Mr. Stern, sir? May I welcome you on behalf of Alfred Somburn, sir."

"You may indeed," I said. "Who is Alfred Somburn?"

He deflated visibly. "Oh, didn't you know? You're working for Mr. Somburn. He's a very important producer on the lot, sir. I work for him, too. These are a gift from Mr. Somburn."

He proffered the two bottles of champagne.

"How very kind of Mr. Somburn."

"He's a very fine gentleman, sir."

"You're Mr. Wadsworth, I take it?"

"Yes, sir. Would you like my card?"

It was out of his waistcoat pocket in a flash.

"I have the limousine downstairs, sir. It's Mr. Somburn's personal limousine, which he's placed at your disposal."

"Well, I don't think I'll drive it just now."

"Oh, no, sir. I have to take you to him."

"Why don't you come inside?" I said, totally confused by now. "Would you like a drink? As you can see, I could open a bar. Perhaps you'd like some champagne?"

"Thank you, no. The fact is, Mr. Somburn is expecting us."

"Now?"

"Yes, Mr. Stern."

"What is he expecting us for? Dinner?"

"Gee, I don't rightly know, sir. All he said was to bring you to the studio. I'm sure he'd give you dinner if you're hungry."

"No, I was just asking. Well, we'd better go then. I'll just put on a clean shirt."

"May I use your phone, sir? I'd better advise Mr. Somburn of the delay."

"Take your pick."

I splashed some cold water on my face and changed my shirt. "Does your Mr. Somburn always operate at this pace?" I called into the next room.

"Oh, yes, sir. He's noted for it. He has no fewer than seven motion pictures under consideration at this present time."

One of the longest cars I had ever seen was drawn up outside the Wilshire Boulevard entrance. A black chauffeur opened the door for me (they still called them 'Negro' in 1952) and I sank into the custom-made interior. It was like climbing into a feather bed. Wadsworth occupied one of the jump seats. Throughout the twenty-minute journey to Culver City he gave me a sobering run-down on the many qualities of Mr. Somburn, leaving me with the firm impression that I was shortly to be ushered into the presence of a man of genius.

I was deposited in front of the Thalberg building, having

been closely scrutinised by the studio police at the gate. It was quite obvious from young Mr. Wadsworth's behaviour that he felt he was leading me into a holy place. I noticed he straightened his tie and pulled the points of his waistcoat before entering the building. I was given a printed security pass by another policeman sitting at the desk in the lobby. It bore my name and the description 'Contract Writer – valid for one month' which was not exactly reassuring.

Somburn's office was on the second floor, which I later learnt denoted that he existed somewhere between heaven and the ghetto. He had three secretaries, all of whom looked like Varga girls to my innocent eyes, and all three greeted me as though I was the sole survivor of Pearl Harbor. It was flattering but unnerving. The senior of the three, distinguished by her slightly larger desk devoid of a typewriter, buzzed Mr. Somburn in the inner sanctum. The office itself was of dazzling whiteness.

"Why don't you go right in, Mr. Stern?"

"Congratulations," Wadsworth said, as he opened the door for me. There wasn't time to ask what for.

In alarming contrast to the outer office, Somburn's room appeared to be in total darkness. The shutters were drawn, the only illumination coming from a picture light over a framed photograph of Louis B. Mayer, and I found it difficult to move through the wall-to-wall carpet, the pile of which came up to my ankles.

"Mr. Stern from England, sir," Wadsworth said.

I peered in the same direction as Wadsworth and finally made out a figure lying on a couch at the far end of the room.

"Did you get the champagne?" a voice said.

"I personally handed it to Mr. Stern," Wadsworth said.

"Of course you did, you prick!"

The body on the couch heaved itself up to a sitting position. By now my eyes had more or less adjusted to the gloom and I was able to make out Somburn's features. He had the face of a prize fighter gone to fat – the beard sparse and reddish in colour where he had neglected to shave, reminding me of the scalded skin of pigs in a slaughterhouse. I had no idea of his real age and he was careful not to volunteer it. When I looked him up in a trade reference book his entry merely said, 'Born Pittsburg, the only son of Stanley and Miriam Somburn.' He was a snappy dresser, had his finger nails manicured every day and affected two-tone brogue shoes.

His first rejoinder to the immediately craven Wadsworth took me off guard. At that time I was totally unfamiliar with his species.

"Tony, I'm sorry I didn't meet you myself, but I had a mess of dailies to look at. They take care of you at the hotel? You got everything you want?"

"Well, I've just arrived, but everything seems fine, thank you."

"You want anything, just tell Helena outside. You met Helena?"

"I imagine I have."

"She's terrific. The best. You want a drink?"

"No, I don't think so, not just for the moment."

"Pour me a Jack Daniels then fuck off, will you?" he said to Wadsworth, then added, "But hang around, I may need you later."

He opened a drawer and took a paper cocktail mat from it on which he placed his whisky glass. I noticed that the paper mat had a motif on it of two naked bodies closely entwined. This was repeated on his personal stationery with the words *Things to Do Today* printed underneath.

"Tony," he said. "I hired you for your reputation. You've got a great reputation. In this town that counts for something. Most of the writers around here couldn't write their way out of a fucking paper sack. But I've read your books, that's why I didn't turn a hair at your price. It's cheaper to live at the Ritz, that's my philosophy. Don't you agree?"

"Absolutely," I said.

"I treat my people well, you know. You work for me, the best ain't good enough. And you know something else? That man . . ." He poked a thick, pink finger at the photograph of Louis B. Mayer. ". . . That man is like Jesus Christ to me. Fucking saviour of this industry. What he doesn't know ain't worth knowing. I worship him. When you meet him you're going to worship him. He put me here because he trusts me, because he know's my heart's in the right place, because I'm not a fucking pinko like some of the pricks who really sold him down the river. They sold that beautiful human being down the river. Took his money and sold him. But he's going to have the last laugh. We're going to run every one of those commie motherfuckers out of town. Let me show you something, see if it's still on."

He pressed a button and pointed at an oversized television set. After a few seconds a picture appeared. It was a commercial for a local beer called Brew 102. When this came to an end I found myself looking at Senator McCarthy's blue-chinned face. He was smiling.

"That's the man who's going to save America!" Somburn said.

At that point I had only the vaguest idea of the day-to-day workings of the House Un-American Activities Committee, but I remember being immediately appalled by the spectacle of witnesses being interrogated like participants in some spectator sport. It was so alien to my very British conception of justice and the fact that it was being presented on television like some grotesque soap-opera was more shocking than anything I could have imagined.

The close-up of McCarthy was replaced with live transmission from the actual sub-committee rooms. Not wishing to rely on the hazy memories of that afternoon, I have since verified the actual date of the first hearing I witnessed. It was May 21, 1952 and the witness on the stand that day was Lillian Hellman. The staff member who conducted the interrogation was a Frank S. Tavenner. There in Somburn's shuttered office I heard for the first time the constant reiteration of the basic question, and the monotonous denials by the witness.

"Were you at any time a member at large of the Communist Party?"

"I refuse to answer, Mr. Tavenner, on the ground that it might incriminate me."

"You might refuse to answer it. The question is asked, do you refuse?"

"I'm sorry, I refuse to answer on the ground that it might incriminate me."

"Are you now a member of the Communist Party?"

"No, sir."

"Were you ever a member of the Communist Party?"

"I refuse to answer, Mr. Tavenner, on the same grounds."

And so on. Somburn might have been watching a football game.

"Listen to the communist bitch!" he said. "She's fucking lying. They're gonna nail her like they nailed the rest of those red cocksuckers. You got any like her in England?"

"I don't think there's anybody like Miss Hellman," I said, but the nuance passed over his balding head.

"You know, sooner or later you're gonna hafta get after your own commies, because you take my word for it, your woodwork's infested just the same."

His mood suddenly changed and he switched off the sound and turned to face me again. The rest of the conversation was conducted with the mute face of Miss Hellman confronting her accusers always in my vision.

"Now, you're sure you're being taken care of? You want to change your room at the hotel?"

"No, the room's splendid. I haven't even unpacked yet."

"That's good, that's good. Long as you're being taken care of by my people. Now I expect you're wondering why I got you over here?"

"Yes, I did wonder about that."

"When you get to know me better, you'll get to know how I work. You got to keep moving in this town. Stand still and they'll take you to the cleaners. You're sure you don't want a drink?"

"Quite sure, thank you."

"Coffee? Hey, what about a cup of your English tea?"

"Well, maybe a cup of coffee. When in Rome."

"You been to Rome?"

"No, it's just an expression."

One of the girls appeared in the doorway in response to his buzz on the intercom.

"Get Mr. Stern a cup of coffee. How do you take it? You want cream and sugar?"

"Just as it comes."

"Well it comes black."

"A little milk then."

"We don't use milk, how about half and half?"

"Yes, fine," I said, not knowing what he was talking about. I could lip read Miss Hellman as she again stood on her constitutional rights.

"So, where were we?" Somburn said. "Yeah, let me tell you about my operation. I've got a wide open deal here, very kosher. I don't make waves for them, they don't make waves for me. Anything I want to do, L.B. listens to. You know what he's a sucker for? Pictures with heart." He thumped his initialled shirt pocket as he said this. "He likes to be hit right here. Because he's got a big heart, that man, and he likes to share it. I hired you because I like what you write. I loved that one, the last one, *Last Call For Dinner*."

"*First Call For Dinner*."

"Yeah, something like that. I was going to option it, but train movies are dying this year. And one thing I always stick by. Don't knock the public. They don't want to buy it, don't give it to them."

The girl returned with a welcome and excellent cup of coffee and the liquid called 'half and half' which turned out to be thinned cream. Before the door had closed behind her, Somburn again switched his train of thought.

"Listen, any time you want a little action, just drop the word. What are you, a leg man, or do you like to eat off the candy counter?"

"Tits," I said descending to his level, since subtlety seemed a lost cause. "I go for tits."

"You've come to the right town." Much to my horror he made a note on his pad, tore off the top sheet and handed it to me. "Have that on me," he said. "That little baby has a pair of jugs that'll put your eyes out."

"Very kind of you," I said.

"My pleasure. So listen, the point is, what L.B. likes, what I like, is class. I only make pictures with class. That's why you're here. You're a class writer and I'm a class producer. That's a great combination."

"Do you have any particular subject in mind or do you want me to think of something?"

"No, I've got something for you. Only we've got to keep it under wraps for the time being. Know what I mean?"

I didn't, but I forced my face to register renewed interest.

"You ever heard of a book called *Harriet's Day*?"

"By Theo Gittings?"

"That his name? Another English guy, right?"

"Yes." Something warned me not to blurt out my relationship with Theo.

"What d'you think of it?"

"It's a very good novel. Very good."

"You bet your ass it's good. The point is, and you're going to be part of the family from here on in, so I'm going to take you into my confidence . . . what's happening is that some guy who calls himself a producer over at Warners has got this Gittings character knocking out a script for him. But what he doesn't know is that we bought it from under him. And I'm going to put you on it."

I stared at him. On the television screen the committee room seemed to be in uproar. Photographers were clustering around Miss Hellman as she and her attorney prepared to leave.

"How does that grab you?"

"You mean, you now own the novel, but this other producer doesn't realise you own it?"

"You got it."

"Won't he object when he finds out?"

"He can object 'til he's blue in the fucking face, who cares? I wanted it, L.B. said you go buy it, I bought it. He's going to wake up to find his balls have been cut off."

"Does this sort of thing happen very often?"

"Sure. Like I said, you've got to keep weaving. It's just business. Warners weren't going to make it anyway. They grabbed at it when I made the offer. Grabbed at it."

"Amazing," I said.

"Listen, you stick close to me and I'll teach you the ropes.

297

When I like somebody, I share everything. That number I gave you, I don't give that out to everybody."

He opened another drawer in his desk and took out a copy of Theo's novel which he pushed across to me.

"Tony, we're going to get rich with this one. You start tomorrow. Helena'll show you where your office is. Now, I'm going to take a little steam and a rub. You want to join me?"

"No, I think I'll get back to the hotel. I've been on that train for four days."

"You take it easy tonight and in the morning you can start nice and fresh. But if you feel a little tense, use that number. She'll take very good care of you. You're going to love it here, believe me. You're never going to want to leave."

Safely back in my hotel room I found it difficult to believe that the entire scene had taken place. Somburn's personality and dialogue were a grotesque background to the tragic happenings on the television screen. I had strong premonitions of disaster and they sobered me more quickly than the coffee. I looked around the unaccustomed opulence of the hotel suite, taking in the gifts of fruit and flowers, thinking of the telephone number on the piece of paper in my pocket, and wondered how on earth I had been trapped. Survival was my immediate concern, and I reached for the telephone and asked to be connected to the Beverly Hills Hotel. When that operator answered I gave Theo's name. I was in luck because a moment later I heard his familiar English voice.

"Where are you?" he said. "Are you here?"

"Here and frantic. I must see you."

"Look, I know what you're going to say. And I take back everything I wrote about this place. It's a nightmare. You've no idea what's been happening to me."

"I think I do."

"You remember I told you they wanted to cast a lady called Maria Montez? Well, last week I found out she's dead."

"Shall we meet for dinner?"

"Can you believe that?"

"After what I've gone through this afternoon I could believe anything. Where shall we meet?"

"Why don't you come here? Have you got a car?"

"No. I've got a room full of flowers, some champagne and the telephone number of a tart, plus a copy of your novel."

"My novel?"

"Yes – *Harriet's Day*. I'll tell you about that when we meet."

"I'll pick you up. Half an hour?"

"Fine," I said. "Hurry."

At Theo's suggestion we avoided the more popular eating places and ended up at a small restaurant on Wilshire which was Belgian owned, had Mexican waiters and served pseudo-Italian food. We wasted no time in comparing horror stories and I gave Theo a blow by blow account of my encounter with Somburn.

"They're quite shameless," Theo said. "In a way I admire them. I mean they have this unbelievable capacity for self-deception."

"So what are we going to do? I simply can't rewrite your script."

"Why not? I don't mind. The whole thing is a farce anyway."

We ordered a second bottle of imported wine, being European snobs.

"I tell you what," Theo said. "I've got a brilliant idea. We must put our heads together – after all, we weren't in Intelligence for nothing. Play them at their own game. Is there anything in your contract which says you can't collaborate?"

"I don't think so, why?"

"Let's both write identical scripts and turn them in on the same day. I mean, do you care if you ever work here again?"

"Right now I don't."

"Me neither. I mean, I'm slightly ahead of you. My reading of the situation is that although they've bought my book from under Zeidman's nose, they won't tell him. They'll keep him in ignorance and let me go on writing as though nothing had happened. They like getting their pound of flesh."

"It's a great idea," I said.

"I'll let you see what I've done so far. Working to Mr. Zeidman's inspired instructions I've already turned Harriet into a demur girl from West Virginia – the whole thing's set in America now, by the way."

"You're kidding?"

"Alas, no. Look, like you I was seduced by their hospitality in the first few weeks, but then gradually I woke up to what was really happening. They've perfected the techniques, of course. They're all so scared, they grasp at any straw. Actually, I like them. They mean well, they're generous with the studio money, they're so sincere they make you puke, and the whole set-up is a fantasy."

"What happens when we've finished?"

"Well, now," Theo said. "Let's think it through." He finished his glass of wine. "The really clever thing would be for us both to plant a few rumours. You go around saying that you're amazed they rejected my script – because it's so brilliant – and I'll let it be known to Warners that they were insane to let the property go because you're turning in a work of dazzling originality."

"Will they take the bait?"

"They'll get the hook right down their throats. Yes, I know! I've got it. I know exactly how to do it. You get your story to Louella Parsons – you know who she is, don't you?"

'I've heard the name. Doesn't she write a column?"

"She's practically gaga. She doesn't write much of it herself. She has leg-men, or leg-women who collect most of the garbage they print. Then her great rival is she of the amazing hats, Miss Hedda Hopper. Between them they practically run this town. And they hate each other."

"And you think that's the way to do it?"

'I'm sure. I might even hire a press agent for a few weeks. In fact, that would be the smart way to do it."

We spent another half an hour embroidering the scheme before going to our separate hotels, highly pleased with ourselves.

Theo sent over a copy of his work-in-progress before I left for the studio the following morning. I had been allocated what to my eyes was a palatial office complete with a bright-eyed secretary called Carol who seemed to be dressed in a negligee, plus a generous supply of paper, sharpened pencils and two more bottles of champagne. Wadsworth was in attendance for my arrival and over-anxious to ensure that everything was to my satisfaction.

"I think I'll spend the morning reading the novel," I said.

"If you don't like your desk, we can change it," Wadsworth said. "Likewise . . ." he rolled his eyes in the direction of Carol in the outer office. "No sweat."

"Everything seems perfect."

"I'll call for you at lunch, then and take you to the commissary."

I had no sooner closed the door when my telephone rang. It was Somburn.

"How's it going? How many pages?"

I was not sufficiently tuned in to his subtle sense of humour in those early days and simply remained silent.

"Just putting you on, Tony. Did you get the champagne?"

"Sitting in front of me. Unopened, of course. I never drink when I'm working."

"That's my boy! How did you make out last night?"

"Last night?"

"Did you meet the little lady?"

"Oh, that. Er, no, I didn't feel I could do her justice last night."

"Well, she's on ice for you. Listen, I just want to leave you with one thought. The book. It's not the Bible. Understand?"

"The book? Oh, yes."

"You want to change anything, you go ahead and change it. Have you had any thoughts?"

"Well, the only thing that occurred to me, is that possibly the heroine, Harriet, is too English. I suppose you wouldn't want me to make her an American girl?"

"Tony. Let me say something. You're one of my people. You're thinking like I am. That is one *hell* of an idea. I can't wait to read the pages."

Begin as we mean to continue, I thought as I put the phone down and started to read Theo's unfinished script. This took me most of the morning and I made notes as I went along. I resisted ringing Theo to exchange progress reports: if our scheme was to succeed we had to maintain radio silence.

My first lunch in the studio commissary proved to be another emotional experience. I had a place reserved for me at Somburn's table in the executive dining room – the caste system was still rigidly enforced in Hollywood 1952. Like any other first-time tourist I confess I was impressed to come face to face with a dozen household names, but I found the locker-room conversation strangely disconcerting. The humour of the film industry is savage – 'as funny as a baby's open grave' explained one local sage when I questioned him on the subject. An onlooker at the perpetual feast, I had the feeling that most of the regular guests would self-destruct given time, for they all seemed to be living on their nerves, their keenest pleasures originating from the failures, artistic, commercial or marital, of their colleagues. Most of them appeared to be living on borrowed time, borrowed money and borrowed ideas and they kept one eye trained on the permanent officials – those who controlled the books. Everything seemed to be expressed in numbers: you scored with a tally of wives, girlfriends; inflated budgets, busts and box-office returns rated high; six-figure salaries, the profits that *Variety* were encouraged to exaggerate, even the gin-rummy stakes were discussed with a reverence never before encountered. Their total dedication to the pursuit of affluence was stunning when it wasn't frightening.

Surprisingly – for the place was inhabited by over-anxious gossips – our deception was not uncovered. Pleading devotion to duty, we resolutely declined the many social invitations; having sampled two or three we felt we could exist outside the Beverly Hills Circuit – that perpetual round of the same tight group going to the same parties, making the same conversation night after night. Equally, we felt it prudent to avoid being seen together in public. Our meetings and exchanges of progress reports took place in unfashionable restaurants.

The schoolboy prank we were playing visibly excited Theo and he could hardly wait for the dénouement. It was the sort of joke that appealed to him, just as years before his friend Raymond's impersonation of Miss Angela Pritchett had given him such lasting pleasure. If I had any misgivings about the eventual outcome Theo swept them aside.

"They deserve everything they get," he kept insisting. There was a touch of the old Cambridge élitism in his all-embracing dislike of the American scene. He was often unnecessarily supercilious with waiters when discussing the menu and wine list. He embarrassed me sometimes – unpleasant echoes of his father. I suppose I should have been more perceptive and realised that his frequently absurd anti-Americanism was a symptom of some deeper resentment.

Our stay in Hollywood came a year after Burgess and Maclean's flight. Given past associations, it was inevitable that we several times discussed their defection. Even at the time Theo's reaction struck me as odd, though I attached no particular significance to it: he was frequently perverse in argument.

I think I was morally shocked by the Burgess and Maclean affair, coming as it did in the wake of the Nunn May and Fuchs trials. I found myself curiously torn. Part of me abhorred the current American obsession with communist treachery, but at the same time I could not embrace the liberal theory that Russia's atomic programme would miraculously enhance world peace. Theo, on the other hand, appeared to have no such divided loyalites.

"I was questioned, of course."

"Were you?"

"Yes, I expect they'll get around to you in due course. Anybody who ever knew them."

"Well, I didn't really *know* them."

"No, but their knickers are in a right old twist. They've got to find a few victims to excuse their own total incompetence. I mean, I told them it was always right there under their bloody noses. Imagine putting Guy in Washington, or anywhere else for that matter! You only had to take one look at him to know he was a degenerate liability. He'd have sold anybody on a first come, first served basis."

"Now they're saying it's only the tip of the iceberg."

"Yes, well, it's equally obvious they weren't operating alone. Guy could just about find his way to the nearest toilet, but you'd hardly cast him as a master spy. There must be others."

"This Third Man theory they're pushing?"

"Oh, that's just journalese."

'The trouble is that when anything like this happens a great number of innocent people have their lives wrecked. Look what's happening over here – all these kangaroo courts. Have you watched any of it?"

"Yes."

"Well, don't you find it horrifying?"

"Not really. They all look as though they've got something to hide."

"You serious?"

"Yes, absolutely. I don't think it's all that horrifying. I mean, this great show of standing on their famous Fifth Amendment. They should try that in Russia, see how far it would get them."

"But most of them are just writers and actors."

"So?"

"Well, what threat could they pose, even assuming they are converts or party members or what-have-you?"

"Now you're being naive. We're writers and we did it. We were up to our necks in it during the war."

"But that was during the war."

"Well, the war's still on. Russia's the enemy now, Russia was always the enemy. Hitler's war was just the dress rehearsal."

"You are a cynical sod."

"I'm being bloody serious. And I'm certainly not going to get morally indignant because a few boring film stars and Hollywood hacks are asked some perfectly legitimate questions. I've got no particular love of all things American, as you well know, but I think in this instance they're perfectly within their rights. If these would-be martyrs are innocent they don't need to stand on anything; if they're not then they deserve anything they get."

I still thought he was merely goading me for the sake of effect. But there was another incident that made me wonder whether his new covictions were perhaps genuine, even though unfamiliar.

I don't quite recall how it came about, but on one of the

rare occasions when Theo and I did not have dinner together (he was cruising the bars on Santa Monica Boulevard after an enforced period of sexual abstinence) I accepted an invitation from a fellow writer on the lot. He had a pleasant house out in the Valley and had promised me that he and his wife had not 'gone Hollywood' and that I would meet some interesting people. 'Not the usual crap merchants,'' he said.

When I arrived I found there were about twenty fellow guests, a small gathering by local standards, none of whom I had ever met before. The hospitality was generous but informal –barbecued steaks *al fresco* around the modest-sized pool – and it was my first glimpse of anything approaching normal standards of human behaviour. The conversation was still mostly film-industry shop, but it lacked that vicious cutting edge which characterised the higher echelons of Hollywood society, and I relaxed and accepted it. I gradually became aware that, unofficially, the guest of honour was a male star who had 'sung' before the Un-American Activities Committee, and had paid dearly for it. A few years previously his career had been one of the most publicised even by Hollywood's standards. Now it was non-existent. I have no idea what motives drove him to make his confession – fear assumes many disguises – or what he expected from it, but he could hardly have envisaged the eventual outcome. Reviled by his fellow travellers, he had also been shunned by those very reactionaries who should, logically, have applauded him. He was in limbo, a star name that nobody would put above the title, an embarrassment to friends and foes alike.

My host (described by another guest as a 'closet-liberal') was at some pains to tell me that he was acting purely out of charity.

"I don't sympathise, I don't condemn. He's just a considerable human being and right now he needs a little compassion."

I have frequently observed that the cardinal American sin is getting found out. It doesn't matter too much what you do, but don't get caught doing it. The fallen star had managed to violate all the codes at once, and they were making him pay for it. He seemed to me falsely, irrationally cheerful about his predicament, over-anxious to confide that this was just a temporary pause in his career, that good things were just around the corner. He still had that carefully groomed, slightly unreal look of the old-fashioned Hollywood leading man. "I go to class every day, just to keep in trim," he told me. Even his agent had abandoned him, and his wife was just about to, but he hung on for another eighteen months, keeping in trim, holding himself in readiness for the call that never came, unemployed, unemployable, until his savings ran out and then he opened his veins in his king-sized bath under a framed photograph of himself in his first major success.

The grapevine was visited by many little foxes that year and the following morning I had no sooner sat down at my desk when Somburn asked me to come and see him. He got straight to the point.

"Tony, you're my guest over here and a very important guest. I respect you, so don't take what I'm going to say the wrong way. I understand you had dinner out in the Valley last night."

"Yes, very pleasant."

"Look, me, I don't take sides. I'm strictly neutral, Switzerland on Coldwater Canyon, that's me. But I think you ought to stay clear of those people."

"What people?"

"You know what people. I don't have to spell it out for you. Some of your fellow guests last night are bad news in this town. One in particular. And who needs it?"

He took a Kleenex, blew into it and then carefully scrutinised the results before screwing the tissue into a ball.

"Assuming we're talking about the same man, I thought he'd washed himself in public," I said.

"You could be right. But I repeat, who needs it? You could have a ball here, Tony, write your own ticket, but you have to play it by the house rules. That guy is a no, no. Off limits. *Verboten*, you understand?"

I didn't answer him.

"See, I know you're innocent, but it doesn't look good. A lotta people are running scared. They jump to conclusions, and it's easier to jump to the wrong conclusions, you take my meaning? So why run the risk, for what? What d'you care whether this guy is kosher or not? I'll tell you something, he aint that kosher. Personally, and I'll deny it if you ever quote me, I think he's paid his dues. I mean, I'm a great believer in justice and I think he had a lotta guts. But I'm not calling the shots. You either get off the pot or piss in it. Am I right?"

"I don't know," I said.

"Tony, I'm right. Believe me. I know the way this town works. Play your cards right and you've got it made here. So, let's talk about the script. How are the pages coming?"

"It seems to be coming along okay."

"You having a good time? Everybody treating you right?"

"I've no complaints," I said.

"So take a little advice. You're my boy, remember?"

I reported this nauseating conversation to Theo that evening. He gave me the second surprise of the day.

"Well, allowing for the fact that your Mr. Sunburn is as ghastly as my Frau Zeidman, he does have a point. Why get mixed up in local politics?"

"Nobody's going to tell me who I should or should not see."

"Oh, don't get all high hat and indignant. You betray your origins."

"I insist, nobody has that right. Certainly not a super prick like Somburn."

"Yes, but the way to get even with those characters is not to take up moral attitudes. Hit them where it really hurts, in the wallet. We're well on our way to doing that."

We argued backwards and forwards for most of the meal, but Theo refused to shift his position. I retired none too gracefully to my own corner, irritated, as one always is when somebody we know very well reveals that we know them scarcely at all.

Perhaps jokes of that nature never succeed after adolescence, or perhaps we underestimated the enemy, but in the event, despite the fact that our collaboration on the screenplay was a masterpiece of inspired mediocrity, the last laugh was on us. I hadn't realised that the Somburns of this world always take out insurance policies, and whilst Theo and I were happily engaged on our involved deception, Somburn hired a third writer – a tame, local boy noted for his ability to serve any number of masters at once. It was quite common practice (and probably still is) owing much to the industry maxim that 'you can't bullshit an old bullshitter'. We turned in identical scripts on the same day, then sat back to await the explosion. There wasn't even a whimper. After forty-eight hours of silence, I phoned Somburn to enquire what he thought of my effort. Theo did the same with his Mr. Zeidman.

"You did a great job," Somburn said. "Maybe just needs a little polish, which we won't bother you with."

I compared reactions with Theo. His Mr. Zeidman had said: "Theo, it's a classic example of the art form. Too good for these bums, they can only recognise crap."

On balance, we felt that Zeidman won by an expletive.

We suffered a feeling of let-down. I still have a tattered copy of the script somewhere and the last time I glanced at it I formed the opinion that manufactured dross seems to age in the wood. The awful thing is it was rather a good, bad script, despite our efforts. When the film eventually appeared it had been retitled *Heaven, Hell and Harriett*, our names had been removed from the screenplay credit, and the only reference to Theo's original was a line of small type which read: *Based on a novel by Theo Gittings*. I never saw Mr. Somburn again, though I still get Christmas cards from him. Full of the spirit of the Nativity they are always specially posed colour photographs of our hero himself and give details of his latest epic. They are collectors' items.

22

I T WAS SOME years after our foolish escapade in Hollywood that I finally accepted his invitation to take a working holiday in Barbados. Things have changed now, I believe: with the coming of independence the new government saw fit to rescind most of the labour permits for Europeans so that the islanders would have a better chance of advancement. Friends tell me that the exodus included most of the trained chefs and that subsequently the over-ambitious hotel menus lacked a certain piquancy, to put it mildly. But at the time of my first visit there was a happy lassitude about the whole island; the package tourists had not yet started to descend in their jumbo-loads and imports of plastic commercialism were still of modest proportions.

I took an ancient taxi from Seawell Airport and drove across the island through lanes shadowed by the tall and impenetrable fields of sugar cane. My local driver appeared to work on the same principle as those shire horses one used to see at harvest time in Norfolk: finding his way by habit. At one point I looked up and saw his reflection in the rear-view mirror: both his eyes were closed. Since the road we were travelling on was only wide enough to accommodate one vehicle at a time, I felt the need for urgent action if we were to survive the journey. I hastily engaged him in a conversation about cricket and at the mention of the national hero, Garry Sobers, his eyes flickered open and some resemblance of energy crossed his face. He stayed awake for the rest of the trip and in time we descended from the high ridge where the cool winds blow and drove along the coast road, reaching Theo's house at last light.

Theo greeted me with drink in hand, and appeared to have gone semi-native. He was dressed in tattered shorts with a loose fitting cotton shirt flapped over them. He was tanned and relaxed and seemed genuinely pleased to see me. I had brought a bundle of English newspapers with me, always the most welcome gift, I have found, for those who profess to have turned their back for ever on the mother country.

There was a young male house-boy called Thomas to attend to my luggage and it did not escape my notice that his relationship with Theo was hardly formal. We sat and chatted on the verandah, strangely contrasted in appearance, for like most arriving travellers I felt vaguely ashamed of my pallor and crumpled city clothes.

"Get out of them," Theo said. "Nobody wears anything here. I can lend you a beachcomber outfit. Take a swim."

"Now?"

"The best time. The sea is always warm, and bathing at night is sybaritic. But let me show you where. One has to avoid the coral and the sea urchins. Very painful if you tread on one of those and the cure somewhat bizarre. The natives piss on the soles of your feet and then apply hot wax."

"I think I'll give that a miss on my first night here."

"Yes. Personally I cheat and use lemon juice."

After my swim, which I found as relaxing as Theo had promised – the sea warmer than anything I had imagined and of a strange consistency – we had a meal of flying fish and sweet potatoes, expertly cooked and served by Thomas. He had threaded freshly picked hibiscus blossoms on thin wires and these fanned out from the centre of the round table and hung down over the sides.

"He's so artistic," Theo said with noticeable pride in his acquisition. "A positive little Lady Chatterley with flowers."

The house itself was cool and surrounded by greenery, so that one hardly noticed where the walls ended and the garden began. It was in the pre-air-conditioning days, but the room had a large circular fan on the ceiling and when I lay down to sleep that first night I found myself thinking of Kipling and the early travel books of Somerset Maugham. The sea broke on the coral shingle only a dozen yards from my bedroom window, and the small night frogs called non-stop. I felt the tiredness slake from me like a useless skin, and slept as I hadn't slept since childhood.

310

Theo had gone to immense pains to make me comfortable. He had set aside a small, bare room close to the beach for me to write in, and explained his own working method.

"One can't write after lunch," he said. "It's too hot and one must surrender to the customs of the island. My routine is to rise early, have a swim, then breakfast and work until about eleven. Then another swim and laze around all afternoon. Other good intentions prove ultimately useless. One can see why the natives burn the sugar-cane fields rather than go to the trouble of harvesting them. Why should anybody work hard in a climate like this?"

There was a cane factory set back from the beach about half a mile from the house, and on two days a week the heavy, sickly scent thrown off by the refining process would penetrate every corner of the house. More frequently the air would be full of floating black ashes as a distant field was fired, arson being the local pastime, and an ancient fire engine would race past with a crowd of naked children in its wake. These were the only excitements, and for the rest it was day after day of blissful sameness – perhaps gentle rain in the early mornings, which freshened all the foliage and steamed the verandah. There was a tulip tree outside my bedroom window and humming birds hovered round it, their wings beating so fast that they appeared to be china models suspended on invisible wires.

Some mornings Theo and I would walk the half a mile to the local market and choose fresh fish and vegetables. There was none of the clamour and dirt of the Middle East, no beggars or professional cripples, just brightly coloured women and school-children sedately walking in crocodile file, the girls wearing smart blazers and straw hats and white stockings. On Sunday mornings I could hear their voices raised in song from the church across the way, and in the afternoon they would rush to the beach, naked, gleaming, screaming with pleasure, turning cartwheels as they dived and leap-frogged into the foaming surf. I would watch the young men play beach cricket, utilising driftwood, roughly-shaped, for bats, making miraculous catches with headlong lunges that often ended with the fielder in the sea. It was a world apart, innocent and joyful and within a few days of my arrival I had totally surrendered to it and could scarcely recall the life I had left behind.

For the first time I could understand how some people come to such islands and never leave, the lotus existence seducing them away from old realities. In such a climate the past seems like a pawn ticket one cannot be bothered to redeem, for it is easier to cut one's losses. Time no longer retains its city meaning; clothes have no importance, personal appearance matters for little. After two weeks my skin was tanned and taut, cleansed and salted by the hour-long swims we took each day. I began to lose my writer's paunch and smoked less, though I had yet to learn the trick of Theo's discipline. I tried to write in that perfect setting, but the very nothingness of it defeated me. It was a time to contemplate my navel in traditional beachcomber fashion, to take stock. I had ideas for a new novel, but they swam beneath the surface – multi-coloured plots darting about in the coral of my mind.

I think Theo was amused by the transformation in me and kept reminding me I could have sampled this life style many years earlier.

"You see," he would say, "I told you what it was like, but you never believed me."

One night under the influence of too many rum punches prepared by the ever-solicitous Thomas, he talked with un-characteristic sadness of his life.

"I've always envied you," he said.

"Me?"

"Yes. For as long as I can remember."

"Well, that's odd, because really I could say the same thing. I remember, if we're going to let our hair down . . ."

"Not so much to let down these days . . ."

". . . I remember feeling, well something stronger than envy, hate almost, the day you told me your first novel had been accepted. There I was struggling with my pathetic first attempts, and you just sailed home on the maiden voyage."

"Really, I never knew that. I dedicated it to you."

"Not very perceptive of you."

"I'm sorry," Theo said. "But I didn't really mean that, I

312

wasn't talking about your writing. That sounds very rude. What I said was – God knows what Thomas put in these tonight. Lethal! – when I said I envied you, I was thinking more of your love life."

"Which could be written on the head of a pin."

"Not always. You're just going through a temporary lull. At least . . . at least you've had one *grand amour*."

"Have I?"

"Yes. Judy."

"Ah," I said. "Dear Judy. That seems a long time ago."

"But while it lasted it was all or nothing."

"Catastrophic," I said.

"I never had that . . . Some queers don't, you know."

It seemed odd to hear him use the word 'queer' but I sensed he wanted for once to unburden himself.

"Even when we're settled and happy," he said, "we never stop looking. That's the main difference. It's a compulsion, a kind of love-death-wish, if you like. I sometimes think it's not really me. I'm standing outside a lighted window, looking in and seeing myself behave in a totally alien manner. It's the horror of a long dream. You know you're doing it, that you'll do it again and again, yet you can't stop yourself. That and the risks you take. The endless . . . stupid, hideously exciting risks. And I'm not talking about what you might call 'camp', not that. I don't mean those sad creatures who swish about the West End, defiantly female under their blue chins. Not them, that isn't me. They revolt me as much as I'm sure they . . . well, you must find them grotesque. No, the types I'm attracted to whenever I'm back in my own familiar hunting grounds . . . And that's what they are, you know: hunting grounds;" – he lingered over the phrase, bringing his eyes to meet mine and smiling – "well, you'd never suspect, not in a million years. Bank managers, postmen, long-distance lorry drivers, quite a few of them married with dull, mousy wives if one is to believe what they tell me . . . And of course, their risks are greater than mine. It isn't like the proverbial dirty weekend at Brighton with your secretary – two single rooms and clean sheets. It's usually somewhere exposed, dangerous and with a complete stranger. You often don't even exchange first names. Everything's anonymous and you get it over quickly, in a car parked on a bomb site, or else in a railway station toilet between trains . . . the risk, you see, that's so important, the need to feel that even the quick pleasure might be interrupted, that you'll be caught in the act. Fear is a very powerful aphrodisiac . . . Am I disgusting you with all this?"

"No," I said.

"I expect I am. Here, it's different, of course. There's a kind of pagan innocence about it. Perhaps it is something to do with the sea, the cleansing sea. I'm very happy here . . . fulfilled, as they say . . . and yet, I miss the danger, it's not quite the same without the danger. Did you ever feel like that?"

"I can't say I have. But then my sex life has always been very ordinary."

"What's ordinary? . . . If we knew that we could all live peacefully. No, I have the feeling that one day it'll destroy me. But I have to go on, I'm driven, I can't help myself."

"You've never brought any of this into your novels, have you?"

"No."

"Why not?"

He hesitated. "If you give people a murder weapon," he said, "sooner or later they're tempted to use it."

"But you could disguise it."

"Not well enough. Not and be honest. And there doesn't seem to be any point in the half-truth. Like all those boring novels which skirt around it, getting heavily praised in the *New Statesman*, written by lapsed Catholics."

"Can I ask you something? I presume Thomas has talents that extend beyond the kitchen and the bar?"

"Oh, yes. There have been quite a few Thomases over the years. As you probably suspected. I find them very good for the morale, though a little short on stimulating conversation. That's why it's so good to have you here. Quite like old times. It's funny our friendship, isn't it?"

"In what way?"

"Oh, I don't know. We've nothing in common, really and yet . . . at the risk of embarrassing you . . . you're one of the very few people I actually care about. I must have been a bit of a pain at times. Especially at Cambridge. I used to lord it over you, didn't I?"

"I don't think so. I was very dreary, always mooning over the delectable Judy. I wonder what became of her?"

"Yes, I wonder," Theo said, and looked away.

We replenished our glasses yet again and swopped anecdotes of those years, lapsing into mild hysteria at our own jokes. Our mood was half-induced by alcohol, half brought about by a nostalgia for things lost – a searching back for innocence.

The next morning Theo studiously avoided any mention of our previous discussion, and I did not press him. We spent the day like any other, and that evening enjoyed a sunset that was vividly unreal. The sea was without ripples, though far out to the right we could discern the glinting surf breaking on the reef. Small fishing boats were silhouetted against the fast-changing sky. One was closer to the shore than the rest and we could see two young, naked fishermen standing in it.

"Look at them," Theo said. "They're so beautiful when they throw the nets."

"What do they fish for?"

"I don't really know. 'I'm not very up on such things." He was silent for a while. "I don't think they catch much."

He turned away and walked back into the house. "Perhaps they only catch my eye," he said.

23

THE FIRST BAD omen that day was the discovery of a dead
suckling pig at the water's edge. It was white against the
sand and seemed weightless in the slight swell. It was
perfect, like an exquisitely moulded bone china replica. The
umbilical cord was still attached to the body, floating from
the belly like a strand of purple coral. I carefully moved it
with a piece of driftwood so that it remained in the sea, but
when I returned an hour later it had again been shifted higher
up the beach. After lunch I went back to the same spot a third
time but could find no trace at first. Then I saw the
membrane with the cord still fixed to it had come away from
the carcase and was floating on its own like some giant
contraceptive. The rest of the tiny body was trapped on the
coral and was being pounded to pieces. I was somehow glad
that it hadn't been devoured by the sand crabs, for at least the
sea was cleansing and its very ruthlessness mitigated against
the horror. I stood and stared at it for a while but the afternoon sun in a cloudless sky seared my shoulders, and I
retreated to another section of the beach and plunged into the
clear water, swimming alone for half an hour in an attempt
to wash away my strange feeling of guilt – the guilt I felt for
being human and alive in a world of meaningless cruelty.

Later, walking to post a letter in the village, I came across
death in another form. There was a dead toad lying in the
centre of the debris-strewn roadway. It had been flattened like
a cartoon character so that it resembled nothing more than a
brown suit of clothes for a toad: one expected to see buttons
on the jacket, and it reminded me of a theatrical costume for
The Wind in The Willows.

The whole day seemed filled with sinister portents. Leaving
the post office I was approached by a total stranger, a
European, quite well spoken and dressed with an insane dis-

regard for the intense heat. His suit was dark with perspiration; the sweat must have been running down his body as rain from a roof, for I noticed that even his shoes were discoloured around the lace-holes. He asked me who I was, without any polite preamble, but when I told him betrayed no further interest. Then he told me he had been fishing on the North Coast earlier in the day and had caught some barracuda.

"D'you know what?" he said. "I'll tell you something fascinating. This man, this man I hired the boat from, very interesting character. D'you know how he killed the fish once we'd landed them? You'll never guess. He poked a finger through their eyes, straight into the brain. Never seen that done before."

Having distributed this information he trotted off. There was a small patch of wet where he had stood. The encounter left me feeling nauseated, for I could not rid myself of the image he had conjured up. I began to feel that I had somehow been selected as the receptacle of everything that was repulsive on the island: horror is always more pronounced, I find, for being introduced into idyllic surroundings – one expects it in graveyards and empty houses, but never in strong sunlight.

I took a stiff drink the moment I returned to the house, but even so I was witness to yet another incident. Two men suddenly appeared on the beach, one minus an arm, the other minus a leg. They undressed awkwardly, then helped each other in and out of the sea, all the time shouting at each other in German, which is not a language which lends itself to immediate humour. Theo joined me while they were still cavorting.

"There's going to be a storm," he said. "I can always tell. I saw the rain bird this morning when I got up, and now these. That's probably a rain dance."

"Oh, don't be ridiculous," I said. "They're just two cripples having a good time."

"You'd be surprised. Everything gets shaken up before a storm, people go slightly mad. I've seen it many times."

"You're not going to run amok, are you? Warn me if you are, because I've had quite an afternoon." I told him about the various incidents.

"Yes. Well, there you are, you see. Proves my point. By the way, changing the subject, or perhaps staying with it, we've been invited to a party this evening. But you don't have to go if you don't feel like it. I must, I'm afraid. I'm so antisocial most of the time that I have to make the occasional effort."

"No, I'll come. I assume I'm invited because I'm here with you and not because of my so-called literary reputation?"

"Oh, they'd invite anybody new," Theo said, ungraciously. "They're always desperate for new faces."

"Who are they?"

"A couple called Neisser. There's a standing local joke. The nicer they are, the more you should watch out. She's passable providing she doesn't get at the gin too early. He's a monster. Very rich, of course, which he needs to be, since she goes through it at a rate of knots. I don't know where he made his money, there's a kind of mystery about that. Some have it that he made a killing during the war, cornered the South American copper market or something. One thing I will say, they don't stint on food and drink. The guest list is pot luck, but I've found I usually come away with some good copy."

"Sounds intriguing," I said.

"It's formal, of course. At the beginning of the evening, that is. Most parties on the island tend to fall to pieces very quickly. They're so bored, you see, they drink to forget how lucky they are."

The Neisser's house was situated inland, near the golf course and standing in some thirty acres of land: a long modern structure, with two guest wings forming a pair of protective arms around an enormous swimming pool. The driveway was hung with lanterns and a steel band was playing at a discreet distance from the illuminated patio around the pool. We arrived slightly late because Theo's water pump had shown some temperament and delayed our showers. There seemed to be fifty or sixty guests with almost as many servants, coming and going with endless trays of food and drink. Introductions were haphazard, and it was some time before I met either of my hosts. We had no sooner been offered an enormous drink when we were approached by a tall, gangling man wearing a white dinner jacket at least two sizes too small for him.

"Theo!" he said. "Why you're just the man I want to see. You've saved the day."

He had a pronounced American accent, and pushed his very large hands towards your face as he talked to you. Instinctively one wanted to duck.

"Hi!" he said, turning to me. "I'm Bill."

"Bill is a society photographer," Theo explained.

"*The* society photographer, thank you. Not here, of course. I'm from Palm Beach."

"From whence you should never have strayed," Theo said.

"Listen, Theo, old dear, I need you desperately. I'm here on assignment and there's simply nobody on the island worth exposing."

"Say it louder," Theo said. "I don't think everybody heard you."

"Oh, shit to them," Bill said. His hands punched out within an inch of my nose. I stepped back and trod on somebody's foot.

"Excuse me," I said. I had nearly crippled an enormously fat man. He took my apology graciously and passed on.

"What I need," Bill was explaining, "is a really challenging lay-out. Something out of the ordinary. How I see it, is if I could get you against one of those really broken-down shacks with lots of naked little local kids – you looking very suave and terribly, terribly British, contrasted, you know what I mean, you get the picture? I mean, I think it would make a terrific set which I know I could place, and believe me I need the bread. I'll make you look like Edith Sitwell."

"What is the point of the pictures?" Theo asked.

"The point? The point is to pay my rent, dummy. Now listen, you loved the last lot I took of you. Your publisher used one on the jacket, though I can't say he paid my going rate. Listen, can we fix this? Can I ring you? Do I still have your number? Give it to me."

I heard Theo give him a false number, changing the last digit, though I had the conviction that Bill would not be put off so simply. I eased myself away before he knocked me flying with one of his expansive gestures, and went in search of the fat man, feeling that I owed him a more detailed apology.

He was sitting in a corner, taking up at least half of a large sofa. He was even larger at a second viewing, though like many fat men, his face seemed out of proportion to the rest of his body. He was gripping an unlighted full corona between his lips, turning it round and round to saturate the tip with saliva.

"I do so hope I didn't do you a permanent injury,' I said.

"Not at all. It was nice to feel my feet. I haven't seen them in years," he said with unexpected humour. "Do you have a light, by any chance? My name's Mannix, by the way."

"Tony Stern."

"Pleased to meet you, Mr. Stern."

I offered him a light and he went through a ritual with the cigar.

"Do you live on the island, Mr. Stern?"

"No, I'm just visiting."

"Likewise. I just came to case the joint. Thinking of buying a house here if I like it."

"And d'you think you'll like it?"

"What's your opinion?"

"Depends what you want," I said.

"I want somewhere peaceful to die," he said. "See, I've got a little problem." He tapped his chest with a pudgy hand. "Here. I've got a pacemaker. Quite a dandy, as a matter of fact. Made of plutonium. Ticks away at a steady seventy-five a minute if I behave myself. Got enough power to keep going for thirty years. Even if the rest of me falls to pieces, this little baby will still be pumping away."

"That's quite a thought."

"Sort of Edgar Allen Poe brought up to date." He regarded me quizzically. "What's your line of country?"

"I'm a writer."

"Do me a favour, will you? Reach me that ashtray. Do you accept commissions?"

"For books? Yes."

"How'd you like to write a book about me?"

The question took me by surprise. Although at several

stages in my career I have been approached to write what are known as 'house biographies' – the history of some brewery or chocolate manufacturer – I have always resisted. I'm sure it's an honourable way of earning a living, but I have not yet felt the need to succumb to it.

"Does the idea appeal? I'd be willing to pay generously."

"Why don't you write it yourself?" I said.

"Me? I can't write two words. Well, maybe two words. My name on a cheque." He smiled. He had a rather slack jaw which the most extensive dental surgery had been unable to correct.

"I take it you've had an interesting life?"

"I think so."

"What d'you do?"

"I make money," he said. "You know, that stuff that buys people who do the work that makes more money."

"I've heard about it," I said

I began to feel slightly uneasy again, as though some of the earlier happenings of the day had been warnings of worse to come. Far out to sea the sky was illuminated by violent electrical discharges and I felt the wind freshen on my face and saw it disturb the surface of the swimming pool. Behind me the crass photographer suddenly screamed: "The faggots won the war in the desert, not your Monty!" The party was beginning to fragment as the lethal drinks loosened tongues. The general level of conversation seemed shriller, rising above the insistent music of the steel band. I caught a scent of burning, something acrid, transporting me back to the Blitz, and saw that on the lawn a troupe of limbo dancers were preparing to stage an exhibition.

"Take my card," Mannix said.

He fumbled in a pocket and extracted it with some difficulty. Before putting it away I glanced at the address. There were three: Miami, Zurich and Hong Kong. "Any one will get me," Mannix said. "I'm computer-linked. I'll keep the offer open."

"You're taking me on trust. How d'you know I can write?"

"You can write." He rattled off the titles of my last three books. Then smiled again and tapped his cigar against the side of the ashtray. "I never make guesses in the dark. Glad to meet you, Mr. Stern."

It was with a feeling of some relief that I turned towards the limbo dancers. The performance started with an exhibition of fire-eating. I thought it particularly impressive set against the backcloth of an angry sky, though I noticed that many of the guests behaved with noisy indifference towards the artists. I have always had a sneaking sympathy for any form of cabaret act, forced as they are to display their talents to audiences intent on other pleasures, but to have to ignite methylated spirits for a living and still not gain attention seems particularly cruel. The steel band increased the monotonous rhythm and the spectacle on the lawn took on savage splendour. The leading man in the troupe imposed silence on the watching spectators, breathing out tongues of flame I swear must have been three to four feet long. It was then that tragedy struck.

A drunken girl, teetering on the edge of the swimming pool, suddenly veered towards the performers. The leading fire-eater, head thrust back as he brought the flaming taper close to the vapour he was expelling, did not see her and when he breathed the next jet of flame it shot across her face. Screaming, her hair on fire, she fell backwards into the pool. Two male guests immediately dived in fully clothed to rescue her. She was brought to the side and I could see that part of her face was blackened and that most of her hair was charred back to the scalp. The limbo dancer responsible for the accident came forward to help, his lips still wet with methylated spirit, but he was pushed away in the panic and confusion. Mrs. Neisser collapsed, moaning, as the half-drowned girl came to and began to scream. As the girl was carried into the house I could see that the skin on the burnt side of her face had bubbled and peeled away. Too many people were giving advice, but eventually a car was manoeuvred as close as possible and the girl carried into it. As it drove away the first heavy drops of rain began to fall, beating into the pool, the surface of which was blackened in places.

I heard the American photographer complaining, "Jesus!

why the hell didn't I have a camera? I knew I should have brought one."

I went in search of Theo and again stumbled into Mannix.

"What happened? I was inside."

"A girl got burnt."

He nodded. I might have been telling him that the Dow Jones Index had shifted half a point.

"That was nasty," I said, when I found Theo.

"And the rain," Theo said. "I told you. There'll be other things before the night's out."

"Don't be too cheerful, will you? I need a drink."

Outside, in the rain, the troupe of limbo dancers were packing their props and the members of the steel band were grouped together in a forlorn huddle as though they shared a collective responsibility for what had happened. Mrs. Neisser had been taken to her bedroom, and her husband moved amongst the guests attempting to save his party from total collapse.

"Silly little cow," I heard somebody say, "she was drinking like there was going to be no tomorrow."

"What d'you think?" I asked Theo. "Shall we ease our way out?"

"I don't think so," he said. "It's all part of life's rich pageant."

"Does that mean you've found something?"

"Could be."

"Well, let me know, won't you, because I'll need to get transport."

"Oh, I won't abandon you."

There is something primeval about a tropical storm. For a few moments the rain was so solid that it stifled all conversation and we stood gaping at it. Small rivers formed on the previously immaculate lawn and, as though seized by madness, some of the younger guests who must have come prepared for such an eventuality, changed into swimming costumes and plunged into the pool. Coming so soon after the girl's tragedy their antics filled me with revulsion, but most of the guests applauded them from the safety of the covered patio. I drifted around, wishing to God I had never come, and

323

caught a glimpse of Theo in the distance. He was standing in the doorway of one of the bedrooms, earnestly in conversation with a young man with floppy, thin hair. Theo had one hand on his shoulder, and their faces were close together.

"Talk to me," a voice said. "I'm worth talking to."

I turned to find a woman of about my own age, flamboyantly dressed in a Pucci print dress.

"Where did you come from?" she said. "I haven't seen you before. You haven't got a drink. Don't tell me you're on the wagon, I couldn't bear it. Everybody's going on the wagon these days. It's so boring."

"I've just put one down."

"Oh, you've just put one *down*, have you? Well, why don't you pick one *up* and be sociable? This bloody party's gone to pot! First decent party for weeks and it's all ruined because of that dreary little Hamilton girl."

I looked around for an escape route.

"Don't look away when I'm talking to you. Most people like talking to me. I don't suppose you even know who I am, do you?"

"No," I said.

"Well, guess."

"I'm no good at those sort of games."

"My husband – he's that fucking bore over there – that dehydrated Prince of Wales – talking to, I don't know who he's talking to, nor do I care – well, anyway, he's one of the most important people on this shitty little island, and I'm his wife, thank you very much, though you wouldn't know it because he doesn't do it very often. Not with me at any rate. Are you from jolly old England? You look as though you're from jolly old England. Well, let me give you a tip. Don't, repeat don't, come and live here because it's fucking death. Death! Believe me, and I know. Sun, sand and the dear little blackamoors who don't do a fucking thing. They can't even pour water, most of them. Do you think I'm attractive?"

"Very," I said.

"Fucking liar. Let me tell you something. I don't know who you are – did you tell me who you are? – but I thought you had a pleasant face and that's why I talked to you. I've given up talking to everybody else, because they're all fucking bores. And the biggest bore of all is my husband. I am attractive, whether you think so or not. Very attractive. I'll show you, if you like."

She pulled her dress open, exposing one breast. "Does that do anything to you, or are you like the rest of the men on this boring island? You can see the rest if you like."

"Oh, put it away, Doris," somebody said. "You're always flashing those tired old tits."

She flung the remains of her drink in the man's face, and I was able to escape.

The whole party was like that, and as the evening wore on I glimpsed those hatreds that always lurk just below the surface in any closed community. As the interloper, I was therefore a new audience for old resentments, the recipient of many un-asked-for confidences and slanders. Perhaps only strangers could be trusted; those who remained on the island were too close for trust.

I finally went and sat next to Mannix again. He seemed reasonably aloof from the mob and shared my detachment.

"Have they come back from the hospital yet?"

"No idea," he said. "Tell me about your friend."

"My cousin, you mean?"

"Oh, he's your cousin, is he? Then you must know him very well."

"Reasonably well."

"He interests me. I seem to have seen him somewhere before. The face looks familiar. I was trying to place him."

Something in his voice put me on my guard.

"Mention my name to him. It might jog his memory. I'm staying at the Sandy Lane for a few more days. He might care to have lunch with me."

"I'll ask him," I said.

He heaved himself up out of the sofa and I noticed his neck turned a different colour with the effort.

"It was good to meet you, anyway. Think about my offer. It's worth thinking about."

I waited until Theo joined me with the fair-haired young man. By then I had drunk rather too much.

"Ready?" Theo said. "I think we've had the best of this. Quite an amusing party, as local parties go. This is Adrian, by the way."

I nodded. Adrian was swaying on his feet and needed Theo's arm to guide him through the crowd. Just as we were halfway to our car I heard the American photographer give one last shout. "Theo, you old queen, don't forget you're going to pose for me!"

It was fairly obvious that Theo had acquired another house guest in Adrian, who sat with lolling head in the front seat while Theo drove with a caution I was thankful for. Reaching the house was a triumph of concentration.

"I think bed, don't you?" Theo said. "Poor Adrian lives on the other side of Bridgetown, so I suggested he stayed the night."

"Where's the bathroom?" Adrian muttered.

"Let me show you," Theo said, grimacing at me behind his back. "We've got everything you need here."

They disappeared in the direction of Theo's bedroom. I was too tired and too irritable to care what they did, and for once slept very badly, waking at frequent intervals to hear the rain beating down on the flat roof. The sound of the phone ringing woke me another time. I listened to see if Theo would answer it, letting it ring a dozen times before groping my way into the living room. It was a long distance call, I could tell that from the echo on the line, and a slurred man's voice said: "Theo?"

"No," I said. "This isn't Theo."

The man did not speak again but the connection wasn't broken immediately and I thought I could hear an operator's voice in the background. It seemed to be Arabic. Then nothing. I waited, but it never rang again. On my way back to my room I heard somebody running past on the beach and registered that it had at last stopped raining.

I was awake again just after dawn. My lungs felt as though they had no air in them and I walked out on to the deserted beach. Evidence of the storm was everywhere – driftwood and bottles, broken but washed smooth by many tides, ugly, greasy piles of seaweed, and a palm tree, half-buried in the sand and sticking up at an angle. It looked like part of a dead elephant. The sea was calm now, just lapping the beach, and the sand was rippled in symmetrical patterns, reminding me of a yellow lawn that had recently been mown. Far out to sea was a single fishing boat, the sound of its outboard motor bringing back memories of Sunday mornings in suburban gardens. Fallen green coconuts lay like the heads of massacred brigands, and ravening hordes of sand crabs scrambled to unseen holes as I walked along the water's edge enjoying the feel of cool damp sand.

That particular stretch of beach ended after a couple of hundred yards and fingers of rock encrusted with limpets poked out into deeper water. The body was jammed into a crevice, pushed there by the last of the storm waves. I didn't register it at first. I was walking into the sun and the rays came back at me off the water. When I reached the rocks I sat down on them to enjoy the peace, elated as always by the sheer, deserted tranquillity of the beach. Putting out a hand to steady myself I touched something soft and looking down I saw it was a black arm, bent at an obscene angle. I pushed myself off the rock, losing balance so that I ended up on my knees, and there, with my face only inches from the water, I found the rest of Thomas.

His black head was under the water and even as I looked, shoals of small silver fish darted from the scene, and the ripples seemed to move his features, waving them in the same way that old movie close-ups used to dissolve into each other to denote the passing of time. I don't know how long I remained in that supplicant's position, for the shock had crippled me. He was naked except for a pair of striped shorts, but apart from the fact that the body was grotesquely twisted I could see no marks of violence.

I suddenly became conscious that the noise of the fishing boat was much closer and looked up to see it passing. I struggled to my feet and shouted to its single occupant, but he mistook my panic for a greeting, waved and kept on going. I ran all the way back to the house, heedless of the broken glass, straight through and into Theo's bedroom.

He and the young man called Adrian were both sprawled asleep in the bed, and Adrian had one arm thrown across

327

Theo's chest as though warding off a blow. Theo's eyes opened at my first words, but he couldn't take in the news immediately and I had to repeat my story before the full impact penetrated. I don't think Adrian had any comprehension at that moment, but he was forgotten as Theo and I raced back to the beach. Together we managed to drag the body out of the crevice and on to the dry sand.

"Twice," Theo said.

"What?"

"Twice, oh, God!" He didn't seem to be talking to me. "He's dead, isn't he?"

"It must have happened during the night," I said. "During the storm. He must have been caught by a wave or something, knocked against the rocks, maybe, and drowned."

"Why would he drown?" Theo said. "Thomas wouldn't drown, he could swim out of sight."

"Well, there's nothing we can do now, except call the police."

"I'll do that. Don't you leave him. Stay here, you stay here. I don't want him . . . I don't want him left."

He went back to the house while I stayed crouched by the body. I tried to brush some of the sand off Thomas's face while I waited, then I got up and walked to the water's edge to bathe my feet. I had cut myself on the broken glass during that first dash for help. As I swished my feet through the shallow water I saw something white floating close to the rocks. I bent to retrieve it. It was a small card and when I turned it over I saw that it was Mannix's visiting card, the one he'd given me at the party.

When Theo returned he brought a sheet with him that he placed over the body and weighted down with pieces of driftwood at each corner. Adrian appeared in the distance, but made no attempt to join us.

"Are the police coming?"

"Yes," Theo said. "I don't suppose they'll hurry. They never do."

"Well, I suppose there's not much to hurry for."

We had both smoked three or four cigarettes before a sergeant and a constable from the station at St. James' strolled across the beach. By then the sun was hot enough to be uncomfortable and the dead body was attracting flies. After the briefest of examinations the two policemen carried the body up the beach to the house and deposited it alongside Theo's car. Eventually an ambulance arrived and with it the inevitable crowd of sightseers, for the news did not have far to travel.

It took the best part of an hour for the sergeant to take down my statement, writing one word at a time. I thought he might have questioned Theo as well, but the effort of getting my statement seemed to have exhausted him, and when I had signed it he left us.

Adrian had spent most of the time in the bathroom during this; now he surfaced and immediately excused himself. "I'm sure you don't want me here," he said.

Theo didn't answer at once.

"I'll give you a call later, Theo. It's all been such a shock. Nice to meet you," he said to me.

"Don't you want a taxi?" Theo said.

"I think I'll walk. Fresh air'll do me good."

"I wouldn't talk too much about it. You know what this place is like."

"Oh, I won't. I won't say a word."

Theo made no attempt to see him to the door and he walked out of the house and presumably out of Theo's life, for I never saw him again, nor was his name ever mentioned.

"What did you mean out there?" I asked Theo during a sparse brunch we forced ourselves to eat. "You said 'twice'."

"I said what?"

"Twice. Has it happened before? Did somebody else drown out there?"

"I don't know what I meant. I don't even remember saying it. It was just too ghastly for words."

"I suppose there'll be a post-mortem?"

"I assume so."

"Does he have a family?"

"I believe so. I've never met them, but there's bound to be dozens of them. Practically everybody's related to everybody else."

"Well, quite a night, one way or another. What with the storm, and that girl getting burnt. I take it all back."

"Take what back?"

"What you told me. You predicted something like this."

"I wish to God I'd never brought that other creature back here."

"Well, that wouldn't have made any difference."

"It might. Thomas wouldn't have been out."

"Oh, I see."

"I'm such a bloody disaster." He got up from the table, and I was embarrassed for him. "Why can't I just be faithful to one thing, one person?" he said. "For what? I mean, for what?" He was close to tears, working himself into a bout of self-pity. "I didn't need it, I didn't enjoy it but I still make the same bloody mistakes time after time. And while I'm rutting in that bed with that bloodly little pouf my poor baby, my darling Thomas is dying out there. I wish you'd help me, I wish someone would help me sort it all out once and for all."

"Of course, I'll help."

He began to drink again. I took a few to keep him company, but the alcohol didn't touch either of us. I tried to put myself in his position, because it became more and more apparent that his relationship with Thomas had been a turning point in his life.

"You're the only one I can tell," he kept saying. "Nobody else would understand," but I didn't really understand, because even confronted with his anguish, part of me remained appalled.

"We all do stupid things for sex," I said.

"That's not what I'm talking about. I'm not talking about that. I should have protected him."

"You make it sound as though he was murdered or something. Was he promiscuous?"

Theo stared at me as though I had used a word he had never heard before.

"Is that all you ever think about us? Queers are promiscuous. Heteros aren't, I suppose? Christ, every bloody woman on this island is at it like knives."

"I was only asking. You've told me yourself you all pick up

strangers. Perhaps he picked up the wrong stranger."

"Perhaps." His burst of anger was over; he seemed crumpled again. "I'm sorry I shouted like that. Don't you turn against me, will you? I couldn't bear that. Just ignore me when I lash out . . . I can't really expect you to understand. He wasn't anything very special, poor Thomas, not to other people, but he never wanted anything from me. He was just a boy who was kind to me, and that's rare enough."

24

A s a result of the tragedy I stayed longer than I had intended. There was a post-mortem, the verdict being,
predictably, death by drowning. I gave evidence of finding
the body, but nobody seemed unduly concerned. It was, after
all, only the death of a house-boy; an excuse for a colourful
funeral. Thomas appeared to have many friends and relatives, and the size of the cortège amazed me, since I was a
stranger to the customs of the island. The procession of cars
passed Theo's house along the coast road, preceded by a
band, a rather ragged band to be sure, but playing with gusto.
There must have been at least twenty cars following the
coffin, reminiscent of a Mafia ceremony, except for the
incongruous gaiety.

Theo did not go to the funeral or the wake. "They wouldn't
want me there," he said. "I'd only inhibit them.
They're very touchy about such things." He sent a generous
cheque to the family and a week later the father appeared,
dressed more sombrely on this occasion than anybody at the
actual funeral, to thank Theo and pay his respects.

He invited us both back for tea to meet his wife. We could
not refuse. His home was some ten miles away in a village
that bore no resemblance to the area around Theo's house.
Everything was on a miniature scale, dolls house versions of
Tara, built on precarious piles of rocks. I learnt from Theo
that this meant the occupants did not own the ground the
house was built on. If they couldn't pay the rent they moved
the whole house elsewhere; only those with freeholds built on
solid foundations.

The house, although a patched wooden wreck from the outside, was spotlessly clean within. We were shown into the
main room the size of an average British bathroom. Thomas's
mother and six or seven other children of various sizes and

ages stood clustered in a doorway while we were offered the only two chairs. There was a picture of the Queen on the wall, framed in gilt. Two odd cups and saucers had been laid on the table, together with a packet of Peak Frean's cream crackers. We were solemnly introduced to everybody present, but nobody spoke to us. Tea was poured and we drank it self-consciously, feeling, as Theo remarked afterwards, like the royal family at Versailles. Theo made a charming and I am sure sincere little speech about Thomas, extolling his virtues and saying what a good house-boy he had been. The mother smiled nervously, but none of the other children betrayed any emotion. And after a decent interval and one cream cracker each, we said our thanks and left.

"Do you think they really like us?" I asked on the journey home. "Politically this is a comparatively stable island, isn't it?"

"Yes. But change is on the way. I dare say in a few years all those charming little children will be making petrol bombs and throwing them in our direction. You can't blame them. They must see what we've got and what they haven't got. The only thing is, when we've gone they still won't have anything. Chances are they'll have even less. Still, that's progress these days."

He pulled into the side of the road to let an overladen cart of sugar-cane pass. It left a trail of green stalks in its wake.

"Something occurred to me the other day," Theo said. "I was watching two people on the beach, visitors, smothering themselves in sun-tan oil to fry quicker. And I thought, somewhere back in the States there are a lot of underpaid blacks making that stuff. There's irony for you, yes?"

"Yes. You should use it. Make a good short story."

"Too modern for me. You can have it."

In an effort to take his mind off recent events I suggested we dined out that evening, something we had studiously avoided until then. Theo was none too enthusiastic but allowed himself to be persuaded.

The restaurant was British-owned and like many similar establishments on the island hideously pretentious. The decor suggested that Butlins had been taken over by the Speer organisation – a mixture of plastic and Germanic wrought iron with a conflicting colour scheme of purple and orange.

"We must drink a great deal," I said. "And don't get the giggles. I've just spotted the Maître d'."

The gentleman in question was one of those Englishmen who can only succeed abroad, and had imposed a public school accent on top of Streatham Cockney, with the result that when he highlighted the *plats du jour* he sounded like a strangulated railway station announcer.

"If I maybe so bold, gentlemen, I think you'll find the veal done Viennese style with just a hint of garnish to your liking."

"How about the local fish?" I said.

"It's all fresh, sir, unless, of course you'd like the imported Dover sole which we have flown in from New York every day."

"That sounds enterprising."

"Then of course there is the boeuf Wellington, a speciality of the house."

"No, I think fish," Theo said, and kicked me under the table.

"We have dolphin, sir. Or flying fish."

"He doesn't mean our kind of dolphin," Theo said. "But it sounds off putting."

We settled for the plainest dish on the menu and ordered two bottles of Puligny Montrachet at a price that would have embarrassed the wine waiter at The Mirabelle.

As we ate bugs immolated themselves in the flame of the candle burning in the middle of the table, great green and brown things which stained the cloth with a strange charnel dust as they fluttered and died. The food when it came was tepid and the vegetables, overcooked, reminded me of childhood holidays in lodgings. But the wine was cold and had somehow weathered the long journey from the Côte d'Or. We made a determined effort to enjoy ourselves despite frequent visits from the proprietor. He was so obviously out of his depth that I began to like him. I wondered if he had been the author of the menu, which was prefaced by a greeting in Gothic Script which read: *Bon Ape Tit.*

334

"Now, how about dessert, gentlemen. I can personally recommend the pot au chocolat. Oh, wait a minute, that shouldn't be on the menu tonight."

"I think the crème caramel," Theo said.

"I cannot apologise enough, sir, but it's Friday and the man who comes in specially to make the crème caramel unfortunately didn't appear today."

"Right. Well, what about the ice cream, then?"

"Oh, yes, we have ice cream, sir."

"What do you have? What flavours?"

"Well, normally we have vanilla, strawberry, orange and cassata."

"What do you normally not have on a Friday?" Theo asked with a straight face.

"Tonight we've got the lime sherbert, sir."

"Just coffee," Theo said. "And another bottle of wine."

We were halfway through that third bottle when Theo's mood changed abruptly in the middle of an anecdote he was telling about his literary agent.

"Oh, God," he said. It was an involuntary exclamation.

"What?"

He was staring past me and I turned. Mannix was just entering the restaurant with a scrubby-looking young blonde tourist on his arm. Even from a distance I could see that she was a newcomer to the island, for she wore a topless dress which exposed the white strap-marks of her bikini on inflamed shoulders.

"Let's get out of here," Theo said. "There's somebody I want to avoid."

"You mean that man. I met him the other night at the party. Mannix. He gave me his card."

"That isn't his name," Theo said. "Look, do me a favour, will you? Pay the bill and let's get out."

He kept his face down, picking up the menu again to shield himself as Mannix was shown to a table on the far side of the now-crowded room. It didn't seem worth arguing about, so I called for the bill. Theo didn't wait for me to pay but got up and went outside. As I left, Mannix suddenly spotted me and waved, beckoning me to come over to his table.

"Thought any more about my offer?" he said. He made no attempt to introduce the young girl.

"I'm giving it a lot of thought."

"You on your own? Why don't you join us?"

"No, I am with somebody." I gestured vaguely. "Very nice to see you again."

Theo was already sitting in the car.

"Do you think he saw me?"

"No. Definitely."

"Thank God for that."

"Why the panic?"

"No panic. He's just one of the locals I try and avoid if possible."

"But he told me he'd only just arrived," I said.

"Well, he comes and goes. What else did he tell you? Did he mention me?"

"Yes, he did come to think of it. Nothing much. Just asked the odd question. He didn't seem to know you. He was mostly interested in me, wanted me to consider writing his biography, which seemed odd."

"Stay clear of him," Theo said.

"Well, I don't intend to take him up on the offer."

Theo drove very badly, mashing his gears and braking far too late on every blind corner. I found myself braced for the inevitable crash, though stupidly much too British to urge caution. About half a mile from the house our dim headlights picked out a group of natives far too late, and Theo reacted violently, swinging the wheel and hitting the accelerator instead of the brake pedal. We ended up in the ditch. It was not a serious accident and the natives pulled us on to the road again, but because I had been so tense I knew that I had pulled something in my back. When finally we reached home, the pain was intense and by the following morning I could hardly get out of bed. I asked Theo if he had a doctor.

"I don't use the local doctor," Theo said. "She's a woman and it puts me off. I always go to somebody in Bridgetown. He's a genius. Not everybody's cup of tea, but I swear by him. He's got healing hands. He's your man."

He ordered a taxi for me and gave complicated directions

to the driver, then watched us out of sight, which at the time I thought strangely touching.

We drove in sweltering heat for the best part of an hour, and at one point the heavy traffic forced us to stop by a lunatic asylum on the outskirts of Bridgetown. Half a dozen of the inmates rushed to the iron railings. They had demented, zoo-like faces, but seemed sadder even than the caged anthropoids they so closely resembled. They made no gestures, but just stared at us from a distance of ten feet.

The doctor's surgery was close to the harbour in a side street. It was a wooden building with a decrepit verandah running round it on three sides. There was a queue of patients waiting to be seen, most of them squatting against the slatted boards of the house. It was obvious that I had a long wait ahead of me, but having come that far and being still in pain, I told my taxi driver to park nearby.

It was a scene that closely resembled a television documentary on the life of some Schweitzer-like character. The biggest difference between the rich and the poor when they are sick is the attitude of resignation that most of the poor assume, like another symptom of the terminal diseases they carry. Nobody looked at me as I joined the back of the queue. We moved up one position every five minutes or so and I accepted the fact that my original estimate had been optimistic. There was a cinema opposite and I read the handwritten posters a dozen times, learning them off by heart. The programme being advertised was VILLAGE OF THE GIANT and THE TERRORNAUTS. There was an added encouragement, for the legend beneath one title read: *Teenagers Zoom. See them burst out of their clothes and bust up a town.*

I was sweating profusely from the combination of heat and the pain in my lower back. Looking at my wrist-watch I saw it had taken the best part of an hour for me to reach the entrance to the waiting room. There were still a dozen patients ahead of me, but at least I had gained my quota of shade. Ten minutes later I was inside the room and able to claim a cane chair. For the benefit of those waiting, there were some faded magazines mostly of a religious nature, and one tattered book. I picked it up, desperate for anything to take

337

my mind off the pain. Worms had eaten into the pages, making strange patterns, but I could still make out the title: *William Carey of India* by Percy H. Jones, Author of *The Young Browns Abroad*. I didn't have time to study the text, for the queue started to move at a faster pace, and we played a sort of crippled musical chairs. Now I could hear the doctor talking quietly in the surgery, for the fanlight above the door was broken. There would be a few muttered questions and responses and then a strange sound, like somebody faking a sneeze. It came at regular intervals. "Ha-shoo! . . . Ha-shoo!" I had no idea what it meant or who was responsible for it.

Finally I was at the head of the queue.

The surgery was no different from the rest of the building. It contained a rocking chair, a card-table, a couch, a tattered arm chair and some ancient green matting on the floor such as one finds in the pavilions of impoverished cricket clubs.

The man who greeted me was an old Bajan. I guessed him to be in his late seventies. He was wearing white American ducks with black shoes. When I came into the room he was sitting at the card-table writing something on the fly-leaf of a Bible. He motioned me to the couch. I sat looking at an eye-testing card on the wall opposite, but sweat, rather than poor eyesight, blurred the words. It was incredibly hot in the room and I became aware that it was windowless.

The doctor closed the Bible and moved to me.

"Where's the pain?" he said.

I put my hand on the tender region. He felt it, pressing hard into the spine so that I could not help crying out.

"Lie down," he said.

I climbed up on to the couch and lay on my back.

"Other way."

I turned over. Nothing happened. Then I heard the same noise again. "Ha-shoo!" and seconds later he seemed to jump on me with all his weight. I felt something crack in my back, and a pain so intense that my whole body poured with sweat. I waited, but nothing else happened.

"Five dollars," he said.

"Is that all? I mean is that all the treatment?"

"In a few hours, later this afternoon, you'll be better."

I paid him and he went back to the Bible and started to write again. As I left a woman with pendulous breasts under a cotton shift took my place.

The treatment seemed to have made the condition much worse, and it took me a few moments before I felt able to go in search of my taxi. I found the driver parked across the street. He was fast asleep and made no effort to assist me. The taxi itself was like an oven. I think I passed out the moment I was inside and when I next became conscious of my surroundings I found we were outside a native bar. My driver was nowhere to be seen, but before I could panic he appeared with a can of ice-cold beer. I drank half of it, wanting to die.

"I think I'm very ill," I said. "Drive very slowly. No bumps." Then I passed out again.

He must have taken me literally for it was late afternoon before we reached the house. Amazingly, I woke feeling almost normal. There was an ache in my back, but the blinding pain had gone and my legs, when I gingerly tested them, no longer felt as though they were joined to the pelvis by hot wires. I gave the taxi driver double what he asked for in an excess of gratitude.

I don't think I noticed anything particularly different about the house at first; ever since Thomas's death there had been little to disturb the normal quiet, for the garden foliage cushioned the traffic noise and the background of surf was so constant as to pass unheaded. The sudden absence of pain made me feel lightheaded and I could hardly wait to tell Theo the good news. He wasn't in his room as I had expected, so I walked down to the beach, since it was roughly the time when he took his afternoon dip. There were two or three people in the water, but no sign of Theo. I came back into the house to change into some clean clothes. Pinned to the door of my bedroom was a handwritten note.

Dear Tony,

Forgive me, but I've had to leave in somewhat of a hurry and there was no way of contacting you. Please don't be alarmed, and I'll explain when we meet up again in London. I had some urgent business to attend to in New

York, but I shall be moving around after that. Treat the place as your own for as long as you like. There's nothing worth stealing anyway. Excuse haste.

Ever,
Theo

I was reading the note a second time when a voice called from the living room.

"Anybody home?"

I walked into the room to find Mannix.

"I know it's not done to call without any invitation," he said. "I did ring but there hasn't been an answer all day."

"No, I've been out. I had to go to the doctor in Bridgetown."

"Nothing serious, I hope?"

"I don't think so. Not any longer anyway."

"Nasty business, being ill away from home. Something to avoid. Look, actually I came to apologise for my rudeness. I'd no idea that your cousin was such a distinguished literary figure. Somebody at the hotel told me and since I pride myself on being a keen student of literature, I wanted to pay my respects."

"What a pity," I said. "You've just missed him."

"Oh, he's not here?"

"No, he had to go away on business."

"You mean he's left the island?"

"Yes."

There had been something bogus about his reason for calling and something about his general manner which put me on my guard.

"Well, that really is a pity. I was really looking forward to meeting him. Do you know how long he'll be away?"

"I don't think he's coming back for some time. I shall be leaving myself shortly."

"That's too bad. Perhaps you'll tell him I called when next you see him."

"Of course."

"Tell him I'm always willing to pay a good price for original manuscripts. It's a hobby of mine."

"Yes, I'll tell him. I don't know that he ever parts with his manuscripts. We authors tend to feel very maternal about them."

"Well, you can always find me if he changes his mind."

He was staring at Theo's note in my hand.

"Take care of your health, Mr. Stern. You don't want to end up like me. You know what they say. Neglect your health and you end up dead. And once again, forgive me for coming in unannounced."

"That's all right. Have you made up your mind about buying a house here?"

"I think I've decided against it. There's not enough activity. Enjoy the rest of your stay, Mr. Stern."

He was surprisingly light on his feet for a man carrying that much weight. A few moments later I heard the sound of his car scattering the gravel on the drive, and poured myself a much needed Scotch. Perhaps it was only my novelist's mind at work, but Mannix's visit seemed more than coincidence. Reading Theo's note again, remembering his anxiety in the restaurant, there seemed reasonable cause for alarm.

There is something disconcerting about being left alone in a house that doesn't belong to you. One is tempted to do irrational, sometimes shameful things. An alien personality takes over. It becomes in one's mind, a hotel, impersonal, a place to which one will never return and therefore towards which one has no responsibility. I have to confess that disorientated by Theo's sudden exit, I examined his work room, sifting through the papers on his desk, opening drawers, behaving like some sneak thief. I found nothing that would explain his panic and after a while my behaviour shocked me.

I phoned the B.O.A.C. office in Bridgetown to make my own arrangements for departure, only to be told that the next available flight to London was in three days' time. I booked a seat, then spent those remaining days lazing about on the beach – which I mostly had to myself, the solitude being not unwelcome – and the enforced rest enabled my back fully to recover.

It was a night flight and before take-off the stewardess came

341

round with an armful of English newspapers, the first I had seen for some weeks.

"They are today's, sir. They came out on this morning's flight."

I selected the *Telegraph* and the *Daily Mirror*, intending to break my fast with the best or worst of both worlds, settling down with seat-belt fastened in masochistic mood to enjoy what, in all honesty, I had not missed. News from England after an absence has a depressing sameness about it: the government and the T.U.C. were locked in one of their usual contortions, a former vicar of Balham had been charged with 'open and notorious sin', a Labour M.P. had made a speech criticising the cost of the Royal Family and the film of *Cleopatra* was still in difficulties following Elizabeth Taylor's illness. But the item which caught my eye was not given much prominence in the early editions. It was tucked away in a small paragraph at the bottom of page one and gave the first news that a Soviet spy named George Blake had been arrested.

25

I DON'T SUPPOSE I shall ever know for certain why Theo
left Barbados in such unimagined anguish. At the time,
of course, I made no sinister connections, inclined to the
belief that the fat man was somehow part of that world of
twilight sex which, without benefit of any reliable maps, I had
neither the ability nor the inclination to explore in depth.

He seemed to have disappeared without trace, putting the
island house on the market a few months later. I saw an
advertisement for it in the pages of *Country Life* and noted that
it was being sold complete with furniture and fittings through
an agent. I contacted his British publishers, but they had no
knowledge of his whereabouts and in fact were somewhat
irritated by my enquiry; the editor I spoke to said they were
anxiously awaiting delivery of his next manuscript. "We've
announced it in our list," he said. "You've no idea what this
does to our sales conference. It throws everybody out."

I was concerned for him, for I felt that we had once again
grown closer, our relationship dovetailing as of old. My own
life was not so stimulating that I could afford to dismiss the
absence of somebody like Theo without a moment's thought.
It was a period when I was drifting between two women, both
of whom satisfied me in part, but both lacking that spark that
might have led to a more permanent relationship. I sat down
every day at my desk to fulfil my quota of words, but my
writing lacked any real inspiration.

I followed the Blake trial with keen interest, for it touched
upon some of my own wartime experiences, and perhaps
because of this I was not so shocked as some at the apparent
viciousness of British justice when his sentence was
announced. I felt no pity for Blake, then or now. He was one
of the coldest of operators, sending many of his colleagues to
their death − a useful man, I suppose, if he's on your side,

like one of those footballers who perform professional fouls with total indifference if their team is behind. Blake was a supreme cynic in a cynical game.

Now, of course, I am better placed to pull together most of the threads. I realise the significance of the word 'twice' and why Mannix's visiting card was floating close to Thomas's drowned body: it was just that – a social reminder to Theo as to who had come calling – except that, by chance, I found it and not Theo. At the time I had assumed it to be the card Mannix had given me in the restaurant, and which I must have dropped.

Then there was the phone call during the small hours of that same night. Blake's arrest had finally led the authorities to close in on Philby. He was in Beirut at that time, on the verge of flight, his well-documented bouts of drunken violence blurring his previous, ice-cold confidence. It could have been Philby, or somebody close to him, attempting to warn Theo. That seems plausible enough now.

I think Theo wanted out by then. He felt he'd paid his dues. His employers felt otherwise; they had to let him know he wasn't yet in line for a one-way ticket to Moscow. They'd left him alone for a few years, allowed him to put down roots on the island, cover his wartime tracks, and be lulled into believing that he was out of the wood. Now, with Philby spent, they reactivated him. I suspect the coincidence of my visit complicated matters. They hadn't bargained for me and for all they knew I might be there doing their business, with a brief to turn him a second time. So instead of the direct approach they killed Thomas to let Theo know they were in earnest.

None of these possible explanations occurred to me at the time. Why should they have done? Theo's behaviour may have been odd, but I didn't attribute anything sinister to it. Listening to him explain his way of life I realised it was something I could never fully comprehend so I didn't try. I had no strong moral views about his homosexuality, and I certainly understood his grief at the death of Thomas, even if it wasn't my sort of love.

No, I was too conventional in my outlook to harbour

deeper suspicions. I had left the war behind. It is only in recent weeks that I have begun to dredge my memory. Recalling the whole episode of Blake's escape, I've remembered an occasion, some years ago, when I was in Long Island researching a novel that I ultimately aborted when Mr. Mario Puzo's best seller about the Sicilian Forsyte Saga beat me to the post. I was tracked down to my motel by two men, one a lawyer who is still practising so I will not reveal his name. His companion was a man introduced to me as Herbert Hoover, which I thought was ironic. They came with a proposition for me to write a screenplay based on the Blake escape. It was all very businesslike. Their story was they were acting on behalf of a consortium stuffed with tax-haven money which could be used for financing a film. Until the United States Government passed new laws, it was perfectly legitimate a few years back. The idea was sufficiently intriguing for me to pursue it, but at the moment when formal contracts would normally have been exchanged the dialogue mysteriously came to an abrupt end, and I heard nothing further. In the interim, however, I had what facts were available and had made contact with several people who had been connected with the case. There was one detail, never satisfactorily explained at the time, which fascinated me.

Students of the case may recall that, oddly, Blake's mother and sister refused to provide him with the modest amount of capital necessary to finance his escape. Yet the money was eventually obtained and despite prior tip-offs to the authorities by an ex-safe-breaker that the attempt would be made, Blake walked out of his English prison with embarrassing ease. I felt that I needed to know more about this aspect and closely questioned my American contacts. For the first time during our dialogue they were curiously reticent. All I could extract from them was the admission that the identity of the benefactor would surprise me. "The person involved was a member of your artistic community," the lawyer said, using that curiously stiff vocabulary that Americans sometimes employ. I pressed them further, but that was as far as they would go. "A well-known name," they said with irritating smugness. Once the entire episode had petered out I took the trouble to look up one of my old colleagues who was still connected with the Special Branch. I told him what I knew and he thanked me for my trouble, but nothing ever came out and doubtless my information, together with other documents on the case, still await the statute of limitations on such matters.

Now when I think of it, I wonder if they were talking of Theo? The expression 'artistic circles' is loose enough and American legalese is just as obscure, if not more so, than its British counterpart. It could have been Theo. He was back in England by the time Blake made his escape.

Seemingly his old self and making no immediate reference to his long absence or the manner in which we had last parted, he turned up at the Garrick one day while I was having lunch. He'd been travelling, he said, doing what he had meant to do long ago. "I always regretted I'd never seen the Far East. So one day I just decided to take a boat and go."

I wasn't going to let him off the hook that easily.

"You did disappear rather quickly. I mean I went off to that witch doctor – and you were right by the way, he did have healing hands, though an alarmingly unorthodox technique – and when I came back, you'd gone. Not a trace."

"Yes." He smiled. "I felt badly at the time, but . . . well, anyway, I'm sure you've forgiven me, Tony; you were always of such a forgiving nature."

"I didn't at the time. I was frightfully worried. So were your publishers."

"They should worry. As a result of my trip they're going to have a best seller on their hands next autumn."

"Tell me something," I said. "Just to satisfy my insatiable curiosity, and then we'll forget it. Did your sudden exodus have anything to do with that gross character who called himself, Manic, no – Mannix? Do you remember who I mean? Looked like Sydney Greenstreet and boasted he had a plutonic device to boost his heart."

"What was your question again?"

"I'm asking whether he had anything to do with your headlong flight from the island."

"I doubt it. Did I ever give that impression?"

"You didn't give any impression. You just upped and went."

Theo merely smiled.

"He came looking for you on the day you left. I thought he was very bogus."

"So were most of the people on that island. I'm not sorry I sold the house. Got a reasonable price for it, too. I could never go back, of course, not after the way poor Thomas died."

"Was that the real reason?"

"Yes. I was very fond of Thomas. Very fond."

"And Mannix had nothing to do with it?"

"What a persistent character you are, Tony. You should have been called to the Bar. If you must know I once allowed Mannix to do me a favour. A great mistake, because he asked too much in return. He liked them very young. Much too young for my tastes. I draw the line at chickens. That's our slang for small children." He grinned at me. "I hope you're shocked but satisfied. Now let's talk about more fragrant subjects. I hear that the Duchess of Argyll is trying to stop her ex-husband publishing the secrets of their married life. This generation of aristocrats are such spoil-sports. Don't they realise that the only thing that keeps them from the tumbrils is the occasional really juicy scandal?"

There was a brittleness to his humour that almost made me suspect he was on drugs, but I was so delighted to have him back I refrained from further questioning. One sure way of losing friends is to criticise their morals.

He had taken a pleasant flat in some mews off Eaton Square and for the first few months after his return we again saw a lot of each other. Theo wanted to catch up on the theatre he had missed and seemed quietly confident that his new novel would surprise both his admirers and detractors. His confidence was not misplaced, for when *Pastoral with Rising Sun* was published he was 'rediscovered' and seemed not to have a care in the world, though like most of us he complained bitterly about income tax.

Reading his journal entries for the period confirms this, for they are mostly taken up with witty, often libellous accounts of his social activities. Fame in his case was a spur to a lighter

347

view of human nature. He no longer tabulated his sexual encounters in such lurid detail. There are occasional references to brief affairs, but mostly he confines his sharp powers of observation to describing aspects of the so-called smart set.

Vogue is an obscene irrelevance, in itself a cause for revolution. Exclusive high camp, a strong lesbian influence in all the models who have mouths like sabre slashes, photographed in contrasting disaster areas, just to emphasise the fact that there are two worlds. There is also a monthly column purporting to be about People In The News, whereas in fact it is mostly about jet-setting layabouts famed for their unattractive behaviour. What fascinates me is the slavish way in which women allow themselves to be de-feminised annually by a few French poufs, paying through the nose for clothes that cannot be worn outside the fashion houses without arousing ridicule. Western civilisation deserves all it inevitably will get. To thumb through the pages of this and other similar magazines is to read advance news of the coming apocalypse – a glimpse of hell in which all the occupants will be condemned to the Royal Enclosure at Ascot for the rest of the time, dressed in last year's fashions, listening to readings of Jennifer's Diary given by a trendy Church of England bishop.

He moved in more exalted circles than I and the pages of his journals are dotted with references to Cabinet Ministers and the new plutocrats who made the headlines in the dizzy Sixties. I could wish that he had once attempted a contemporary novel, Trollope brought up to date, or a new look at the political scene. On one occasion he writes glowingly of having met the Beatles, his prose as awestruck as any teenage fan.

Lennon's remark about Christ is just, that is why they have turned on him. They *are* the new religion, and less harmful than the old. Their lyrics are the Gospel for the young, and at least they preach love and not pestilence and guilt. People cannot bear to be told the truth, especially when it is the young who are telling them. Reality is the ultimate outrage.

This was about the time I moved into Albany. We met fairly regularly and once a month went to the theatre together. I felt he was more relaxed, less inclinded to bridle at some imagined slight. His reputation as a major British novelist was now secure and since it was the age of instant punditry his opinion was often solicited to dispense wit and wisdom on a number of subjects about which, as privately he was the first to admit, he knew little or nothing. I remember him showing me a commissioned article he had written for one of the popular women's magazines. The piece was entitled *Why I Never Married.*

"It'll give you a laugh," he said. "It's in the great tradition of British fiction. Every queer writer I know has always responded to this particular call. I cribbed most of it from the collected writings of Godfrey Winn."

"I'm still impressed."

"My dear, if they're foolish enough to pay me four figures to tremble all those suburban wombs, who am I to reject them?"

Even allowing for the fact that his steady sales and such extra-curricular activities must have pushed him into the higher income brackets, I remember thinking that he seemed to enjoy a very affluent life style. It was a source of irritation, because I sold more copies of my own books, but lived on an overdraft.

"I have this amazing accountant," he said when I tackled him on the subject.

"How does he do it, then?"

"I never enquire. A little knowledge of tax affairs is a dangerous thing."

The explanation irritated me even further. My own accountant was a boring, pedantic little man, self-satisfied with his own lot, and a stickler for the fiscal truth.

Theo appeared to enjoy his money; there was no hint of the self-inflicted misery to come in Englefield Green, that last decade when he withdrew from everything and everybody. He must have been receiving regular payments from his Russian friends, for nothing else could explain the comparatively large sum that came to light when his Estate was proved. Novelists

349

of the calibre of Theo are not in the habit of amassing small fortunes in modern-day Britain.

The paradox of his situation is that although blackmailed, he did not pay in money but in services rendered. He had no lovers to keep, no demanding kept boy with a wandering eye and a greed for Gucci trivia and Cartier cigarette lighters that seem the trademarks of their calling. It is true he always had to buy affection, but it was obtained from the bargain basement from creatures as driven as he was, who wrote on cheap notepaper and met with him in sad bed-sitting rooms. The last journal entries do not reveal a single splurge such as the lonely sometimes indulge in – money spent on an impulse in solitary desperation. On the contrary, the meticulous book-keeping is of a kind that would have impressed the small mind of my erstwhile accountant: every item detailed, journeys taken by public transport, depressingly ordinary meals taken in squalid restaurants, everything noted down to the last penny as though he was some old age pensioner too proud to ask for national assistance. I don't think he could have bought a new suit or shirt in the last ten years of his life, for all the clothes I found were out of fashion. The major expenses he incurred were all medical. He had a collection of patent medicines, many of them lethally deteriorated – infallible cures for what I suspect were mostly imaginary ailments. He subscribed to a number of nature-cure magazines, combining the orthodox with the unorthodox, backing every horse in the race as it were, and alongside the daily expense sums he recorded – sometimes hour by hour – his physical condition and the remedies he applied.

Perhaps nobody has ever prescribed a relief from deceit, and that is why he cast his net so wide, sampling herbal potions alongside the latest wonder drugs. I found homoeo-pathic powders in small white envelopes stiffened by the half-used contents, boxes of suppositories like bullets laid in for a long siege, pills for every organ, ointments for every joint, even a home enema kit. He kept careful note of his periodic and invariably unsuccessful attempts to give up smoking, recorded his own bowel movements – the list is hideously disconcerting, reading like one of those *Lives of The*

Saints that used to terrify me so much as a child, the pornography of the devout.

Those were the lost years I did not share in any part, for when he moved to Englefield Green he closed all previous accounts. By then, of course, Philby had surfaced in Moscow and the espionage fraternity were apparently happy to balance the books. The complicated game they all played had ended in a tie. Our side and the C.I.A. had given Philby a few years rope, a last attempt to save face by planting a final seed of doubt in Russian minds. Although nothing will ever surprise me again, I don't subscribe to the theory that we tried to turn Philby a third time: in the end, I think, we frightened him into defection. He was spent by then, just a husk, one of those old retainers who has been around too long and is an embarrassment to family and strangers alike: he couldn't lay table any more, or polish the silver, without making mistakes, and to top it all he was heavily into the wine cellar. A careful study of the journals reveals only one small reference to the event. 'It seems that Kim Philby has finally gone home to his elephants' graveyard' – that burial ground, a long way from Granchester, that was shortly to receive the remains of Guy Burgess. But old habits die ponderously, and shorn of his routine Philby kept his hand in with the oldest deceit in the world: stealing another man's wife.

I don't find it surprising, as some may well do if the truth ever comes out, that Theo escaped detection. The history of our security forces during that period is hardly one of continual success. The democracies have demonstrated time and time again how much they are prepared to conceal rather than admit to their political illiteracy and lack of foresight. By the time Philby had been granted Soviet citizenship there were juicier local scandals in the offing, plenty to divert the popular imagination, lurid tales of Cabinet ministers dressed as waitresses, orgies in high places, the very lifeblood of Fleet Street.

Theo, I believe, like Philby and the rest, had simply out-lived his usefulness, and if they knew him as well as I think they knew him, they realised he posed no threat. He retired himself, shuffling off into that backwater. Perhaps they

351

prodded him from time to time, just to keep fear one of his ailments, something that none of his drugs could remove. And in the end the remnants of a once distinguished life I found in his cupboards were just as threadbare as the memorabilia that Burgess left behind in that grace and favour flat he occupied in Moscow – both exiled in their separate ways, both broken in the last analysis by self-interrogation, a torture that leaves no marks.

26

THERE HAVE BEEN many moments in my life when I have regretted my lack of perception, but never more so than now. Some people have no such worries; their minds work instantly, reminding me of that phenomenon occasionally witnessed at sunset in the West Indies. There is a fractional second which occurs just as the sun disappears below the horizon and the sky is slashed with an intense green light. It happens so quickly that the onlooker is often uncertain as to whether he has seen it or not. Theo introduced me to it, and often we stood on the sanded verandah of his house in Barbados to watch for it across the tranquil sea. I don't think I ever saw it.

Yesterday, on an impulse, not inspiration, I drove to Westfield, hoping I might resolve one of the imponderables that remain. I went unannounced.

The house seemed smaller than I remembered, but what was immediately obvious as I drove up to the front entrance was the neglect. The garden was unkempt, great clots of black ivy obscured some of the windows and the drive was scarred with pot-holes. As I rang the bell I realised I had no idea of Harry Gittings's second wife's Christian name. Water dripped on to the back of my neck from a broken guttering as I waited.

The door was finally opened and I came face to face with a woman who, although past her prime, had obviously been trim and attractive in earlier years. She had good bone structure and her face was still pert.

"Mrs. Gittings?" I said.

She nodded, but looked blank.

"You won't remember me . . . We did meet, once, many years ago, in somewhat sad circumstances. I'm Tony Stern . . . I was a cousin of Theo's."

353

"Oh, yes. Yes, at the funeral. I remember."

"I'm sorry I didn't warn you in advance. I should have done."

"That's no matter. Please come in. Have you driven up from London? The place is in a bit of a muddle, I'm afraid. I live alone and I sometimes don't bother."

I've noticed that women always make the same apology, no matter how tidy they keep their houses.

Something from those distant childhood years came back as I stepped into the hallway. Perhaps it was a certain scent, or the fact that the pictures on the walls were still hanging in the same places, but I had a rush of memory and could feel again that mixture of fear and excitement that always attended my visits there. The whole house had that chill that comes when many of the rooms are unused and unheated. I felt Gittings's presence still, the more so as his wife led me into his study. This was virtually unchanged except that I noted that the bound sets of Law Reports had been replaced with popular works of fiction from the Book Society. His desk stood where it always did, and beside it the brass spittoon Gittings had used for his cigars.

Mrs. Gittings bent to switch on an electric fire.

"I expect you'd like something warm after your long drive. What would you like, tea or coffee?"

"Coffee, I think. Thank you."

"Anything to eat?"

"No, I stopped and chanced my luck at one of those motorway places. Just coffee will be fine, Mrs. Gittings."

"Call me Angela, please."

"Fine. If you'll call me Tony. Look, don't go to any trouble."

"No trouble. It's nice to have a visitor for a change. I shan't be a moment."

Left to myself I could not resist sitting at Harry's desk once again, and, taking care not to rattle the handle, opened the top drawer. It was empty. I looked around the room and I could see Theo's ghost, white-faced with adolescent concern, standing nervously in front of the desk that afternoon we made the great discovery. I got up, not wanting to be dis-

354

covered there when Angela returned and passed the time examining the titles of the novels in the glass-fronted bookcase. I found one of Theo's, but none of my own.

"I don't know why I showed you in here," Angela said when she returned with a tray of coffee and chocolate biscuits. "It's not the most comfortable room in the house."

"No, it never was," I said honestly.

"Well, let's take our coffee in the sitting room."

She led the way. It was quite obvious that she had made the sitting room her own, for it was furnished in a taste entirely alien to Harry Gittings and for the first time since I had arrived I lost that feeling of unease.

"I was sorry about Theo," she said. "Not that I ever knew him. Harry wouldn't have his name mentioned."

"No, they really never got on," I said.

"He wasn't easy, Harry. He had many good qualities that perhaps other people didn't always see." She looked me straight in the eye. "But he left me comfortably off, and I went into it with my eyes open, so I've got no complaints." I had the feeling that she was warning me away from any criticism of him.

"You read the reports of Theo's death, I suppose?"

"No, I didn't. I'm somewhat cut off here. First I heard was when somebody from the local paper called. Just a young boy who'd been sent round to find out if I knew Theo."

I could imagine the young reporter bearing some resemblance to my old self – sent on one of those depressing assignments to the recently bereaved.

"I had to say I didn't know him at all, and he lost interest after that. How did he die?"

After I had told her the bare details I waited, but she did not pose the expected question. Most relatives, no matter how distant, usually cannot wait to ask the value of an estate.

"I suppose I should have contacted you before now."

"Why? No reason why you should. I'm not family."

"No, but it would have been polite. How long ago did Harry die?"

"Oh, about six years. Yes, be six years this coming March.

355

He suffered a lot towards the end, so I was glad I was here. I was trained as a nurse, you see."

"I'm sure you were a great comfort to him."

"I doubt that. He wasn't a man given to much happiness, as you probably know. He just wanted somebody to take care of his needs. And look after his cats. He had a thing about cats."

Again she stared straight at me.

"Yes, so did Theo."

"I haven't got any now. I had them all put down when Harry died. Not my favourite animals." She poured me a second cup of coffee.

"I expect you're wondering why I suddenly turned up like this, out of the blue? You've a perfect right to be curious."

"No," she said. "I had a feeling you'd show up one day."

"Why was that?"

"I don't know, I just did. Perhaps it had something to do with that man."

"What man?"

"Oh, about two weeks after Theo died it must have been, this man suddenly appeared on the doorstep. He mentioned your name, you see, otherwise I don't suppose I would have let him in."

"My name? Well, who was he?"

"He said he'd known you both. Something to do with the war, I think he said. About your age, I'd say. Now he did give me a name. Matlaw? I believe that was it. Does that mean anything?"

"Matlaw?" I said. "No, doesn't strike any bell. What did he want?"

"Well, that was the odd thing. He first of all said he was in the district and had merely called to convey his sympathy. I thought that was a bit odd, because why would he come here? Anyway, I suppose because I see so few people, I felt I ought to ask him in. Stupid of me, that's how people get murdered or robbed, so the local police say. Then, once he was inside he started asking questions."

"What sort of questions?"

"About Theo mostly. I mean, they weren't questions

356

exactly. How shall I put it, they weren't direct questions. Sort of, well, the way insurance men talk when they're trying to sell you a policy. But he kept mentioning your name, and he seemed genuine enough. I hope I didn't do anything wrong?"

"No," I said. "It's just that I can't think who he could have been. Did he leave any address where I could contact him? I mean, it's quite possible that I do know him. The war's a long time ago."

"No, I asked him to leave an address, but he said he was moving around a great deal and spent quite a bit of time abroad."

I must have looked anxious because her next question to me was right on target.

"There was something odd about Theo, wasn't there?"

"How d'you mean odd?"

"Oh, I don't know. It's none of my business. Just something Harry once said right at the beginning. You won't shock me, you know. I'm quite broadminded. Nurses usually are. I guess he was queer, wasn't he?"

"Yes," I said. There didn't seem much point in denying it to her.

"Harry couldn't wait to send them to jail. He was a J.P. you know, when he retired from his practice. And he had real malice on the bench towards anybody like that. That was the really evil side of him."

"Was this character, Matlaw . . . do you think he was queer or gay or whatever they call it now? Is that the connection?"

"No, I didn't think that. Very smooth, but, no, I wouldn't say anything else. He just said he was a great admirer of Theo's work and if I ever wanted to sell any of his first editions or papers, he'd be more than happy to pay a good price for them. But I didn't have anything. Harry wouldn't have Theo's books in the house. The only ones I've got I bought after Harry died."

"So he just went away, did he?"

"Yes. And I've never heard from him or seen him since. The only . . . well, I don't know whether I'm doing him an injustice, but about three weeks after that, after he called, the house was broken into. One afternoon, when I was at the

357

cinema. The curious thing is, nothing was taken. None of the silver or anything of value, which they could have had. Just the books and Harry's desk – they'd been gone through. Everything thrown all over the place. I can't imagine why, can you?"

"No," I said. "It does seem odd if they didn't take anything."

"It unnerved me for a while, and the police didn't find anything. I mean there weren't any fingerprints or anything. Still, that's something we have to live with these days. It must be worse in London."

"It seems general," I said. "Don't you find it lonely here?"

"Yes and no. I was lonely enough with him. So there isn't much difference." She smiled when she said this, as though to head off any more sympathy.

We chatted for another half hour and then I excused myself and left.

I drove back to London in obscuring rain, a sense of being on the brink of something keeping me alert, and when I woke the following morning the conviction was still with me. I set about trying to trace some of Theo's wartime colleagues. It was a difficult and mostly unrewarding quest, involving several long journeys with little to show for them at the end. Most of those I interviewed were seedy and suspicious; they were only really forthcoming about their present discontents, for almost without exception they were living on fixed and inadequate pensions. They remembered Theo, but as just another ghost from their shining pasts, and in any case the patterns of caution were too deeply engraved. The only time I felt close to the truth was when I managed to locate the woman who had originally interviewed him – the one he had called 'Miss Malcolm' in his would-be fictitious account.

Her real name was Upward, Dame Margaret Upward. She was a sprightly eighty-year-old living alone in a cottage in the Chalfonts. Her memory was still sharp, even though she was partially deaf and had cataracts on both eyes. She had been retired and made a Dame at the end of the Macmillan administration.

"Yes, I remember Mr. Gittings," she said. Her head

turned towards some dusty bookshelves. "You'll find a set of his novels over there somewhere. I used to read them a lot, when I could. He was one of my gentlemen. What's he doing these days?"

I broke the news of his death and explained my own background and relationship. "I've been thinking of writing a biography," I said. "But there are a lot of blank spaces. It's his wartime activities that interest me most and I can't discover much about them."

"Well, you wouldn't, would you?" Dame Margaret said. "And you won't now, I don't suppose."

When she chuckled she passed her hand over the top of her head, smoothing down the snow white hair which was cut in a severe, mannish style. Like many women of her ability and generation she had kept herself spruce even in ever-reducing circumstances. I don't suppose a grateful government allowed her much of a pension; in her day to be made a Dame Commander of the Order of the British Empire was considered reward enough. I noticed that she served me tea in odd cups. All that took the chill off her damp sitting room was a single-bar electric fire with a frayed lead.

After a few general questions, I guided the conversation around to the Burgess and Maclean episode.

"Never thought too much of Burgess," she said. "Something about the mouth. I used to go a lot by mouths. Very charming, of course. He could get around most people, but not me. I put in a report long before he took off. Got nowhere. He had friends in high places, or so I was told."

"What about Philby?"

"Ah, well, now you're talking about a thoroughbred. No, none of us suspected Mr. Philby." There were still traces of a grudging admiration in her thin voice.

"Did you ever believe in the Fourth Man theory?" I asked.

She took another sip of tea and her partially blind eyes came up to meet mine. "There had to be more than four," she said.

"Why d'you say that?"

"I've had a long time to think about it."

"Did you ever suspect anybody in particular?"

"I suspected everybody," she said slowly. "That was my job."

"Would it be anybody close to home?"

The question was out before I could stop myself and I knew at once it was a mistake. Dame Margaret was not the type to be put on the spot. She murmured something I did not catch.

"I'm sorry?"

"Dead," she said. "And if they're not, they should be."

I was committed now. "Theo's dead, my cousin's dead," I said. "Could it have been him?"

"More tea, Mr. Stern?" she said, and groped for the pot with the loose lid.

I tried to think of ways and means of putting the same question more obliquely, but she was not to be drawn again. Perhaps she was tired of the whole game. I couldn't blame her. I might even have misjudged her waning powers. All I know is that after my visit to her all further enquiries were discreetly blocked.

Denied any assistance from official sources I went back to the journals and papers yet again, hoping that I had overlooked something in previous searches that would provide the final answer. With a writer one can never be sure where deception begins, with what ease the practised author twists fact into fiction. And Theo had proved himself a master of the art.

The carefully hoarded contents of that room in Englefield Green reveal not only a man I never knew, but a man who, despite his many betrayals, is still deserving of my pity. Those fading cries for help, duplicated on cheap paper – box numbers answering box numbers, as though the war was still on and he had the need to communicate in code: I could take any one of them at random and be grateful for my own life of ordinary human despair.

Friday

Dear Friend, I still don't know your name, so it is a little difficult calling you anything when I write. I thought you might be disappointed when we didn't meet last Wednesday, and I'm sorry you had to be, but it couldn't be helped. You suggest

Monday. Can you come here at 6 p.m. or soon after? The flat I am in belongs to a Miss Harding – her name is on a card by the bell push. Ring this twice for me. If you only ring once it will bring her out. She is around most evenings which considerably restricts my activities and I must warn you of this, so do be prepared for disappointment in this respect. But we can always chat and for the rest just trust to luck. Will sign myself Charles which has always been a favourite name. I wish I'd been christened it. My own is a joke.

There is one phrase in that letter which haunts me. It seems to sum up Theo's last years, if not his whole life. 'Do be prepared for disappointment.' He was not given 'love with a capital L' that Philby once confessed to; no 'peace and stability at last'; no flight, no spurious glamour or sanctuary in a foreign country, just the slow working out of a familiar sad routine, passion with strangers who had to trust to luck.

The net was cast wide, some of the correspondence coming from the Continent from members of an organisation called The League of Pals. Across one such letter, originating in Germany, Theo had written *Where there is no hatred there is no need for forgiveness.* There were also glimpses of those serious charades played to an audience of the three cats. 'I can assure you I am prepared to be used for humiliation;' 'I am a practising Christian and always put Christ first;' 'I do not know from your letter whether your emphasis finally would be oral or anal (or both). I have become fully dentured within the past week and am anxious to know whether you would consider this a disadvantage;' 'I long for a true and sincere friendship and you will find that I love with a gentle strongness.' I found many of them unbearably poignant.

Then I came across a letter that at first I was inclined to skim through. The writing was miniscule and the opening page taken up with quasi-religious matters: 'What do you think about Montefiore's contention that we cannot rule out the possibility of Christ being homosexual?' There was much more in the same vein and I was just about to move on to the next when a name I had heard in recent weeks leapt at me from the page.

361

I thought I should warn you I'm almost certain I have seen a familiar face in the region of Temple Fortune on two occasions during the past month. If it was the person I think it was we both have reason to take care. I'm fairly certain he didn't recognise me either time. He was in the company of a younger man than himself – a foreigner from the look of him. I think you once knew him under the name of Mannix, but from my enquiries he uses a variety of aliases and now calls himself Matlaw. Please be on your guard. I suggest we don't meet again until I can be sure the coast is entirely clear. I will make contact when satisfied. Don't contact me.

The letter was signed 'A' and dated three weeks before Theo's death. I read it several times, then phoned Angela Gittings.

"Look, I'm sorry to bother you again, but that man you told me about – the one who came to the house, and called himself Matlaw, I think you said – how would you describe him? Would you call him fat man?"

"Yes and no," she answered. "Put it this way, he was a big man and his clothes hung on him. As if he'd once been much fatter, but had lost some weight. Why?"

"It's just that I do remember him . . . He was somebody I once met with Theo in Barbados. Have you been . . . has anybody worried you since?"

"No."

"Well, if they do, if anybody does, let me know."

I obviously hadn't kept the anxiety out of my voice. There was a slight pause and then she said: "You make it sound rather ominous."

"Did I? I didn't mean to. Forgive me."

"Theo wasn't mixed up in anything, was he?"

"No," I said quickly. "No, he just had a few odd hangers-on. People, strange people, sometimes latch on to writers, you know. They start out as fans and then sometimes they make our lives a misery. It's one of the hazards of the trade. Actors suffer in the same way."

"Well, I'll watch out," she said, "and let you know."

I regretted making the call the moment I put the phone down and hoped my explanation had sounded plausible. There was no point in embroiling a totally innocent person. I

362

think it was then I made up my mind to put an end to the whole business. After I had read the letter once more, I destroyed it, afterwards consigning the whole sorry mess to the dustbin. I hesitated over the journals, going back once more to read the final entries. A few of the pieces of the puzzle did fit. The letter mentioning Mannix tied in with the last page of the journal.

> Had difficulty finding A.'s address . . . He kept me waiting . . . said I could not stay . . . the whole thing was impossible and had to end . . . that it was madness, the place was being watched . . . I am past scaring.

I suppose I could have made more determined attempts to trace Mannix – but for what? By the end of his life Theo admitted he was past scaring. Why not take him at his word? For a writer there is no such thing as a happy ending, anyway: there are always more blank pages to fill, and others who come after me will undoubtedly fill them; the gaps in this story won't remain blank for ever.

All the rumours of a third man that preceded Philby's unmasking will one day be restitched to a fresh canvas. There had to be a fourth man. He wasn't Mannix; Mannix was just another pawn, like Theo. Perhaps if I had the resolve I could dig deeper and chance upon him, or then again, perhaps he, too, is dead and past scaring. But somewhere, at some time, in that Cambridge of the lost generation he placed the right advertisements and got the right replies; just as Theo, conditioned to the pattern, pursued his own converts to the very end. Politics, like sex, is so often the last resort of the lonely and unfulfilled – a conceit that few will admit to since 'duty' is a cleaner word than 'power'. He knew what he was about, that recruiter. Perhaps not always successful – for the proposals of marriage must sometimes have been rejected – but successful enough, claiming those we know of, promising them they could love, honour and obey the doctrine of deceit. As far as we can tell he confined his activities to Cambridge for selecting members of that 'élite force' Philby was so privileged to serve.

Is he there still – some cloistered, respected figure pointed out to visitors, made holy by the eccentricities of age so that what once would have betrayed him in turn is now accepted as wisdom? None of his converts ever gave him away, not even Theo who had greater cause than most, and from this we could deduce that his secret is still worth preserving, that the seductions still continue. There are, after all, future generations to betray, new privileges to bestow. Because we cling to our beliefs in a society he is dedicated to destroy, we shall never be proof against his kind. As long as we remain free, we are the prey.

Postscript

I THOUGHT I HAD written the finish to this story when I burnt Theo's journals, adding my own quota of treachery by destroying the evidence on Chobham Common – a necessary journey since Albany is now in a smokeless zone and my Adam fireplace houses a bogus log fire.

A week or so later I was sitting in Hatchard's Piccadilly bookshop signing copies of my latest novel. Such events do little for the ego. They can best be compared to feeding times at the zoo: the majority of the spectators merely come to gape, a few of the faithful actually buy copies, and the whole operation is conducted with painful embarrassment.

On the day in question I fared slightly better than usual, and in the course of three quarters of an hour managed to satisfy some forty customers. At one point there was a respectable queue of middle-aged ladies doubtless inflamed by a reference in one review to an isolated racy passage which, quoted out of context, gave the impression that I had written a sequel to *Tropic of Cancer*. Their gushing enthusiasm flustered me, so much so I found myself unable to look in their faces.

"How would you like it signed?" I asked the last of the few.

"You could put 'to Judy with love' if you felt like it," a voice said.

It was then that I looked up. Shock made me blotch the title page. Why is it that the sudden reappearance of someone we have once loved to excess has this power to destroy us? Seeing Judy standing there immediately made me feeble. Some of the old pain returned and my mind was swept back to our first meeting in that Cambridge tea room.

"I read in the evening papers you were going to be here," she said, "and I couldn't resist it."

She hadn't altered as much as me. There were no grey hairs and the face that smiled at me so guiselessly from under the permed perfection had retained all its old warmth.

"I don't believe it," I said.

"I'm sorry if I gave you a shock."

By now there was a middle-aged man waiting his turn and slightly irritable at the delay. He thrust his copy at me. "Sign it 'To Marjorie'," he said. "Don't want it for myself." I winked at Judy and signed.

"Can I buy you lunch?" I asked, as Marjorie's copy was snatched from me. "I'll be through here in a few minutes. I don't think my services are going to be required much longer. We could go next door to Fortnum's."

"That would be nice. If you're sure you want to."

"Don't be ridiculous. Of course I want to."

"It'll be crowded," she said. "I'll go ahead and get a table."

I watched her leave the shop. She still walked the way I remembered, and although her waist had bowed to the inevitable her legs were shapely.

She was just as blunt as ever. The first words she said to me when I joined her in Fortnum's were typical of her old self. "I bet I know what you thought in there."

"What? What did I think?"

"You said to yourself, 'I'm glad I don't have to wake up and find that on the pillow every morning.'"

"You're quite wrong."

"I always told you I'd go fat."

"Where?"

"Where it matters."

"Well, not as bad as me."

"As a matter of fact I was thinking just the opposite. Wondering what your secret was. I've given up trying. I went to one of those la-de-da health farms once, starved myself rotten for a week, then ruined it all by cramming down a pound of chocolates the moment I got home."

"Where is home now?"

"Nowhere special. I'm quite the traveller these days. I keep a small place in Dolphin Square, but I'm not there very often.

366

I'm mostly on the go, seeing the world, making up for lost time."

"Is . . . are you still married?"

She shook her head. "No, he's dead. George passed away, oh, nearly eight years now. Left me very comfortably off, mind. Enough to see me out anyway. How about you?"

"No, I'm not married."

"Were you ever?"

"Yes."

"Didn't work out?"

"It didn't have much of a chance," I said. "It was during the war . . . Was yours a happy marriage?"

"I suppose so. Yes, happy as most. Least, he seemed happy enough and I kept my side of the bargain."

I touched her hand briefly as we shared looking at the menu. "It seems a long time ago since you took my order, Mrs. Fraser."

"Have you forgiven me?" she said. "I almost lost my nerve at the last moment. Walked past you twice. Guilty conscience, I suppose."

"No need to forgive when there's never been any hate."

"That's nice. You always said nice things. Did you write that?"

"No," I said. "So . . . tell me more about yourself."

"Not that much to tell. I go on cruises most of the year. Get in the warm, away from this bloody climate. I like cruises. You get a nice type of companion and it's never anything permanent. I mean, I still like a bit of that, if I can get it, even at my age. Isn't this nice? You and me sitting here. 'Course, bit different from where I first served you. That's gone now – it's a sodding great office block. Oh, I shouldn't swear in here, should I? No, it's all gone, your cinema, the lot. Still, I like change, keeps you young."

"The old cinema went in the war," I said.

"Were you in the war?"

"Sort of. I didn't do much fighting."

"Just as well. They might have killed you, then we wouldn't be here." She smiled. "You've got those white patches on your cheeks. You always got those."

"It's the effect you have on me. Where do you go on your cruises?"

"Oh, I'm not fussy, long as it's somewhere hot. Australia, all around there I've been, Hong Kong, then the other way round through the whatsit, that canal named after a hat, and round the Cape. I like the West Indies best, though. Ever been there?"

"Once," I said.

"I know what I had to tell you. Yes, that reminds me. On one of those trips down there, round the islands and that, I bumped into that cousin of yours."

"Theo?"

"Yes. Wasn't it a coincidence? Well, life's like that, isn't it? I mean, take us now. 'Course, I'd read about him from time to time. Used to get his books from the library. I never really understood them, but George was very taken. Bit deep for me."

"'Deep' was a good word for him."

"Was?"

"He's dead now," I said. "He died earlier this year."

For the first time in the conversation she didn't have an immediate answer. I wondered if she was thinking the same thing as I was.

"I'm sorry to hear that," she said, and her voice was quieter. "I expect that upset you. You were always so close."

"We shared a lot of things." I watched her face but her expression did not change.

"Got quite famous, didn't he? Well, you both did. Didn't mean to be rude . . . I don't suppose he ever married?"

"No."

"No, I didn't think so. As a matter of fact . . . I suppose I can say it now he's gone . . . there was a bit of trouble on the boat. One of the crew, some young boy he took a fancy to. He was a bit that way, wasn't he?"

"Yes, you could say that."

"Well, I didn't want to say it. Not come out with it like. Live and let live. Those sort of things never bothered me. People can't help the way they're made, and I was never the one to throw stones in glasshouses. As well you know. No, I

368

don't care overmuch for the real whatsits, unless they're hair-dressers. Don't mind them. How did we get on to that?"

"You were telling me you bumped into Theo."

"Oh, yes. Yes, well, he was asked to leave the boat in Panama. I felt sorry for him really. Must be difficult if you can't say no. That's good, coming from me. But some of those cabin staff do flaunt it a bit. Very bold, some of them. Bring your breakfast at eight and stay for elevenses . . . It was all hushed up, being a British boat. If it'd been French they wouldn't have cared less. But I knew all about it. He came to me the night before we docked in Panama, told me all . . . I suppose he thought . . . well, after all, we weren't strangers."

She looked straight at me as she said this, and it was my turn not to betray anything.

"I think he just needed somebody to talk to, and you know me, never could resist a sob story."

"You resisted mine."

"I was right, though, wasn't I? You wouldn't be signing all those lovely books if you'd married me. We'd have both dragged each other down long before now. I'm right, aren't I?"

"I don't know," I said.

"Well, Theo agreed with me. We talked a lot about you that night. He was very fond of you. Said you were the only true friend he'd ever kept, that friendship was a fatal gift. Always remembered that."

"I wonder what he meant?" I said. "It's a quotation of Byron's, but he got it wrong. Theo, that is. I think the real quotation is 'the fatal gift of beauty'."

"Never mind, it was still nice, wasn't it? I know men like to keep their secrets, but it's always better to get it off your chest. He talked about so many things that night. Got himself in quite a state. Funny thing about you men, you can never quite bring yourselves to admit you're frightened, can you?"

"Was Theo frightened?"

"I thought so. I could be wrong. Not so much frightened about the trouble, but just things in general. Said he'd done everything wrong in life, that he could escape from what he was. 'Course, I'm not religious, I don't believe in all that afterlife stuff, so I couldn't help him much; I just listened."

"I'm sure you were a great help."

She dug her fork into a second slice of Black Forest cake. I stared at her, this woman whom I had once loved so obsessively. Don't, I thought. Don't remind me of the past any more. I've had my fill of love and betrayal.

"What's your new book about?" she said, changing the subject abruptly as though she had read my mind. "Will I like it?"

"Depends on your tastes. It's another thriller."

"Don't you ever write love stories?"

"Not for publication."

"Harold Robbins. He's my favourite. He gives you a slice of life. Well, that's what it's all about, isn't it? When I was young I used to give it away, then when I was older I sold it . . . Now? Now I'm buying it all back," she said, and laughed. "Fancy you and me, meeting like this after all these years. That's a book in itself."

She wiped her mouth with a tissue she took from a cluttered handbag, then reapplied her lipstick with generous strokes. "I gave him my address and he said he'd write one day and tell me the whole story, but he never did. Had better things to do, I expect."

We were practically the last to leave and the waitresses were anxious to go off duty. I paid the bill and bought Judy a box of hand-made chocolates. We said goodbye on the pavement in Jermyn Street. It was crowded with shoppers, their faces desperate with affluence. I asked her if she wanted a taxi.

"No, I think I'll walk. Shake down the lunch and get myself in shape for the chocolates." She leaned forward and kissed me. I could taste her lipstick.

"I'll let you know what I think of your book. If I finish it, that is," she said, with some of her old candour. "I usually cheat and turn to the last page first."

I watched her until she was lost amongst the crowd, then I walked back across the road to Albany. It was cold in my study. I switched on the electric fire and poured myself a drink. Somebody gave me a pocket calculator last Christmas.

It is only the size of a cigarette packet, but it has a memory and can tell the time in various parts of the world. By a process that is beyond my limited knowledge of modern technology it can also serve as an alarm clock. The source of power, like Mannix's pacemaker, is guaranteed to work the thing for years. For some reason at three-thirty every afternoon it repeats a bleeping sound for several seconds. It went off that day as usual to remind me of time passing, times past.

I thought of Judy as I had once known her and of that day we had all spent together on the river when the choices were simple and clear cut. It seemed like a way of life I had once invented for another of my fictions. But we can always cheat with fiction, turn to the last page first to find out if the solution fits our needs. We forget that it is the necessities of life – the need to be human and fallible – that determine ideas of right and wrong.

Theo's necessity was that he had to choose between the risk of betrayal and the risk of love. It seems now that I inherited that choice from him. It would be comforting to think that what he told Judy was finally reality, something that, for once in his life, he didn't have to betray for. But if all I gave him was only another fatal gift, then I doubt it. It will be my turn to sit here and listen to the warning note that sounds every day, if any of us care. Sit and wait for the batteries of conscience to run down. When that happens we shall need all our strength to remember we once had illusions – a deep innocence we thought we could protect forever.